LUCIENNE DIVER

BLOOD HUNT

The Latter-Day Olympians #5

QUOTES

"Lucienne Diver writes the story beautifully giving you enough information from other books so you're not lost if this is the first one you have read. It also motivates you to read whatever you have missed! The investigations and people surrounding Tori are a blast to read, and you will enjoy every moment of it. I look forward to the next book in the series and following the antics of Tori and Apollo. Blood Hunt is an excitement-filled mystery with great characters and a good twist at the end."

—*Fresh Fiction*

"Blood Hunt is a fairly fast paced read and it's all sorts of enjoyable! There's snark, action, steamy romance and just all the goodness one expects from a good paranormal read I will definitely be looking forward to reading Tori's next adventure!"

—*A Great Read*

"We are fond of mythological based stories so particularly like this series. Tori is the every-day girl who ends up in extraordinary

circumstances that we all wish we were! The magic is generally in line with characters from mythology, so the relative magical strength of different characters reflects many facets of traditional myths.

"If you like your urban fantasy with a large helping of magic and mythology then this is definitely the series for you!"

—Bull Spec, A Magazine of Speculative Fiction

Blood Hunt
by Lucienne Diver

ISBN: 978-1-61475-614-9

Cover painting by Kanaxa

Cover design by Janet McDonald

Kevin J. Anderson, Art Director

Published by
WordFire Press, an imprint of
WordFire, Inc.
PO Box 1840
Monument CO 80132
Kevin J. Anderson & Rebecca Moesta, Publishers

WordFire Press Trade Paperback Edition 2018
Printed in the USA
Join our WordFire Press Readers Group and get free books,
sneak previews, updates on new projects, and other giveaways.
Sign up for free at wordfirepress.com.

❀ Created with Vellum

DEDICATION

To my absolutely amazing grandmother, Vincie, who first made me believe in magic in the form of two imaginary crows named Jack and Jill.

PROLOGUE

Shhh!" Ian scolded him, index finger mashed up against his lips and pushing his nose out of joint.

Richie rolled his eyes at his twin and then waited for the room to come back into focus. *Shhh ...* as if the museum guard they'd locked in the closet wasn't already making enough noise to wake the dead.

And as if Ian was any more sober than himself. Still, Ian wasn't the one who was going to be bruised tomorrow from accidentally hip-checking that cabinet.

"If the cabinet's a'rockin' then don't come a'knockin'," he sing-song-sang to himself. He didn't think that was quite right, but he couldn't remember the actual words to the song. *House,* that was it. House, not cabinet. No matter.

Ian glared him silent. *All right, already!* He got it. Heists required secrecy. And silence.

And copious amounts of liquid courage.

Really, he had no idea how things had gone this far. Sure, Ian had fantasized about bringing home a *real* souvenir and had pointed out casually the closed areas and the lack of guards at the small museum—possibly because of funding issues. But he never dreamed Ian would really go for it … or that his brother would convince him to come along.

Probably that sixth—or was it seventh?—drink had been a mistake.

"Hold this," Ian ordered, handing over the flashlight he'd brought with him, as if maybe there'd been a bit of premedication. No, that wasn't right. Premeditation. Sheesh. He needed to lie down, not to be skulking around dusty museum vaults.

He held the flashlight as still as he could on the cabinet Ian was poking through, opening drawers, rifling contents, sometimes bringing them closer to the light to inspect them … like the thing he held now, which was about the size of a half dollar and gleaming gold.

"What do you make of this?" Ian asked him.

Richie did his best to focus on the disk … or was it a medallion? Yes, definitely a medallion, chain and all. It seemed to flash in the light. Almost definitely gold, Richie thought. But, if so, why wouldn't it be on display? Seemed like the sort of thing that would be a major find for a small museum.

"Cool," Richie commented. "Grab it and let's go."

He hadn't actually seen any other guards, but someone was bound to miss the one they'd locked up sooner or later. Plus, the place gave him the creeps. Those two sarcophagi they'd passed … Well, he'd seen *The Mummy*, the old black and white version *and* the newer version with Brendan Fraser and Rachel Weisz. *Ah, Rachel Weisz.*

"But *look* at it," Ian insisted.

Richie sighed. He liked the vision in his mind's eye better, but obediently he gave it another glance. "What's that thing on the front? Looks a dog, but for those funny knobby things on top of its head. Maybe a giraffe? I didn't think the Egyptians had a giraffe-headed god."

"It's Set, you dummy."

"Who?"

"Bad boy of ancient Egypt. You know, god of chaos? Cut his brother Osiris into itty bitty bits."

"Oh, *that* guy."

Ian dropped the chain of the medallion over his head and went back to rifling through the cabinet. He came back with several more gold disks, smaller than the last, but each one bearing the image of the same strange animal.

"Such a waste to lock these away in dusty old vaults," Ian said, pocketing the coins. "They should be appreciated."

"Ian, I don't think this is such a good idea."

"Relax, we're not going to get caught."

Richie wasn't so sure. This wasn't like shoplifting for laughs back in California. Or "borrowing" that Batmobile replica for a joy ride the one time. This was art theft, wasn't it? They could create some kind of international incident.

He opened his mouth to say something, but Ian had already moved along. "Come on," he said, "bring the light. I want to check out those sarcophagi."

It was the last thing in the world Richie wanted to do, but he knew he'd get out of here sooner if he just went along. Arguing would only waste time and in the end, they'd do what Ian wanted anyway. They always did.

He dragged his feet in approaching the sarcophagi. He wasn't quite the expert Ian was on Egyptian stuff, but he knew there was something very wrong with these two coffins.

"Check them out!" Ian said, awe in his voice. "I'm thinking First Intermediate period, maybe." On the other hand, *Ian* wasn't quite the expert he thought he was either. *First Intermediate period.* Who was he trying to impress? All Richie really knew about it was that it was a period of unrest. All the intermediate periods were. "But ... look, no prayers for the dead. No names. No spells to unite their *ba* and *ka* in the afterlife...."

A chill swept in out of nowhere, raising gooseflesh all over Richie's body. "There's Osiris," Ian continued, "but ..."

Richie could see it now for himself. The images on the sarcophagi, still weirdly crisp after all these years, showed Osiris, the weigher of hearts ... only these had clearly been found wanting. Severely wanting. Something that looked like a demon crouched beside the scales waiting to devour the atrophied organs. It was as though the priests had carved a sentencing recommendation into the sarcophagi. Those inside were never meant to pull enough of themselves together to reach the afterlife, and if hey did

Richie shivered, as though to shake off the thought. The flashlight beam went wild and then Richie lost it all together. It rolled on the ground and under the cart on which one of the sarcophagi rested.

Ian cursed and reached for it, bumping into the sarcophagus and then ... something happened.

Richie watched in terror as his brother's body went suddenly rigid and he sparked, as though zapped by electricity. Against his chest, something glowed gold and then red, strobing. The medallion ...

Crazy stupid terror flashed through Richie, and for a split second, he couldn't move. Couldn't do anything but watch, all those horror movies flitting through his head. And then he steeled himself. This was his brother. His *twin*.

He grabbed Ian and yanked, trying to separate him from the sarcophagus, to get him outside and away from this insanity, but Ian lashed out, landing a palm forcefully against Richie's chest. Richie's whole body convulsed as some kind of energy flashed between them, a bolt of pure power that blasted his heart and exploded outward until he lost control of his limbs, fell against the other sarcophagus ... where something waited to grab hold.

More electricity zapped through him as he hit the coffin full force, branching out like lightning. Everything flashed through him. His past, his present ...

His future, red-washed and full of pain.

He bit back on the pain, tasted blood. It flooded his mouth like memory.

But that flood was quickly blown away by the sandstorm that raged behind it—a dry, hot wind flecked with thousands, millions of stinging shards, scouring everything in its path, leaving him a husk, a shell. Dry, desiccated.

And then something filled him like a bellows. Pumping him full of so much—hunger, rage, lust ... Pure animal need, startling in its intensity.

A sudden noise blew away the haze, breaking him from the sea of pain ...

At a second sound, he and the one beside him looked up simultaneously, sighting in on the source.

Somewhere a door opened. Footsteps. Then a woman appeared, calling "Hello? Bakari, was that you?"

She spoke in Egyptian, but he no longer struggled so hard to understand. At the sight and sound of her, something inside went mad. Clawing at him, tearing and scraping, howling for release. Filling him with rage and hunger and a thirst for blood.

He saw red. Saw it and liked it and wanted more.

He and the other circled silently, closing in on her from either side. She saw them, but too late. Her screams fed his strange new hunger, but they were not enough. Would never be enough.

1

Apollo was waiting for me as I stepped out of the shower. He was naked as the day he was born, striking a pose as the sun streamed in through his beach-facing windows. He looked just like a statue from the National Gallery ... except that he was perfectly proportional. And erect. And ...

"Yes?" I asked, amused, one brow quirked in a way I'd finally managed.

"That's it? That's all I get? Two weeks together and already you fail to swoon at the sight of me in all my glory?"

"When have I ever swooned?"

"Well, you could try it just once," he said, striking a new pose and looking at me hopefully. It did emphasize certain muscles he knew how to put to good use. I felt my resolve wavering.

"I have an appointment," I said. It didn't come out as strongly as I'd meant it to, but then ... naked sun god absolutely in his element. I was lucky I could form a complete sentence.

"You can be late," he said, his eyes making promises he was clearly ready to keep.

When I didn't respond, he dropped his pose and stalked me instead, prowling like a mountain cat, gaze pinning me in place. I was suddenly hyperaware of the rough towel wrapped around my body and how much better the smooth warmth of his hands would feel. Or his lips ...

I put out a hand to stop him, and it met the smooth, hard planes of his chest. He felt like sun-warmed silk. I swallowed hard and he leaned in to kiss my neck, tilting my head to the side. I moaned as his teeth scraped lightly along my pulse point. Next thing I knew, my towel was on the floor, and I was pressed up against him.

It was all I could do to push him away.

"Rain check," I said, my voice sounding breathless. "I can't believe you're even ready to go again. We just ..." I took another step back so that I could look into his eyes, study his face. "Wait, why the sudden interest? You could have joined me in the shower ..."

His gaze flitted away for just a second.

"Ah ha! Something's come up. Spill," I said.

Apollo closed his eyes and then rubbed them, along with the bridge of his nose. Not that I was looking at the bridge of his nose. Not when there was so much else to see.

"Fine," he said after a second, taking his hand away so that he could look into my eyes. "I was hoping we could skip right to the make-up sex."

I crossed my arms over my chest, which, unfortunately, still left the rest of me exposed.

From his reaction, he was fully aware of that fact.

"What did you do?" I asked, bending at the knees to reach for the fallen towel.

"You know that movie premiere I'm committed to on Saturday?"

"Yes," I said dangerously, beginning to twist the towel again and again in my hands as if I might wring his neck with it rather than use it to cover up.

"I've just confirmed you as my plus one."

It might not be the towel he had to worry about. My gorgon glare was stronger than ever, and I was seriously considering hitting him full blast.

"You did what?" I couldn't have heard him right.

"Hear me out," he said, reaching for the towel before I could lash out with it ... or anything else. We couldn't actually read each other's thoughts, but back when he'd touched me with the gift of foreseeing, we'd become linked in some intimate way, and feelings came through loud and clear. "My publicist called while you were in the shower, which is why I didn't join you. She says the only way to counteract all those tabloid photos with you and your wings is to take you out in public and let you be seen. It'll put all the crazy rumors to rest. Maybe even save your life."

"Or give the zealots a perfect opportunity to get at me."

Curse the damned wings. Ever since I'd gotten wrapped up with the Latter-Day Olympians—the old gods in their Greek or other guises who were still with us and still as fractious as ever— my life had gone kablooey. The gorgon blood that ran through my veins, dating back to the god Pan beer-goggling one of the gorgons, seemed to get stronger all the time. What had started with the ability to stop men in their tracks through eye contact and sheer force of will had evolved to the point where a drop of my blood could turn them to stone. The wings had been the most recent and, I hoped, final surprise. Not pretty little fairy wings, all gossamer and shimmery. Or feathered phenomena that might fool friends and enemies alike into seeing me as something angelic. No, mine were big ole bat wings—long and leathery.

They'd been out in full-force when we'd fought the lord of all plague-demons for New York and, ultimately, the world.

And like everything these days, they'd been caught on camera. My old Homeland Security pals Rosen and Holloway had done what they could to keep the footage from getting out and to spin all the devastation we'd left in our wake—or rather that Hecate and her cadre, who'd tried to take advantage of the chaos, had left in their wake, but there was just too much. The conspiracy theorists, the religious zealots who liked ranting about end times, the average citizen with trust issues ... they weren't buying it.

I didn't blame them.

"It's a red carpet event," Apollo said. "Do you have any idea how much security there is at those things? No one is getting to you. Besides, I want to show you off."

Now that called for a look. Not the gorgon glare, maybe, but a dubious look nearly as effective. "You've been linked to some of the hottest starlets of our time ... of various times ... and you want to show me off?" I snorted. "Try again."

He risked life and limb by approaching despite the stranglehold I now held on the towel.

"I do," he said. "Because you're the real deal. Beautiful—" I started to protest and was instantly hushed by the emotions that roiled out of him, overwhelming me, "—strong, powerful, incredible. Mine."

Even he couldn't fake that kind of sincerity. Not with me.

I let him kiss me when he stepped in. Let, hell, I grabbed him around the neck, pressed myself up against him and gave as good as I got ... until he began to back me into the wall. I gasped as my butt hit and he leaned himself against me. I knew what came next, and I didn't have time for it, though I wanted more. I wanted it all.

I was breathless when I broke off the kiss. Aching and desperate for him, but ... "You're changing the subject," I said, practically gasping in the necessary air.

"Am I?"

"And I'm late."

"Are you?" His hand was stroking down my side, over my thighs. He shifted just enough so that he could stroke somewhere more central. The shift also allowed me to escape. Reluctantly.

"Yes, I am," I said. "And we're not finished with this discussion. I never agreed to go."

"I can convince you."

I looked him up and down, gaze catching on certain spots. I was sure he could convince me. Absolutely sure. He could do things that would make me forget my own name, the day, year ... anything but the pleasure.

Gah, I was hopeless. This was what I'd been trying to avoid, why I'd resisted him all those months. I didn't want to be subsumed. I wanted to stay the same special freakin' flower I'd always been.

* * *

I TURNED AWAY, headed for the walk-in closet where I kept some of my clothes. Thanks to the Grey Sisters and a runic tattoo, I could now fold my wings right into my body, magically absorbing them into their permanently inked likenesses on my back. My clothes would fit again. Which was a good thing, because clients tended to be put off when you showed up au naturel ... with gargoyle wings besides.

Apollo followed me to the closet, but didn't loom in the entrance. Didn't block my path. "Tori?" he said, his voice low and intense. "You went away from me just now."

"No," I said, knowing he'd sense the lie. "I just have to get to the office. We'll pick this up later."

"Want company? I'm free until lunch."

"No," I lied again. I did want it, and that was exactly why I had to do without. Unless ... unless I was overthinking things.

Wasn't it always this way at the start of a relationship? All hot and heavy, painful to be apart. Maybe.

I had to stay strong.

"O...kay," Apollo said. He didn't understand. Hell, I didn't understand. Maybe I was just too ornery to be in a relationship. Any relationship. Maybe I should just ... stop thinking.

I grabbed an amber silk-blend cami, black pants, and a blazer that wouldn't last through the client interview—not in the LA heat. Then I pulled on my black low-heeled boots from yesterday and was off before I could change my mind. Leaving Apollo felt like leaving behind a part of myself.

I squashed the feeling mercilessly. I couldn't think about any of that now. I had a client, one I hoped came with a big, juicy case rife with distraction. No cheating spouse or missing money, but something I could sink my teeth into. Like a chocolate croissant.

Speaking of which, my favorite coffee shop was on the way, and after my earlier aerobics with Apollo, some sustenance was definitely in order. I'd probably earned myself a cheesy omelet, an entire side of bacon and whatever else I could carry back from an all-you-can-eat buffet, but I didn't have time. Carbohydrates and caffeine would have to do the trick.

I was already late. It wouldn't do to arrive faint with hunger as well. Better to take the five-minute detour and show up with pastry-shaped peace offerings.

I pushed through the door of the coffee-shop/art house I frequented to find, mercifully, only one man ahead of me, already paying for his cuppa.

Barry-the-barista greeted me by name and asked, "The usual?"

"Yeah, but make it three. Wait, four. Make one soy just in case and hold the sugar on two. Three chocolate croissants and three regular."

"Oh, so it's a party," he said, drinks already in progress.

I smiled. "Don't know what everyone else is going to eat."

"Isn't that why you ordered the plain?"

"You know me so well."

And all I knew was his name. Well, and the fact that he'd proposed to his girlfriend last month and been accepted. And that the wedding was next spring. And … okay, so I knew quite a bit. Probably, I'd even financed a good part of the big day.

While I waited, I looked up at the ever-present TV screen tucked away in a corner of the cafe, practically a necessity out here between weird weather, riots, and all-important air quality updates. The sound was down or off, but the subtitles scrolled across the bottom of the screen—all about a murder in the upscale Hollywood Hills. As I watched the external footage of a body being loaded into the back of an ambulance, I caught the flash of a familiar figure—Detective Nick Armani. My ex. He looked as amazing as always, all dark hair and midnight blue eyes. I knew those eyes in all of their moods; right then they were troubled, his usual poker face nowhere in evidence.

A zing went through me and I froze. It could not be about Nick's eyes. It couldn't, but … It happened again and I laser-focused on the foot disappearing into the ambulance, the door slamming on it with the finality of death. Something was not right at the scene, even beyond the taking of a life. Something …

Barry called my name. For the second time, I thought, and I shook myself out of my fugue to grab the coffee carrier and pastry bag he offered me. Only to set them back down on the counter so that I could root around in my pocket for payment. I left the change in his tip jar. Maybe I could help toward a down payment on the hall. It was my feeble attempt to counteract the bad in the world with just a little bit of good.

The office was only another minute away, located in old Hollywood, home of iconic theaters like the Orpheum and Rialto, sadly long since past their prime, most no longer operating as theatres. My office was in an old art deco building with a lift so ancient there was always a chance the doors wouldn't open again once they closed. But there were rules against messing with historic buildings by doing things like updating unsafe equipment. I decided to live dangerously and take the elevator anyway. I lived to tell the tale.

The door to the office opened while I was still trying to juggle coffee, pastries, and keys.

A haughty Jesus (pronounced Hey-Zeus) stood in its place, glaring his disapproval. "You're late," he said.

"No kidding," I answered.

"The client is waiting."

"She wouldn't be waiting anymore if you'd let me in."

He relieved me of the coffees and graciously allowed me to pass. "Would you carry those in for me?" I asked.

"It depends. Is one of them mine?"

"Yes."

"Well then, *chica*, by all means."

I breathed a sigh of relief. *Chica* meant all was forgiven. Boss lady would have meant I was still in the doghouse, which could mean anything with Jesus from him changing the password on our computer network to selling my story to the tabloids ... not that he knew the half of it. One did not thwart Jesus's iron will.

I expected to see the client almost immediately, sitting in the small waiting area in front of Jesus's desk. Instead, he led the way to my office, and as we approached the door, I understood why he'd tucked this one away, despite my prohibition on seating anyone in my office when I wasn't there to watch over them. The sound of her sobbing carried all the way through the door. Big, sloppy tears from the sound of them. Jesus abhorred a scene ... unless he was creating it. And messes were right out. He'd probably handed her the tissue box, toed my garbage can closer to her, and run for the hills.

"Good luck," he stage-whispered as I reached past him to

open my door. As soon as I had that hand free again, he passed the coffee tray into it, ushered me forward with a hand to my back and closed my office door firmly behind me.

The girl, because really she wasn't much more than that—nineteen, twenty maybe—looked up from the tissue she held over her nose. Her eyes were watery and red where they weren't cornflower blue.

"I'm so sorry to have kept you waiting," I said. "Can I offer you something? Coffee? A pastry?"

She stared blankly at first, as though the words were in some foreign language she had to translate for herself.

"I'm lactose intolerant," she said finally.

"One of these is soy."

The girl gave a wobbly smile. "Thanks then, I could use it."

I wondered if my foreseeing had played any part in the order, but if it had, I wouldn't have paid for the fourth cup ... I set the coffee carrier down on my desk and handed her the one marked soy. Then I set the sugars—I'd gotten a fistful of each—out where she could reach them and in lieu of a plate, tore the paper pastry bag down the center to reveal the yummy goodness inside.

She went for sugar in the raw and eyed the croissants as if she hadn't eaten in an age.

I grabbed a chocolate croissant to show her the way and bit into it immediately. The taste—butter and chocolate and flaky sweet goodness burst onto my tongue. I did not moan, but it was a close thing.

She sniffled, used the edge of the tissue in her hand to swipe at the moisture on her face and to give a good hard blow of her nose, then dropped it into the wastebasket and reached for one of the plain pastries. It was a good thing, I thought, that I wasn't the germaphobe Jesus was. I could just picture his reaction.

But once grabbed, all she did was hold the croissant in her

hand. I half feared she'd forget it wasn't the tissue and we'd have a big ole mess on our hands.

"Do you want to tell me about it?" I asked. The girl's eyes filled with tears again. "Why don't we start with your name?"

"Jessica," she said. "Jessica Roland."

That zing from back at the coffee shop struck again and I knew instantly where I'd heard the name Roland before ... the teletype about the Hollywood Hill murders.

"And you're here today because ..." I prompted.

"Because of my parents," she said, finishing my sentence on a sob. As I'd feared, she started to raise the croissant to her face. I quickly dropped my own like a hot potato in order to head her off with the offer of another tissue.

The Hollywood Hill murders ... Allowing Jessica a moment to compose herself gave me all the time I needed to imagine just how overjoyed Nick would be about my interfering with his new case. He'd be positively giddy.

But Jessica had made her appointment yesterday. Before the killings. Or at least before the bodies had been found. Maybe this was about something else? Inheritance or ...

"What about them?" I asked gently.

"They're dead. Murdered," she said, holding my gaze, the tissue unused in her hand. "And ... and the worst is ... I think my brothers did it."

And I thought I had problems. "Explain?"

She took a huge sip of her soy latte first for sustenance. "I mean, not them exactly," she said, looking away, "but ... Let me start at the beginning."

"That's usually best," I said. I could imagine Jesus rolling his eyes at me for that, but I wasn't trying to be a smart aleck ... not this time anyway.

Jessica stood with her coffee and paced as she talked. "I called yesterday because ... Look, this is going to sound crazy, but someone told me you sometimes handle things ... a little outside the box."

I nodded to encourage her to continue. There was no point in denying what was, especially when it was so severely understated. Gods, plague demons, dragons, apocalypsi ... or whatever the plural might be of apocalypse ... Yes, we certainly handled things outside the box ... Pandora's Box, specifically.

She took a deep breath. "Here's the thing. Ian and Richie got back just this past weekend from the graduation trip my parents sent them on to Egypt. My brothers had always been fascinated with it. Ian was even planning on going to college for archaeology, Richie probably for the drinking. Anyway, the thing is, they came back ... different. I don't know how to describe it. They've always been trouble. Not bad, just ... they don't really have any impulse control. If something occurs to them, it has to be done ... right that instant. Especially if it's new or exciting or dangerous. Mom and Dad have always had the influence or the money to get them out of any trouble they've gotten into. Still, they've always been fun-loving and have always looked out for me as their little sister. Well, not little, but younger."

"But now?"

"When they came back, they were ... scary. Different. Ian said ... I don't even want to tell you what he said to me. I'm his sister. He's never been like that. He would have punched out any of his friends who talked to me that way, and ... I was freaked. I mean, seriously. For the first time ever, I locked my door against them, and the night before last, I was sure I heard the door knob rattle, like someone was trying to get in."

"You mentioned Ian. What about Richie?"

"Richie's been ... quiet since he got back. Not pensive-quiet, but more like a predator of some kind, waiting and watching, looking at me like prey. And the way he looked at Mom and Dad ... Yesterday my parents got into a knockdown, drag out fight with the boys. There'd been a call from the tour company about them. Mom and Dad were trying to protect me, I think. They wouldn't tell me what was going on, but sent me away to a friend's house. That was when I called you and now ..."

Her hand was shaking so hard I could hear the remains of her coffee sloshing about in her cup. I rose to guide her back to her seat so she could sit down before she fell down. She followed my guidance, and when she was back in her chair, she looked up, tears glittering in her eyes as she speared my gaze. "Do you believe in possession or ... I don't know, is there some kind of drug or disease that can totally change someone's personality? I mean, there's no doubt these are my brothers. The way they walk and talk, their mannerisms, but ... but at the same time, they're not. I've heard about the curse of the pharaohs. Do you think that somehow they disturbed an ancient tomb or ... I don't know. Can you even investigate something like that? Especially if it happened an entire continent away? Please tell me you can help. I don't know where else to go."

I'd get to "the curse of the pharaohs" in a second. "Have you talked to the police yet?"

She looked away now, and I knew she hadn't. "N-no," she admitted. "I mean, they're my brothers. They're not themselves, but the police aren't going to believe that. They're only going to look at the boys' records, assuming my parents left any behind, and the evidence, and ... I don't know what to do."

"Jessica," I said gently. "You have to talk to the police. I know the detective in charge. He'll listen. He has to pursue the investigation, of course, and go where the evidence takes him, but ... Well, he'll listen. That much I can promise you."

She lunged forward and grabbed my hand across my desk. "You can help me then? You'll take the case?"

I couldn't do anything else. If she was right about her brothers, I might be the only PI who could help her.

"I will. First, you need to tell me everything you can about your brothers. Their friends, their resources, places they frequent, what they drive, anything you can think of. Most especially, I need to know what tour they were on. I'm going to need to contact the tour company. I presume the police didn't find them at the house? They haven't yet been arrested?"

"Not that I know of."

"Then step one, I call my friend the detective. Step two, we find your brothers. If they're dangerous, we need to get them safely under wraps while we figure out what's going on."

Her hand still clutched mine, and now she squeezed. "Thank you," she said in a voice gone hoarse with emotion. "Thank you."

I squeezed back and smiled reassuringly as I took my hand back so that I could call Jesus on the intercom. "Jesus, will you bring in a standard contract for Ms. Roland?"

He agreed, and I turned back to Jessica. "Now, about this *curse of the pharaohs ...*"

It was superstition nonsense, of course ... A few early archaeologists had met with misfortune, but no more than normal, and Howard Carter, the infamous discoverer of Tut's tomb, had lived to the ripe old age of sixty-four. Science didn't allow for "curses." It did allow for deadly mold or bacteria which could have accumulated in the tombs or burial boxes over the years and made people sick when the spores were unleashed, but none of those, that I knew of, made people into crazed killers.

Not that I thought science held all the answers. I knew better than most that Shakespeare had been right—there were far more things in heaven and earth than were dreamt of in my philosophy.

"What about mad cow disease?" she asked when I finished. "Or, like, syphilis? Not that I'm saying they have syphilis. I know that can take years to make a brain into Swiss cheese, but ...

something like that. It can happen, right? Maybe if I can convince them to get tested ..."

"No!" I said, a little too quickly. "I mean yes, it's possible, but I don't want you alone with them. I don't want you to confront them. If it's true that they're responsible for what happened to your parents, it's too dangerous for you. You need to let me handle things."

Jesus knocked on the door and didn't wait for me to give him the all-clear before coming in with the contract in duplicate.

Jessica didn't delay signing. "Do you take credit cards?" she asked. First world problems. Nobody carried cash or checks anymore.

"Sure," I said, letting Jesus know with a look that this time we'd make an exception. Generally, cash and checks were a lot harder to dispute if you didn't like the way an investigation turned out.

As soon as the paperwork was done, I had her list out all the things I'd asked her—people, places, hangouts for her brothers, cell phone numbers. Everything she could think of. While she was writing, I made the call.

As predicted, Detective Nick Armani was beside himself to hear from me. No, really.

2

———

I followed Jessica to the police precinct. She had her own car, but I wasn't entirely sure she was fit to drive, and anyway, I wanted to talk to Nick myself. I needed to prime him on what she was going to say and pick his brain about the case.

He hadn't loved my "interference" in his cases before we'd dated. Now that we had history I suspected he'd love it even less. Especially now that I kept company with his former rival. "Kept company with" sounded so much more and less than "dating," which was far too normal for whatever was between Apollo and me. Now that we were trapped in each 'others' orbit? Now that inescapable forces pulled us together ...

Gah, this thing with Apollo was dangerous. Certainly for my concentration. He wasn't even here and he was messing with me.

So, *Nick*. Detective Armani. Whatever we were calling each other these days. Neither one of us was going to be leaving LA. We'd have to find a way to work together sooner or later.

It was a good thing I'd taken that fourth coffee with me

when I left the office. I finally understood what I'd bought it for in the first place. It wasn't for me, though I'd toyed with the idea, even knowing that me on caffeine overload was something like a Chihuahua on speed. It was for Nick. A peace-offering of sorts. It would be cold, but still better than the swill they served at the precinct.

I met Jessica at her car in the parking lot and we walked in together.

The desk officer who ruled all traffic in and out of the precinct with an iron fist raised a brow at the sight of me. I wondered if he'd seen the stories about the wings or whether he knew about me and Nick and the breakup. I hadn't seen him since I'd returned from my trip back to Greece to meet with the Grey Sisters. I didn't know what tales Nick might have told about us or the miraculous healing from his third-degree burns. Very possibly we should have gotten our stories straight on the phone, but I'd had an audience and, really, it hadn't even occurred to me.

"We're here to see Detective Armani," I said quickly, before the sergeant could ask anything unprofessional in front of my client. "Tori Karacis, PI, and my client Jessica Roland. He's expecting us."

At the name *Roland*, his brows rose even higher, actually disappearing into his hairline.

"One minute."

He picked up his desk phone to make the call, but had to leave a message. As soon as he hung up, he picked the phone up again, probably to call Armani's partner. *Armani* ... best to start thinking of Nick that way again, to distance myself. The officer covered the mouthpiece of his phone when he spoke into it this time, but my precog didn't set off any warning bells, and so I just stared all the while.

When he hung up, he waved us to one of the few chairs in the entryway. "Someone will be out in a minute."

It took five minutes before Nick appeared, and when he did I caught my breath. Not because my heart still skipped a beat when I saw him ... really it was more of a delay than an actual skip ... but because of how tired he looked. Exhausted, really, like he hadn't slept in a week.

"Come on back," he said, barely meeting my gaze.

We followed him in. He bypassed his desk entirely and headed straight for one of the interview rooms.

"Can I talk with you first?" I asked before he could shut us in.

He turned to me, and it hurt more than it should have to see the cop look on his face, as though I was just another perp he was prepared not to believe whatever I had to say. The look was pretty effective. If I really was in the hot seat, I might be revising my strategy right about now, considering whether it was even worth the effort to lie to him.

"Please," I added.

He sighed heavily. "Do you mind waiting for just a second?" he asked Jessica.

She looked at me, and I nodded. "Just for a second," I said. "I want to make sure the detective understands the situation."

She blinked, new tears catching in her lashes. Not that I didn't understand, given the situation, but if she kept up like this, she was going to dehydrate in no time. "Maybe someone can get her a bottle of water," I suggested.

Nick ... Armani ... looked into my eyes, searching for hidden meaning. Finding none, he glanced toward his desk and gestured to someone nearby. I turned to look and found an attractive Latina woman headed toward us, her hair pulled back into a tight queue at the back of her head.

"Detective Reyes, can you get Ms. Roland something to drink? I'll be back in just a second."

Her gaze raked me dispassionately, and when she turned to Jessica, her lips quirked up in a smile that transformed her face.

The warmth of it made her more than just attractive. It made her compelling. I felt a pull at my heart at the thought of her working so closely with Nick and knew that it was totally unfair.

Detective Reyes motioned Jessica away from the door, off to another room, and Nick held the interrogation room open for me to precede him. I did, and he shut the door and leaned against it.

"For you," I said, holding out the coffee.

He stared it down, his eyes crinkling at the corners momentarily. "That your idea of a bribe?" he asked. Still, he took the cup. "It's not even hot."

"Fine, I'll take it if you don't want it."

"I didn't say that." He took a long sip and then fixed me with a look. "Okay, so talk."

I took a deep breath and let it out again. "It's going to be one of those cases," I began.

"One of your kind of cases, you mean?" He suddenly looked even wearier than he had before, despite the coffee.

"I think so. At least, Jessica thinks so. I know it sounds crazy —well, probably not after all you've seen—but she says the Roland boys came back from their trip to Egypt ... different. Not her brothers. At least, not entirely."

"You're right," he said. "To anyone else that might sound crazy." He took another supersized sip.

"I know. I mean, there are cases of brain injuries or whatever changing a person. If it had just been one ... but both strains credibility."

He laughed, but without much mirth. "And you're about to propose something much more credible? What—possession? Body snatchers? Cyborgs? Changelings? Stop me when I get close."

I rolled my eyes at him. "I don't know. I just started on the case. Literally. Jessica made the appointment yesterday. We met this morning and then we came straight from my office to yours."

"Wait, she called you yesterday? The murders only happened last night."

"Yeah, she called before the murders. Her brothers scared her. She wanted me to find out what happened to them over in Egypt. I think she was hoping for a solution. She didn't expect ... this."

"Did she tell you her whereabouts last night?"

"She did. She stayed with a girlfriend."

"But left her parents alone with her brothers?"

"Again, she wasn't expecting murder. Would you?"

"I don't know. I won't know until I talk to her."

"You'll do that soon enough. First, I need to know whatever you can tell me," I said, glancing into those deep blue eyes.

He gazed back and I couldn't read him. I hated that. "Like what?"

"First, whether you've found the Roland boys. I'm assuming not or it would be all over the news that you had them in custody."

"You assume right. There's been no sign of them. And they're not exactly answering their phones."

"And I'll need to see the crime scene."

He stared like I'd grown a second head. Given my sudden sprouting of wings not so long ago, it wasn't entirely out of the question. I had to resist checking just to be sure. "You don't ask for much, do you?" he asked. "The crime scene techs probably aren't even done processing yet."

"Call me when they're done? Same deal as always—you show me yours and I'll show you mine."

I didn't quite realize what I'd said until the words were out of my mouth, and then I wished to gods I could recall them.

His eyes darkened, and he didn't say anything for a full minute. "Professionally?" he asked finally.

I looked away. It hurt too much otherwise. "Professionally," I confirmed.

"Damn shame," he said, and left it at that.

"No promises on the crime scene," he said after a moment, "but I'll see what I can do. I'll call you later."

It was his turn to look away at that. Such a simple thing, and so loaded.

"Um, good. Great. Thank you. I'll let you talk to Jessica right now. I'm going to explore some of her brothers' haunts, see if I can find them."

"Be careful," he said, meeting my gaze again.

"You too," I said.

"Always," he answered, though we both knew that wasn't true.

"It's good to see you back. How did you explain the miraculous healing?"

Nick pulled at a gold chain I'd barely noted around his neck and brought a pendant out from where it rested next to his heart.

"A St. Christopher medal?" I asked.

"Jude. Saint of impossible cases. You mentioned miraculous healing. That's exactly what I went with."

"Your mother must be so proud," I said with complete sincerity.

If there was one thing Nick had told me about his mother, it was that she was a diehard Roman Catholic ... the kind who went to church not just every week, but *every day*. Oh, and that she was, literally, a little old lady from Pasadena, just like the song.

His lips quirked. "In hindsight, the miracle might have been a mistake. Now she expects me to drive up and take her to church every Sunday to show proper thanks. And she likes to show me off to her friends."

I tried not to smile at the thought of Nick among the church ladies. He'd be quite a catch. No doubt eligible daughters were being flung at him left and right.

"Matchmaking?" I asked.

"Don't even get me started."

It was my cue to go. I knew it. Even so, I hesitated just a second. "Call me about that crime scene," I said as a parting line.

He just nodded, letting me have the last word.

IN THE CAR, I looked at the list Jessica had given me and tried to prioritize. Mentally, I came up with a most-likely/closest-by-scale that helped me pinpoint my first few stops ... after the crime scene. I knew I couldn't get in right away. That would have to wait until Nick ... Armani ... called. *If* he called. But I had a burning need to see what I could myself. To begin at the beginning, move on until the end, then stop, as Lewis Carroll would have said. My reasoning was twofold. One, there'd be looky-loos—reporters, neighbors, passersby, any local scanner-jockey who'd rather chase police cars than ambulances. If I was lucky, one or both of the Roland boys might even return to the scene of the crime. Or ... well, I wouldn't know until I got there. My hope was that I'd find someone who knew something they hadn't told the police, or that the police would never tell me, maybe something crucial they were withholding. I needed to gather all the intel I could. Knowledge was power.

Which brought me to reason number two.

Just seeing how and where the Roland boys had lived would help me build a profile that could lead me to them. Maybe even allow me to bring them in without bloodshed. I could dream. Maybe my own Saint Jude medal was in order.

I GPSed the address Jessica had given me, but the roads up in the Hollywood Hills were narrow and the closer I got, the harder it was to get through. Cars were parked illegally all along the way—up to a mile from the house. I drove carefully past them all ... for about a half mile until I met a car coming the other way on a road that had been artificially choked down to a single lane. One of us was going to have to back off, and it was clear it would not be the lady in the other car.

Her heavily kohl-lined eyes burned like lasers, boring their way through both our windshields until I could feel the heat of them. Her face was broad and symmetrical, which seemed a weird thing to notice, but it was almost too perfect. Most people had something—a scar, a brow slightly higher than another, one lid droopier or ... something. But even the intricate braids of her hair perfectly matched from one side to the other.

I memorized her for later, just in case. Maybe it was my precog. Maybe it was the sense of purpose rolling off her in waves, but I had an idea she'd be important later on.

Her eyes seemed to flare as we continued to face off, as though she could move me off the road through sheer force of will. The odd thing was, it worked. One of us had to give, and in this case it was clear it would have to be me.

Scowling, I backed up until I found a driveway I could pull into to get out of her way, and then she drove past without raising a hand in thanks or even looking my way in any sort of acknowledgment. I flung a few choice words after her and stopped when I realized I'd come back around to the beginning.

Vocab exhausted, I shrugged off the encounter and found a place to park down the hill, probably illegally. I had to hope the cops were too busy to ticket me. I set my parking brake and trudged up the hill to the murder scene. And trudged. As much as I'd bemoaned their existence when I'd had them, I now mourned the temporary loss of my wings. My back kept twitching, as though my wings wanted out. I could have flown to the scene in no time ... if I wanted to expose myself to the reporters and half the police force. But I didn't. I climbed up the old-fashioned way.

The news vans alerted me when I got close ... those and the kick to the gut delivered by my precog. There was something important here. As if I needed my precog to tell me that.

The danger might have moved on, but it hadn't passed.

The scene was controlled chaos. The Roland mansion stood behind seven-foot tall wrought iron fencing with even higher gates done up in scrollwork that culminated with a medallion containing the house number in a fancy font. The medallion was, in fact, about all I could see of the front gates beyond the spectators, most with cameras or phones held over their heads to capture what they couldn't see themselves. The mansion wasn't far beyond the gates, space being such a premium on the hills. Unlike most of its neighbors, it was a boxy brick colonial, complete with two-story white pillars, and wrap-around front porch, rather than something more hacienda in style.

In the foreground, two reporters stood several feet from each other, each on a raised platform to bring them to the level where a cameraman could get the mansion in the shot, a trick of perspective, as they delivered their sound bytes. They were from competing networks. I wondered how their sound guys would do with cutting out their rival's background chatter. I was nearly past when one, a woman in a red power suit with flowing chestnut hair, called out, "Wait!" and jumped down from her box.

I was startled enough to turn and ended up with a camera in my face. I put a hand up to block it, and then realized that walking away would work even better.

A hand landed on my arm, and I was tempted to remove it

with prejudice ... if only the camera weren't rolling. Anyway, I supposed that if I got really desperate I could just give her and her cameraman the gorgon glare to get away. Enough to freeze them in their tracks, of course, not turn them to stone. That could be accomplished too, but it required blood I was not ready to spill.

I halted but didn't turn, so the woman circled around in front of me, her four-inch heels putting her at about eye-level with me in my boots. "You're that girl," she said, eyes wide.

"Girl might be a bit of a stretch," I answered ungraciously.

I recognized her, I thought. A stringer from Channel 9. Not a tabloid journalist or a sensationalist—that I knew of—but an on-site reporter, someone they sent to various scenes so the anchors would have someone to talk to from the comfort of their desks.

She smiled, and it did good things for her. "Sorry, let me introduce myself. I'm Susie Tallios from News9. I ... I recognize you from the trouble in New York last month."

I snorted. "Trouble" was possibly the understatement of the year. Zombies, plague demons, godly cabals, none of which had been limited to the Big Apple ... Trouble didn't cover the half of it. But then, neither had the news.

"Rumors of my involvement have been greatly exaggerated," I said, meeting her gaze in a way I hoped projected sincerity.

"And now you're here," she said.

I bit back a comment on her mastery of the obvious.

"Can we talk?" she asked.

I considered that. I was looking for information. It was just possible she had some.

News was her business, after all.

"Maybe," I responded. "If you'll turn off your camera."

She looked to the cameraman as if she'd forgotten all about

him, and made a hand gesture that looked something like cutting her own throat.

I glanced back to see him making a few gestures of his own. When he saw me looking, he sighed heavily and lowered the camera. "Fine. I'll get some crowd reaction. But don't be long. They might want you to interview some of the neighbors or ..." he shrugged, "... you know how it goes."

"I do," she said. "I'll be right with you."

I waited for the cameraman to go off before facing Suzie again. My precog hadn't kicked up at her presence, which meant she didn't present a danger. It didn't mean she was my friend.

I crossed my arms over my chest. "So, what do you want?" I asked.

She looked after the cameraman to make sure he was really gone. "Listen, I'm ambitious, okay?" I did not roll my eyes. I'd seen it coming. "I've done some checking. Whatever else you might be, you're a PI. You work here in LA. You've been connected with Apollo Demas and with the murder earlier this year of that talent agent Circe Holland, the details of which are still hazy at best. You were photographed fighting off a crazed mob in Central Park." It was fascinating the spin the press and everyone else had put on the sudden profusion of plagues and other insanity. But then, magic and myth were out of the realm of most peoples' experience. Conspiracies, on the other hand, were almost an everyday affair. Plus, they had the advantage of selling papers. I'd seen speculation blaming everything from killer viruses escaping the CDC to radical groups like ISIS and al-Qaeda.

She lowered her voice, looked surreptitiously left and right. "And now," she near-whispered, "here you are, right on the scene where two people were murdered, their brains literally scrambled ..."

"Wait, what?"

She had my full attention now. She grinned as if she knew it. "I'll tell you what I know if you'll give me something I can use."

I eyed her. It wouldn't be the worst thing in the world to make a reporter friend. It didn't seem like I could avoid the news anyway. Might as well use it to my advantage. Wasn't that what Apollo wanted? Would making my own friend keep me off the red carpet?

"I'll have to hear what you have first," I said.

She eyed me back. "You good for it?" she asked.

"Cross my heart and hope to die."

She turned a little green at that for some reason. It looked like she might even have lifted a hand to cross herself but caught herself first. Interesting.

"Okay then." She looked around again to be sure no one was close enough to overhear. A few of the spectators had turned from watching the nothing they could see through the crowd of people between them and the fence to watching us, but unless anyone had super hearing ... a deeply underestimated superpower in my book ... "Look, the rest of that saying, 'Cross my heart and hope to die' is 'stick a needle in my eye,' right?" She didn't wait for an answer. "Well, that's pretty close to what happened."

"More," I said.

Her eyes scrunched shut for a minute. Her lips twisted. These weren't just words for her. Whatever had happened had left an impression. "Okay, this is going to sound crazy, but ... well, look, I caught an officer losing his lunch over the scene inside. He talked before he could think better of it. Really, I think he was just trying to vent the horror. He swore me to secrecy. I can't use this ... yet ... but ... Those poor people inside had skewers stuffed up into their brains and ... when I say scrambled, I meant liquefied. And the police didn't find the fluids all over the floor, which means ..."

"They were carried away," I said. "Or ..."

"Or drunk," she whispered, barely forcing out enough air to form the words. "Or drained away down the toilet or the sink or any number of things."

Our eyes met and held. "What else?" I asked, sensing there was more.

"Their chests were torn open."

"Torn how?"

"I don't know. He just kept repeating, 'So much blood.'"

My precog chose that moment to chime in, as if I might not recognize that a ripped-open chest and missing brain were somehow significant. Dangerous. Deadly.

The blood cemented it. If the killers were worried about bodily fluids, the site would have been clean. To soak up the gray matter somehow and leave the blood ... No, there had to be a method to their madness.

I didn't know a hell of a lot when it came to ancient Egyptian practices, but I'd had a childhood fascination with mummification ... hadn't everyone? The brain, strangely, wasn't one of the organs the priests had deemed important to preserve. It was actually ripped out in pieces through the nose and discarded so that the cranial cavity could be packed with cotton and resin and various preservatives. The important organs were saved separately—the lungs, liver, stomach, and intestines—all except for the heart, which they considered the seat of intellect as well as emotion. That stayed with the body.

What did it mean that the killers had gone for both? Modern sensibilities coupled with ancient superstition? After all, Jessica said her brothers had come back different, but they had come back. That meant they still knew how to get to the airport, suffer through security, use cell phones and credit cards and all that jazz.

"Wow," I said, knowing I'd been silent a little too long.

"Yeah, wow. Your turn now. What can you tell me?"

I debated. I couldn't give up my client or anything she'd told me, clearly in confidence, but I suspected that if it hadn't been already, a BOLO—be on the look-out—would be issued for the Roland boys at any moment. I'd only be jumping the gun by a little bit tipping her off. Anyway, it couldn't hurt for the world to be warned against them.

It was my turn to look left and right, to make sure we weren't being overheard. "I hear the sons are 'sought for questioning.'"

She stared at me. "Really? Like the Menendez brothers all over again?"

Another sensational LA homicide—years ago brothers Lyle and Eric Menendez had murdered their wealthy parents. It had been a bloody, sensational crime, but not like this ... nothing like this.

"Something like that," I said. "But remember, the investigation has just begun."

"I'll be cautious."

"And I'll be anonymous. I don't even want to be a 'source close to the investigation' or anything like that."

"But—"

"No," I said firmly. "We might be able to help each other, but only if we play by my rules."

She blew out a hard sigh. It ruffled her perfect hair. "Yo, Simon," she yelled, calling back her photographer. I aimed to be out of range before he got back.

"Bye," I said, fair warning, just to be polite.

"Wait," she called to my already-turned back. Reluctantly, I glanced over my shoulder to see her holding out a business card. I had no idea where she kept it in that skintight suit, but as warm and slightly damp as this one was, I could guess. "Call me if you want to exchange any more information."

I tucked the card into my pocket. It was, after all, what they were for. "You too. I suspect you know where to find me."

And I was off before the camera could hit. I'd gotten what I came for—information. Or, at least, all I was likely to get without access to the crime scene. Susie must have been one of the first reporters to the site if she'd been there early enough to witness a cop tossing his cookies over the scene. If she had her ear to the ground, not unlikely given her ambition, she might be a useful contact. Seemed about time to have the press working for me rather than against.

3

———————

I walked a little way down the street, back toward my parked car, and stopped to consult the notes Jessica had given me. I decided to start at the top—calling the numbers I had for the brothers and their friends. I didn't really expect an answer, not from the brothers anyway.

I wasn't disappointed there. I *did* get an answer on my fourth call, but the voice that answered wasn't the one I'd expected. From the name Viktor Ramone, I understandably expected a male voice. What I got was a female, exotically accented.

"Yes?" the voice said. Clipped. Precise. A don't-fuck-with-me voice.

"I'm looking for Viktor," I told her. At the mention of his name, my gut felt like something ... or someone ... had given me a sharp kick to the solar plexus. Something was wrong.

"I'm sorry, Viktor can't come to the phone right now." That sounded ominous. "Who is this?"

"Who is *this*?" I countered, because *oh yeah*, I was a master of interrogation.

"I am Neith," she said, like that answered everything. "You do *not* want to get in my way."

"You know what? Maybe I do." I hung up on her.

Immediately I dialed Jesus, who answered after two rings, as always. According to him, "One ring says we're too hungry and three that we're too busy."

"*But two is just right,*" I said in a singsong voice the first time he'd shared his philosophy.

My next coffee came laced with cayenne.

"Karacis Investigations," he said in his uber-efficient voice.

"Jesus, it's me. I need you to do an Internet search on Neith."

"Neith who?"

"Just Neith. One name, like Cher or Madonna."

"O-kay," he said. "Do I get a please?"

"You get a paycheck."

He huffed.

"Okay, please and thank you."

"That's better."

He was going to train me yet.

I hung up on him too—I'd never really gotten the hang of good-byes—and programmed Viktor's address into my GPS.

Probably it hadn't been the smartest move to let this Neith lady know I was coming. I could be setting myself up to walk into an ambush, but I couldn't help myself. I was ornery. If you told me to go one way, I was bound and determined to go another. She didn't sound like the type of woman to put up with that.

Well she didn't know who she was dealing with.

My GPS guided me to a house farther down the Hollywood Hills. Bungalow-type. One floor, low to the land, probably open floor plan inside. Quite a step down from the Roland mansion, but given the location—and as they said in Hollywood, it was *all* about location, location, location—it was still probably a few mil above my pay grade.

My precog hammered at me now with a knocking in my stomach like I'd just left an all-you-can-eat burrito bar.

"Shut it," I growled, like it would listen. Miraculously, it did.

I sat for a second outside the house doing recon. Like the Roland mansion, it had a wall—this one a low brick wall with rose bushes poking over the top. It also had a gate, though it only rose to chest height. Easy as pie to just reach over the top, lift the little bar and let myself in. I didn't even understand the point of a gate that wasn't secured, unless it was for curb appeal.

Because I was impetuous but not crazy and didn't want to deal with the scolding later should anything happen, I texted Jesus to let him know where I was. There was no telling what I'd find inside the house ... or who ... but since the voice on the other end of the phone had made it clear that Viktor was indisposed, there were better than even odds I was walking into a crime scene. Maybe even walking in on the perp. If I let someone split my head open, I'd be in no condition to weather one of Jesus's lectures. Or Armani's, for that matter.

Reluctantly, I added that if I didn't check in after twenty minutes he should call Nick.

I didn't wait for his response before I was out of the car and headed for the house. I reached over the gate and let myself in. The walkway beyond was paved unevenly, probably years ago before the ground had settled or the latest quake had shifted the earth, but the path was short and I was at the door before I'd finished the thought. Then I listened. Inside, as far as I could tell, was silence. The fact that the front door was ajar was worrisome, but also made it easier to listen in.

My precog jumped and fluttered in my gut like ... something that jumps and flutters. A flying grasshopper, maybe. But I couldn't hear a thing inside. It was deadly silent.

In case I was in for an ambush, I gave the door a good swift kick to knock it into anyone who might be hiding behind it, but all it did was bounce loudly against the wall, probably leaving a mark, before coming back at me. I stopped it with a hand.

As usual, my gun was elsewhere. Anything that couldn't be stopped by my gorgon glare was only going to be seriously pissed off by a bullet wound.

So I entered the house with nothing drawn but my nerves. The foyer was nothing special. It opened almost immediately into a large living room with the focal point a large wood-burning fireplace. Not a television? I wondered, but then I spotted it just above, a huge flat screen hanging on the wall in place of a painting or fancy family photo above the mantel. The coffee table was entirely obscured by used cups, dishes, two pizza boxes, a round of empty beer bottles and a humungous work boot, which I realized after a second was still occupied. I traced it to the body around the other side of the coffee table; worried I'd find the rest bloody and brainless, but the man's chest rose and fell as I approached. He didn't so much as bat an eye or turn in his sleep. There seemed to be a coin resting in the center of his forehead. Or ... I leaned in closer ... a round metal disk, anyway. Not gold but maybe bronze, pressed with some kind of symbols but worn to the point where they were barely readable, at least to me.

I took out my phone, clicked on the camera, and snapped a close-up. For now I left the disk in place and moved on from the body, needing to be sure I was in the clear before I took things any further. I could see the dining area beyond the living room. Just a simple dark wood table and chairs with a buffet behind it and a hutch off to the side holding an alpine-designed set that looked more Yosemite than LA.

That was as far as the open concept went. The kitchen was its own contained space with two entryways—one leading toward the dining room along one wall, the other leading to the living room/foyer on the other. I wouldn't be able to see in without exposing some part of myself in the doorway.

My precog didn't like that idea one bit, by which I knew that whatever waited for me, waited there. But in poker terms, I was all in.

I jumped into the doorway, glaring around to catch the eye of whoever waited for me. Before I could, my head was grabbed and wrenched around so that I was propelled toward the wall. Just as quickly, one of my arms was yanked and twisted up behind me. I bit my cheek and as blood flooded my mouth, I muttered the ancient Greek words I'd been given to recall my wings. They flared out with the force of a parachute opening, and my attacker howled in surprise as she was thrown back. I heard her impact with the kitchen cabinetry and whirled to meet her.

She recovered quickly. A booted foot was already headed my way. I blocked with an arm, countered with a kick of my own. She grabbed my foot in mid-air, lightning fast, and twisted so hard I had to spin with it or wrench my ankle. I used the momentum and my wings to whirl me all the way around, catching her upside the head with my other foot as I twirled.

She *oophed* and staggered to the side, and I landed hard on the ground as she let go of my foot a second too late for a smooth landing. My wings took the brunt, but I used them to kip back to my feet. She hadn't fallen, but stood facing me, her eyes burning. Not like Hades's with their natural hellfire. Not even with hatred. Bloodlust, I'd say. Or battlefire.

It was the woman I'd faced off with for the right of way at the Roland crime scene. She was stunning. Not in the sense of beautiful, but in the way that would have been called handsome back in the drawing room days. Or fierce. She wasn't tall. Maybe five foot eight. Her skin was mahogany, her brows arched in that perfectly manicured way some women came by naturally. Her hair was braided back tightly to her head into a dozen or so rows, so no grabbing possibilities there. She was outfitted in bounty-hunter black from head to toe, with some kind of padded vest, maybe Kevlar, over her chest with a shield and crossed arrows design in muted red, black, and brown across the front. Very *Hunger Games*.

Since she was so determined to stare me down anyway, I seized the moment. *"Freeze,"* I told her, putting everything I had behind it.

I was stunned when she didn't, instead becoming a blur of motion, coming for me. I didn't have time for a sigh, though I certainly felt it. Instead, I countered, blocked, countered again, lashed out, was denied. We were a flurry of strike, counter-strike, each getting in our blows but never enough to disable the other. Finally, I was just a second too slow, and the next thing I knew I was pinned to the refrigerator, the handle digging into my chest and a knife to my throat.

"No fair," I said before I could stop myself. Moving sound through my throat brought it into more direct contact with the knife, and I felt it bite into my skin. I wondered if it was enough to make me bleed and whether I could use that. My blood on the knife wouldn't do a thing to me, but if I could turn it on her ...

If I turned it on her, she'd be stone and I'd never get any answers.

"Who are you?" she asked, backing the knife off just enough to let me answer.

"I'm Tori Karacis, a private investigator. I have ID." I wasn't stupid enough to reach for it. Not without her permission or an opening where I could take the upper hand.

"Show me," she said.

"I'm going for my wallet," I said.

Slowly I did, reaching into the pocket of my jeans. When I had the wallet out, I flipped it open and cautiously turned to show her.

She studied my license with so little interest I wondered why she'd asked.

"I've heard of you," she said, grudgingly, knife still at my throat. "Why are you here?"

"I'm working a case," I answered, replacing my ID. "I'm trying to find the Roland brothers. You know, the boys whose parents were killed. I saw you at the crime scene."

"It's too dangerous for you," she said, pulling the knife away, but not sheathing it. "This is outside your expertise."

I slid out from between her and the refrigerator, toward one of the entrances so that there was nothing new for her to pin me against. Not without effort anyway. I'd gotten used to being a badass. I'd faced down gods, goddesses, plague demons—hell, even sea monsters—and, okay, I'd had help, but I guess I'd started to take for granted that there was nothing I couldn't handle.

Being bested by a mere mortal ... But wait, Neith hadn't responded to the gorgon glare.

The only beings I'd ever seen unaffected were the older gods. Surely she wasn't ... Oh crap.

My phone buzzed just then. And buzzed. I had a call coming in. Had it been twenty minutes yet? Surely not.

"Sorry, I've got to take this," I said, but I waited to see if she was going to take advantage of my distraction. Instead she nodded regally, granting permission.

I didn't trust it, but I didn't want Jesus calling in the cavalry if I didn't respond, at least not yet. I pulled the phone from my hip holster and swiped to accept the call.

"*Chica,*" he said, without even a hello, "you ask me to research the strangest stuff. I'm assuming you're not talking about the video game character, but the Egyptian deity, yes?" He didn't wait for my answer. "In brief, Neith is a warrior goddess and a goddess of domestic arts, weaving especially, which doesn't all seem to fit together, but there it is. At least that's how it all started. Later she seems to have gotten confused with Isis and became a protectress of the dead. She's also known for being chaste." He said that like it was a bad word, "which with the warrior goddess thing might be why she's seen as some kind of corollary to Athena. Her fetish is two crossed swords on an animal skin or shield."

"Oh," I said, eyeing the insignia my attacker wore on her vest, "that Neith."

"I can send you all the research."

"Yes, please."

"You sound funny. Do I need to call Detective Armani?"

"No, everything's fine," I said, hanging up once again.

Neith and I stood eyeing each other. If she'd "heard of me" before, she knew who I was, probably knew I had gorgon blood running through my veins. Maybe that was even the reason for the instant animosity. If she'd been Athena, she didn't have the best track record with the gorgons. Myth had it that she was responsible for making Medusa into the monster she was, and all for something that wasn't her fault—being defiled by Poseidon. I knew all about how stories could be distorted, but until I knew another angle on this one I couldn't squash the ... dislike was too weak a word. Hatred was poison. The very strong feelings I had for her. Or rather, against.

"So, warrior goddess," I said finally. I tried to keep my voice cool and even. I mostly even succeeded.

"So, PI to the Pantheon," she said back.

"Tell me about the man dead asleep in the living room." I wasn't asking. I was commanding. She liked that about as much as I would have had our positions been reversed.

We walked back into the living room; watching each other warily, and stood over the unconscious man as though we weren't tromping all over a crime scene. Come to think of it, I didn't have any evidence of a crime. If he'd been drugged or knocked out with blunt force trauma or any number of things, I could call this in. But if he was bespelled ... I didn't think there was a police code for that. Calling all cars, calling all cars—there's a 666 going on at the Ramone residence....

"See the image stamped into the coin?" Neith asked me.

"Sort of. Seems like it's been worn away."

"Nearly, but if you look closer—" she grabbed the nape of my neck and pushed me down closer to the body. I had to remind myself that I couldn't take her in a fight—not the goddess of warfare and, particularly, strategy—so I couldn't rip her arm off for manhandling me. Instead, I ground my teeth. "You see?" she asked, now that I was right on top of the thing. "It's nearly sphinxlike, but instead of a man's head, it's a dog's."

"It doesn't look like any dog I've ever seen."

"Extinct species. Anyway, it's the symbol of Set, a dog if I ever saw one."

"Set? As in ... Set? The chaos god who chopped Osiris up into a million pieces?"

She let go of my neck and I rubbed it, glaring at her. She glared back. "Yes, that one. Worse, he fed his ... er, never mind ... to the fishes."

His "never mind"? Wow, chaste was understating things if in all her years she hadn't come to terms with the word penis. I was tempted to pull a George Carlin and run through all the alternate words for a guy's man parts, but I suspected she might wash my mouth out with soap ... or worse.

"Okay, got it. Really bad dude. You think the Roland brothers have fallen in with him somehow?"

"'Fallen in' might be overstating things. Set is still bound. His wife-jailor, Taweret, assures it. But it seems the brothers have encountered some of his talismans—an amulet and six smaller tokens, based on what's missing from the museum inventory—and it appears they might be under his influence."

"That can't be all there is to it. Objects are objects, aren't they? I mean, power might be stored or they might be built to do a specific thing, but ..."

"And if that thing they're meant to do is create chaos? Or put a man into a coma-like sleep? Anyway, you don't understand spellcraft. Everything is representative. You know those thousands of terra cotta soldiers found in China, each different from the others? They were put there to become an actual army for the emperor in the afterlife. The same is meant for the clay representations of food and animals that were sealed into tombs with the bodies in ancient Egypt. So, if an object is created with Set's likeness ..."

"There's some kind of connection to the man himself," I finished for her.

"God," she corrected. "And he's a right bloodthirsty bastard."

"Okay, but how do you know all this? Not about the spellcraft. I'll grant you've probably learned a thing or two in all your years. But how are you tracking the Roland boys? The murder only just happened."

"This murder only just happened. There's been at least one other."

Neith pulled out a phone I'd never even noticed. I guess that with her ancient goddess aura I assumed she sent ravens or doves or psychic messages. The modern device in her hand seemed so out of place, especially when she started scrolling through it for photos. The first one she showed me nearly made me lose this morning's chocolate croissant.

I couldn't even tell at first whether the body was male or female. There was so much blood. Pools of it. It seemed like she'd been torn open, painted in her own lifeblood and ...

"What happened?" I asked, swallowing back bile.

"She was killed. Right in the museum from which the artifacts were stolen. Mutilated, as you can see and ... well, best not to talk about that."

I filled in the blank—*assaulted.* Given Athena's history with Medusa, I wanted to lash out and ask her if this was somehow the victim's fault as well, but despite my efforts to choke it down, bile still flooded my throat. Besides, that was ancient history. It was possible she'd changed with the times. Hera certainly had, no longer revenging herself on Zeus's lovers, but now an actual woman's advocate.

"But that's not even all of it," Neith continued. "She was found in the museum's vault. The museum had just gotten in two very unusual sarcophagi. The names have been lost to history, their spirits not commended to the next life, but ... Osiris knows the hearts of all those who have died. These were very bad men. Killers, rapists. They'd managed to kill nineteen women and two men back in their day before they were taken down."

"And yet someone went to the trouble to embalm them?" I managed.

"They weren't embalmed so much as interred. Spells were set to bind them in, to confuse their spirits so that they'd never reach the afterlife. And if by chance they did ... the demon Ammit would be waiting to eat their souls."

"Fun," I said. "But I'm not sure—"

"I think it was a ... perfect storm, as you would say? Set's amulets alone—others have handled them and not gone on rampages. I don't know, but I suspect that there was a sort of sympathetic magic set up when the two brothers, in commission of a crime, came upon the confused spirits of the criminals and that Set's tokens played some part in joining them."

"Awesome. Oh, Armani is just going to love this."

"Who?"

"You'll meet him soon enough."

Viktor suddenly jerked and uttered a low moan, drawing our attention to his sleeping form. "Why haven't you woken up Sleeping Beauty here?" I asked Neith. "Is it dangerous?"

"I wanted to have an uninterrupted look around first." She gave me the hairy eyeball as she said it, since clearly I'd put the kibosh on that.

"Well, then, I'll do the honors."

I pulled my jacket sleeve down over my hand and went to lift the coin from the forehead of the man I presumed to be Viktor Ramone.

He came up kicking, his booted foot landing hard on the table, knocking over used beer cans, and sending one pizza box crashing to the floor. Neith instantly dropped down on top of him, nearly sitting on his chest with her arms outstretched to capture his wrists. I grabbed for his feet, catching a mule-kick to my thigh before I got them under control. He screamed, incoherent with fear, his eyes rolling in his face like he was a googly-eyed doll in the hands of a child. It took a full one minute for him to calm down and his eyes to focus. When they did, they were still spooked, but they latched on to Neith.

The look changed from fear to bafflement. "You're not a demon," he said.

She huffed and said in her melodic voice, "Nice of you to notice. Are you okay? If I get up, will you hurt yourself or others?"

Us, she meant.

He looked around wildly before answering. "Where are Ian and Richie?"

"They were here?" she asked. We both knew that they had been, but he might clam up later, so better to get the confession now before he had his wits about him to invent whatever story would serve him best and keep him from an accusation of aiding and abetting.

When he didn't spot them, he relaxed. His legs slumped in my hold and it seemed safe enough to let them go. They thumped down on the table, knocking around the bottles that remained.

Neith wasn't ready to do the same with his arms, but speared him with her gaze while she held him bound.

"They're gone," she told him. "Had you invited them in?"

He tried to shrug in her grasp and found he couldn't "They're my friends," he said instead. "Well, were my friends, anyway. Something's gotten into them."

"Like murder?" she asked, studying his response. From where she was, holding his wrists, I realized she could probably feel his pulse. I wondered if she could sense his truth or lies from the pace of it.

I watched his face. His eyes got really big at that. Huge. And he started to struggle again, less wild but more desperate, as though he suddenly felt his vulnerability.

"Murder?" he said, his voice shaky. Then, "Let me up. Who are you, anyway? You're not the police."

Neith seemed satisfied by his reaction and eased up off of him. She even reached down to help him stand. He was taller than her by several inches, so it was odd I had the impression she towered above him. It must have been the force of her personality. If she'd worn six-inch heels, like all movie heroines seemed to do regardless of their ridiculous impracticality, she'd have been totally over the top.

"I'm a bounty-hunter," Neith told him, flashing me a glance daring me to contradict her. "And Ms. Karacis here is a private investigator. You really don't know about the murders?"

"What murders?" he asked, clearly frustrated.

Viktor Ramone was a big man. With his work-boots, jeans and serviceable shirt, he looked far too blue-collar and work-a-day for the Hollywood Hills. He looked maybe like a stuntman or stunt coordinator ... until you got to the mullet. I didn't know how he expected to be taken seriously with that. But then, Dog the Bounty Hunter rocked a mullet, and I didn't see too many people underestimating him.

"The Roland boys killed their parents," she said baldly. In

her Oxford English spoken with her melodic accent it came out sounding a lot less harsh somehow than if I'd said it.

"Allegedly," I added, for form's sake. And in case it made him more apt to talk. "The entire LA police department is looking for them. We want to find them first."

"But ... why?" he asked, face scrunching in bafflement.

"Why do we want to find them or why did they kill their parents?"

"Either," he said. "Both?"

"First, because it's our job. Second, we'd like to ask them the very same question. And you—what happened here?" I'd answered his questions. Only fair I got in some of my own.

Neith took a step closer, as if to intimidate him into answering, but I didn't think that was going to be necessary.

"I was just heading out the door when they showed up out of nowhere," he said, eyes still a bit glazed over and wide with sincerity. "They didn't call first. Nothing. I told them I was running late, but Ian practically pushed me back inside. His eyes were ... not right. I thought he was maybe on something —crack or meth or ... I don't know. Then Richie stepped in and closed the door behind us, leaning against it. I'm twice their size, but something felt off about the whole thing. People can do anything hopped up on drugs, you know? I told them they had to go, that I was on my way to a set, but they wouldn't leave. Ian asked if they could stay, but not like he was asking, if you know what I mean. When I tried to force the issue, Richie said something strange. I'm not even sure it was English. And then I woke up to you in my place and ... all this."

He gestured to the mess. "I mean, the pizza boxes are mine, but the rest ..."

"You woke up fighting. What did you expect to find?"

"Nightmares."

"Can you be more specific," Neith asked, micro focusing on

him, taking another step forward until she was right in his personal space. He stepped back and she moved with him.

"Whoa, babe, boundaries," he said to her, taking another step. He waited to see if she'd advance again, and when she didn't, he went on. "It's all fading now. And it wasn't that clear to begin with. You know, kind of like a Michael Bay film—all action and explosions, very little storyline. There was blood and violence and ... stuff. And there was a man ... or ... something. He didn't look like any guy I've ever seen. His skin was white, but not like albino-white, where it's really more pale pink. More like birch-bark white. And he had flaming red hair. His eyes were ... I'm not a words guy. They were, like, agony and pain and bat-shit crazy all rolled into one, if that makes any sense. Like, worse than Charles Manson's shark-eyes."

He stopped, swallowed hard, and waited for us to show some sign of sympathy or understanding. We both nodded.

"And he was wrapped all in chains. They cut into him in places and in others the skin was rubbed clean away ... He was screaming something, but I don't know what. And there was something about a hippo and a scorpion, like I was on a really bad acid trip ... Not that I'd know anything about that."

Neith's eyes were blazing. "You're sure he was still chained?"

"What, you know this guy?" he asked. "He's ... he's for real?"

But Neith was looking to me now. "As I said, Set. Thank the gods he's still bound and only acting through agents."

"And if he gets free?" I asked, afraid for the answer.

"Take your greatest nightmares and multiply them exponentially. He's got millennia of scores to settle and ages of pent-up chaos. I can only imagine."

Viktor looked at us like we were both crazy. It was nice to have company for a change. Hermes, aka Mercury, aka Iemisch, Spider, Coyote, Loki, and a gazillion different gods throughout history, had done his best, I thought, to keep chaos alive. I didn't guess Set was going to be satisfied with that. Oddly, now that I thought about it, Hermes had been associated with about all the trickster gods through the ages and yet Set seemed to be entirely separate ... or was he?

I asked, and Neith answered. "Set was ... set apart." A twist of her lips said she understood the verbal irony. "He was infertile, and so he had no offspring. He was responsible for fratricide and attempted incest and other atrocities. Some sources link him to Typhoeus—you might know him as Typhon—but since Typhon was the Father of Monsters ... No, Set's line stopped with him. Some of his powers were mirrored in others, who took on his attributes, but he was ... discontinued."

I stared at her in shock. Viktor stared at us both.

"What are you talking about?" he asked.

Neither of us answered. I had to imagine that being so completely packed away and forgotten had to be the worst torment for a god, one used to being worshiped and revered, especially for a god from a culture that believed in the continuation of life ever after. The rage that must have built up over the millennia ...

No, he could never be allowed free. I had no idea what connection the Roland boys might have to Set, but they were a link at the very least, and one we had to sever. Belief and worship fueled a god's power, and if they were able somehow to make him strong enough, it was possible he could bust his bonds and we'd be in a world of trouble.

"Where would they go?" I asked. "Richie and Ian? They came to you, but you weren't in a position to help. Where else would they go?"

"I don't know. They have lots of friends ... or, at least, people they party with. I can give you some names and numbers, but ... do you really think they killed their parents."

"Yes," I said, meeting his gaze dead on. "I really do."

4

I'd put it off long enough, but I was going to have to call Armani ... again. He had to talk to Viktor. He'd want to take a statement, go over the place, find out if anything was missing or if anything from the Roland crime scene had transferred.

And he was *really* going to want to meet Neith, see the photos of the museum crime scene, talk about what happened in Egypt. Luckily, she wasn't law enforcement. There weren't going to be any international hoops to jump through. No joint task force and Homeland Security getting all involved. The Roland boys were undeniably human, so she couldn't even argue that the gods policed their own. If everything went the way it should, which, sadly, it rarely did, she could see about Set and let Armani worry about the brothers. It seemed perfectly fair to me. Armani had already been hurt more times than I could count fighting gods and monsters. Maybe he could sit this one out. But there was no way he was going to let the murders go unanswered.

The front door to the bungalow blew open right then and

two figures suddenly appeared in the doorway, guns out and aimed our way.

"Police!" the front figure said. "Everybody, hands up."

Viktor and I raised ours instinctively, but Neith looked thunderous.

"Hands up," I said out of the corner of my mouth, oh so subtly. I gave my hands an extra little raise-the-roof motion so she'd get the point.

Slowly, with a glare all around, she complied.

I recognized the woman giving the orders. I'd seen her back at the station with Nick ... Armani. She was the one he'd sent Jessica off with. His new partner?

Her gun lowered only slightly when she recognized me. "What's going on here?"

"Did Jesus call you?" I asked, wondering if I'd taken too long to get back to him.

"Jesus?" she asked, clearly at a loss. She sighed. "Stand down," she told the uniformed officer with her. "Tell Detective Armani the place is secure. And tell him ... well, just tell him," she said.

Armani must have gone around the back to secure other exits.

Then she fixed us with a *look*. She and Neith could easily have done a stare down and I'd have had a tough time calling a winner. But it didn't really faze me. Unless she could shoot lasers out of her eyes, I had her beat.

"What's going on here?" the detective asked. Reyes, I remember Nick calling her. "And who are you?" she asked Neith.

Neith inhaled, and it seemed to blow her up an extra inch or two. She reached into her vest and pulled out a wallet, which she flipped open, showing some kind of badge. She reached behind it to pull out a card as well and to hand it to Detective Reyes.

"Neith Sais," she said, "insurance investigator. I'm tracking Ian and Richie Roland for suspected antiquities theft."

I should have known that the goddess of strategy would have a cover story. Maybe it was even true. So many of the old gods had day jobs now that their worship and tribute had dried up.

"For ... theft?" the detective asked.

"Well, that and murder, but that's a little beyond my purview. Largely I'm here to recover the artifacts ... and see justice done, of course."

Nick arrived in the doorway then. Again, I didn't think the little kick to the gut had anything to do with my precog. But it didn't matter. I was with Apollo now and Nick ... I didn't know if he'd moved on yet. I didn't want to think about it.

He took one look at his partner, one look around the room and froze on Neith.

Or rather, her gaze snagged his and wasn't letting go. I knew how powerful it could be; like a tractor beam. I looked from him to Neith, prepared to be amused, but found myself startled instead. Neith looked ... transfixed. As though she'd suddenly been struck by something. If it was one of Eros's arrows I was going to find him and tear his little bow to kindling. Not that I had any claim on Nick anymore; I knew that even if I couldn't internalize it. But, well, now was not the time for Neith/Athena to finally make a love connection. Not in the midst of what was looking to be a serial killer case with the chaos god all up in the mix.

"I didn't do it, man," Viktor chimed in right then, breaking the tension. "I didn't know they were killers or I'd never have let them in. Anyway, I didn't really. I just opened the door and they did the rest."

His outburst *should* have broken the tension, but it looked like it took a monumental effort for Nick to turn his gaze that way.

"Why don't we talk about it outside," he said, gesturing for emphasis, "so that my partner can check out the rest of the place." When no one moved instantly, he made it an order. "All of you, *out here.*"

He was looking at me now in a way that promised trouble. At a guess, he wasn't happy that I'd been a step ahead of the police on where the boys had been. It smacked of not sharing information, as I'd promised to do. But I had no idea what I would find when I arrived, and since then I'd been a little busy.

"How did you end up here?" I asked Nick quietly as I passed him on my way out into the yard.

He glared at me as though I was the one who should be answering questions, but he relented enough to say, "We activated the Lojack system on the car the Roland brothers made off with. It pinged close by, and since this was one of the addresses their sister provided, we came looking for them."

"Well, they were here," Neith said, drawing his attention. She still stood puffed up, an inch or two taller, I thought, as she'd been with Detective Reyes. Her eyes were so incredibly intense they were almost mesmerizing. "They knocked out Mr. Ramone here, raided his beer, and then, it appears, took off. We missed them."

Despite catching on her gaze, Nick's professional face was in place. His poker face. I couldn't read anything—not whether he saw her as witness, suspect, ally, or potential pick-up. Not that he thought in those terms, but ... Gah, not my business.

"Mr. Ramone," he said, switching his focus to Viktor, "is that true? What did they want? I doubt it was just beer. They could have found that anywhere."

Viktor looked scared at that. He'd been so intent on the fact that he'd unwillingly harbored fugitives; I didn't think he'd even considered the rest.

"I don't know," he answered. "Wait ... you said their car is still in the area. If they took off ..." He ran to the garage that looked like a later addition to the bungalow and glanced quickly through the small windows in the electric doors. Whatever he saw had him dropping his forehead to the doors and sagging against them.

"What is it?" Nick asked.

"My El Camino!"

"El Camino?" I asked, probably not as quietly as I intended. "You've got to be kidding me."

"It's a classic. It's worth ... it doesn't matter what it's worth. It's mine, and it's all original, and if they do anything to that car ..."

"What else did they take?" Nick asked.

"What else?" Viktor turned on him. "Isn't that enough?" But then he seemed to think about it and instantly patted himself down. "My wallet. They have my wallet. My money and all my cards. But ... why would they need any of that? They're rich."

"Not if their assets are frozen," Nick said. He grabbed his phone and rang through to someone, maybe back at the station. "Janice? We need an APB out on a—tell me everything about the car," he ordered Viktor. He relayed what was said. "A '64 metallic blue El Camino with white side panels and detailing, license plate LBZ 32A. Stolen. Perpetrators considered armed and dangerous. Approach with caution. Yeah, thanks." He hung up.

"Wait right here," he said to Viktor. "As soon as the place is cleared, we're going to need you to do a walk through, find out if anything else is missing."

Viktor only nodded.

"You," he said to me, "we need to talk."

"And me," Neith said, stepping up beside me. Nick looked from me to Neith.

"Tori?" he asked.

"Oh, let her come. She's got something to show you and ... I don't think you're going to like it. I was actually about to call you when Detective Reyes came busting in. New partner? How's she working out?"

Nick ... Armani ... had no trouble working with women, I knew. Not only had I fought alongside him, but his last partner, Detective Helen Lau, had been about as badass as they came and had left the force only to become an honest-to-gods dragon rider. Dragon, as in flying, scaly, fire-breathing beasts—well, some of them anyway.

"We're not talking about Detective Reyes."

"Oh, right, because, well, murder." Matricide. Patricide. Scrambled brains.

I pulled Nick off toward the gate. It wasn't very far from the house, but it was far enough that probably Viktor couldn't overhear or oversee, and it put us between him and escape ... not that I thought that was likely. "Show him," I told Neith.

She pulled out her phone again, pulled up the pictures and handed it to Nick. He took it, slid a finger over it every once in a while to scroll through or used two fingers to enlarge a section for better viewing. He didn't turn green, but neither did he look ready to break for lunch.

"I'll need copies," he said. "And details. Case files, if you have them."

"I'm not law enforcement," she told him, going through the whole museum thing again, "but I'll give you what I have. Maybe we can work together."

"And me," I said, echoing her. "I'd like copies and ... whatever."

"I told you to stay out of this," she said. "It's too dangerous."

"What about Nick? And Detective Reyes? It's not dangerous for them? No, thank you. I have a client and a case, and you don't have the authority to remove me."

Neith tore her gaze away from Nick and took a step toward me until we were chest to chest. All I could think was that Hermes would have paid money to see it. Hell, Hermes probably would have snapped his fingers to make it a cage match. Or, more likely, bikini wrestling or something equally ridiculous.

"Do you want to test that theory?" she asked.

"What, you're going to beat me down to protect me? That makes a helluva lot of sense. And here I thought you were the mistress of strategy."

"If by maiming I protect you from death ..."

"It's not your job to protect me."

We weren't just chest-to-chest now. We were breathing each other's air. And there wasn't enough for the two of us.

"Ladies," Nick said, voice tinged with amusement I kind of hated him for at that moment. "There will be no maiming."

When neither of us moved, he stepped up to us, shoved his hands between us and pried us apart like he was the Jaws of Life.

I went only because it was pretty silly not to. Also, a uniformed officer jogged toward us, squinting into the bright sunshine after being inside the darker house. "Place is clear. Shower is still wet, like it was used recently, so there might be some trace there. Also, we found the packaging for prepaid phones." He shot a glance toward Viktor. "Detective Reyes says I can escort him in to tell her what might be missing."

"Then by all means," Nick said, nodding toward the house. "I'll be right behind you."

He waited for the officer to escort Viktor and for them to disappear through the doorway.

"You will wait and give statements," he said to us. Us ... as if Neith and I had a common bond.

"Of course," I said.

Neith didn't say a word, but apparently Nick took it as agreement, because he also vanished into the house.

She stared after him. "No," I said. "Just, no."

Her head swiveled back toward me, eyes blazing. "You dare?" she asked.

I'd thought Neith/Athena/Minerva and whoever else she might have been was supposed to be a virgin goddess. Chaste. Untouchable. Beyond such things as human entanglements.

But if the way she looked at Nick was any indication ... "He's been through enough," I told her.

"You have history." It was a statement, and she made it as though it tasted bitter on her tongue.

"We do. Not so long ago, he had third-degree burns over a good part of his body from taking on a fire-breathing monster. He's tough and he's dedicated and he won't stop. If you can't protect him, you need to just let him go."

"Like you did?" she asked, voice quietly deadly.

I stared back, not answering. That wasn't what I'd done. At least, it wasn't the whole story. But the truth was complicated.

"I am not you," she said, each word clipped, bitten off, heavy with what should have been meaning but came out as menace.

Wow, did I know how to make friends or what?

There was a choking sound from inside the house, and when I looked up, Viktor was stumbling out, gagging. The officer with him was dragging him off the path to the gate, away from any potential evidence. I looked away while he emptied his stomach of the pizza he'd eaten, which didn't look or smell as good coming up as I was sure it had going down.

When I glanced back around, Neith was gone and Nick and Detective Reyes were striding back out, the former holding a clear plastic evidence bag full of what looked like a dead mouse, but which on closer inspection was a clump of wet hair and other detritus probably pulled from the shower drain. I wondered if that was what had sent Viktor reeling. She sealed the bag while I watched and Nick called for a team of crime scene techs.

When he ended the call, he stared me down. "Where's the other woman? Neith." The way he pronounced it, it rhymed with Beth.

"Gone," I said. "Don't worry, she left Detective Reyes with her card, and I don't think you've seen the last of her." As much as I wanted it to be so.

"Well, then, for now, you can tell me everything."

The Set coin burned a hole in my pocket where I'd put it after I'd removed it from Viktor's forehead. It was on the tip of my tongue to say something, but I bit it back. Neith hadn't ratted me out about the coin when she'd shown him the crime scene photos on her phone, but it was probably only a matter of time. And then I'd be in deep trouble for withholding evidence. If it came to that, I'd turn it over. But not until I absolutely had to ... and not before I was sure any enchantment it held had been broken. Until then, it was safer with me. Anyway, it seemed too small and too pitted to be good for prints and the police had no means of tracing the magic. I, on the other hand, just might.

I gave my statement and then headed straight back to the office. Jesus could scan the coin and start an online search, and while I waited for that to come back, I could check in with Yiayia to see what dirt she had on Neith and show the disk to Apollo to see what he had to say. I wondered who he'd been in ancient Egypt. My first thought was Ra, who was known for being the sun god, but I thought Ra was more on the level of Zeus. Whoever Apollo had been, no doubt he'd known Set and what he was capable of. He might be able to shed some light.

The coin might even kick up a prophecy or two that could help us catch our killers. One could hope.

5

———

I hadn't had anything since the latte and croissant that morning. It was amazing how much of a hunger two crime scenes and a little hand-to-hand combat could work up.

Apollo'd had to go into the management office he owned since his partner Circe—yes, *that* Circe, who'd long ago turned Odysseus's men into uncultured swine—had been murdered in the case where we first met. He'd mentioned being due in around lunchtime. It was significantly after that now. He might be up for a late lunch. Or an early dinner. My precog couldn't tell me a thing, but then, that was why man had made cell phones.

I wondered if there'd ever been a deity responsible for the gift of gab. If so, he or she had blessed LA inordinately.

Apollo's secretary answered, twice as perky as Jesus. She put me on hold as she checked in to see if the big man would speak with me and sounded three times as cheerful when she discovered I was worthy. Apollo came on the line a second later.

"Good news," he said without taking a breath after "hello."

"I've just taken on Thalia Day. I'm meeting her on set later to sign the papers. We have to celebrate."

"*Thalia?*" I asked, like we were on a first name basis. "As in *Silent Solace*, *Tilting at Windmills*, and, like, every single Clairol commercial ever?"

"The same. I'll tell you a secret." He dropped his voice, though I had no idea who he expected to overhear. "She's one of mine."

"Yours?"

"The muse of comedy and frivolity, though she's pretty damn good at drama as well."

"Why didn't she come to you sooner?"

"She was worried about nepotism. And also, she loved her agent, but he's retiring, and so ..."

"Great! Something to celebrate. How about you order in and I swing by for a late lunch? I need your help."

He let out a breath. "I didn't even ask about your client. Cheating husband? Stalker? Search for a long-lost heir?"

"Murder," I said, ready to kick myself for the little thrill I had in throwing that into his mix.

It wasn't that I was glad of the killings. It was that all the rest were so insignificant after all we'd been through. Since Apollo and I had gotten back from stopping yet another apocalypse, the small stuff just wasn't cutting it with me. Panacea and Asclepius were changing lives, making and distributing the drug that had brought the world back from the brink of zombification. They were mass-producing miracle cures, and what was I doing with my life?

I couldn't save the world every day. I knew that. I didn't even want to. The stress was too great. What if I was out that day with the flu or Apollo was filming or our sometimes-helper Hermes was in a snit ... Still, I'd discovered I wanted to make a difference.

"Murder?" he asked before I could continue along my mental track.

"I'll tell you all about it when I get there. Actually, I have a bit of show and tell."

"What kind of food do you want?"

"Surprise me," I said.

"Salads?"

I blew him a raspberry. A wet one. He knew better.

He laughed, and it made me tingle straight through the phone. "How about Thai?"

"Now you're talking."

I hung up. He knew what I liked, and with LA traffic, there was no telling how long it would take me to get to him.

As it turned out, avoiding the freeways meant I was able to make it just inside a half hour. Apollo's perky receptionist greeted me. She looked sent from central casting to play the part—stylish black and gray tweed skirt, black silk top, dark hair with thick bangs, librarian-esque glasses and a smile that could have booked her tooth-whitening commercials. And maybe had. She did look vaguely familiar.

She showed me back and I tried not to be jealous of how well she could walk in her four-inch heels or the fact that her calves could have been carved out of stone. My boots had heels —the nice chunky kind. I *could* wear stilettos—would probably be forced to for Apollo's red carpet shindig—but the world had better watch out. I was just as likely to step on a foot or fall into someone as I was to make it without mishap. Oh, who was I kidding. The odds were *not* ever in my favor.

Apollo rose to greet me when receptionist-lady—I really should learn her name—showed me in. He put hands to my shoulders and gave me a kiss to each cheek.

I pulled back in shock and fixed him with a look that said if that was the best he had, I'd take my order to go.

"Sorry," he said with a laugh. "I get in the zone. Its office brain as opposed to, well, Tori brain."

He pulled me in again and this time the kiss curled my toes and stopped my breath. When I remembered the need for oxygen, I tried to take it in discretely but ended up sounding something like a vacuum hose that had suddenly cleared an obstruction.

I looked over at his desk like we might continue things there, but it was covered in papers.

Our link kicked in, and his eyes flashed. "Nothing important," he said. "I can have Victoria sort them later."

Ah, Victoria. I'd have to remember. "Lunch will get cold," I said.

"Do you think I care?"

"Besides, there's that great big picture window behind your desk."

He walked over to it and grabbed a remote from a drawer. Pressing a button brought a curtain across the window, blotting out the view while still allowing some light through. Things suddenly took on a cozy intimacy.

My stomach chose that moment to growl and the emptiness I'd been too busy to feel hit me all at once. "I, uh, might need sustenance first. I don't think that croissant is going to get me much further."

Apollo sighed. "Just as well. I lied. Some of the papers are important, but I didn't think it would be terribly sexy for me to move them off in nice orderly stacks. Might kill the moment."

"I think I've already done that."

He grinned, and it was wolfish. "Nah, eating can be sexy. Haven't you ever seen *9 1/2 Weeks*?"

"I think crystal noodles might be a little too messy to eat out of a belly button."

"What about *Lady and the Tramp*?"

"You think *Lady and the Tramp* is sexy?"

"Romance is always sexy."

Gods, when he said things like that ... suddenly, my hunger could wait. I stalked toward him and he stood his ground, waiting. He realized he still held the remote and tossed it into a drawer. When I got close, he slid his arms around me and I stood on my tiptoes to reach him, fitting my mouth to his and forgetting to breathe again as he devoured it. My heart did all sorts of complicated dance moves. I pressed my body into his and felt more than heat rising between us. Just to be absolutely certain, I swept one of my hands down his sides, across his washboard abs and then let it dip a little lower.

There was a firm knock at the door before I vaguely heard a click and a much less vague gasp. "Oh, uh, sorry. I should have waited ... Your food is here."

Apollo had turned toward the door, but didn't let me go. "Thank you, Victoria," he said, and I was pleased to hear that he sounded every bit as breathless as I felt. "Just, leave it by the door."

She did and retreated, her face aflame.

My stomach growled again. "Rain check?" I asked.

Apollo smiled at me, and the effect was devastating. I fought it.

"Rain check," he said, voice full of promise, as though there would be interest attached.

I shivered at the thought.

He could sense it, even though I managed to keep the shiver inside rather than out, and I felt the full force of his arousal echoed back at me. It hadn't bothered him at all that Victoria had walked in. And why should it? I reminded myself, as always, how different we were. Apollo dated back to the time of orgies and offerings. Before he'd made the move to more mainstream theatre and then dipped into management, rumor had it (and I'd since confirmed) that he'd been a star in the adult film world. If I lived ten lifetimes, he'd still have more experience. It was shocking I hadn't bored him already.

"Stop," he said.

I wished the Grey Sisters had taught me to hide my thoughts as I could my wings. "You know it's true," I said out loud, since it really wasn't my thoughts he could read so much as my feelings. Everything else was context.

"I know no such thing. First off, you are anything but boring, and if ever there was someone less predictable and more faceted, I'm not sure I'd like to meet her. I don't think I could keep up."

I didn't answer.

"Do I have to do you right here on this desk to prove my feelings? It's a sacrifice, but one I'm willing to make ... for you. Though your stomach rumblings may be a bit distracting."

I balled up a piece of paper from his desk, hoping it wasn't one of the important ones, and threw it at him.

He caught it and lobbed it back at me.

"I'll get the food," I said as though it were an answer.

Really, it was. These very same thoughts had chased around in my head ever since I'd met Apollo and yet I'd fallen into bed with him anyway. I'd resisted him long enough to prove I could. And now ... Now it was too late. I'd been hooked ever since, just as I'd been with my first taste of ambrosia.

Anyway, the food smelled heavenly. I wasn't sure I could resist that. Not for much longer. Hunger was even bossier than my hormones.

While I carried it to the desk, Apollo was shifting piles of paper away and off to a side area with a small buffet—coffee maker, sugar, creamer, minibar—under which was a mini-fridge containing, I knew, various kinds of water, sparkling and otherwise.

I set the delivery containers out on his desk, making sure the shrimp and crystal noodles were closest to me, although the Khao Phat smelled mouthwatering as well. I took some of each, leaving enough for Apollo. There was also some kind of soup, which I ignored entirely. I was half way through my plate with barely a word spoken. I was hungry, dammit, when Apollo said, "So, you promised me show and tell?"

I would have smacked myself in the head if I wasn't afraid of stabbing myself through the eye with a chopstick.

"Right!" I answered. I'd pulled off my jacket at some point when the heat of the meal had started sweat beading on my forehead. Now I reached for the pocket, forgetting my aversion to touching the coin with my bare hands. My precog kicked hard, though, and I yanked my hand back, going for a napkin and using that to grasp the disk and hand it to Apollo.

He put his chopsticks down and took it, setting the napkin in the palm of one hand and opening it up gingerly like the corners were delicate flower petals.

All the color drained from his face. No mean feat when he was so California tan. "What is it?" I asked. "Apollo, are you okay?"

He looked up at me without really seeing and back down at the disk.

Alarm was coming through our connection and ... something else. Shame? Horror? Immediately, I felt him crash down on those feelings, trying to lock them away, but it was too late. Like closing the cage door after the lion had escaped, as Pappous would have said. Circus folk, go figure.

"Apollo?"

He swallowed something down, possibly bile, and looked at me again. This time there was a little more awareness there.

"How did you get this?" he asked.

"You recognize it?"

"Not the piece itself, but the symbol. It's Set."

"That's what Neith said."

"Neith? She's here?" He looked around as if she might actually be there in the office and he'd somehow missed her.

"In LA. I met her at the crime scene where I got this. Apollo, what's going on? Your emotions are all over the map."

"Are they?"

"You know they are."

He put the coin down and covered it back over with one corner of the napkin. When it wouldn't stay down, he grabbed a penholder from his desk and placed it over top.

Finally, he looked up at me again, but his eyes were ... shadowed was the only way I could put it, as if clouds had moved between me and the sun, dimming its brilliance, hiding its face.

"How much do you know about Horus?" he asked. I blinked.

"Horus?"

"You know that most of us have been many things in many cultures, sometimes doing double duty, since civilizations don't rise and fall like dominos."

"Yes."

"In Egypt, I was Horus."

"The falcon-headed god?"

"The sky god. He ... I ... was portrayed as a falcon. It was said my right eye was the sun and my left was the moon and that they traveled the sky when I took to the air. Poetic more than strictly accurate, but it worked just as well as a golden chariot or anything else. But ... okay, Set ... there's history there."

I waited for him to continue. When he didn't, I jumped in tentatively. "I know some of that, I think. Set supposedly killed Osiris, right? He dismembered him and sprinkled his parts all over the earth. Isis, his wife, recovered them all. All but his penis." Take that, Neith. "And she resurrected him. Or, wait, was Osiris the one who was tricked into lying down in a coffin, which was then locked up and thrown into the sea and then grew into some kind of tree that Isis, um ... that somehow impregnated Isis to produce ... uh, you?" Okay, it sounded crazy when I said it like that.

Apollo's lips twitched. Not quite into a smile, but almost enough to chase away the shadows still hanging over him.

"There's truth here and there," he answered, which was completely unenlightening.

"Anyway, Set did plot against Osiris. And kill him. And Isis, who was a powerful sorceress as well as a goddess, did resurrect him. But ... Osiris wasn't the only one he plotted against."

"You?" I asked.

"And Isis too. He was equal opportunity."

"I don't know Isis," I said. "I know you. Tell me what happened."

He used the pencil holder to push the coin away to the very edge of his desk. I didn't think we were going to be playing around on it anytime soon.

"He attacked me. He tried to ... Well, anyway, he didn't succeed. Myth has it that he put out my left eye and that Thoth helped regenerate it, but that it was never the same, hence the fact that the moon waxes and wanes and sometimes is blood red. It recalls the trauma." I reached across the desk and put my hand over the one he'd drawn back from the covered-up coin.

"Is that true?" I asked, looking into his eyes. He wouldn't meet my gaze, and he was still bearing down on his swirling thoughts. I got torment and a mix of emotions so complex it would take a master to unravel.

"About the eye? That much is true." He glanced up just briefly. "As you can see, I got better."

I squeezed his hand. "But you've never forgotten."

"You don't just get over something like that. I mean, you move on, but something like that tends to leave a mark. Anyway, the long and short of it is that Set isn't just petty or vengeful or any of those things the rest of us might be. He's evil.

Pure, unadulterated, no-holds-barred evil. If there's a god of psychopaths and murderers, he's it."

"But the other gods locked him away, right? He's imprisoned."

His eyes locked on mine then, as if to drive his next words home. "He is, but … I've been worried for ages that with our power so weakened, he might break free. The only thing that lets me sleep at night is the knowledge that he's likewise weakened. Probably even worse, since he hasn't been around to draw new followers, which is a good thing, because mankind gets into enough trouble on its own."

The wheels in my mind were turning, and I didn't like any of the thoughts they were churning up.

"What is it?" Apollo asked.

Unlike him, I didn't have the ability to quell my thoughts. I kind of lived out loud.

I looked to the coin he'd covered as though it might produce answers. "What if …" I wanted to voice the thoughts even less than I wanted to think them. "Look, you've read the Harry Potter books, right? Or at least seen the movies?"

He nodded and waited.

I sighed and plowed on, knowing that denial was best left as a river in Egypt. "What if Set left something of himself behind, like Voldemort did with the Horcruxes?"

He stared. "Come again?"

"Look, Neith explained to me about sympathetic magic, like clay figurines standing in for the actual animals and food and stuff that were supposed to accompany a person into the afterlife. What if these coins hold a piece of Set's ba … or is it ka? Anyway, a piece of his spirit? I'm sure the gods would have tried to erase images of Set like the Pharaohs tried to eliminate the names and all of their rivals, but some tokens always survive."

Apollo froze like I'd hit him with the gorgon glare. But not just externally. His thoughts stopped entirely as though they'd just met an immovable barrier, one they couldn't brush past.

"No," he said, horror now starting to slip through.

"And what if ... what if just like the grave goods and all, the bloodshed and violence somehow nourishes him?"

"It can't happen."

"It can't happen or we can't allow it to happen?"

"Both." He pushed away the remains of his meal. "How can I help?"

My gaze shot to the coin again, and I considered for a minute whether I really wanted to put him through remembering everything he clearly wanted to forget. But people's lives were at stake, and he was made of sterner stuff. He could handle it, and he wouldn't thank me for babying him.

"There's a god or goddess for everything," I said. "I thought there might be someone for tracking who could help me trace the coin back to the killers ... to the Roland boys."

"Like a bloodhound?"

"Yeah, but more, you know, mystic."

"Well, there's Ichnaea, but ... I haven't seen her in a dog's age. I don't know where she might be."

"One way to find out."

"Yiayia?" he asked.

"Yiayia," I sighed.

My grandmother ran the gossip rag of the gods. She knew all there was to know about everybody ... at least, everybody interesting. I had no idea whether Ichnaea was interesting or not. This was the first I'd heard of her.

"What's her story?" I asked, so I'd be prepared.

"Funny thing," he said. "You know how Cinderella had those three fairy godmothers show up at her birth?"

"Hey, you made a pop culture reference!"

"Yeah, one that's ages old. Anyway, I had three witnesses at my birth as well. Goddesses—Ichnaea, Nemesis, and Theia. In a very real sense, they are god-mothers, even though they didn't grant me beauty and grace."

"Um, have you *looked* in the mirror lately? Any more beauty and I wouldn't be able to stand you."

"Thank you, I think."

"You're welcome. Anyway, I'll see if she's got contact info on Ichnaea."

"Good. You call Yiayia; I'll call Hermes," he said.

"Hermes?"

"I hear he sometimes uses her to track lost packages. He might have a current whereabouts."

Right, packages. For his worldwide messenger service.

"Don't tell him more than you have to," I said. We had enough chaos already without him deciding to add to it. I trusted Hermes about as far as I could throw him, but he'd just gotten back together with his wife, Sigyn, from his Loki incarnation, and I didn't trust her even that far. Sure, under duress, she'd helped us save the city of New York, but she'd also put runes on me at one point to make me compliant, and I still bore a grudge.

Apollo fixed me with a look. "You know the less I say, the more curious he'll be."

Something dropped from the ceiling at that instant, and I'm not ashamed to say I shrieked like a banshee, considering that it was the grandpappy of all spiders— about the size of my hand, black and brown furry legs, flashes of red. I rose from my seat so fast it fell over and I whirled away, ready to head for the door if the thing so much as moved. Spiders and heights were my kryptonite, though ever since I'd sprouted wings, the latter was fading, moving arachnids up to first place. Yay team.

It jumped to the desk and my heart nearly beat its way out of my chest. I backed up an extra few steps, not wanting to leave Apollo to fend for himself, but ...

"Watch out!" I called, as though he might not have seen it for himself, but I couldn't spare a glance away from the spider to see what he would do. Smash it, I hoped, even though I was primarily a live-and-let-live type. I knew in the rational part of my brain that spiders were good. They kept down the insect population and all that jazz, but the rational part of my brain had been chased away by the jumping spider and now crouched in some corner of my brain rocking and sucking its figurative thumb. I *couldn't* look away, because if it moved again and vanished from sight I'd never be able to enter the office again, sure it hid in wait for me.

So when it started to grow ...

When it started to grow, I froze, staring in horrified fascination. *"Freeze!"* I yelled at it, but it laughed.

Laughed, I swore it. That or I was losing my mind.

In terror and desperation, I tore my gaze away to look at Apollo, who knew my fear. I'd met Arachne. *The* Arachne. I'd nearly been killed by millions of her minions.

"Hermes, cut it out," he snapped.

The spider clicked out something with its mandibles and began to change shape.

Anger started to replace fear. If this was Hermes and he was pulling some kind of prank ...

I yanked off my shoe, ready to smash him flat, only to realize he was already too big for that. The laughter got bigger as he did, and I wished, probably for the first time ever, that I had my gun.

Half a second later there was a full-sized Hermes sitting on the edge of Apollo's desk, legs crossed, grin splitting his face from ear to ear.

"How long have you been here?" I asked, thanking the universe at large that Apollo and I hadn't used his desk as intended and given Hermes a show.

"Long enough," he said. "Funny thing. People always say how they'd like to be a fly on the wall, but flies are so vulnerable, don't you think? Spiders are much more fun. Just think of Little Miss Muffet sitting on her tuffet ... whatever the hells a tuffet is. I'm thinking it's not her badonkadonk, but ..."

"Hermes!" I cut in, frustrated as always.

"Right, anyway, don't worry; I haven't been here long enough to know about that birthmark above your right buttock.

It's just a simple little spell Sigyn helped me with. Kind of a 'speak of the devil and he appears' sort of thing."

"Hermes!" Apollo growled. Hermes's head swiveled toward Apollo, turning far enough around that I'd swear Owl was one of his aspects, though I'd never heard of it.

"Apollo," he growled back.

"You will remove the spell at once."

I limped around the desk to stand beside Apollo, so I could see Hermes assume an expression of wounded innocence. It sat surprisingly well on his face, even knowing it was all an act. "But it's come in so handy," he said. "No sooner do you want me than I appear. Almost as though I am at your beck and call. Really, I think that thanks are in order."

"You're lucky I didn't pound you flat," I said, waving the shoe I still held in my hand.

"Well," he said with a huff. "If I'm not wanted, I can simply scamper off."

I thought again of the vanishing spider. I might never sleep again. What if Hermes decided to drop in on me while I slept ... or hide under the blanket to tickle my toes. Or ...

Apollo shot me a glance, apparently reading my stress level.

"You're here for a reason," Apollo said, neither chasing him off nor begging him to stay. "Out with it."

Hermes looked put out. Not nearly as put out as I felt, but I did my best to hold it in. He was a trickster god. It was in his nature. He couldn't help himself. And, well, he had helped us save the world a time or two, even against his self-interest. I just crossed my arms to keep from involuntary swattage.

"I'm bored," he admitted, sounding like a five-year-old on a long car ride. "Titans rising, skeleton armies, plague demons, zombie hordes ... there's just no going back to the daily grind. It's like ... it's like drinking Dom Perignon and then finding all you have left is water. It's like Icarus soaring to the sun and then crashing to the ground. It's like ..."

"Okay, we get it," Apollo said. "You could always pick up a phone."

Hermes fixed him with a look. "Can I? Can I really? Think who you're talking to."

Apollo sighed heavily. I finally let my arms drop to my sides, anger ebbing. I let my boot drop as well and worked my foot back into it.

"Fine," I said with bad grace. "Maybe you can help. Do you know how to find Ichnaea?"

"Yes and no."

"Which is it?" I asked.

"I know her number, but she's no longer tracking packages for me. Not even the really important ones."

"What's she doing?" Apollo asked.

"She's moved on to bigger and better things. Right now she's working for a group that helps track missing kids. Why do you need her?"

"Hermes," Apollo said gravely. He paused a second, waiting for the tone of his voice and the look on his face to bring home to Hermes the seriousness of the situation. "Set is back." Hermes didn't say anything for a full minute. I wasn't sure I'd ever seen him speechless.

I didn't imagine it boded well.

"Not back, exactly," I said, needing to cut the tension, "but possibly on his way."

"I'm in," Hermes said. "You tell me what you need me to do."

Apollo and I exchanged a glance, and he shrugged.

"Right now, we need a tracker," I answered. "Someone who can help us with this."

I pushed Apollo's pencil holder away and lifted the napkin carefully to show Hermes the coin inside.

He sucked a breath in through his teeth with a low whistle. "Where did you find it?"

"On the unconscious body of a man left behind by two brothers on a murder spree."

"So this guy came into contact with it? Direct contact? And they left him alive?" Alarm sharpened his voice.

"Yeah, why?" I asked, his concern infectious.

"He might not be entirely safe."

"In what way?" Apollo asked.

"Let's just say that Freddy Krueger isn't the only monster who can reach you in your dreams."

Fear shot straight through me. Viktor had mentioned dreams. Horrible dreams, and a man with white skin and flaming red hair. I said as much.

"Then he's been touched."

"But what does that mean. Is he in danger?"

"He may be the danger."

"What?" I asked, not at all excited over the concept of multiplying murderers.

"Have you ever heard the expression 'touched in the head'?"

"Yeah."

"It's not just a figure of speech."

I groaned. "So how do we find out for sure?"

"Well, we can wait until he kills someone or we can take the coin to a specialist. Someone who's good with spells might be able to figure it out."

"Like who?" I asked.

"Before Hecate joined the dark side, I'd have recommended her, but since she's not an option, I'd say Sigyn is the next best thing."

"I thought her specialty was runes."

"Many things in many cultures, remember?"

I wanted to hit my head against Apollo's desk ... repeatedly. Not so long ago, Sigyn had been part of a cabal bent on remaking the world. She seemed to have come to her senses, but what if it was all an act? What if she'd loved the trickster god for so many years, she's adopted some of his antics? If that was the case, there was no way I could turn over to her a direct link to the god of chaos.

"Um, Apollo, can I speak with you privately for a minute?" I asked. He looked dubiously at Hermes.

"You could try," he answered.

I looked at Hermes as well. He had on an innocent look and was pretending to study the ceiling.

"Oh, fine, whatever," I said. "I'll ask you right here. Do you think Sigyn is trustworthy?" Hermes started to speak and I held up a hand. "Not you," I said.

Apollo thought about it. I couldn't hear the thoughts, but I could feel his mind whirring. "As far as I know, she's always been loyal. Even that thing in New York ... she was doing the wrong thing, but for what she perceived to be the right reasons. Like fallowing a field or setting a controlled burn to save a forest."

"Great. And if she perceives we could all use a little chaos in our lives?"

"Fffftttt," Hermes said. Or something like that. It sounded a lot like air escaping a tire. "She won't do it again. If you don't believe me, you come along. Watch her the whole time. Hell, record the whole thing." He paused for a split second. "Although, I've got to say, if you two are going to go at it in any appreciable way, I want to be the one holding the camera."

I picked up Apollo's pencil holder to lob at him and he held his hands up to protect himself.

"I give, I give!" he said, although we both knew it wouldn't really do him any harm.

"Look, I have a couple of killers to track down. I need to know right away about this coin, before Neith comes after it or rats me out to the police ..."

Hermes shot up and met Apollo's gaze. "Is that true? She's back?"

"That's what I hear."

"Well, holy hells, that woman knows how to hold a grudge. I'd better make myself scarce. More soon," he said, and then vanished into thin air.

Neith must have him spooked. Usually he liked a little more pageantry. I looked at Apollo. "Tell me I did the right thing."

"You did the right thing."

"You really believe that?"

"Yes."

He didn't sound so sure, but I chose to believe him.

7

I let myself into my car before calling Yiayia. It wasn't that I couldn't call her from Apollo's office or even from the street, but there were bound to be awkward questions up to and including my sex life with a god, and I preferred to deal with them in private.

"*Egona!*" she answered on the first ring. The Rialto Bros. Circus was back in the States. I couldn't remember just where they were at the moment, but at least we were close to the same time zone.

"Yiayia!" I answered, not having to work very hard to match her enthusiasm. Despite her special brand of crazy—or maybe because of it—she was one of my favorite people on earth. "How are you doing?"

"Wonderful! Lenny gave Fergus a job with the circus. He's the new two-headed goat wrangler."

I had to process that for a minute, since Fergus only had one head, last I knew, but in my world the acquisition of another was not necessarily out of the question.

"Great," I answered.

"The goat likes to head butt. Twice as much as the normal goat, if you get my shift." It was *drift*, but I let it go. "They do a little thing where the goat chases him around the ring. The audience goes wild."

"Can't wait to see it."

"The left head is very sweet. The right one bites."

"Um, okay."

"Fergus has a big old bite mark on his right buttock. It didn't break the skin, but oh, the bruise ..."

I did *not* want to think about how Yiayia knew what the bruise looked like. Fergus was her ... boyfriend. *Boyfriend!* I knew it was silly of me to be so freaked out by the idea with Pappous two years dead, but somehow, I'd anticipated her mourning him forever. Or that the prodigious beard that had earned her a place in the circus sideshow would make dating difficult. But she and Fergus had met at a beard competition and it had practically been love at first sight. For some reason, my over-curious brain kept trying to figure out how they kissed without the Velcro effect. It failed miserably. Probably just as well.

"But enough about me," she said, saving me from my thoughts. "How are you and that great god of yours? Is he behaving himself? Do I have to come yet to kick his—"

"Yiayia! He's fine. No kicking necessary. But—"

"Ah ha, I knew there would be a butt. I will come kick it."

"Yiayia, the but has nothing to do with him."

"There is another butt in your world? Tori, I'm shocked!"

She didn't sound shocked. She sounded intrigued, but I let that go too.

"No! Listen, this isn't about Apollo at all. Or romance. Definitely not romance. It's about murder."

There was a dead pause on the other end of the phone and then. "Oooh, tell me more."

"Off the record." It had to be said. When Yiayia wasn't busy with her bearded-lady duties, she ran the *Goddities* website, which was basically a gossip blog on the Latter-Day Olympians. She was usually my one-stop shopping on current whereabouts, aliases, and who might be consorting with who.

She answered with a heavy sigh. "Always 'off the record.' I help you, but where is the tit for that?"

"Tit for *tat*, Yiayia. And anyway ..." I sighed. "Just listen. As long as you leave the names out of it, maybe there is something you can use. I suppose the gods should be warned."

"Well then, I'm your girl."

At nearly seventy, she was a little more than a girl, but she was also eternally young. I loved her for it.

"There have been some murders here in LA that might be linked to Set. You know, the Egyptian god of chaos. As far as we know, he's still all chained up and out of the picture—if you hear differently, please let me know right away—but before he was locked away, he left some talismans behind, and one found its way out here. I'm hoping you might know how to find Ichnaea. We could really use her help tracking the talisman back to the killers."

Yiayia sucked in a breath. "Murders! Are they juicy? You will tell. Anyway, Ichnaea ... I think she consults for the Center for Missing and Exploited Children or some kind of law enforcement. She was in the news just last year for the Annabel Jenkins case. You might have seen it. She goes by Naya Frain. Anyway, I'm not sure of current whereabouts, since her tracking takes her all over the country, but I can find out. Have you considered asking Hades?"

"For tracking?"

"For one of his hellhounds. He used them to track down the Titans who escaped during Rhea's uprising. Surely they can help you."

I let my head hit the back of my seat. It wouldn't be fair to say that I hated hellhounds exactly, but we weren't best buds. There had been times they'd been turned on me, and others when we'd fought side by side, but I was never comfortable with them. I'd also never considered them anything but extensions of Hades's will.

"I'll see," I said with significantly less enthusiasm than when I'd begun the conversation.

"Meanwhile," she said, "I will see if I can find Ichnaea and you will tell all."

I rolled my eyes at Yiayia's thirst for lurid details. Then again, given my chosen profession, I supposed I was hardly one to judge.

I left Neith out of it, but gave her everything else. I concluded with, "If you hear anything about Set ... anything at all, please let me know. Not to sound cliché, but it's a matter of life or death."

"I will check in with his jailor. I don't know her personally, but I hear that Sigyn spent some time with her. They had that in common, you know, both cooped up with their imprisoned husbands, although in Sigyn's case it was voluntary. And in Taweret's case, at least she has help."

"Help?"

"His other wives—Anat and Astarte." Great, an ever-expanding cast of characters.

"Yiayia, I've got to go. It's been great talking with you. Talk again soon. And love to Fergus."

That cost me to say, but I got it out. Probably only because I was completely preoccupied.

I had to get back to Hermes. And Sigyn.

As soon as I hung up, I bellowed, "Hermes!" at the top of my lungs. The sound bounced around the car but had no other effect. Maybe three times was the charm. It always seemed to work in stories—Rumpelstiltskin, Beetlejuice ...

I tried it twice more. Nothing.

Then I remembered I actually had his number on my phone. Sometimes the mystical messed with your mind.

Unlike Yiayia, he did not pick up on the first ring. Or even the fourth when it clicked over to voicemail.

"Hermes, this is Tori. Call me RIGHT NOW." I made the caps perfectly clear. "We need to talk."

There was a great pop of air, and suddenly he was right there in my passenger seat with a great Cheshire Cat grin on his face. His dark eyes lit from within by some kind of mischievous fire and his black hair rakishly disheveled.

"Uh oh," he said. "'We have to talk.' You're breaking up with me, aren't you? Hold on, you can't break up with me. We've never been together. But wait! That's it, isn't it? You've finally realized how desperately you love a bad boy and you're throwing Apollo over to be with me. Oh, he won't take it well. There may be fisticuffs. Do people say that anymore— fisticuffs? No matter, I will be fleet of foot and stout of heart. I will—"

"Hermes!" I cut in, trying desperately not to laugh. "Be serious. You're with Sigyn. And that's not why I called."

He clutched a hand to his heart and one to his head. "You wound me. You wound me to my core."

"I will wound you if you don't cut out the dramatics."

He dropped the hand held to his forehead so he could see me with both eyes. "See, that's why we'd be perfect together. You call me on my bullshit."

"Again, Sigyn. And if you hurt her again, you answer to me." Wait, when had I joined the Sigyn fan club? I flip-flopped more than a politician.

"Oooh, will there be whips and chains?"

"Worse, Republicans. No, wait, Tea Partiers."

He looked stricken. "The horror."

"Exactly. Have you talked to Sigyn? I really do need to meet with her. It's not just the coin now. Yiayia says she and Set's wife are friends. Or maybe were friends, I'm not sure about the tense. You gods are impossible."

"Oh, I promise you, we're perfectly possible. More than possible. We're highly probable, considering the fact that I'm right here. Unless you think you're talking to yourself, which is also perfectly plausible."

I gave him a *look*.

"Okay, okay," he said. "So, Sigyn and Taweret. Lucky for you, I already have everything arranged. Drive."

"Sigyn is here? In LA?" With Hermes, I assumed, but he usually made his home on the East Coast. I'd thought he was popping in from the other side of the country.

"Sure. There's a big movie premiere tomorrow night, and as one of the backers, I've been invited to attend. Sigyn will be on my arm."

"Wait, the *Dark Reckoning* premiere?" I asked.

"But of course!"

I didn't know how to feel about that. It was the same red carpet event Apollo had inveigled me into. On the one hand, at least I'd see one friendly face in the throng. On the other hand, there was no telling what mischief Hermes might get up to.

"Great," I said, trying to work up the enthusiasm. I was going to have to practice my game face in front of the mirror for hours. I'd take inspiration from the *Penguins of Madagascar* ... *Just smile and wave, boys. Smile and wave.*

"So, where are you guiding me?" I asked.

"A special spa we know. Sigyn treats primping like it's an Olympic event and she's in training. Right about now, she'll be getting paws and claws done. There might even be waxing and threading and ..." He shuddered. "I don't even like to think about that."

I started the car and pulled out into traffic. "Sure, because the old days of sanding it all off with pumice were *so* much better."

"Don't knock it until you try it. Very exfoliating. Makes your skin feel like a baby's bottom."

"Just what I've always wanted."

8

————

Something hit me when I walked into the Sulis Day Spa. It was a smell—strong, pungent, and even ... invigorating. I tried to place it, and the closest I could come was lemongrass and, maybe, ginger? Or cucumber? It seemed tart and awakening and soothing all at the same time. I distrusted it instantly.

It should be entirely up to me whether I felt happy or sad ... or homicidal, for that matter. Still, I put on my best smile for the professionally perky girl behind the counter with the sleek blonde hair.

"I'm looking for Sigourney Skalda," I told her, giving the name Hermes had provided.

"And?" she asked, her smile going hard.

"And what?"

"Exactly."

I took a deep breath, hoping to find the lemongrass-scented Zen needed not to knock her into next week.

"Look, her—" How was Hermes representing himself these days? Her husband? Boyfriend? Lover? Best just to use his street name. "Um, Herman Molyvos called ahead. Sigourney is expecting me. I believe we're scheduled for mani-pedis together."

I displayed my pitiful excuse for nails, which hadn't been done since my cousin's destination disaster wedding and had since survived two near apocalypses. Well, *survived* might be overstating things. They'd cracked, split and been righteously ripped, but the polish on the remaining portions was still glossy as all hell. I figured any self-respecting spa girl would rush me back into the salon stat.

"Doubtful," she said, unimpressed. "We book up weeks in advance."

"Well, then, it wouldn't hurt to check," I answered smugly.

She sighed heavily, rolled her eyes, and typed away at her computer, all with the air of doing me a vast, unrepayable favor.

I wasn't worried. Hermes and I had discussed this. If the trickster god couldn't wrangle a little scheduling glitch, then it really was time to give up the title.

"Your name?" she asked, looking up as though to assure herself I wasn't leaning over the counter reading over her shoulder.

I gave it to her.

She froze as if zapped. She hit a key on her computer two or three times as though it might alter the view.

"Um, here you are, Ms. Karacis. I'm so sorry. I was sure ..." She looked up at me with pleading eyes, willing me to understand. "Anyway, the changing room is right through that door." She took a key from her desk and held it out to me. "You have locker number forty-eight. You can leave your things inside and put on the robe. Someone will be right in to escort you."

"Oh, there's no need for a robe. It's just a pedicure and ..."

"I'm afraid that's how we do things here. No clothes beyond this point ... except for our therapists, of course."

"Of course," I said wryly.

Out in the real world, people were losing their lives. I supposed I could lose my skivvies for the cause.

"When you're ready, Adriana will escort you into the spa."

Well, I certainly couldn't be left to wander willy nilly among the filthy rich and nearly naked of Beverly Hills.

I nodded and went through the door she'd indicated into a fairly typical if upscale locker room. The paint was the color of sandstone. Supplementing the recessed lighting were antiqued bronze wall sconces molded like vines and laurel leaves, holding up fan-shaped travertine light covers. The locker doors had frescoes on them that looked like they'd come straight from ancient Roman bathhouses. It was a nice affectation that made me wonder whether Sigyn had chosen the spa for nostalgia's sake or whether there was something more to it. Given all the gods, Titans, demons, nymphs, djinn, giants and others that had existed over the course of history, it seemed impossible to swing a dead cat without hitting one of them. Of course, swinging a dead cat—sacred in ancient Egypt—might rile up some musty spirit that would haunt you until the end of days. Not to mention, it called up a pretty strange visual.

Anyway, I shed my clothes and thoughts of dead cats, hung the clothes up in the locker I was assigned, frisked the robe in case of anything odd, frisked it again because it felt like a cloud and it was worth another feel, then wrapped it around myself and belted it tightly. I slipped the Set coin into my robe pocket.

No sooner had I done so than a woman appeared out of nowhere. I supposed that in such a fancy spa they'd have calculated to the millisecond the exact amount of time it would take to strip down and belt up.

The woman had mounds of flaxen curls pulled up on top of her head from whence they came tumbling down again. Her spa uniform was stunningly white, the blouse a wrap-around that tied at the side so that it would be an exact fit, the pants wide-legged and free like resort wear. Her face looked naturally bronze, almost the color of her wall sconces, and if she wore any makeup, I couldn't tell ... unless it was what gave her those impossible lashes. I could slave all day and still not look like she managed to look effortlessly.

"I'm Sulis," she said, her voice deeper than I expected it to be.

"Pleased to meet you," I answered. I debated offering a hand when she hadn't done so. Sulis ... surely they wouldn't have sent the owner herself to deal with me, unless I'd already been marked as trouble.

"Hermes called to say that you're to get the star treatment. I'm so pleased. Any friend of his ..."

"Hermes?" I asked. Surprised she hadn't called him by one of his aliases.

"Oh!" She looked suddenly disconcerted. "You probably know him as Herman."

"No," I said, "I don't. Well, I do, but ... How do you know him?"

"He didn't tell you?"

I shook my head.

She laughed, and it was like water bubbling through a brook. "Sulis," she said. When I didn't register a reaction, she added, "Goddess of the healing waters. Well, at Bath, anyway. I was fairly localized."

"Oh." Since that didn't seem to be a suitable reaction to meeting a goddess, at least based on the expectation on Sulis's face, I added a huge smile and asked, "What brought you here?"

"No one believes in the healing waters of Bath anymore—especially not since mankind discovered the dangers of the lead piping! I understand, though, that they still charge a pound or two for people to drink the dreadful stuff."

I didn't know what to say to that. How could waters through

lead pipes ever have been healing? Unless that was all part of the goddess's special magic.

"Do you have healing waters here?" I asked.

"Of course. Mud baths that drain a body's impurities. Herbal baths that do the same. Both leave the skin feeling fresh and rejuvenated. In fact, I'm taking you to the mud room right now. Sigyn is already there."

"Uh, mud room?" I'd thought paws and claws were bad enough. She laughed again.

"Hermes really didn't tell you. Classic."

She led the way, and I followed her swishing, pristine pants through the locker room door to the rest of the spa, which followed through on the appearance of an old Roman bathhouse. She used a keycard on a lanyard she'd tucked away inside her top to buzz us into a room that was all frescoed plaster, except for the mosaic-tiled floor. A kelpie or something like that —front part horse, back part fish—frolicked beneath my feet. There were three bubbling mud baths set into the floor, looking like freshly turned graves or the La Brea Tar Pits. The fourth was occupied by a figure with cucumbers for eyes ... or over her eyes anyway. Her raven hair escaped in moist curls from under a tuque that twisted her hair out of the way of the mud.

I looked at Sulis. "Uh, I'm good. I like my impurities. Or, as I like to call them, preservatives. They may be all that's holding me together at this point. Maybe I can just ... keep Sigyn company."

"And disturb the peace of this place? No, I can't allow it. If you're here, you soak." Her eyes glowed for a second, like amber suddenly superheated.

"All due respect—"

"Soaking will show me all due respect."

"But—"

"No buts."

"It's my butt, actually, and I don't want it getting grit where the sun don't shine."

A muddy hand rose out of the one occupied bath, and a cucumber flipped up. "Tori, you're such a hardass. I promise you'll love it."

"I promise I won't."

"Well then you'll get to be right."

Sulis was watching me expectantly, and I realized that I was essentially in her temple, expected to comply with the tenets of her religion. I supposed the damage to Hermes's credit card wasn't tribute enough.

I sighed. "Okay, but there's something I need you to look at first. Sulis, can you give us a moment?"

She looked from me to Sigyn, and at the latter's nod, she gave one of her own. "A moment. I'll send Adriana back to care for you."

And with that, she left through a door I hadn't even noticed at the other end of the room. It blended so nicely with the frescoes.

As soon as she was gone, I pulled the sleeve of the robe down around my hand, but it was too thick to fit into my pocket and still grasp the coin. Considering the problem, I squatted down and dipped the thumb and forefinger of my right hand into the closest mud bath to coat them and provide some layer of protection between me and the coin. Only then did I reach into the pocket and bring forth the Set disk, leaving mud smears on the pristine white robe.

As it cleared the pocket, Sigyn's eye widened, as though she could feel the power. Her hands and all the rest of her was so coated in mud that she couldn't take the coin from me, so I set it on the mosaic tile between us and brushed away the mud I'd left behind with the belt of my robe. We both stared at the face revealed, the mud in the cracks bringing it into better relief than it had been before.

Sigyn removed the cucumbers from both her eyes and shifted for a better look. Then she glanced from the coin to me.

"Set," she said in a hushed voice.

"Hermes talked to you about it, yes?"

"Yes, but ... I hoped he was wrong. Taweret was certain she and her sister-wives had cut him off from his power."

"You feel it then? What does it do?"

She started to raise a muddy hand out of the bath and then thought better of it. "It's not my work. It would take me time to unravel, but it is dark magic. Not that I would expect any other kind. If I could have time with it ..."

I wasn't so sure that would be a good idea. "Would you be able to track this coin back to those who'd carried it?"

"Set's taint overpowers any other. I could trace it back to him, but that's not what you asked."

"No." If Set was locked away, it was his acolytes we had to stop. And his influence. "Could you ... neutralize it?"

She looked back to the disk. "Have you tried a sacred salt circle? Or, better yet, a salt bath?"

"Um ... no." I didn't know the first thing about sacred circles, and my only use for salt involved steak and eggs.

"Leave it with me," she said. "I'll decipher the magic and then you can tell me what you want to do with it."

I studied Sigyn. First Hermes and now she had tried to get me to leave the disk behind.

I wasn't equipped to deal with it. I knew that, but still ...

"I'll get back to you on that. I've got feelers out on Ichnaea. I don't want to do anything right now to the disk that might keep her from tracking it back to the last guys who used it." She eyed me back, aware of my distrust.

"I would not use it for ill," she said.

"Maybe not intentionally." But what if she succumbed to Set's influence? With Sigyn on his side ... Sigyn, like Hecate and Isis and others, was a powerful sorceress, a mistress of runes and other magic. She could control others, paralyze them, send them to sleep; possibly for good and all ... It was a risk I couldn't take.

The door on the far wall opened again, and a new woman appeared—petite and unassuming. She carried a tray of what looked like jars of oils and a plate of cucumber slices. I quickly pocketed the coin without first coating my fingers. I felt a flash of power, something dark and almost greasy, and immediately pulled back my fingers, wiping them on my robe, rubbing until the tingling gave way. Suddenly, I couldn't wait to enter the bath and soak out any impurities.

The new woman—Adriana—twisted my wild hair up into a rose-colored tuque, helped me off with my robe and let me sink down into the mud bath.

To my surprise, it wasn't nearly as icky as I expected it to be. The temperature was perfect, and the mud oddly silky. It still smelled like mud, but ... not the kind mucked up from the earth. More ... aromatic.

I'd come about murder, mayhem and the patron god of both. I didn't see how relaxation was possible, and yet as I sank into the mud, I actually heard an "Ahhh," escape my lips. I even felt a muscle unkink.

Ariana moved my head like I was a ragdoll and put a pillow under it, heedless of how muddy it was likely to get. Then she gave Sigyn a new set of cucumber slices and rubbed something that felt like cold cream and smelled like lemons into my face before placing cucumbers over my own eyes. Cutting off my sight. My eyes were already closed by that point, or I might have been upset over the curtailing of my vision.

And then she was gone, leaving me alone with Sigyn and a weird new mud fixation. "So, tell me about Taweret," I said, before the sleep-inducing heat of the bath dragged me under.

"Set's first wife," Sigyn said, her voice quiet, soothing, "but you know that. It's very sad, really. She's the soul of devotion.

Faithful through all of Set's many affairs … I know all about that. She's the goddess of childbirth and yet married to a man not only faithless but infertile."

"That's horrible," I mumbled.

"Worse, have you seen representations of her? Her people gave her the head and back of a crocodile, and the body of a pregnant hippo. Don't even get me started on the use of a hippo to represent a pregnant woman."

"Horrible," I said again.

"She's really a very lovely person."

"She's not bitter?" I forced myself to ask. My body seemed to have become one with the mud, and even my lips, which were above board, wanted to go slack with relaxation.

"Yes, some. But the whole world is her family, in a sense. People may not call on her much anymore, but she still feels every birth, provides strength when she can. Unlike Set, she's been called on in many incarnations in many different cultures. Procreation is universal. Her worship was once immense. All that doesn't just go up in smoke."

"So she's strong?"

"I'd say that if anyone was made to endure, it is she. But you do know she's not his only guard, yes? Anat and Astarte take their turns as well."

"Tell me about them," I said, almost dreamily. The peace of the mud was taking its toll.

I had to shake it off, but shaking seemed downright undesirable.

"Sister wives," she said.

I raised a brow and a cucumber went with it. She'd used that expression before, but it hadn't really penetrated. Did she mean it in the sense that they were actually sisters? And to Set or each other? Either way, it wasn't the shock it might be. Many ancient cultures and the pantheons that represented them were polygamous … or at least polyamorous. Many kept the dynasties all in the family. Bad idea from an inbreeding perspective, good for the maintenance and consolidation of wealth and power ... assuming assassination stayed out of the mix.

Familial relationships aside, I couldn't see it. A single relationship was hard enough to maintain, even over the course of a human lifetime. I couldn't imagine the complications of a full house, especially for an eternity. The stresses that would build ...

"Lovely," I said. "All above reproach? None of his wives want to see him freed?"

Sigyn snorted. "See him dead, maybe. Freed? Not on your life."

"Even if it meant they wouldn't have to play jailor any longer?"

"I think they rather enjoy it. Certainly more than having Set free to claim conjugal rights. And Anat and Astarte are much less gentle than Taweret. I'm quite certain they yank his chain, perhaps even wrap it around his neck from time to time," she seemed to take a certain glee in that, which made me hope Hermes slept with one eye open. "But either way, I'm sure they're quite dedicated to keeping him bound."

"Maybe you can arrange a visit for me? Just to see for myself."

I heard Sigyn move, the mud sucking at her, and I forced myself to move as well ... only far enough to slide a cucumber off one eye so that I could see what she was about. She sat up in her mud bath, cucumbers fallen into the muck, staring at me as though I'd grown a second head.

"Are you crazy?" she asked.

"Popular opinion says yes," I quipped.

She didn't smile. "Set is a natural born killer. No, worse, he's an unnaturally born killer. He ripped his way out of his mother's womb, and he never stopped tearing a path of destruction until the gods rose up against him and bound him in his chains.

Taweret, Anat and Astarte, they are goddesses. You ... you would be like Clarice in *Silence of the Lambs*, and you know how that ended."

Yeah, Hannibal Lector had escaped to kill and kill again.

"Okay then ..." My precog kicked me in the gut, doubling me over and making me lose both my cucumbers and my cool just as Sulis came running back into the room, shattering any lingering sense of peace.

"Come quickly," she said, thrusting a huge towel at me, regardless of the fact that I couldn't catch it high enough to keep it from the mud. "There's been a horrible accident at Dynastic Studios. The police are asking that you come right away."

My heart beat double-time, and I wrapped the towel around me, mud and all. "Who called?" I asked. "What accident?"

"A Detective Reyes called," she said. "Accident on a film set. Five dead or injured. Carly took down the information."

The hell with double-time. My heart stopped.

I didn't know what it meant that Reyes had called and not Armani. Was he hurt? Or ... was it Apollo? He'd mentioned heading to a set to sign papers with Thalia Day. Could it be ... I frantically wiped the mud off with the towel, doing the best I could in under a second.

I still felt the slime between my toes and in other regions, but I couldn't be bothered with them. I dropped the soiled towel to the ground, shrugged myself into the robe, wiped my face on its pristine white sleeve—pristine no more—and ran for the locker room, Sulis's protests ringing in my ears. I didn't care about her floors or her linens. I cared about my men. And murder.

Back in the locker room, I ran as quickly as possible through a shower that had only started to get warm by the time I shut off the water. I grabbed a new towel off a nearby shelf and finished up with that, sure I'd be finding mud later in my unmentionables, but too worried to care. I hustled to my locker, jumped into my cami and slacks, grabbed my jacket, and bolted for the front desk.

The perky girl from earlier now wore an expression of great gravity as she handed me a handwritten note on sage green paper.

I might have thanked her. I might not. My only focus was on the door.

9

It took every ounce of willpower I had to stick with ten miles per hour above the speed limit rather than the twenty or fifty I wanted to go. I couldn't risk getting stopped for speeding. Every light made me grit my teeth and every sudden braking in front of me from tourists who didn't know where they were going threatened to crack those teeth I was clenching so hard.

Finally, I was able to break from the tourists, following the instructions left for me rather than the studio signs for the hoi polloi. I had one turn left to go. If I craned my neck, I could see the gate off to the side, two cars awaiting entrance, but yet another light—the final light, so help me—stopped me cold. I was looking left when my passenger door opened suddenly, and I whipped my head around to see Neith letting herself in. She didn't bother with the seatbelt.

"Go!" she said as the light turned green. As if she wasn't the distraction that kept me sitting there staring.

"The hell?" I asked.

"You got a call, right? I need in. You're going to take me."

"I should do that why?"

"I think the deeper question is 'why not?'"

I chewed on that one. I had no reason not to bring her in, except that if she needed me for entrance, it meant she wasn't on the list and there'd be a hold-up at the gate while they got clearance for her. Probably we'd be asked to move out of line. Minutes would tick by. Time I wouldn't know what the hell was going on, who was hurt and how I could help.

"There's no time," I said.

"What if you need me? You'd lose time calling me in."

Short of a pry bar or maybe some Mace, I didn't see how I was getting rid of her anyway, and the cars at the gate had cleared, one being turned back. We were going to be conspicuous very soon.

I growled, but I turned the corner and drove forward, giving my name when we got up to the gate—not just a lift-bar, but an actual eight-foot or so steel mesh gate. I was assuming on the steel. Guarding it was one studio security guard and one uniformed officer, hand on his sidearm.

The former checked my name against a list. The latter leaned down to look into my passenger seat. "Who's she?" he asked.

"Neith Sais," she supplied, giving him a grim smile. "Insurance investigator." She flashed a badge of sorts. "Detectives Reyes and Armani know me."

He gave me a look as though to see my reaction to her story, and when he didn't get one, said, "I'll have to check you out."

I huffed at the delay, but I'd expected as much. Luckily, a phone call seemed enough to get Neith through. I wondered if I was needed urgently enough to rubber stamp her or whether Nick—oh please let him be okay—or Reyes thought she could contribute. The officer gave us quick directions, but I didn't think it would be a problem. I could see flashing lights even from the entrance. Between his directions and them as a beacon, I should be able to find my way.

I was through the gates so quickly I scraped my passenger side mirror on them going through. I was too worried to care and Neith didn't say a word. Smart woman.

I wanted to ask her how she happened to be at the accident site. I wanted to ask her a whole bunch of things, but I didn't, knowing I'd be out of the car before she could even answer.

I had to pull sharply right to let an ambulance pass us, full lights and sirens blaring, but there was another where that came from, still waiting at the scene, blocking our view of what was happening. An officer stopped us as we got close to it, waving us down a side street and following to check our IDs again before letting us out of a car. We pulled over next to blank storefronts that looked vaguely familiar, probably seen in a million and one television shows and movies done over to look unique each time and mostly managing.

"Who's hurt?" I asked him. I didn't ask about fatalities. I couldn't face the answer.

"Ma'am," he said, "I'm just here to escort you. I'm sure the detectives will fill you in." Any other time I might have taken exception to being ma'am-ed, but for now I power-walked toward all the action, Neith right beside me. Her strides were shorter but faster, as though we were in competition to see who could get there first.

Beyond the ambulance, beyond the crime scene tape, the first thing I saw was a blue car plowed into the side of one of the storefronts, this one all done up like a florist. Flowers lay like bodies all around. The driver's side door, which had crumpled with the front of the car, had been pried open, and blood left behind. Stage blood or ...

From the frantic call, I assumed it was the *or*.

"Action flick?" I asked the officer.

"Romantic comedy," he answered.

"I think they got it wrong."

Comedies didn't usually involve buckets of blood or ... was that a hank of hair left behind in the car or part of a wig?

The real activity was centered around the other car on the scene. It ... I had to look away, but not before I saw what looked like a mannequin trapped under it. Only I knew it wasn't a mannequin.

Detective Reyes spotted us and left the crime scene photographer snapping pictures of the body to come over, giving pools of blood, broken glass and twisted metal a wide berth. My heart sank into my stomach. Where was Nick?

I looked over to Neith, who seemed to be scanning for him as well; her eyes pinched and worried, a furrow in her forehead you could plant crops in.

Reyes was nearly to us when something sharp rang out from the ambulance beside us, along with a howl of rage. Neith and I whirled for it, but I was a step closer and a shade faster, so I was the one in the way when the doors exploded open and Nick came flying out. A cry wrung out of me as I leapt into position to catch him and ended up getting hit with the full brunt of his weight and momentum. It knocked me back a step, and if Neith hadn't been there to steady me, we might both have gone over. Nick's face was overrun with blood, which he brushed away quickly to clear his eyes.

"Run!" he said, bucking himself free and preparing to get back in there. He reached for his gun, but Neith was in his way.

As soon as I was steady, she'd dodged around us and now leapt for the back of the ambulance where Viktor Ramone stood with arms raised like he was King Kong, wrists trailing broken leather restraints. He roared like Kong too, as he swung both fists straight at Neith to keep her from getting close. Quick as lightning, she kicked off the bumper, changed her trajectory for one of the open ambulance doors, and grabbed on to the top of it. Her weight made it swing inward, and she twisted to ride it in, kicking out with both legs to help the momentum and catch Viktor dead center of his chest with both heels. He went flying deeper into the ambulance, quicker than any of the cops who'd come running, Reyes included, could get a bead on him.

Neith dropped into the back before her hands could get smashed by the doors closing. Viktor instantly recovered and grabbed her up in a monstrous grip, as though he might squeeze her to death. Her arms were trapped against her sides, but she was kicking frantically. I raced to help her, dodging Nick's hand as he reached to hold me back.

Viktor was so intent on squeezing the life out of Neith he didn't notice me until I jumped him, arms wrapped around his thick neck to choke off his air, making him let go of Neith to deal with the new threat. I nearly inhaled his mullet-hair and had to cough it out. Instead of letting Neith go, Viktor fell back, letting me smash back-first into the equipment behind me. Pain flared, but I held on, and he rammed forward, trying the same thing on Neith. There were cabinets behind her at head height and she hit with a horrible crack.

She started to go limp, and I was afraid I wasn't going to be able to fell him in time to save her. I changed my tactics, dropped off his back, releasing his neck and hollering his name.

I waited for his crazed eyes to meet mine before I yelled *"Freeze!"*

But at that same moment, Neith came alive again ... or maybe she'd just been playing possum ... and gained enough space to bring her knee up right into his balls. The pain doubled him over, breaking our contact or short-circuiting it because of the pain.

But it didn't last. Angrier than ever, Viktor roared up from his collapse, fists first and caught Neith right under the chin, knocking her head back like a losing Rock'em Sock'em Robot. She reeled, eyes rolled up in their sockets. The back of her legs hit a gurney and she went down on top of it.

Viktor turned immediately for me, a predatory gleam in his eyes and, I noticed, red-stained teeth. I didn't want to think "blood," but my brain went there without me.

The ambulance dipped, and I knew Nick had stepped up next to me, the better to get a bead on Viktor.

"Freeze!" he said. It was my line, but in his case, he backed it up with his service weapon.

Viktor didn't so much as pause. With an inhuman sound, he launched forward. Out of the corner of my eye, I saw Nick's gun level. I had a millisecond to decide what to do. Foil the shot and the fight would go on. Someone might get hurt. Don't, and Viktor would be hurt for sure. Maybe killed. And ... before I knew I'd made a decision, I chopped down on Nick's hand, screwing up his aim and sending his shot into the floor. I stepped in front of Nick to prevent another shot and right into Viktor's charge. He hit like a battering ram and knocked me into Nick, blasting us both backward through the ambulance's loading doors.

The freefall was nothing compared to the impact. I heard Nick's gasp of pain as he skidded along the pavement, Viktor and I falling practically on top of him. My own body screamed at the injustice, especially my already abused back. I twisted as quickly as the pain allowed and tried to get a grip on Viktor, to hold him down. But he recovered the fastest of us all and pulled a meaty hand back to deliver a blow I could see in his eyes would put my lights out.

"*Freeze!*" I yelled, at the same time I heard a shot go off, and Viktor collapsed on top of me ... dead weight. I didn't know whether it was from the gorgon glare or the gunshot, but all I could feel at that moment was relief.

An EMT rushed up. Cops closed in.

Nick was calling my name, pushing at me, trying to get me to respond. It took me a second or so to actually hear him, my ears ringing from the gunshot. Or maybe shock.

It took an officer pulling Viktor off for me to shake out of it. Viktor wasn't so lucky. He rose like a mannequin, stiff and frozen ... and bleeding from the thigh. The blood ran sluggishly, as though it too obeyed the order to freeze, but that was good, I thought. He wouldn't lose too much blood before the medics could patch him up.

Nick rose behind me, putting a hand to my back to comfort or steady me. Maybe I'd swayed, the adrenaline of near-death starting to wear off, leaving me feeling a little shaky.

The EMT took charge of Viktor while his partner tried to get a look at Nick's head wound, but he waved him off and sent him to Neith.

Reyes, gun now down at her side, asked, "What the hell was that? I've seen guys hopped up on drugs before, but never so ... feral."

"New stuff coming on the market all the time," Nick ventured, meeting my gaze as if to tell me to roll with it. Like I was going to argue.

"Or the Roland brothers could have given him a concussion when they knocked him out," I added helpfully. "Maybe there was some kind of damage? Or ... a psychotic break."

"And what were you thinking—you and your friend jumping into the action?" Reyes asked. "Maybe you didn't notice the police all around?"

"What I noticed was the detective who came flying at me. You know, the one I caught," I said, shooting Nick an apologetic look. "Then I saw a woman getting the anaconda treatment and the cops with no clear shot."

She couldn't argue that, though I could see she wanted to. Instead, she bit down her response, which seemed to taste bitter if her expression was any indication. She gave up on me and turned to Nick, studying the blood trails on his face. "You good?" she asked. "I mean really?"

"It's worse than it looks," he said. "I promise." He grabbed a handkerchief out of his pocket and did his best to wipe the blood away, wincing as he touched his forehead. He managed to get some of the blood up. The rest he just smeared around. He was going to need soap and water ... at the very least.

"Fine then, you stay here. Finish up at the scene," she ordered. "Get her statement and ... whatever else you brought her here for. I'll ride with the perp."

I wondered whether she outranked him, but since Nick agreed, it wasn't my place to argue.

"Touch me again and you draw back a bloody stump," we heard loudly from the ambulance.

Neith. Nick and I exchanged looks.

"I think I'd better go save our medic friend," he said.

He went with Reyes to the ambulance and came back with Neith. I noticed right away that she hadn't made him draw back a bloody stump. In fact, Nick had an arm wrapped around her waist and she had one around his shoulders, using him as a crutch to help her walk. I wondered whether it was strictly necessary or whether the goddess of strategy just wanted an excuse to get up close and personal.

As soon as they were on the ground, the ambulance doors swung shut behind them and latched. A second after that, the ambulance took off, slowly at first and then gaining speed. Nick dropped his arm as if he'd been caught doing something he shouldn't, though really he had the right to wrap himself around anyone he wanted ... and I had the right to remain silent on the matter.

I noticed it took Neith a very telling second longer to withdraw her own arm.

"What did you want me here for?" I asked when the silence was in danger of stretching on. "Not that I would have missed this for the world. Murder, mayhem, blood and guts ..."

As usual around Nick, my mouth ran away with me.

Nick looked from me to Neith, and I realized he wasn't sure

she could be trusted. He didn't know who she was. I hadn't told him.

"It's all right," I said reluctantly. "She's one of us."

"Us?" Nick and Neith asked in unison.

I gave them each a look, one at a time. "Us as in ..." Okay, jury was still out on what exactly I was becoming. More gorgon than god, certainly. I gave it up. "Nick, meet Neith. Otherwise known as Athena, Minerva and whoever the hells else she might have been at one time or another."

"So then, not an insurance investigator?"

"That too," she said.

"Well then, you might be the person I really need."

It wasn't meant as a sucker punch, and I didn't take it as such. Really. "This way," he said. At least he included me in the invitation.

We followed him under the crime scene tape and off to the right toward a tall, skinny guy whose tufts of blond hair made him look a little like a cartoon clown ... or Mr. Noodle from Sesame Street. He was holding a shoulder-mounted camera and watching footage.

Nick skipped introductions, except to shrug in my general direction and say, "This is the one I told you about. Show her."

Mr. Noodle, for lack of any other name, looked at me and then at Neith, eyes widening at the sight of her and a "Whoa!" escaping his mouth.

She gave him a smile that seemed a little bit deadly and he swallowed so hard his Adam's apple bobbed like Ernie's rubber ducky in the bath. What was it about me and Sesame Street right now? I was in the middle of one of the bloodiest crime scenes I'd ever encountered, and ... Maybe that was the whole thing. Maybe my brain was trying to protect me by throwing in innocent images to counteract the horror.

"Um, well, here you go," the tech guy said, hitting some buttons and scrolling back footage.

Neith and I leaned in until we would have been breathing each other's air had we been breathing at all.

The scene that unfurled as Mr. Noodle pressed play was standard enough at first, at least in Hollywood. Traditional chase scene. Cars racing toward the cameraman, one ahead, then the other, swerving, weaving, cutting each other off. Someone—the driver of the boring blue car—was hanging half out the window, shouting at the driver of the hot red sportster, which had half a wedding dress hanging out of it, flapping in the breeze. It was amusing enough ... until the face of the driver —Viktor, I realized now—suddenly changed. His head popped back into the car and in the next instant, he was ramming the red roadster, shooting the red car forward, straight toward the fake storefronts.

People screamed. The director hollered.

As if Viktor heard him, the blue car left off ramming the red and veered sharply, right for the camera and everyone behind it. The camera dropped to the ground, but landed at an upward angle, catching running feet and falling bodies. Screams, cries, and curses ... and above it all, someone yelling as though toward the heavens. Viktor, I realized. It sounded like gibberish to me, but Neith's head cocked, and I knew she understood.

"It's ... Egyptian," she said in wonder. "A prayer. One he couldn't possibly know."

Nick and Mr. Noodle were both watching Neith as if every word that fell from her lips was pure gold.

"What's he saying?" Nick asked.

"He's offering his deeds in tribute ... to the god Set."

"Great," said Nick with a groan.

"You get all the best cases," said Mr. Noodle. He turned to Neith. "I don't suppose you'll need to come back to the lab and work side by side with me to develop a translation."

"I just might," she said, but it was Nick she was looking at.

The techie didn't seem to notice. He went on, enthusiasm

undampened. "Could this be related to that other case, where the kids came back from Egypt and killed their parents? Maybe there's some crazy kind of possession going around. Something like in the *X-Files* ... or *Supernatural* or ..."

Neith and I both stared at him, and I couldn't help but notice we wore the exact same expression. It was eerie.

"What?" he asked. "Sheesh, I'm just kidding, unless ... don't tell me I'm onto something!" Neither of us said a word. "I am, aren't I? Awesome!"

We neither confirmed nor denied.

Nick grabbed me by the arm and hustled me away from the techie conspiracy theorist.

Neith came with us.

"Why is Viktor Ramone speaking in some ancient Egyptian dialect and what does it have to do with the Roland case?"

Uh oh. There was no way to hold back about the coin now. Nick was going to be pissed. I braced myself and I told him about the coin. And Set. And Viktor's nightmares. "And you didn't tell me this before because?"

Nick's eyes were blazing. He was not irritated. Not irked. This was full-on I-will-throw-your-ass-in-jail anger.

"Because," I said, keeping calm, "it was more use to me than it was to you. If you had it in evidence, I wouldn't be able to track the signal."

"Are you tracking the signal?"

"Not yet, but—"

"Hand it over."

"But—"

"Now!" he said. And just for a moment, it almost seemed that Nick was more than human himself. His anger had weight. His voice echoed off the backlot buildings.

Less than a month ago I'd have given him the coin. We'd have pursued leads together, but now ...

"No," I said. "I need it for tracking ..."

"Tori Karacis," Nick said, his voice harder than I'd ever heard it before, "you are under arrest for withholding evidence and for obstruction of justice. You have the right to remain silent—"

Neith hit him. Just a quick jab to the gut, but ... I don't know who was more stunned—Nick or me. We both stared at her like people always stared at me ... like she'd grown another head, or maybe, just for a change, tentacles.

"Don't be stupid," she snapped. "You need her and you need me, and we need to find those Roland boys before they infect anyone else."

Nick didn't so much as blink.

And then a strange smile started to spread across his face and he looked from one of us to the other. "Tell me the truth; you two were separated at birth, weren't you?"

Neith drew herself up, offended. "Considering that I sprung fully formed out of my father's head—at least in Greek myth—I don't see how that's possible."

"I don't know," Nick answered. "Makes a lot of sense to me. Together you two equal one big-ass headache."

I shot him a look, but it was Neith he'd locked eyes with.

"I know a great cure for headaches," she said, batting her ridiculously long lashes, though not well. More as though her lashes were a fan and she was trying to cool down her entire face.

I rolled my eyes, but no one was paying me any attention. "Something in your eye?" he asked.

I snorted, and immediately muffled it with my hand. "Can you excuse us a minute?" I asked Nick, grabbing Neith by the arm and pulling her away without waiting for his answer.

"Sure," he called after us, "just twiddling my thumbs here. No rush. It's not like lives are at stake or anything."

"What are you doing?" I asked Neith.

"Keeping you out of jail," she snapped. "You're welcome."

"So all that was, what, a distraction?"

"It worked, didn't it?"

"Were you actually trying to flirt ... at a crime scene." Never mind that I'd gone ten rounds of snark with Nick when we'd first met. There'd been absolutely no eyelash batting ... and a helluva lot less blood and guts.

She gave me a sharp glance. "What do you mean *trying*?"

I sighed. I didn't have time to instruct her, even if I was so inclined. "Listen, this is not the time or the place."

"Warrior goddess," she said as a reminder. "Life's one big bloody battle after another." In other words, this was her version of normal.

"Huh," I muttered to myself. "Who'd have thought a warrior goddess would have a glass jaw."

I hadn't really meant her to hear, but in my defense, she had gone down like a ton of bricks in that ambulance.

She bristled at that. "I specialize in strategy," she said. "Not hand-to-hand combat. I'm used to leading, inspiring, not grappling."

And yet, she'd taken me down quickly enough at Viktor's place. And I had to admit that her trick with swinging in on the ambulance doors was pretty impressive.

I moved right along. "Then why are you here now ... down in the trenches?"

"Times change," she said with a shrug. "No one sacrifices livestock anymore for a favorable outcome to a battle. Modern warfare isn't even about warriors. It's about weapons. Devastation. Who has a finger on what button. Besides, every once in a while, you have to get down into the trenches or you lose touch."

Oddly, I got all that. I could even respect it. "Fine," I said, "so what now?"

"You let me get back to Nick. He needs me."

"For translation," she added at my dubious look. "Or do you think experts in ancient Egyptian grow on trees?"

I didn't comment on that. "Fine. How about if we divide and conquer then. You stay and see if you can translate any more of Viktor's ravings. We can connect up later to compare notes."

"Divide and conquer, what a lovely notion."

Meanwhile, I knew I had a statement to give, but I had to get out of there. It was more important than ever that I track down the Roland boys and the rest of those disks before the chaos could spread.

10

I was hurrying back to my car when my cell phone rang. I liberated it from my pocket and checked the screen.

I hadn't even stopped to program my client into my contacts yet, but I was pretty sure I recognized the number. I had that sort of memory.

"Jessica, is everything okay?" I started.

I didn't know why I gave that greeting, exactly. My precog hadn't kicked up, and it wasn't exactly unusual for a client to call for an update so soon. It had been almost a full day, I realized, looking at the angle of the sun. But there was something vulnerable about Jessica that put me in full-on protective mode. I could only imagine how it made her two older brothers feel when they were themselves. I could also imagine that being inspired with abject fear at your former protectors would do a number on you.

"I'm at the police station," she began, voice quavering as I'd half expected.

"Still?"

"I ... it's the only place I feel safe right now. I just heard

Viktor Ramone's name, and ... Tori, what's going on? No one will tell me."

I ran through about a million responses in a millisecond. "I'll be right there," I found myself saying. "Wait for me."

"You'll tell me what's going on?" she asked.

"Among other things."

I tried to remind myself I was her PI, not her caretaker, but the memo didn't take. I drove over to the station knowing I was going to drag her away from there, get food into her, convince her she couldn't stay. There had to be someone who could look after her while her brothers were on the loose. *Somewhere* she could go ...

The drive took me longer than I'd have liked, but I saw Jessica as soon as I stepped inside. She watched the door as if she was waiting for Godot, cell phone clenched in her hand. She spotted me as soon as I entered and raced up. She looked like she wanted to hug me, but stopped just short. "Oh, Tori, oh thank God. What's going on?"

The desk sergeant watched us with something between bemusement and exasperation. "You can't block the door," he said.

I took her by the elbow and maneuvered her back out onto the street. She looked terrified. "Have you eaten?" I asked.

"No, but—"

She probably weighed about a hundred and ten pounds dripping wet. She couldn't afford to miss many meals.

"Come on," I said, hand still on her elbow, aiming her down the street at a diner I knew existed but had never patronized.

It was a diner near a cop shop. That was all I needed to know to make certain assumptions—heavy on starches and proteins, better than even chance at drinkable coffee.

She dug her heels in after just a few steps, and I was forced to either stop or manhandle her along, and I wasn't inclined to do that.

"Tell me what's going on or I'm not going another step."

I glanced around. We were completely exposed standing out on the street. Sure, there were a hundred or so cops just steps away, but it wasn't like they were forming a phalanx around us. If anything happened, they'd come running, but it would be too late.

"You asked about Viktor Ramone. Your brothers ... infected him somehow with their crazy. He lost it today on-set and ..." How did I put this delicately? "Ran his stunt car into another car. And then into a cameraman. There were fatalities."

She gasped, her hand going to her mouth and then falling away. "But ... how?"

"I'd feel a lot better if we could talk about this off the street."

She looked around and seemed to cringe in on herself at that, as if to make a smaller target. But it got her moving again. One foot in front of the other.

I put myself between her and the street so that I was on one side of her with buildings on the other. It wasn't far, and my precog wasn't kicking up any kind of warning, but ... better safe than sorry.

We made it to the diner, and I ushered her in ahead of me, but then zagged around her so that I could lead the way to a booth in the back, where I could sit facing the rest of the place. She automatically sat across from me, and we both took a menu that had been left in a wire rack with various condiments. She stared at hers, unseeing. I wasn't hungry. Not with all I'd seen, but I'd take the coffee. I didn't think my day was going to end any time soon. I should probably try to eat something, if only to insulate my stomach against all the acidity. The waitress arrived, smelling like she'd just come in from a cigarette break, which didn't do wonders for my appetite. Still, I ordered coffee and fries. Jessica tried to wave her away without ordering, but I wasn't having any of that. "You serve breakfast all day?" I asked.

The waitress agreed that they did. "Give her a grand slam … or whatever your equivalent is."

"I'm vegan," Jessica protested.

I checked myself before my eyes could roll.

"Don't worry, honey," she said, "we've got something for that." And she walked away without saying what it might be.

"You get that a lot?" I asked.

"That's actually one of the better responses," she said. "Worst is, 'You mean like Spock?'"

"Isn't that *Vulcan*?"

"Exactly."

She gave a fleeting smile, and then fixed me with a hard look, as though she was about to grill me. "I want details on what happened with Viktor and what you've learned so far."

"You do realize that every second I spend updating you, I'm not out doing my job?"

"You have to eat sometime, right? And, besides, I'm going out of my mind. I don't know what to do or where to go."

"What about the friend you stayed with last night?"

"I don't want to put her in danger. Ian and Richie know all my friends, and … look, I know people can track phones. Mom and Dad put some kind of GPS or whatever on Ian and Richie's phones when they started staying out and getting into trouble, even before the trip. I'm afraid."

A cup of coffee landed in front of me then, a little sloshing over onto the saucer. Jessica ended up with a sweating glass of water, and the waitress walked away before she could ask for anything else, although it seemed the furthest thing from her mind.

"Did you tell the police about the tracer on their phones?"

"Of course."

If the police hadn't tracked them by now one way or another, it likely meant the boys had turned off or disabled their phones … yet when Jessica had come to the office this morning, she'd mentioned her brothers weren't answering. She'd never said anything about her calls going right to voicemail, as they would have done if the phones had been off. They could have since died or whatever, but ...

Just in case, I had to ask. "Have you heard anything from your brothers? Have they responded to your calls? Texts? Anything?"

"No," she said. "I'm almost afraid ..."

"Did you leave them messages? What have you said to them so far?"

She was busy shredding the napkin in front of her into little tiny pieces and failed to meet my eyes. "I asked them what they'd done and why. I cried, asked them to turn themselves in."

I thought a second before responding. "Try them again. Call them. E-mail them. Leave messages on all their social media. Even if they've tossed their old numbers, they might access webmail or other things. Tell them you're sorry you jumped to conclusions. That you know they couldn't have done it. That you want to help."

"But—"

"You don't have to believe it. Just say it. We want them to make contact. Arrange a meeting."

Her hands paused in their shredding, and she shrank back into her seat. "I can't," she whispered.

"Don't worry. I wouldn't let you go alone. You'd have plenty of backup. We'd catch them and stop them before anyone else gets hurt."

"You really think it will work?"

"Only one way to find out."

Jessica picked up the phone she'd put face up on the table and, with shaky hands, started to type.

The waitress arrived at that moment with two plates, one easily identifiable as fries. The other full of something that looked like scrambled eggs if all the color had been leached out of them and then added back in the form of tomatoes and green peppers. "Tofu scramble," she announced, placing it in front of Jessica. There was butterless toast on the side. "Jam's on the table."

She turned to go when Jessica shot out a hand and connected with her wrist. The waitress turned back, trying to turn irritation into a smile.

"An orange juice," Jessica said timidly. "Please."

She nodded, pulled her wrist free, and headed toward the kitchen.

Jessica put down her phone to pick up her fork, looking to me apologetically. "I'll send more in a second. I ... suddenly, I'm feeling shaky. I think I needed this."

She forked a bite into her mouth, and I watched to see her reaction. It seemed to go down just fine, and I reached for my own fries, which were salted to within an inch of their lives, just the way I liked them.

The coffee clashed, but to hell with it. Coffee and carbs were two of my favorite food groups. I let them battle it out.

I let Jessica get a few bites into her meal before I started again, "So, about getting you some place safe—"

"Can't I stay with you?" she cut in.

I stared. "I was thinking more along the lines of a hotel. A nice one. With security."

"But ..." She put her fork down, which I'd been afraid of, and started to tear up, which I should have seen coming, but apparently my precog didn't consider tears much of a threat. "But it's not like security will be at my door. Ian and Richie got to Mom and Dad. They got to Viktor. They can get to me."

"They were living in the same house as your parents, and Viktor let them in."

"The hotel's a public place. I'd have to go out some time for food and they could grab me. Or I could order in and they could pretend to be room service. Or put something in my food. Or ..."

She seemed to run out of ideas, though not fear. That shone in her eyes along with the tears. Jessica was flat out terrified. She'd been sheltered all her life, and now she'd lost her family and her shelter in one fell swoop.

"Please," she said. "I'll pay you double. Whatever you want. Just ... please don't send me somewhere to die."

Holy melodrama, Batman.

"Eat," I said.

"But—"

"Eat. I'll take you to my place for tonight," I said, instantly regretting it. "But I can't watch you twenty-four/seven. I have to be out hunting your brothers. So tomorrow you look into a bodyguard and a hotel, yes?"

She sniffled and used her shredded napkin to wipe the tears out of her eyes. She didn't seem able to speak yet, so she just nodded. "Thank you," she said finally, voice quiet and husky.

She picked up her fork again and started to eat. She was halfway through when the waitress arrived with her orange juice and a check, never asking if we wanted anything else. So, of course, I asked for another coffee. She eyed mine, still half full, huffed and went away. I'd drained my cup by the time she came back with the coffee pot, but I didn't really have any urge for that second cup. I doctored it anyway out of habit.

"And the toast," I told Jessica, when she was about to push her plate away.

Jessica gave me a sad smile. "Yes, Mom."

Then she seemed to realize what she'd said, and the tears sprang up once again. It wasn't long before snot joined the tears. Her shredded napkin wasn't going to do the trick, so I gave her mine, only slightly the worse for fry grease. She blew her nose loudly. Not knowing what else to do, I grabbed the check. I'd expense the meal later. It would be on her bill.

But for now ... I took some cash out of my wallet and laid it down.

Instead of sliding immediately out of the booth, Jessica took up one of the pieces of toast and started spreading it with strawberry jelly. I saw a couple of tears hit as she spread and wondered if the salt would add to the flavor. Oh, bad me. No cookie. Probably I needed sensitivity training.

Or another french fry.

Two pieces of somewhat soggy toast and half her glass of orange juice later, we got out of there. Jessica had her car but didn't want to take it, so we left it in the garage where she'd parked and took mine. A text came in as I started it up, and I checked it before pulling out of my spot.

Apollo: *Where R U?*

I texted him back, *Headed home.*

His reply came almost instantaneous. *Meet U there.*

But someone else beat him to it.

11

I was about as far from a happy homemaker as it was possible to get. Oh, I wasn't a hoarder. That would imply stuff to actually hoard, when in truth most of my possessions had gone up in flames when I'd pissed off Zeus, god of pyrotechnics and nuclear level retaliation, back when I'd first discovered the gods were real. I'd since met Titans and hellhounds and dragons ... oh my! I'd even met vampires, if not exactly your typical type. The deadly *baobhan sidhe* lured people in with their charms and drained them through needle-like nails. Not nearly as sexy as the bitey-bitey babes.

No, I was more a squatter than a happy homemaker. My place was actually Nick's former partner's apartment—try saying that five times fast. She'd literally flown off on the back of a dragon, and though she'd returned to the States, it seemed she'd given up the sedentary lifestyle, and I was on a somewhat permanent sublet.

Since Jessica had asked for it, I didn't apologize for the dishes in the sink, the mail piled up in the foyer that I'd someday find time to sort, or the dust bunnies that hadn't yet staged a revolt. Anyway, I figured I could take them. Apollo had suggested that he could send his cleaning lady over to tidy up the place, and I'd almost lasered him with my eyes. If my powers had run that way, I'd have been short one hot and sexy boyfriend. Somehow, hiring someone seemed too much like surrender. Waving a white flag. Admitting I had a problem. I *would* clean. One day real soon now. When life settled down to normal.

Some part of me laughed maniacally at that thought, and I let it have its fun.

"The guest bedroom is through here," I said, closing and dead-bolting the apartment door behind us and leading her through the living room and off to the left. It was a really simple layout. Kitchen with a breakfast bar to the right, living room dead center, bedrooms to the left with a bathroom between them, all of it vaguely sand-colored to go along with former-detective Lau's fascination with the dead and desiccated, mostly sea life. I'd packed away boxes of dried sponges, sea fans and cucumbers, sand dollars, puffer fish, starfish and shells. I hadn't really replaced it with anything but clutter. It was cheap and effortless decor. I led her to the room toward the front of the apartment, which had a bare bedframe and mattress along with a single dresser and, of course, the closet where I'd stored away most of Lau's sea life. I'd left out the sea turtle painting over the dresser and the shadow box near the light switch with more dried sea fans and shells.

They didn't seem to bother Jessica. She set her big designer purse down on the dresser and turned to thank me.

"It's not much," I said. "I'll get you sheets and blankets. There's no TV in here, but you're welcome to the one in the living room. There are bookshelves out there too with a crap-ton of books. Help yourself. I don't have a lot in the fridge or in the cabinets, but you've already eaten, so hopefully that won't be much of a thing."

"Don't worry," she said, hugging herself slightly. "I really appreciate this. Really. It's great."

The buzzer at my door sounded then, surprising me. Someone wanted to be buzzed up. Which meant unexpected company. I knew Jessica couldn't be expecting anyone. She hadn't had the chance to let anyone know where to find her. Which meant someone was here for me. Someone who hadn't thought to call ahead.

I pressed the intercom button on my end to ask who it was, waiting for my precog to tell me whether or not to worry. It buzzed, but didn't kick, and I had no idea how to take that.

"Tori, it's Neith. I'm here to compare notes."

"How did you find me?"

"Was it supposed to be hard?"

My teeth ground together as I pressed the button to release the outer door and let her up. "Who is it?" Jessica asked, having crept up behind me.

"Someone helping with the investigation."

I debated what to do. On the one hand, if I invited Jessica to stay and meet her, Neith and I would have to watch our words, dance around the realities. On the other, if I sent Jessica to her room, she might only listen in anyway. I knew I would.

I deferred judgment, going to the door to let Neith in. At her knock, I checked the peephole before opening the door.

She breezed in without waiting to be invited and stopped cold at the sight of Jessica.

"I thought you'd be alone," she said, turning accusatory eyes on me, as though I'd broken some kind of promise.

"Neith, this is Jessica, the Roland boys' sister. Jessica, this is Neith. She's an insurance investigator from Egypt."

"An insurance investigator?" she asked.

Neith grabbed one of my upper arms. "Can I talk to you in private?"

I looked pointedly down at her hand on my arm. "No."

She let me go.

"Well, okay then, since we're being polite. In here," I said, waving her toward the kitchen.

It wasn't entirely closed off, and Jessica would probably be able to hear if she really strained, but it should be private enough if we kept our voices down.

As soon as we entered the kitchen, Neith marched over to the faucet and turned it on. When I protested the waste, she said, "This way we can't be overheard."

"Seems pretty cloak and dagger. What's so urgent?"

"I need you to teach me how to flirt."

"Say what?"

She looked like she'd sucked on a lemon and swallowed one of the seeds. "I ... You ..." She stopped, chewed some more on that lemon. "You've been with Detective Armani. You know what he likes. I ... don't. I need you. To teach me. How to flirt."

"Now? In the middle of a murder investigation?"

"When it ends, he'll have no more reason to be in my company. It's like any campaign. You plan, then you strike."

"This isn't a military campaign."

"Strategy is strategy."

"Really? So what are you planning? A frontal assault? Flanking maneuvers? Guerilla warfare?"

"You mock me." She turned away, but not before I caught a fleeting vulnerability. Well, damn.

"No," I lied, trying to make it so. "I'm sorry. It's just ... do you have any idea how weird it is being asked to help someone cozy up to your ex-boyfriend."

Boyfriend. It seemed too juvenile a word for what we'd been through together. Been.

Past tense. I had to get used to it. I'd moved on. He deserved the same. "Then you'll help me?" she asked hopefully.

"I will. I promise. But first ... do we really have to leave the tap on? It's making me have to pee."

We both looked over at the sink. Neith cracked a smile. An actual smile. "No," she said, "I suppose not. But I don't think your houseguest needs to hear our lessons."

"Then we'll start with the business at hand." I turned off the tap and then faced her with arms crossed. "What did you learn at the station?"

It was no good. I really did have to pee. "Wait, hold that thought."

I headed for the bathroom, which left Neith alone in the kitchen. When I came back, Jessica was sitting at the breakfast bar, staring through to Neith, and quizzing her about what an insurance investigator from Egypt had to do with the investigation. Neith told her the absolute truth—about the stolen artifacts. When she got to the part about the girl, Jessica whimpered and put the back of her hand to her mouth to keep any more from escaping. When she pulled it away, she asked, "And you think my brothers did that?"

Neith studied her. "I think ... they may not have been in their right minds."

"That's what I think!" Jessica said. "I just don't know how. Or why."

"That's what we're trying to figure out as well," she said. She turned to me. "You asked what I learned at the station. I translated Viktor's ramblings."

She pulled a couple sheets of paper from an inside pocket of her vest and unfolded them, handing them to me.

Jessica hopped off the stool and came into the kitchen to read over my shoulder. I saw no reason not to let her. The translation sounded like the ravings of a religious fanatic, all about the glory of Set. Viktor asked that his deeds of chaos and sacrifice—he used the word sacrifice rather than murder, proving that he was nothing if not delusional—strengthen the god and weaken his detractors. He commended the blood and the fear to Set, as if they were offerings.

Jessica's eyes widened, and she looked to Neith, then to me. "What's going on here? Is it … some kind of cult? Is that what my brothers got sucked into? And they drew Viktor in as well?"

Neith and I exchanged a glance. It was as good an explanation as any. "Probably something like that," I agreed.

Neith took up then. "Set is the god of chaos. The artifacts they stole were representations of Set. It may be that the theft was some sort of initiation."

"And the woman they … hurt?" She clearly couldn't bring herself to use the real words.

"Maybe that too. Or maybe she just got in their way."

Jessica's eyes clenched shut, squeezing back tears. Pain was written all over her face like one of Sigyn's runes.

"Do you have any Tylenol?" she asked me. "Or maybe a good stiff drink?"

"I think Tylenol will do you better," I said, going to the cabinet for it. "And maybe you want to lie down? Without a lead, there's nothing more we can do tonight. We'll pick up first thing in the morning."

"Viktor … I want to talk to him. If anyone knows what my brothers are thinking …"

"They've taken him to the hospital. Detective Armani's partner says they've sedated him. Even if he was talking sense, you wouldn't get anything out of him tonight. Probably they wouldn't even let you near. He's clearly dangerous."

Jessica didn't like that at all. She took the pills I held in one hand and the water I held in the other and downed them both. She thanked me and handed the glass back. "I just feel so helpless," she said. "But also exhausted. I'm going to lie down. Wake me if anything happens."

"I will," I promised. "In the meantime, maybe you can keep trying to contact your brothers. Try to arrange to meet. Somewhere very public."

She nodded and disappeared back into her borrowed room, leaving Neith and I alone. "What have you learned?" she asked.

"Nothing much. Since we parted, I've been looking after Jessica."

Neith glanced to where she'd disappeared. "She seems fragile. Still, she's bent but not broken."

"I'd like to keep it that way."

"Nick says he can have someone walk you through the Roland crime scene tomorrow. *Us* through," she amended, "because I'm coming along."

"Great," I said. At this point, I wasn't sure what I could learn from the scene, but that was the whole point, wasn't it? If I knew, I wouldn't need to visit.

My door buzzer went off again, and I thought, *Saved by the bell.* Another second or so and I probably would have had to give Neith those flirting lessons. Of course, she might consider it a blessing if we had a real, live man to practice on. Probably it would be wrong to tell her that men were like cupcakes—you licked them to stake your claim.

I went to the door with a smirk on my face and, sure enough, it was Apollo. I buzzed him up and waited by the door to let him in. I no sooner opened it than he backed me up against the wall and gave me a kiss that curled my toes and unfurled a heat deep in my lower stomach that spread throughout my body.

Neith cleared her throat.

I was too strong to whimper when Apollo stopped, but it was a close thing. He whirled around toward her and froze. "Neith?" he said.

"Apollo?" she asked. "You haven't changed a bit. Still catting around, I see."

"Tongue still as sharp as your sword," he responded.

They eyed each other for a second and then broke out into smiles. It might have been the first time I'd seen Neith smile. It was ... nice. Her eyes crinkled at the corners and her entire face lightened up.

"*That,*" I said, turning them both suddenly toward me.

"What?" they both asked.

"Do that," I told Neith. "Smile. It changes your whole face. Makes you ... approachable."

Apollo was staring at me, baffled. So was Neith for that matter. "You don't think I'm approachable?" she asked.

"You're a bit ... fierce. Not that there's anything wrong with that," I said. "But it's better against an opponent than an ally."

She gave that some thought. "You're telling me to be other than I am."

"No, I'm saying show another side of yourself. I know you can smile. I just saw you do it."

Of course, she was scowling now, but the comment still stood.

"I'll consider it," she said grudgingly, then changed the subject. "So, you have nothing new to tell me?"

"Not for the moment."

"Then I will go ... for now. But I will see you tomorrow. And you will remember your promise." It wasn't a question.

She was out the door an instant later, leaving Apollo and I alone ... well, mostly. "What promise?" he asked.

"Oh gods, just kill me now," I said in answer.

He didn't leave it at that, of course. Not when we shared that damned empathic connection and he could sense my discomfort. I had to tell him.

When I did, he laughed so loud, I was afraid he'd wake Jessica. I glared, and he only laughed all the harder.

"I'm sorry," he said finally, taking in great gasps of air to replace what he'd lost. If he hadn't been a god, he might have actually died laughing. "It's just ... the great ice goddess herself, finally falling in love ... with a mortal."

"Hey, I'm a mortal," I grumped. "Or something." I wasn't really sure anymore.

"You don't get it. All these eons she's dodged Eros's arrows—"

"Eros," I cut in. "You don't think ..."

"What?"

"You don't think he's here, do you? That he's behind it? That would be just the thing, wouldn't it? The god of chaos and the god of ... well, it's supposed to be love, isn't it, but he's gotten people in trouble more often than not."

"Eros," Apollo repeated. His voice had gone flat, unreadable, but that wasn't my only cue, and I could feel everything he wasn't saying through our bond. They had history. Eros had once turned Apollo's love against him, shooting the nymph Daphne with the lead arrow of revulsion so that she ran and even begged to be turned into a tree to escape him. "People have gotten into and out of plenty of trouble without his help throughout the ages."

"Yeah, but—"

"Tori," he said gently. "Nick's a big boy. He can take care of himself."

"Yeah, but—"

"*Tori.*"

"Okay, okay, but how on earth am I supposed to teach the goddess of war how to flirt. I mean, if she hasn't learned it in all these years, I don't see what hope I have. I'm not exactly a prodigy."

"You caught me, didn't you?" he asked, reaching to pull me toward him once again now that we were alone.

"You mean I let *you* catch *me*," I said.

"Exactly."

"Hmm." And then the *hmmm* turned into more of a hum as he started to nibble on my neck and that warmth that had spread through me sparked into a raging fire. When my knees seemed about to give out, he picked me up and carried me to my room, kicking the door shut behind us.

After that, I sincerely hoped Jessica was out for the count, because quiet didn't seem remotely within the realm of possibility.

12

The next morning, I stretched like a cat, only to find a gloriously naked god in my bed. For a moment, I forgot about chaos, death, murder and other madness. It was hard to focus on anything but the hot body molded to my back and the growing issue between us.

"Good morning," he said, voice raspy from sleep. He managed to make even those two words sound suggestive.

I answered him by rocking back against him, very interested in dealing with that pressing issue. The arm draped over my waist tightened, and he sucked in a breath. I could feel his arousal through our link. It was fueling my own. That, and the fact that the hand that had been hanging casually as we slept was now stroking my stomach and up just under the curve of my breasts ... enough to tease, but just that. I growled and moved my arms so that he'd have better access to anything interesting, but he seemed content for now. I could feel his wicked smile against my shoulder. He knew what he was doing to me. He knew what I wanted. He wasn't inclined to give it to me. At least, not when I wanted it right freakin' now.

I tried to turn toward him, to take what I wanted, and his

arm tightened around me like a steel band. Holding me in place.

I was about to give him hell for it, when his thumb and forefinger suddenly found my nipple and squeezed. I let out a yelp, but it was more in surprise than pain. A delicious tingle—no, more than a tingle, a lightning bolt of desire—shot through me, all the way down to my hoo-ha, as Yiayia would have put it. I wasn't thinking of her in that moment *at all*, but I didn't have a word myself. Not one that I ever used.

My whole body tightened, every single muscle, including those cradling his more than obvious erection. It was his turn for that lightning strike of desire, and I felt him jump against me.

"Tori," he said against my hair.

A series of rapid-fire knocks came at my door. I tried to ignore them.

"Tori!" a voice came through the door. "Tori, are you up? I heard from my brothers. Richie wants to meet."

Damn and double damn. I could feel the sizzling heat starting to cool, and I wanted it back.

"Now?" I asked, voice sounding a little strangled.

"Twenty minutes," she said. "I just woke and saw the message."

"Public place?" I asked, shooting Apollo an apologetic look over my shoulder, which he kissed.

"Mama's Dim Sum and Donuts," she said back.

"Damn," I said, this time out loud. I got up, and Apollo reluctantly let me go. I grabbed a robe from the back of my bedroom door, hastily put it on, and tightened the belt as I opened the door just wide enough to see Jessica on the other side. I knew for a fact that Apollo wasn't decent, and I didn't look back to see if he'd thrown the covers over himself. "Show me," I said.

She held out her phone, and I pressed the button to light up the screen, which had gone dark.

Richie here, the text said, *don't know how long I have before ... No time. Listen, meet me at the Mama's Dim Sum and Donuts on Freemont at 7 AM. Come alone. But ... if my eyes go dark or if you see Ian, run.*

It was time-stamped 4:58 AM.

"What do you think?" she asked, barely giving me time to read it once through.

I checked the clock on her phone. "I think we'd better get going. If we leave now, we can just make it."

"Do you think it's a trap?"

"It could be. No matter what, you're not going in alone. You said Ian is the leader?"

"He always was when ... when they were in their right minds."

I chewed on that. The message sounded as though Richie—the real Richie—might have come through, but the message could have been framed to give that very impression, to draw Jessica out. And even if the real Richie had popped to the surface temporarily, there was no telling how long he'd remain in control. That much was clear from his warning, which was what led me to think there was a chance this was the real deal.

Gah, no time to analyze. Not if we wanted to get there in time. I had no idea if he'd wait. "Get dressed," I said. "Two minutes or I leave without you."

It was an empty threat. If Richie didn't see his sister, there was a good chance he wouldn't show at all, but it would get her moving.

I shut the door practically in her face, ran to my bedside table, grabbed my cell off the charger, and tossed it down next to Apollo. "Do me a favor while I dress?" I didn't wait for him to agree. "Call Neith and ... Nick. Tell them about Mama's. Tell them twenty minutes and to hold back. You heard everything, right?" He nodded. "So you know why. If Richie shows, maybe we can get him to give up his brother ... if we don't spook him. If we do spook him or something else goes wrong, maybe we can follow him back to Ian. But if it's a trap ..."

"You'll need backup. Go."

There was no time to be picky. I put on the first two things I got my hands on. Since all I owned for bottoms were black and about all I owned for tops were solid tees or tanks that could go under blazers or jogging suits, it wasn't a problem. I finished off with my solid black running shoes and turned for the door, only to find Apollo right behind me, dressed in the same clothes he'd been in yesterday, minus the suit jacket.

"I'm coming with you," he said.

"But the calls—"

"I'll make them from the car."

I had no idea why I hadn't thought of that, unless my blood still hadn't made it back to my brain from other parts of my body he'd been stimulating before Jessica crashed the party.

"Great, uh, thanks."

"You're, uh, welcome."

I stuck my tongue out at him—in the most mature way possible—and yanked the door open.

Jessica was waiting for us in the hallway, and together we all raced for the car. "He said to come alone," she protested on the way.

"You left your car near the police station yesterday. You need a ride. There's no time to hail a cab and go separately. Anyway, I wouldn't trust your brothers not to waylay a cab. I'll drop you off a block away, if you'd like, but we don't have time to argue about this."

We hit my car, and Jessica grabbed the shotgun seat. Apollo didn't even protest, but got into the back. "I'll duck down as soon as we're anywhere close," he said. "If he sees Tori, you can mention a friend gave you a ride."

"But—"

"Take it," I said, "it's the best you're going to get."

I didn't exactly speed—not in the way that would get me pulled over—but I didn't exactly come to a full and complete stop at every sign. Apollo made the first call, and I heard him repeat the name of the place. "It's an LA thing," he said, by which I knew he was talking to Neith. Nick would already have known about La La Land's strange tradition by which Chinese restaurants were able to catch the breakfast crowds as well as lunch and dinner.

"Tell her that unless there's clear and present danger, she's not to interfere. Just watch and follow. Richie's going to lead us to Ian one way or another." He conveyed that and moved along.

Highland Avenue to Hollywood Boulevard was the quickest route, and this early in the morning the Walk of Fame wouldn't be plagued with tourists and street performers dressed up like Spider Man, Iron Man, the President, Marilyn Monroe, Johnny Depp, and any performer with a style recognizable enough that random strangers would pay to have their pictures taken with them, every bit as excited as if they were seeing the real thing. I took the route, miraculously missing most of the lights.

Next up was Nick. From what I could hear from Apollo's side of things, it sounded like he'd had to leave a message.

"Damn," I said. I really was going to have to expand my vocabulary.

Apollo ducked down as I turned onto Hollywood and I sketched out a rough plan as we took it several blocks and then turned onto Cahuenga.

"I'm going to pull into the plaza before the one with the dim sum place. Apollo and Jessica, you get out there. I'll drive on to Mama's and walk in as a customer. Let me get there first," I said to Jessica. "Apollo, you're much too well-known. You'd kick up a fuss that might scare Richie away. Stay out of sight, but somewhere you can get a good view of the place." Luckily, being the god of the sun and all, Apollo could easily blind opponents to the sight of himself and manipulate light and shade. I wasn't worried about him. Neith ... she was the loose cannon, but being the goddess of strategy, I had to hope she'd understand the need for restraint.

"Got it," they both said.

"And take this," I added to Jessica, grabbing the spare pepper spray out of my glove compartment and handing it to her. She'd need it more than I would.

She looked nervous as all hells, but she took the spray and got out of the car. Apollo had to motion her to move on when she would have stood watching after me. I hoped she was up to this. I hoped we weren't sending her into a trap.

I pulled out onto the street and into the parking lot for the next plaza over. The dim sum and donuts place was the only shop open this early in the orange-pink, mission-style strip mall. It looked like any other Chinese take-out place, with pictures of food and lists of specials plastering five-eighths of the front window, making it difficult to see in. It probably made it equally difficult to see out unless you were sitting in just the right place, which, having chosen the time and location, Richie could arrange. I didn't like it. But then, no one had asked me.

Before I got out of the car, I reached into my glove compartment again, this time for the directional microphone I had there from my last job—trying to determine whether a businessman had been giving away company secrets. (As it turned out, he and the rival company exec had been far more interested in hot monkey love.)

The door jangled as I walked in. The smell of soy sauce and powdered sugar was an odd combination. Not that the two things went together into one dish, but the very walls seemed permeated with the smell of each. Only one of the four plastic tables in the place was occupied—by a guy in shades, a baseball hat, and a deep blue hoodie nursing a hot beverage. My precog sent a jolt through me as he looked up, and I let my gaze slide over him and to the menu above the counter. It was Richie Roland all right. No doubt about it.

The lady behind the counter smiled, pushed her glasses up her nose with the tip of one finger, and asked if she could help me. I ordered three of the plain cake donuts and their largest coffee, since I hadn't gotten the chance to down any caffeine this morning, and I couldn't say how long I had before withdrawal symptoms set in.

Jessica walked in before my order was up. I knew it from the jangle on the door, but I didn't turn, pretending absolute disinterest in my surroundings.

"Richie!" she said. In her hushed excitement, it could be heard throughout the small restaurant.

Richie shot a glance at the counter, but I was busy checking the texts on my phone while I waited for my order to come up.

Out of the corner of my eye, I saw him try to hush her with the universal hand sign for keep it quiet—palms down, fingers splayed.

The nice lady with the sliding glasses returned a second later with a steaming cup of coffee I could nearly bathe in and a small paper bag full of donuts. I tried not to notice the grease already staining the bottom. It didn't matter. One of those donuts was definitely for me. Plain cake was the missionary position of donuts, the vanilla of ice cream cones. And yet my absolute favorite.

I moved off down the counter to doctor my coffee, which sadly took me farther away from Richie's table, where Jessica was now sitting. When I finished, I chose a table on the other side of the room, as a normal customer might do and put my back to the glass front wall so that I could keep an eye on them.

I used the donut bag and my coffee to cover the directional mic as I pulled it out of my pocket and hooked it into my phone. Then I pressed Record. I made a big show, though, of unwinding the cords to my earbuds and putting them into my ears. *See, I can't hear you.*

Richie glanced over at me again nervously, before finally removing his sunglasses and setting them up on top of his baseball cap.

"Let's get out of here," I heard him say.

"And go where, Richie?" she asked. "You're a wanted man. Did you ..." She swallowed hard enough that the microphone picked it up before lowering her voice to a whisper. "Did you and Ian really kill Mom and Dad?"

Precog kicked in my gut like a bad bean burrito at the same time Jessica's chair made a horrible screech across the floor. My gaze jerked toward them, as would anyone's at such a sound. Jessica was turned away from me, but I saw what had set her back. Richie's hand clenched his cup so hard he'd popped the top off and splashed coffee over the rim. It was spreading across the table like blood. And his face, what was visible of it beneath the cap, was twisted.

"Richie?" Jessica asked tentatively, fear quivering her voice.

"I ..." He breathed. Heavily. Like a pervert making a late night call. "Just ... give me ... second."

"Richie, what's going on?" Jessica asked. "Is this what you warned me about? Should I run?"

She was half out of her seat already, and I itched to run over with napkins, pretending concern over the spill. My precog was kicking and screaming like a cornered alley cat, wanting me to DO SOMETHING, but I was afraid my sudden appearance would set him off.

More coffee spilled as Richie's hand spasmed. Jessica was fully standing now, ready to run. I was prepared to jump between them with the gorgon glare or a really powerful uppercut. But then he took one more breath, unclenching his hand slowly as he released the breath. Very slowly. As though it took a monumental effort.

"I don't have much time," he said, eyes conveying a scary level of intensity. "He's fighting me, and he's ... strong. I'm going to need to ... Listen, Jessica, it's not us. I want you to know that. I mean it is, but it isn't, okay? Tell the police ... tell them ... tranquilizers, rubber bullets, something. I don't want to die. I don't want you to think Ian and I could ..."

"What about Ian?" she asked, trying for answers before she lost him entirely. It was a brave but dangerous thing. "Where is he? If you turn yourselves in there won't be a need for any kind of bullets. You can tell the police everything. Richie, I'm worried."

His face went through another contortion, and I watched him fight it.

"What I know, he knows," Richie said through gritted teeth. "Remember that. And, stay away. If I contact you again ... Just ..."

He jerked, and suddenly he was up out of his seat with the edge of the table in hand, upending it along with the remains of the coffee, which tipped and splashed at Jessica. She screamed and knocked her chair over in her haste to escape. I'd been coiled to attack, and now threw myself across the room, but not in time to pull her away before the fallen chair tripped her up and the table came crashing down on top of them both. Her legs would have been crushed if she'd still been sitting, but as it was, the table caught on the legs of the chair, holding it off of her.

"Richie!" I yelled, trying to get his attention so I could hit him with the gorgon glare before he could do any more damage, but he was no longer answering to that name ... or to the siren song of sanity. Not based on the crazed look in his eyes as he turned for the woman behind the counter.

I jumped between them, suddenly right up in his face. I yelled *"Freeze!"* as he lifted a fist to smash in my face.

For a second I thought it was going to work. He froze, fist

half-cocked. Then all of the sudden a muscle ticked in his jaw and I had only that much warning before the fist was flying. I leapt back, smashing my spine up against the counter, but the fist only struck me a glancing blow.

But the other one, the one I wasn't watching, smashed into my ribs, cracking at least one. Jessica had never mentioned her brother being a prizefighter. I staggered to the side, and he roared, coming after me.

Now that I had his full attention, I yelled to Jessica and the counter-lady to run, but I couldn't spare the attention to see that they did.

Richie charged me like he was some kind of rhino, but I used the counter behind me to grab on to as I kicked out with both my feet, catching him in the soft part of his stomach. He doubled over and staggered back, but not far. Not far enough.

I pushed myself off the counter, not wanting to be trapped against it with no way out. They no sooner had room than my wings were out, bursting from my back and waking muscles that protested their disuse. I didn't remember calling them, but maybe they had minds of their own, like my crazy curls that refused to be tamed.

Richie stared, his eyes widened, momentarily awed ... and then it passed as quickly as it came. He roared and came for me, and I flew at him, catching his blows on my forearms, which went painfully numb on contact, like they were all-over funny bones. As soon as I knocked his punches away, I threw the heel of one hand straight for his nose, pulling the punch at the last second. I didn't want to drive the tiny bit of bone there up into his brain. I just wanted to make him see stars ... and bloody him a bit.

His head bounced back at the contact, and I heard the crunch of bone. I was afraid for a second I'd gone too far, didn't know my own strength, but then he was up, glaring at me through watery, hate-filled eyes slitted with pain. "This isn't over, bitch. Whatever you are," he hissed, "we're coming for you."

I let him stagger for the door, hoping Apollo had gotten Jessica to safety, along with the woman from the shop and whoever had been working in the back. I prayed Neith was in place to follow him as planned.

It was then that I realized I had his blood on my hands. Literally. It had gushed out of his nose, and I'd caught some of it. It was the fresh red of roses, and before I fully realized what I meant to do, I had it raised to my lips. My tongue came through them to lap at the blood, and it was like I sat back and watched myself, horrified and not all at the same time. The same instinct had gripped me when I'd battled Hecate, my transformation bringing with it the squicky new skill of being able to track blood back to the person from whom it had come, like calling to like. Who needed Ichnaea or hellhounds when I had the bad guy's bloody nose?

My stomach roiled at the thought and I gagged, nearly sick. I forced myself to swallow it down. The blood was the only chance we had of tracking the brothers if Neith lost Richie, and self-disgust seemed a small price to pay to catch a killer. I could think of worse things. Cats licked their own bungholes; puppies ate poo; and monkeys picked lice off each other and ate them. I was downright sanitary in comparison.

Apollo came up as I got myself over it and headed for the door. "You okay?" he asked. I looked up at him, realizing that he would have felt my horror, would have known or guessed the cause. I certainly wouldn't be kissing him any time soon. Not without absurd amounts of mouthwash.

"Yeah," I said. "Sure. Quickly, to the car."

"Wings?" he reminded me.

I cursed and then muttered the incantation I'd been taught to transform them back into their tattooed form.

Apollo had already stashed Jessica safely back in the car, so we only had to worry about ourselves. There were sirens in the distance coming on fast. Maybe the lady from the restaurant had called them or maybe Nick had gotten Apollo's message but decided against stealth. Either way, we didn't have time to stand around answering questions.

I pulled out the second our car doors had closed, before there was even time for seatbelts, and headed in the direction I felt the pull. Richie's blood tugged at me like a puppy tugging on the end of a toy, trying to win it away. It felt like Richie was trying to outrun my reach, though it could as easily be Neith he was trying to outpace. He might have spotted her tail.

"My cell phone," I told Apollo. "Press the Bluetooth setting?"

He toggled it, while I fumbled blindly at the cup holder for my earpiece. "And enable voice commands," I said.

He did that too. Or at least, I presumed he did, because when I said, "Call Neith Sais," the phone rang in my ear through the speaker there.

"What?" she snapped in answer. "Kind of busy here."

"You've got him?"

"Yeah. We're headed for the freeway."

Damn and double damn. If he hit the freeway and it was actually moving, we could lose him. I had no idea the range on my strange power. It was something I had yet to test between crises. The urge to laugh maniacally at that bubbled up, but I squashed it down.

"We're right behind you. A couple of minutes at most."

I turned onto Broadway and just as quickly felt a pull to the left. Richie was taking evasive maneuvers. The backend of the car fishtailed a little as he took a quick left turn and came out immediately behind another car.

"Neith, that you?"

But she'd either thrown the phone down or was too busy to answer. In the next instant, I saw the El Camino skid into a last-second turn onto a new street. I had a flashback to the Dynastic Studios crime scene with the one car through the storefront and another crushing a cameraman to the ground. My precog was hammering at me now, as if I didn't know the danger of a high-speed car chase through LA streets.

The El Cam blasted through a light at the next cross street, only to come up short behind a car going way under the speed limit, occupants probably gawking at something.

I was about to tell Neith to back off before someone got killed when it sped up rather than slowed, ramming the back of the car in front of it.

The slam-bang-crunch of metal carried through the windows, and the car in front of Richie went up on the curb and straight into a light pole. The front hood crumpled, but the passenger compartment seemed intact. Not that Richie waited to see. He blew right past the crash, Neith hard on his tail.

"Neith," I yelled into my headset, hoping we were still connected. No time or attention to spare to check. "Back off. He's made you. We'll get him another way."

As if I had to tell her she'd been made. Richie was never going to lead us to Ian while he was being followed.

There was a light up ahead just turning red as Richie got to it. He hit the gas, bursting through it like the final ribbon at a race. Neith gunned her engine as well and hit the intersection but wasn't nearly as lucky. A car cruising through its legitimately green light hit her dead-on from the right, T-boning her, caving in the passenger side of the car and pushing the whole thing several feet before they stopped.

I just missed them both by yanking my wheel hard and skidding behind them. Jessica was sobbing hysterically as I pulled the car over, and there were more sirens in the distance. I hoped they were headed our way, drawn by the other accident or reports of reckless driving.

I jumped out of the car, Apollo right behind me. He raced to

Neith while I ran around to the driver's side of the car that had hit her. The driver was an older man, whose head was almost buried by the now-deflating airbag. At my knock, he jumped and such a look of pain crossed his face that I was immediately sorry to have startled him.

"Are you okay?" I yelled through the window.

His eyes were glassy and lacked understanding. It didn't bode well. Shock, I hoped, and nothing worse. The front of his car had caved as it was meant to, to absorb the impact, but it didn't look like it had done all it should.

Neith stumbled out of her rental cursing a blue streak. At least, I presumed from the sound of things that she was cursing. None of it was in English.

"Is the driver all right?" she asked when she'd finished.

"Dazed, but no blood that I can see," I called back to her.

The driver looked past me, toward the sound of the siren that seemed about to crash into us at any point.

A police car pulled up, lights whirling, though the siren shut off as she cruised to the side of the street. I could see her hit the dash cam before she got out.

"Anyone hurt?" she asked, which seemed a silly question to me, given that both cars looked about totaled, but I supposed she had to ask.

And then we were sidelined as another police car arrived and shortly thereafter an ambulance. As soon as one of the officers pulled us to the side to question us about the accident, Apollo stepped up. "We'll tell you anything you want to know, but first, you might want to call Detectives Armani and Reyes. We were chasing one of their suspects when the accident occurred."

That made it a whole other kettle of fish. We were still questioned, but a lot more closely and for probably twice as long as we would have been otherwise. Jessica's sobs slowed to a stop somewhere in the first five minutes.

All the time, I could feel Richie's trace growing fainter and fainter until it faded altogether. It might be that I would need Ichnaea after all. Or that I could talk Sigyn into creating some kind of rune or spell that would bump up my range, like my own psychic hot spot. Or maybe, given something of his, she'd be able to scry him. If Nick wouldn't let us take anything away from the Roland house, at least I had his blood. I'd wiped the excess off on my jeans, not having anything else handy.

13

Nick was *not happy* when he met us at the Roland crime scene once we'd finally been released and tow trucks had arrived for the smashed-up vehicles. He was, in fact, spitting mad, which put me in mind of the Tasmanian Devil spitting and whirling and taking down everything in his path.

I had to stifle a smile at the thought, lest that path of destruction include me.

"Why the hell didn't you call?" he asked as he wound down, looking from me to Apollo to Neith. He didn't turn that laser-like glance on Jessica, apparently afraid she'd crack. She looked that fragile.

"We did," Apollo said, calmly. "Check your messages."

"I didn't get any messages," he said. And just at that moment, we all heard his phone give a bleep. He yanked the phone off the holster at his hip to check and then looked up at us strangely. "It *just* came in."

Apollo and I exchanged a look.

"Sunspots?" I asked.

"Chaos," he said, more ominously.

"Oh, come on," Nick said. "These things happen."

"Okay, so it's a coincidence," Apollo said with a shrug, not because he believed it but because disagreeing wouldn't change a thing. "Either way, we called."

"When I didn't answer, you could have tried 911," he grumbled.

"We could have. We didn't. A patrol car might have scared him off."

"So you took care of it yourselves?"

"No, we didn't," Jessica spoke up quietly, but the surprise of it shut everyone else down. "Richie ... changed. He was trying to tell me something—that he and Ian were being controlled or something and that all this wasn't their fault. He wanted me to tell you to use rubber bullets or something when you come after them. He doesn't want to die. And he warned me not to trust him. Or Ian. He won't get in touch again. If he does, I should run."

"So one brother slipped away from the other?" Nick asked, watching Jessica's face. "They're at odds?"

"Yes. No. I mean ... yes, he slipped away, but ... Gah, you explain," she said, looking to the rest of us. I don't think she much cared who answered her plea.

"Look," I said, "She's right about Richie changing. One minute he was her brother. The next he was ... someone else. Darker. Bigger. More deadly. It was like watching Doctor Jekyll turn into Mr. Hyde. Or watching David Banner turn into the Incredible Hulk. And once he did, there was no stopping him. We didn't really try. The plan was to follow him back to Ian. You know how that turned out."

"You still think," he shot a glance at Jessica and seemed to revise his chosen words, "this is something more than just multiple personality disorder?"

Jessica jumped back in before I could answer. "He doesn't have any history of it. Anyway, what would send both my brothers into a psychotic break at the same time? We weren't abused. We weren't ..." The tears started again, but silently this time, and she waved her hand as if to say we should continue without her while she went a short distance away for the illusion of privacy.

"It's happened before," Nick said quietly. "It's called a *folie à deux*, a delusion shared by two. It's rare, but ... they might have come across some crazy cult or a bad drug or something that put it into their heads that it's them against the world. People could suddenly have become aliens to them. Or demons. They may be fighting out of some delusion of paranoia or self-preservation."

"And how would they have infected Viktor?" Neith asked, hands going to her hips.

"Ah, that's harder," he admitted. He started leading us toward the house, ducking under the crime scene tape and holding it for us to do the same.

"I'll ... wait out here," Jessica said, when Nick called to see if she'd be joining us. "I can't. I just ... can't."

"I understand, but I don't like leaving you alone out here."

"I'll be fine."

And suddenly I had a thought. "Jessica, turn out your pockets and hand over your purse."

She clutched it tighter. "What?"

Neith started to pat her down, and Jessica yanked herself away indignantly. "Explain."

Neith and I exchanged a look. Apparently, she'd gotten the idea. "When your brothers visited Viktor, they left something behind, a kind of coin right in the middle of his forehead."

"You mean like you'd see in gangster movies?" she asked.

"I think that would be on top of the eyelids," Apollo put in.

"Then I don't get it."

"It's probably nothing," I said, not sure how to explain without sounding like a lunatic and probably having her terminate my contract. "But I wondered if he'd planted anything like that on you. I'm sorry I was so abrupt. It's just … if the coin had anything to do with Viktor's break with reality; I wanted to get it away from you as soon as possible."

She dropped the purse like it was on fire.

Neith picked it up and brought it over to the front of Nick's car. "Do you have a cloth we can spread this out on?" she asked. "And maybe some gloves?"

He didn't have a cloth, but he did dip into his car and come out with a large evidence sleeve and a few sets of gloves. He handed one to Neith, who removed Jessica's wallet and cell phone before dumping the rest out onto the plastic sleeve. Loose change, receipts, gum, a couple of used tissues, a Chap-Stick and single cough drop tumbled out. Neith rooted among the change.

"Nothing," she said disappointed.

I was too. But no, of course things couldn't be that easy. We couldn't possibly have two out of the six Set coins accounted for. Which meant we still had two known killers on the list and five potentials.

"I should have known," I said. "Probably it would have had to contact the skin. Slipping it into her purse or pockets wouldn't have done any good."

"Until she reached into them," Apollo said, hand going to my back and rubbing.

Nick didn't miss the movement. His lips compressed, but he didn't say anything while Neith gathered up Jessica's things and gave her back her purse. She took it tentatively, as though it still posed some danger.

"If you're sure you'd rather wait outside, maybe you should do it in here," Nick said, indicating his car. "You'll be close to the radio and you can honk like mad if anything happens."

"I'm sure," she said. "And … thank you."

Nick nodded and opened the passenger side door for

Jessica. When it was closed behind her, he turned for the house, asking over his shoulder, "What do you expect to find?"

Neith quickened her steps to be beside him, leaving Apollo and me behind. "I guess the other artifacts would be too much to ask," she said.

"I'd guess."

"Anything," I said from two steps behind. "Richie broke loose of his ... dark passenger or whatever ... once. Maybe it wasn't the first time. He could have left us some kind of message here in the house."

"You really think so?"

I shrugged, but he couldn't see it.

"I wonder what let him break free last night."

"In ancient Egypt, people kept cats, which were not only sacred, they were protectors. They kept away evil spirits as well as vermin. Have you ever seen a cat watching something you can't see? Shadowboxing? Now you know why." Her delivery was absolutely deadpan.

Nick gave her a sidelong glance. "Seriously?"

Apollo snorted, and I echoed Nick. "Seriously? You've fought zombies and a fire-breathing dragon and you draw the line at cats?"

His lips quirked. "Okay, fine. So you think a cat scared the bejeebers out of him ... literally."

"And temporarily," Neith said. "Anyway, it's a theory."

"So all we have to do is pin the brothers down, surround them with cats, and tell them to come out with their hands up?"

"You're mocking me," Neith said.

"A little bit," he admitted.

"Why don't we wager on the outcome?" she asked slyly. "If I win, I buy you dinner."

"And if I win?" he asked.

"You buy me dinner," she said.

We'd reached the front door of the Roland mansion, but

Nick paused on the porch. "Hmm, hardly fair. I'm a pizza and beer kind of guy."

"You can order a porterhouse steak for all I care. You won't win."

They stood toe to toe and chest to chest, chins out, pugnacious as all hell. Nick was fighting a smile, but not for long. "You're on. Hell, if we bring these two in, I'll even buy dinner for the cats."

He put on a pair of the gloves he'd gotten out for rifling through Jessica's things and opened the door, stopping just inside to grab paper booties from a box on the floor and handing us each a pair to go over our shoes.

"Don't touch anything," he ordered. "And stay in sight."

Then he stepped inside, and Neith, before following him, shot me a triumphant grin. She'd gotten herself a date, win or lose. But then, I didn't get the sense Neith found herself on the losing side very often.

The smell hit me as soon as I entered the house, faint at first, because it hadn't happened right there in the foyer, but still, there was no mistaking the scent of violent death—blood, voided bowels, fear. Because fear had a smell—acidic, something like vinegar. It was a combination of sweat and the excess of hormones the body dumped into the bloodstream to deal with fright or flight. Animals could smell fear. Apparently now so could I.

The foyer itself was practically a work of art. A huge *Phantom of the Opera*-appropriate chandelier hung like the sword of Damocles over our heads, unlit at the moment but for the natural light streaming through a high vaulted window. The floor was tile. I couldn't have told you what kind, but it looked like stone. Alabaster, maybe. Something pale and likely expensive as all hells.

Nick led us up a sweeping grand staircase, dark wood with a scarlet runner that made it seem we were walking the red carpet. I supposed I'd have to get used to it if Apollo and I were going to make that premier tonight. As though he could read my thoughts and not just my mood, he sent me an amused glance and I answered by sticking out my tongue.

And then no one was smiling. Nick opened the door to one of the bedrooms, and the smell inside rushed out like it had been lying in wait. I nearly gagged. My donut threatened to come back up, made it halfway there before I choked it back down. Inside …

The whole house seemed to go fuzzy around me and the floor was moving, rippling, doing the wave like Galloping Gertie just before it collapsed. Instinctively, my hand lashed out to grab on to something solid, trying to hold myself upright. I caught Apollo. I was pretty sure it was Apollo, and yet I couldn't really feel him or see him.

The room suddenly settled, and I saw … I saw …

I saw it all. Mr. and Mrs. Roland were being murdered right in front of me. One of the twins held Mr. Roland back while the other dragged his mother flailing and screaming from the bed. She grabbed frantically for the headboard, as though being anchored to the bed would be any kind of protection, but she missed. The bed sheets and blanket went with her to the floor, and she cried out as her butt bone landed hard.

The boy reached for the sheets to rip them away from her and she managed to get a kick in, but hampered as she was, it only connected as high as his knee and not with the force necessary to take him down. He laughed at her attempt, and she cringed back at the sound of it.

"Please," she begged. "Richie, stop! Why are you doing this?"

Her husband begged him to stop as well. For Ian to let him go.

Mrs. Roland started a prayer, and Richie slapped her so hard across the face her neck cracked. She was slow to bring her head back around to face him, and when she did, there was blood on her lip and a huge red mark across her cheek. Richie enjoyed it so much, he did it again.

Ian had his father sitting up on the bed, arms pinned behind him, forcing him to watch.

"Cut her already!" Ian called to his brother.

Richie shot him a venomous look and pulled a knife from where he'd tucked it through his belt. It must have been the biggest knife in the butcher block. His mother's eyes shone with fear, and she cried out at the sight.

His father lurched forward on the bed, straining toward his wife, desperation giving him the sudden preternatural strength to break free from Ian's grip. But not for long. Ian whipped a knife out of his own waistband and with a horrible sound slashed it down between his father's shoulder blades. Blood shot out, catching Ian in the face, and he laughed, licked at it. Feebly, his father was still trying to get to his wife, one arm reaching out as if to at least hold her hand as they died, only he couldn't reach that far.

And then the real bloodbath began ...

I CAME to with Nick holding me up by one arm and Apollo the other. My stomach ... I was going to lose that donut I'd eaten, all the caffeine and probably half my stomach lining as well.

"Bathroom?" I said, voice strangled as I fought to hold things down that long.

Nick pointed me down the hall, and I ran, my legs shaky and my whole body feeling a little unreal. When I hit the bathroom, I fell to my knees, bruising them on the cold, hard tile, and threw up hard. So hard it hurt. And a second time with barely a breath in between. I was gasping for air, tears in my eyes, my throat aching, when Neith appeared in the doorway.

"Chew this," she said, holding out something that looked like a stone out of a rock garden.

I held out a hand to take it. Not a stone. Softer than that. Dried fruit? "What is it?" I asked.

"Candied ginger. It'll calm your stomach and do something about your breath."

I glared up at her. "You just carry it around in your pocket?"

"A whole bag of it," she agreed. "I have issues."

I was sure she meant stomach issues, but my sense of snark dared me to comment. For once I took the high road.

"Thank you."

I put the candy into my mouth and chewed. It was ... potent. Not awful, but certainly an acquired taste. She was right, though, my stomach seemed to settle almost immediately. Or maybe it had just given all it could.

"Give me a minute?" I asked her.

She nodded and retreated, leaving me alone in the bathroom. My face felt so flushed I almost wanted to press it against the nice, cool porcelain, but I was germaphobe enough to let that impulse pass as well. Instead, I rose to my feet, washed my hands, and splashed cold water over my face. It felt so good I did it again. When I wiped it away with the towel, I felt like I was wiping away Mr. Roland's blood as well.

The vision I'd seen ... I felt dirtied by it. I felt like I'd been there, watched it all happen, and done nothing to stop it. I knew that wasn't the case, but I couldn't shake the feeling. My precog had always before been just that—precognition. Never before had I seen into the past. I'd never even really had a vision, just vague warnings of danger. I'd seen Apollo have a full-on vision once, and I'd met one of his oracles, a little girl from New York, but ... Well, it seemed my powers had developed another facet. As useful as it might be, I could only hope it was temporary—possibly a side effect of having touched Set's disk and tasted Richie's blood. Maybe it gave me some kind of connection. But I was really kind of okay with not witnessing any more murders.

Everyone was waiting expectantly when I stepped back into the hall. "What happened?" Apollo asked gently. "What did you see?"

"I saw the whole thing," I said, voice scratchy from having been burned by stomach acid. "It was terrible."

"Tell me," Nick said. "Our crime scene techs and all do a great job on reconstruction, but there's still only so much they can know with certainty."

I told them everything, which meant I had to relive every horrifying moment. When I ran down, Nick asked, "So Richie didn't leave any kind of message?"

I shook my head, but it started to throb and I stopped it right away. "No. I guess the universe picked up his slack."

"Just to be sure, can we look at the brothers' rooms?"

Nick nodded, but didn't move for a second; still studying me as though unconvinced I was okay to go on.

"I've been through worse," I assured him.

We moved on, but the boys' rooms didn't turn up anything but a penchant for action movies in Ian's, based on the movie posters—*Indiana Jones*, *The Mummy*, *Tomb Raider*. Richie's tastes ran more toward animation cels, and he had a few framed and autographed lithographs on his walls. Roger and Jessica Rabbit, the *Animaniacs*, *Marvin the Martian* and *Duck Dodgers*. They almost made me smile ... until the sight of him ripping open his mother's chest to get at her heart had my stomach lurching again.

I put a hand to my stomach as if to hold it steady, and Neith silently offered me another piece of ginger. I took it.

"We'd better get back to Jessica," I said. "We've left her long enough. Too long, probably." All the same, I was glad she hadn't been around to hear the manner of her parents' deaths.

Jessica was vigilantly watching for our return, and when

she spotted us coming out of the house, she sagged against her seat in relief. Minutes later, she was back in my car along with Apollo, and we were headed down the hills toward central Hollywood.

Apollo and I were absolutely silent about what we'd discovered inside. We shook our heads when she asked whether we'd found any clues. She didn't ask any more questions.

"We've got to find you someplace safe," I said after a while.

Jessica hugged herself. "I thought maybe I could stay with you again. I ... I don't want to be a burden. I know it's not part of your job or anything. I just really don't want to be alone." I wondered if Apollo would find Jessica's safety or my hunt for her brothers an adequate reason to miss the red carpet event, but as I shot him a look, I could tell by the thinning of his lips this was not an option. It wasn't like I could play the "my job is more important than yours" card. Not without finding myself newly single. Damn relationships and their rules.

I sighed. "You're not a burden. But, Apollo and I have somewhere we have to be tonight, so I won't be available for protection detail. Besides, your brother made it clear I'm on his hit list. I'm not so sure it's safe for you at my place anymore."

"How about a nice bed and breakfast ... with cats," Apollo put in.

"Cats?" she asked.

He told her about Neith's speculation. Jessica got a very thoughtful look on her face.

She didn't even call him crazy. "Mrs. Barbarosa," she said.

"Who?" I asked.

"Our old housekeeper. Crazy cat lady, now retired to spend more time with her furbabies. I'm sure she'd let me stay."

"Do you know where she lives?"

"Sure, I drove her home a time or two when her car was in the shop. I don't know the exact address, but I can direct you."

And so we headed off to meet the crazy cat lady.

14

A fter we dropped Jess off with Mrs. Barbarosa and her cat cabal, Apollo informed me that we had to get to his place to start getting ready for tonight.

"Tonight?" I asked. I couldn't imagine what on earth could possibly trump driving around LA and its environs in ever-widening circles until I picked up Richie's blood trail. "That's hours away. It only takes me, like, half an hour to get ready. Forty-five minutes, since I want to shower. Right now, we still have killers on the loose."

"Do you have a lead on them?" Before I could answer that, he said, "A *real* lead?"

I didn't. And I knew he wouldn't consider driving around aimlessly an actual plan. I couldn't even argue that he was wrong. The greater LA area was huge, and I had no idea how close I'd have to be to pick up Richie's trail or what my limitations were. Superman couldn't see through lead. Supposedly vampires couldn't cross running water or deal with garlic or stakes or sunlight—now that I thought about it, what the hell good *were* they really? I was spinning my mental wheels to keep from admitting he had a point.

"No," I said, sounding like a sullen six-year-old.

"Then we're going tonight and we have to get prepped. I have a surprise waiting."

"Oh goody, I like surprises," I said, with no discernable sincerity.

Apollo sighed. "Come on. It's important for my career. It'll be good for yours. Just think of the contacts you could make."

"I'm thinking about the cameras. All that coverage will make undercover work a bitch."

"Not in a city filled with special effects artists. You can be anyone you'd like practically at the drop of a hat."

But I liked being me. And that was the real point. Last anyone had seen of me, large-scale, my wings had been out in full force. Apollo wanted to take me out and show me off. *Look, fully human. Nothing to see here.* My fear was that the premiere was really the tip of the iceberg. If I lived through it once, he'd convince me I could and should do more, that I had nothing to fear.

Dating Apollo meant being in the public eye. Period. Which meant our relationship, fights, rumors, innuendos, and potential breakups would all be tabloid fodder. I told myself that I was a nobody. Hollywood would lose interest in me as soon as I showed up sans wings. Soon enough Lindsay Lohan or Justin Bieber or one of the other A-listers would pull their next public embarrassment and no one would even remember my name. Tonight might even be the night. I could have a front row seat. Yippee.

"But the premiere is, like, three hours away," I protested feebly. "I haven't even had the chance to shop."

"Done that," he said.

I gave him a sidelong glance, and he laughed. "What, you don't think I know your size?" He looked me over lasciviously to make his point.

"What if I don't have shoes to match?"

"I've taken care of that too."

"But—"

"Give it up; I've thought of everything. Just drive."

I drove. I didn't want to spend the evening coming up with meaningless banter, answering questions about our relationship or my wings or the near-destruction of New York or anything else. I wanted to spend it working the case. In bed with a hot naked sun god ran a close second.

There was a car idling in his driveway when we arrived with two people seated inside, both texting. They got out as we parked, and I could tell just from the wild hair on the one and the airbrushed perfection of the other that they were here to do my hair and makeup. *This was my surprise.*

"Gee, and I didn't get you anything," I said to Apollo dryly.

"Spike and Roslyn are the best," he said back.

"Great."

He stopped my hand on the latch before I could let myself out of the car. "I promise I'll make all this worth your while later. Twice."

A shiver went through me and heat shot down to ... well, it shot down to the important parts. My eyes closed for a second as I had to breathe back the wave of desire.

"I'm going to hold you to that," I threatened.

He grinned, teeth showing like he was the big bad wolf and wanted to eat me up.

I sighed heavily just to show he hadn't cornered the market on drama, and then I let myself out.

I headed straight for the door so that I could ignore the greetings and all the comments that were sure to come about how much work I would take and how they'd need all the time they could get. I'd heard it all before. My hair alone required a lion-tamer's chair and bullwhip to control. Not to mention copious amounts of product and a protective bubble to prevent exposure to humidity. Otherwise, all the hard work would be for naught in thirty minutes or less. Maybe I was part witch; water seemed to be the bane of my existence. Humidity had never been my bestie, and ever since I fell afoul of Poseidon, the water-divinities had it in for me. Going to the beach was now akin to playing chicken on the Santa Monica freeway.

"Before we get started," I said to Apollo, whirling around at the door and cutting through the chit-chat, "I want to see what you got me to wear in case I have to put my foot down."

I didn't.

In fact, I stopped short just inside Apollo's bedroom at the sight of the dress hanging on the door to his closet, protected in a sheath of clear plastic. It was a deep garnet silk with a V-neck and spaghetti straps cut on a bias so that the top of the gown connected to the bottom in an off-center point. It was simple and absolutely gorgeous. I could tell by the sheen of the silk that it would feel amazing and that it must have cost a fortune. Sitting beneath it were gold wedge-heeled sandals with straps that wrapped the ankles. My own sandals that my best friend Christie had made me buy and that Apollo knew I could walk in without falling on my face.

I turned to him, and while I couldn't see the look on my face, I had an idea it might be tinged with awe. I wasn't usually a vain person, but with the dress doing so much of the work ... I was going to look damned good.

"I have to try it on," I said. Apollo laughed.

"And so you shall." He kicked the primping team out of the room and helped me on with the dress.

And then helped me back out of it again. And then ...

Well, I was very glad that the walls in Apollo's beachfront condo were thick enough to muffle most of the noise we made up against them.

It was half an hour or so later that I was robed and ready to let the two-man team have at me. Apollo could have gone all night, as I well knew, and I'd have been more than happy to miss the event, especially given the trade-off. But there was certainly something to be said for hard and fast, as though he couldn't wait to be inside me....

I was pretty sure the team knew it too—from the smile on my face, if not from our prolonged absence. I didn't even blush as they exchanged a glance. I had absolutely nothing to be ashamed of, and Apollo could be downright proud.

We discussed my hair, which Spike would do up with carefully crafted curls escaping, and my makeup, which would involve smoky eyes, bronzer and nude lips, and I let them have at me. I ended up with a mani-pedi before all was said and done as well, a wine color so deep it was almost black.

When they were finished and held mirrors up to me for approval, my own eyes nearly fell out of my head. I ... didn't look like me. I felt something like the Bionic Woman. Better. Stronger. More fashionable. I looked ... like a starlet. Like someone who belonged on Apollo's arm.

"Wow," I said.

Spike and Roslyn gave each other a fist bump behind my back. "Wow," I said again. "It's like you worked some kind of magic."

Their smiles got even bigger. They could easily give the Cheshire Cat or even Julia Roberts a run for their money.

"I can show you how to do the makeup," Roslyn offered. "Some other time, since you're running short on it tonight."

"And I can teach you what to do with your hair, although without my years of experience ..." Spike began.

"Thank you," I told them both. "Really."

I couldn't believe it. I was almost looking forward to a red carpet event. Then a flashback to my earlier vision made my knees go temporarily gelid. Roslyn reached out to grab me before I could go down, but the weakness passed after only a second.

"Don't eat anything. Have a shake if you need calories,

careful brushing afterward. Do not ruin your makeup." That was an order.

"But—"

"No."

And suddenly I was famished. Or simply ornery. Hard to tell.

But I only smiled, practicing for the red carpet. "Before you go," I said, "would you help me into the shoes and dress? I want Apollo to get the full effect all at once."

"But of course!" they chorused.

I wasn't sure about Spike, but I didn't get the impression he had any more than a professional interest in the outcome of my look, and I wasn't the most incredibly body-shy person in the world, so in the end, I just went with it. Once the dress and shoes were on, Roslyn went off to fetch Apollo, while Spike tugged the lines of the dress into place.

She announced their presence with a dramatic "Bamp-bamp-BA," I supposed in place of a drum roll, and thrust the door open.

I swung to face it, hand on hip, one leg out in front of the other in the way Christie had taught me was slimming, but it was my breath that caught. If Apollo was stunning normally—and he was—in a tux he was the living embodiment of sex appeal. It should not be legal to look so good. It was dangerous. He could stop traffic, cause more cat fights than a Black Friday sale at Neiman Marcus, make a nun reconsider her vows. He was ... "Wow," I said again. And since it didn't seem enough to recycle a word I'd already used on my own image, I added, "Wow." I couldn't seem to deal with anything multisyllabic at that moment. My blood was rushing, but not to my brain.

Apollo, for his part, was staring, and I could feel his reaction through our link. It was ... oh my, I wasn't sure we were making it out of the condo.

"Stunning," he said.

Multisyllabic. Still, it didn't dim my smile. I was going to prom with the hottest guy in creation. Or anyway, Hollywood's version of prom.

"I have something for you," he said, pulling a jewelry box from where it had been hidden behind his back. It was big, velvet and the color of a red carpet.

Wait, I'd seen this scene before, hadn't I? Hoity-toity affair, red dress, velvet box. It was *Pretty Woman*. "Borrowed?" I asked before opening. I didn't want to fall in love with something that might be fleeting. I hoped that wasn't any kind of metaphor for the man I'd be wearing on my arm.

"A gift," he said.

"Oooh," I answered, my heart leaping. I reached for the box, almost afraid. Whatever was inside ... I couldn't wait. I opened the lid, ready to see rubies or diamonds or something stunning and priceless and absolutely wasted on me in daily life. Instead ... I stopped breathing until it became desperately urgent to do so. Inside was a necklace of gold coins. Antique gold coins. Ancient. They were strung onto a gorgeous chain, either equally old or made to look so. It was absolutely perfect. And to go with it, hammered gold hoop earrings. "No tears!" Roslyn scolded sharply as they started to well up. She rushed forward with a tissue and dabbed very carefully at my eyes, preserving the makeup.

"Can I help you put it on?" Apollo asked.

I turned my back for him, catching his eye in the full-length mirror. He gave me a wink and then had to look away to concentrate on the clasp. He brushed his hand down my tattooed wings when he finished, sending a delicious shiver through my body.

I handled the earrings on my own.

When I was finished, I turned and gave him a kiss, regardless of Roslyn's gasp. I was pretty sure kissing was on her proscribed list, and I didn't give a single damn.

Apollo's phone buzzed from an inner jacket pocket, and he liberated it to check the read-out. "Right on time," he said. "That's our limo."

I might have squeaked just a bit. It was the moment of truth. "I have to transfer a few things to my clutch," I said.

"Of course."

Roslyn and Spike packed up their kits as I rushed for my clutch to transfer the things I was likely to need. And then Apollo saw them out and whisked me away into the limo with a hand barely touching my back, his heat still coming through the silky fabric. I felt like Cinderella getting into my pumpkin coach.

"I don't think your plan is going to work," I said to Apollo when we were on the way.

"Why not?"

"You wanted everyone to see me without wings to put to rest all the crazy speculation, but no one's going to recognize me! I don't even look like the same person." My laugh ended in a snort.

"Especially when you snort," he said, a gleam in his eye. "So sexy."

I punched him in the gut, but not hard. Not after everything. He pulled me close and held me against him. Mostly, I thought, so that I couldn't get enough clearance for a decent swing. But it was ... nice. Weirdly domestic, if I ignored the fact that I was in an outfit that all told certainly came to more than I made in a month, headed for a red carpet event where I knew no one but the trickster god and his former wife/my former enemy, about to face a firing squad of cameras ...

There was a reason, after all, it was called a photo shoot. "Breathe," he said, feeling my tension.

I did. In through the nose and out through the mouth. It worked so well, I did it again. There was traffic around the theatre, and we encountered the police directing it well before we arrived at the limo line letting people off at the red carpet. Apparently, there was no question of pulling out of the line of cars, parking around a corner, and slipping into the theatre through a side door. I knew, because I asked.

"Five minutes on the carpet," Apollo whispered in my ear. "I promise."

He lied. The butterflies in my stomach turned into vampire bats, flapping in a frenzy, as we pulled up for our turn on the walk of fame. Apollo got out first and reached in for me. I willed myself not to trip on my heels or step on the hem of my gown or anything else and, for a wonder, it actually worked. I got out—if not smoothly then at least without bloodshed—and hit the on-switch for my smile. Luckily, I had some experience at that anyway from my circus days. My fear of heights had kept me out of my family's high-flying act, but I'd still had to make myself useful with dancing bears, hoop-jumping poodles and about any other act that made patrons go "Awww!" Once I'd gotten too big to be cute, the Rialto Brothers had tried to make me sexy with sparkly leotards and the whole nine yards. If they'd had Spike and Roslyn at their beck and call, they might even have succeeded.

As soon as my feet hit the carpet, I felt overwhelmed. Fans screamed from behind barricades, security guys easily the size of a circus strongmen stood by to hold back trouble. Cameras aimed our way like the eyes of a thousand spiders, with which I had some experience. They were nearly as terrifying.

I kept my smile in place and my arm through Apollo's. My clutch gave me something to do with my other hand. Otherwise, I'd have been at a loss.

Then the first microphone came our way. It stopped in front of Apollo, and a short male reporter with spiky hair, hipster glasses and a bright purple ascot in lieu of a tie stepped up to ask what lovely lady he was escorting and whether it was true that he'd just signed Thalia Day away from her former agency.

Apollo had a ... I'd never known what to call it—a glamour, an aura, a presence? Something that was as natural to him as breathing that he had to focus on dimming down when he didn't want to get tackled by willing women ... or men, for that matter. Now he dropped the shield or whatever kept it in check, and I almost staggered back with the power of it. The entertainment reporter in front of us, who I was fairly certain I should know, suddenly licked his lips and gasped for air as though Apollo had stolen it all.

Apollo smiled and I heard women in the crowd sigh and shush each other for the chance to hear what he had to say.

"This lovely lady is my girlfriend, Tori Karacis."

"Tori Karacis!" the reporter repeated loudly, a hand going dramatically to his cravat. "The same woman who was pictured with you in New York with, dare I say it? Wings." He leaned in closer with the microphone, and if I wasn't mistaken, his cameraman leaned in as well.

Apollo laughed, and it was enough to send shivers all through me. The good kind. "As you can see, she's completely wingless tonight. Well, except for those tattooed on her back." He gave me a little spin, and I followed his lead, showing off my ink for the camera. "The only thing that flares is her nostrils when I make her mad."

I swatted Apollo and the reporter laughed, all very theatrical. "Who could stay mad at you?" he asked.

"No one," Apollo answered, "which is just the way I like it."

Another limo must have pulled up and disgorged its passengers, because suddenly the reporter's gaze flitted past us.

"Enjoy the premiere," he said, by way of dismissal, and rushed forward a few steps, leaving us in his wake while he tackled the next guest.

It went on and on like that. A woman aimed her way toward us and then ran interference, guiding us to the reporters she wanted us to chat with, body-blocking us from others.

"Tori, Natashya. Natashya, Tori," Apollo said in rushed introduction to our body-blocker. "Natashya's my PR person."

"Charmed," she said. "Now, you're going to want to talk to Nicole Kent. She's the one with the hot sheet ..."

And on it went.

"Who are you wearing?"

"Is it true about Thalia?"

"What do you say about the rumor—"

"Is it true the mishaps on your last film cost—"

Sometimes we were pulled off into small alcoves with banners or other insignia, sometimes not.

My teeth were in danger of breaking from how hard I was clenching them together to keep my mouth shut. The reporters didn't really want to hear from me, although every once in a while I was called on to do my spin and show off my ink. I didn't mind this so much, as it gave me a moment to relax my smile before my facial muscles went into spasms.

And then we came to a stop as we waited for the trio in front of us to finish up. A sudden throaty laugh rose up above the others, and I felt Apollo ... flare. There was no other word for it. Through our link, I felt a sudden awareness, maybe even sexual. No, definitely sexual. As if all of the sudden his libido had sat up and taken notice.

"Who is she?" I whispered. "And also, down boy."

The woman with the voice was in an electric blue dress with side seams that ... didn't exist. Instead there was silver lacing holding the front of the dress to the back. Very thin silver lacing leaving a couple of inches of honey-gold skin clearly visible all the way up her sides.

"Aphrodite," he said quietly ... and not happily, I was glad to note.

"Yes," she said, spinning around as though she'd heard him, which I couldn't imagine was possible with all the background noise. Still ...

"Apollo!" she said, pushing aside the men to either side of her—one silver-haired and the other blond and twenty to thirty years his junior. She threw open her arms, and Apollo had no choice but to snub her or disentangle from me so that he could receive her embrace.

They stopped short of an actual hug, grabbing each other by the elbows and doing the kiss to each cheek. "What a pleasure to see you!"

The cameras were full on us now, and I wondered what would be made of the spectacle. I'd browsed Yiayia's godly gossip site a time or two for research, and I knew from it that Aphrodite was essentially the current Mayflower Madam. I wondered what she was doing on the red carpet.

"Oh, but where are my manners?" Aphrodite asked. "Let me introduce you." She let go of Apollo to latch on to the silver fox beside her. "Apollo, this is Fletcher Alvarez, world famous producer. We're discussing production of my memoirs. Fletch, this is my dear old friend Apollo Demas."

Fletch held out his hand dutifully, but it was me he was looking at. "Well, well, and who is this?"

He took his hands back from Apollo as soon as humanly possible and grabbed my hands in his tightly enough so that I couldn't easily escape. It struck me that he and Aphrodite were perfect for each other. Both had that predatory gleam in their eyes.

"This," I said, tired of letting Apollo speak for me, "is Tori Karacis. I'm a friend of Apollo's."

"And a media darling in your own right, isn't that true?" asked the blond boy ... because now that I looked, he really wasn't much more than a boy. Twenty-one or twenty-two, maybe, but in such a way that he could play a teenager if the role required it.

"Ah, the feathered femme fatale," said the reporter who'd

been interviewing the trio, trying to insert herself back into the conversation. Apparently, she'd seen my tabloid photos ... and who hadn't. But I'd been war-battered then, far less femme fatale than an avenging angel. And my wings were not feathered.

"I prefer silk to feathers," I said, showing off my gown.

The reporter tittered, and the blond boy, surprisingly, came to my rescue. "I'll drink to that. In fact, I shall. Let us be off in search of champagne."

He took my other arm, leaving Aphrodite with a single escort. I glanced at her to see how that went over, but she looked more fondly amused than irritated, and I was relieved not to have made yet another enemy as we headed into the foyer. It was absolutely opulent with its high, frescoed ceilings, gilt accents, chandeliers, and wall sconces giving off soft golden lighting. Arrayed all around us was more beauty than the mind could possibly process ... and that was just among the assembly. I expected familiar faces everywhere I looked, and I wasn't disappointed, though I was surprised by the number of faces I didn't recognize.

Blond boy flagged down a passing server, liberated two flutes of champagne, and handed me one, leaving Apollo to fend for himself. Luckily, snagging champagne was well within his capabilities.

My new friend clinked his glass against mine, made as if to drink, and then paused with the glass nearly to his lips. "But wait, I haven't introduced myself yet, have I?" There was a certain glint in his eye that made me think for a second of Hermes. It was set off by a trench-deep dimple on his right cheek.

"No, you haven't."

"Roman. Roman Accor." He said it like *Bond. James Bond.*

"You might know him better as Eros," Apollo said, his voice distinctly dry. "Or Cupid, but that brings to mind cherubic little boys flitting around in cloth diapers, and we all know you're not nearly so innocent."

I froze with my champagne halfway to my lips. I'd seen Eros once on a battlefield when the Titans were rising, but I'd been a little possessed at the time. Possibly delirious with pain. I could probably be excused for not recognizing him without his wings and weapons.

"Now, now," Aphrodite cut in, snagging her own champagne and one for her companion. "Can you still be so bitter after all these years? He said he was sorry."

Apollo shot a glance at Fletch, but the producer was scanning the crowd, raising his glass here and there, presumably to acquaintances or business cohorts, and paying no attention whatsoever to the conversation.

Still, Apollo leaned in closer to Aphrodite. "He turned Daphne against me. She begged to be turned into a *tree*. *A tree*, for gods' sake. Even leaving aside the heartbreak, do you know what that does to a man's ego?"

Aphrodite rolled her eyes. "Oh, like you had a shot to start with. Daphne had taken a vow of chastity." She said it in the same way someone might mention drinking hookah water or licking Steve Buscemi's toes.

In a few thousand years, a god was bound to have some bad relationships, but Apollo seemed to have accumulated more than his fair share. The story with Daphne had started with Apollo taunting Eros about his archery skills and Eros taking offense by unleashing one of his golden arrows on Apollo to inspire love for the nymph Daphne and then taking aim at her with one of the lead arrows that caused revulsion. The resultant pursuit was the stuff of epic poetry ... and ended with her begging for escape and her father turning her into a tree. Why a tree was a mystery to me, but myth and legends were full of those kind of stories.

I looked to the blond boy, Eros, who seemed content to let

them battle it out. He met my gaze and winked, dimple still clearly in evidence. Weirdly, it was not entirely without effect.

"Darling," Aphrodite said suddenly to her companion. "Isn't that Layton Jennings over there? Didn't you want to have a chat with him?"

He dropped a quick kiss to her cheek and was off before the words had faded; raising his glass to catch the attention of a tall, gorgeous, African-American man with a smooth head that needed absolutely no adornment.

Oddly, I felt a pull of my own and looked up to scan the crowd. Even more oddly, some instinct had me not only searching, but sniffing, scenting the air as though I could catch a whiff of ... blood.

Only it wasn't a scent. It was a pull, a tug, as though something called to me blood to blood.

Richie had to be somewhere close by.

I couldn't see him, not in the throng. But I knew he was there. I could feel him. I didn't imagine Ian was far behind ... or that it meant anything but trouble.

15

———

Through our link, Apollo sensed my sudden high alert. "What is it?" he asked, quietly.

I leaned in close to murmur, "They're here."

As if on cue, the "they" who actually joined us were Hermes and Sigyn.

Hermes actually dressed up very nicely, his mischievous eyes a glittering accompaniment to his night-black tux and his gold vest. Sigyn was in a matching dress of liquid gold which left one shoulder and arm bare and the other covered by a long sleeve ending in a crystal cuff. But I didn't really have time to appreciate the cut.

I was so distracted searching out the Roland brothers that I missed it when Hermes stared too long at Aphrodite's décolletage, though my attention was drawn back when he gasped suddenly at Sigyn's elbow in his gut.

"I think we'd better mingle," I said to Apollo. Meaning, of course, hunt down our killers. I'd never thought to find them here and didn't even want to think about who they must have killed to get in.

"After you," Apollo said, sweeping a hand out to lead the way.

I took a step forward and realized that Apollo wasn't behind me. Aphrodite had stepped into his path. "Not so fast," she said. "I've heard that Athena is in town, which means something big. You need to tell me if something's brewing. I have to protect my investments."

Apollo stared down at her, though he didn't have to look far. She was a tall woman. Apollo seemed to weigh the advantage of moving her bodily out of his path versus simply answering her question.

"This is not the time or the place," he said tightly.

"Oh, lover." She said it for my benefit, I was sure. "When else am I to ask? You don't call. You don't write. I never, ever see you anymore."

I shot him a glance at the clear implication that she *had* seen him in the past ... possibly in a professional capacity. He didn't blush, but then he'd had ages to get over that sort of thing. It wouldn't have taken him very far in the entertainment industry ... especially not in the direct-to-video films in which he'd gotten his start.

"Fine then. Quickly. We're not looking at a war—yet anyway —but if Set gets free ..."

"Set?" she asked, loud enough in her alarm to draw glances from all around us.

"Right now we're searching out his new recruits, which is why we have to go. A word of advice—if the Roland boys are patrons of yours ... you might want to put them on the black list. If they call, notify the police ... or us ... right away."

Her eyebrows arched nearly to her hairline. "Then they're guilty? Truly? I never kiss and tell, of course, but it's hard to imagine such fine young men having anything to do with murder."

Fine young men? Was she kidding? Jessica said they'd been a handful even before all of this ... but if they'd at least been respectful of women, whether by nature or fear of losing their privileges at the escort services, then maybe Aphrodite had seen them on their best behavior.

"Er, they may not be quite themselves," I said politicly.

At that moment, Apollo's head snapped up, his attention riveted by someone across the room, over Aphrodite's shoulder. "I'm sorry," he said suddenly. "I see someone I have to talk with. We'll have to continue this another time."

Aphrodite gave a pursed-lip pout at the clear dismissal, but Apollo was already moving past. "Later then," she said, her voice full of promise. "Don't be such a stranger."

I could tell through our link that it wasn't one of the blood-lust-boys who'd caught Apollo's attention, and I stood for a second in indecision. I could go after him or I could use the moment of Apollo's distraction to search for the Roland twins myself. I hesitated, focusing on the call of the blood I'd consumed to the blood still running through Richie's veins. My prey, it seemed, lay in the same direction Apollo was headed.

I excused myself from the group and made to follow the path Apollo had opened in the throng when a hand to my wrist pulled me up short. My fists clenched into claws, and I knew the look on my face was anything but friendly as I glanced up ready to fight whoever held me back.

It was Roman ... Eros, pressing something into my palm. He released me before I made an issue out of it and met my glare with a wink and a dimple. "In case things don't work out with Apollo," he said. "My personal number is on the back."

My mouth fell open, but I bit back a response. There was no time and, really, I didn't have the words for his cheek.

I tucked the card down into my bra and kept going in the direction I felt the tug.

Apollo had stopped beside a doe-eyed brunette with Sandra Bullock's girl-next-door approachability mixed with Cindy Crawford's abundance of hair and Julia Roberts's smile.

In other words, Thalia Day ... in the flesh. She was smaller than I thought she'd be. Even with her sky-high heels, she only came up to my shoulders. Unlike most of the other starlets, her dress was positively demure in a pale peach fabric with shimmer but no sequins, crystals or bangles. The only embellishment was on the straps that held up the top of the dress and then ... as she turned, I saw that all the detail was in the low back with more of the beaded straps crisscrossing.

I wanted to stop. Oh, how I wanted to stop. I'd been a fangirl of hers ever since *Still Waters* and *Becky with a Brain*, which hardly anyone else even remembered.

As I went to pass, Thalia threw her arms up and cried, "Apollo!"

She enveloped him in such a hug I felt the smallest little twinge of jealousy. Thalia hugged with her whole body. Her whole heart, it seemed. I'd always wondered if all the warmth that came across on screen could possibly be genuine. Now I knew.

I was nearly out of her orbit when she spotted me, freezing me in the intensity of her smile like it was a searchlight and I'd been pinned down in my escape. "And you must be Tori!" she said, releasing Apollo and clasping me in a hug every bit as encompassing as the one he'd received.

I stood frozen in her embrace, anxious to track Richie down before I lost him again, but unable to bust free. Or maybe unwilling. Social conventions were as hard to break as other bonds.

"Thanks for making him happy," she whispered in my ear.

I wobbled just a little bit when she let me go. Star-struck, I had to admit. A little overwhelmed.

"Yeah, I get that a lot," she said, at the look on my face. "Don't worry, it'll pass!"

Someone—a small, unobtrusive man with dark hair, a close-cropped beard and an impeccable suit in a room full of tuxes—whispered in her ear, and she said, "Oh!" and smiled around, including everyone in her sweep. "Trevor says they're opening the doors. I'm just going to pop into the ladies' room to freshen up. I'll see you all inside."

Suddenly something kicked in my chest so hard, I thought it would burst open. That call, blood to blood, was abruptly more like a sonic boom than a pulse. A combination of the proximity of Richie's blood and my precog trying to tell me it meant very bad things ... as if I might think otherwise. I whipped my head around, trying to spot him, sure he must be right behind me or somewhere close enough to kiss ... or kill. Apollo caught my concern through the link and looked around as well.

"Close now," I said. "I'm going to follow Thalia to the ladies' room." The precog had kicked up at her announcement. Either the danger was to Thalia and I'd be there to protect her or it was to me and maybe I could lead the bloodthirsty brothers off to somewhere isolated and take care of the problem. Richie said he'd be coming for me. Maybe he thought getting me somewhere public would hamstring me. I wouldn't want to go all Gorgon in the face of so many cameras. But he and Ian would be captured on film as well ... Of course, if "Richie" wasn't in control of his own body, maybe the power calling the shots didn't give a hot damn.

"Go," Apollo said. "I'll keep watch out here."

The man in the suit started to usher others toward the door, and I heard Apollo make some excuse, but I was off like a shot in the direction Thalia had gone, cursing that I'd already lost her. The crowd had swallowed up her petite form, and I wasn't tall enough to see over them.

My ankle twisted as I swerved suddenly to avoid crashing into a tuxedoed gentleman built like a linebacker.

"Hey, pretty lady, what's your hurry," he asked as I grabbed on to a bicep the size of my head to steady myself.

I sent him a smile of apology, nearly breaking my neck I had to crane it so high, and released his arm to stumble off. If I could have kicked the shoes off, they'd have been long gone.

I hit the art deco bathroom door and burst my way through. Inside was … no one. No threat. No battle. No starlet even.

"Thalia?" I called.

"Um, yeah," she said, with an undertone of *what the hell* in her voice.

"Just checking," I said feebly. "Show's about to start."

I started in on the buckle of the sandal on my twisted ankle. When danger struck, I wanted to be ready. It meant leaning temporarily against the wall for support. If I'd been smart, I would have moved away from the door first, but I'd been so sure everyone else was headed into the theatre …

The door smashed open, bashing my hip rather than hitting the wall. The blow overbalanced me in my one-footed stance and sent me reeling. I stumbled a few steps until I caught myself on a sink and looked up to see two demonic faces behind me in the mirror. The Roland brothers, suited up like ushers and each leering like a devil on a bottle of diablo sauce.

I wanted to yell to Thalia to stay where she was, but if they weren't aware of her already, I wasn't going to call her to their attention.

"You boys are in the wrong bathroom," I said instead, hoping to warn her.

"Oh, I don't think so," one said. I could tell instantly that it was Ian … or whoever was riding along on his soul. The pull of Richie's blood gave him away. He was the twin closest to the door … between Thalia and escape.

Worse yet, he was the brother with a wedge in hand, which

he kicked into place to jam the door shut and keep out any hope of reinforcements. A blow rocked the door just as he got the wedge into place, and I could hear Apollo calling my name, but I didn't have a second to respond.

Ian launched himself, coming at me dead on; Richie rushed me from the left. I dodged right, and my stupid ankle turned beneath me again. I vowed that if Apollo wanted to take me out in public again, he could damn well do it in combat boots. But that wasn't going to help me now.

There was only one thing to do—take footing out of the equations. I chanted the spell under my breath and felt the pleasure-pain of the wings bursting forth, unfurling, and stretching in relief at their release from captivity.

The brothers had pivoted on a dime and were coming at me again, though Ian was a half-beat behind his brother, having checked himself momentarily at the sight of the wings. I flapped them hard, blessing the high ceilings, which gave me the room to launch. I kicked at Richie's hands, knocking them away as they tried to latch on to my feet and yank me down, then kicked off his head to leverage a blow at his brother, catching him right between the eyes.

If my wedges had been steel-toed or otherwise weaponized, they have packed more of a punch, but at least his head jerked back with the blow, and his eyes when they latched back on me were not entirely focused. Still, his grasping hands found my ankles and he yanked to pull me out of the air. I kicked hard, but he held on tight. The next thing I knew, he had a grip on my calf and then my thigh, pulling me down hand over hand. My wings beat frantically, but it was no good.

I cursed myself as a fool. I'd become so reliant on my supernatural arsenal, I'd forgotten the one absolutely mundane weapon I carried. I snapped open my little clutch, grabbed my pepper spray, and dropped the rest. Before the contents hit the ground, I had the safety thumbed off on my canister and the stream aimed at Ian's face. I let loose with a burst, right in his eyes, and he screamed—one part fury and two parts pain.

He let go to claw at his face, and I kicked off, hoping to gain height before Richie could grab me in his stead. I nearly managed it, but he leapt up and grasped my shoe, twisting and yanking me down, a snarl on his face. Ian stumbled to the sinks and opened the faucets, splashing frantically and cursing at the burning. I knew from experience his face would be on fire.

I decided screw it and let myself drop like a stone. Richie couldn't handle the unexpected weight and had to let go. As soon as I touched down on the floor, I grabbed his head in both my hands and head-butted him full force. Pain bloomed, but I'd always been hardheaded, and he was the one to stagger back in pain. I followed up by mashing his instep and letting loose an uppercut to the chin. He wavered but didn't go down. Tougher than I'd thought. Preternaturally tough, as though he'd gotten something from Set's talismans besides bad dreams and bloodlust.

I planted my feet and whirled like a dervish, wings and feet flying, giving added force to the roundhouse kick I planted in his stomach. He grunted and toppled, but I didn't get to watch the fall. Ian hit me out of nowhere, tackling me at the waist, taking us both down to the floor. My right wing took the brunt of the fall, and I felt something snap between us. The pain flared like a supernova, but I grabbed Ian back, wrapping my arms around him and grabbing one of my wrists with the other hand to secure him tight. Locking him up like I was a human twist-tie.

"Run!" I yelled to Thalia, while I had both brothers down.

Apollo, I knew, was on the other side of the door. Maybe security as well. If Thalia could get it open, this could all be over. There was a split second's worrying delay, and then she burst out of the stall, running for the door.

Richie twisted like a snake, grabbing for her even in his

pain, but he missed, and Thalia came down on the palm of his hand with the heel of her spiky shoe.

He howled and retracted the hand, cradling it against his body, and that was all I could see before Ian, eyes red and squinted shut with pain and swelling, reached blindly for my face and got a thumb hooked up into my nostril. He jabbed it in, and it hurt like hell, tearing sensitive membranes ... and then burning them up with the pepper spray he'd tried to wipe away from his face which had transferred his hands. Immediately, tears filled my own eyes, and my nose welled with something a lot grosser.

I heard Thalia struggling with the doorstop, and pounding from the other side of the bathroom, which probably wasn't helping. Richie must have jammed the wedge in good.

I wanted to help, but Ian was now fighting like the Tasmanian devil on speed. I knew from my experience with Richie that my gorgon glare couldn't penetrate Ian's crazy, but still I watched for his pepper-burned eyes to open enough for me to give it a try. The other option was my blood. If I could get it into his bloodstream through one of his already vulnerable membranes, I could turn him to stone, but I didn't want to do that except as a last resort.

Just to be ready, I bit down on my cheek and tasted blood. It filled my mouth with a tang. Meanwhile, I squeezed Ian tighter and rolled toward Richie to grab him before he could recover enough to try for Thalia again. But grabbing him meant read-justing my hold on Ian, and it gave him just enough space to reach up between us—groping at my breasts, I thought at first, before I realized it was something that rested against his own chest he was going for.

Set's amulet? I knew what the coins did, but had no idea about the amulet. In the very next instant, I found out.

All at once, Thalia got the wedge free with such abruptness that it slid across the floor. The door burst open, spilling in our reinforcements ... but the real explosion came from right beside me. Right about chest level. It blasted the entire room, blowing me back against the wall until I hit with such force it seemed I'd crack open. If I'd thought my pain was supernova before, I'd been mistaken. This blast was a world ender.

16

I woke to a bright light shining in my eyes, and the very first thing I did was flashback to *Poltergeist*. Hadn't the creepy medium lady said not to go into the light? I didn't see that as a problem. Light was pain. I tried to flinch away from it, but someone was holding my eyelids open and maybe even my head in place. Which meant that I still *had* eyelids and a head and, now that I thought about it, an entire body that seemed made up of more pain.

"Now follow the light," someone was saying, but it had become torture. My eyes burned, and regardless of whatever held them open, I squinched them shut so hard my tormentor had to let them go or do me damage.

My reward was blissful darkness and a downgrading of the pain in my eyes. Everywhere else was still screaming.

"Okay then," said the person behind the light—EMT? Paramedic ...? "—at least tell me what day it is."

I had to think about that, and it scared me. And then ... and then I remembered it all.

The premiere, the fight, Thalia, the wings ...

Oh gods, Apollo was going to kill me. This whole thing was

supposed to lay speculation to rest, not provide incontrovertible proof.

I tried to move, tried to flap, to see whether they were still in evidence or whether, mercifully, they'd faded with my consciousness, but my body felt flattened, compressed, as if the explosion had crushed me like a soda bottle and I hadn't expanded back into my regular shape. Since my more dormant gorgon genes had activated, I'd experienced a lot of strange things, including the amazing ability to rebound from just about anything, but it still took some time, and while I recovered, the Roland brothers were getting away.

My eyes seemed to work anyway. I forced them open again and looked around the room, as much as I could from my prone position knocked flat against the back wall. Knees right in front of me, belonging to whoever had tortured me with the bright light. Other feet over by the doorway. Black shoes, shined but not shiny. Security? Law enforcement? I couldn't look high enough to find out. No Thalia. Not that I could see.

"Thalia?" I asked, ignoring his question about the day of the week for my much more pressing concern. My chest ached with the effort to force air up into my vocal chords, and in the end I couldn't manage very much. The word was barely a whisper.

"What?" the EMT asked, leaning down, first looking into my eyes and then resting his ear centimeters from my lips.

"Thalia Day ... where?" I ran out of breath and thus sound and waited for a response while I tried to recover from the effort.

The EMT pulled back again and looked into my eyes. I could tell it was bad. He seemed to be gauging how much I could take, whether he dared tell the truth.

I begged with my eyes.

"Gone," he said, as gently as he could.

I heard the sound of squeaky wheels coming from the

entrance into the bathroom and shifted my gaze to see more shoes and a gurney coming at me.

"This is going to hurt," said the guy by my side. "We have to get you onto a back board. There's no telling how much damage there is. And the police are going to want to talk to you, to see what you remember."

I shut my eyes again. *Gone*. Thalia was gone. Somehow I knew he didn't mean *escaped*. Like me, she'd still been in the room when Ian had triggered the explosion. Muses weren't invulnerable. There was no way she could have walked away under her own steam. Which meant the Roland boys had taken her with them. Given their track record for murder and ... worse ... time was ticking away. We had to find them. Had to save her before they could do their worst.

The person who'd come in with the gurney—a woman this time I saw, as her face appeared above me, biting her lip in concentration—helped the other EMT get me onto the back-board. I could tell from their movements that my wings weren't getting in the way, which put at least one worry to rest. They must have vanished on their own once they weren't needed ... or maybe retracted self-protectively at the explosion. So the EMTs made short work of lifting me up onto the gurney and whisking me out through the door.

Apollo waited in the hallway, held back by security, along with others from the premiere who'd decided the real-life action was more intriguing than that on screen. But the other faces were a blur. I was riveted on his—the fear in his eyes, the pain I felt through our link, which, for all I knew, was a feedback loop of my own. I was almost past the point where I could see him, since the board immobilized me, and I couldn't have twisted my neck even if it would obey when he pushed his way right past the security guard and ran up beside me, taking my hand even as the female EMT tried to block his way.

"You all right?" he asked.

Even breathing hurt, but I forced air through my vocal chords again for him. "Get them," I told Apollo. "Save Thalia."

"Sir, are you with her?" the woman asked.

"No," I said, before he could respond. They'd want him to come along. To answer questions I couldn't or to make decisions if I passed out on them. But I wasn't the one who needed him. Not at that moment.

He looked hurt and let go of my hand as the gurney continued on. But I knew he'd understand. If not in that moment then as soon as he thought about it clearly. Or I'd have time to explain when I healed up to the point where I could check myself out of the hospital. Thalia might not have that kind of time.

A car pulled up, siren and lights blaring as I was loaded into the ambulance, but a jostle as the wheels bounced over the bumper set all my pain receptors to flaring, and I blacked out for a minute ... or two. When I opened my eyes again, they were swimming with spots, as though the world had been blotted out by purple-black bruises.

When they faded, I was face to face with Nick's partner, Detective Reyes, who stared down at me emotionlessly, either hardened to or uncaring about my pain. "Tell me everything you remember," she ordered.

I closed my eyes again for a second, blocking her out, trying to free a synapse or two from screaming about pain to focus on a response. How was I going to explain an explosion with no incendiary device?

"Tori," she said sharply. "Ms. Karacis, stay with me. I need you to tell me what you can. Every second counts."

I'd had the same thought, but ... In the end, the words slipped out without any filter on them. I didn't have enough available brain cells for misdirection. "Do you believe in magic, Detective?"

I'd said it so faintly I wasn't even sure she'd hear, but I'd opened my eyes to see her reaction and watched her reel back as if I'd slapped her face.

"What did you give her?" she asked the EMT who'd stayed in the back with us while the other put on the sirens and the speed.

"Nothing," she answered, sounding mildly offended. "We don't dare until we get her to the hospital. Make sure there's no brain injury."

"So she has a concussion?"

"She was unconscious and non-responsive when we arrived. Her pupils were uneven. There's a good possibility."

"Damn. How soon before I can get anything useful out of her."

The EMT shrugged. "Can't say. Doctor might be able to tell you more, but it can come with amnesia or confusion."

And there was my out. Amnesia. *I have no recollection of these events.* Except the ones that mattered. Richie and Ian Roland had taken Thalia; the police had to focus on them.

"The Roland boys," I said, forcing enough air from my lungs to make myself heard. "They have ... Thalia."

"Did they say where they were taking her?"

I started to shake my head, forgetting I couldn't move it. "No."

"What the hell?" asked the EMT up front.

"What is it, Jake?" asked the one back with us. When he didn't answer, she said, "Jake?"

He cursed and swerved suddenly, and Reyes left me to poke her head through the window into the front of the cab. She cursed sharply in Spanish and grabbed the phone on her belt, voice dialing dispatch. "We've got a massive brawl on Hollywood Boulevard. We're just passing Highland now, and it looks like ..." She trailed off for a second and then, "Oh, holy hell!"

"What?" the EMT asked, coming up beside her. "No

freaking way. Is that Captain America fighting Bizarro? They're not even in the same universe."

I couldn't see a thing. Couldn't move. But I heard shouts and screams, the sound of shrieking metal ...

"It's like all the characters on the strip have suddenly gone insane."

Chaos. That was the only explanation. The boys must have come this way. But did they carry some kind of chaos field, maybe Ian's amulet, or did it naturally follow them wherever they went? Was there a way Apollo and Neith could use it to track them?

And how twisted was it that with everything else going on, I felt a little cheated that I didn't get to watch superheroes fighting? Fake superheroes, but still. I pictured the old-timey Batman, *Oooph!* and *Kapow!* signs appearing above heads, though I was sure the reality was nothing so campy.

"Turn here," the female EMT ordered her partner. I felt the ambulance give a heave to the right, and then swerve almost immediately to the left.

"Holy hell," he said, echoing Reyes, "was that a *Transformer*?"

Something hit the side of the ambulance hard, and it rocked from one set of wheels to the other before falling back on all four. Every part of my body screamed in protest, my brain most of all, because I wanted out of this damned back brace, off this damned gurney and into the hunt. It wasn't even a possibility at the moment, but I hated being sidelined. Helpless was just two four-letter words jammed together.

"Dammit!" the EMT cried, gunning the engine and racing us away faster than was probably safe or legal, but Reyes didn't say a thing.

Behind us I could hear more sirens as, I assumed, police cars poured into the plaza, trying to contain the insanity.

I had to hope the hospital wasn't far now, because even

strapped down for minimal movement, every swerve hurt the hell out of me.

"Reyes," I called. I had to try again, hoping she could hear me over the sound of the sirens. She turned, finally, "Tell Nick to follow the crazy."

She looked at me like I was nuts, especially after the magic comment, but she pulled her phone from her hip and hit a button. "Tell him yourself," she said, holding the phone up to my ear as it rang.

He answered before the first ring even cut off. "Reyes, how is she?"

"She's ... stable," I said, knowing he'd recognize my voice instantly. He'd also get the subtext. "I'll heal, but listen. You have to follow the chaos."

"What?" he asked.

"Reyes will tell you. And call Neith."

My eyes wanted desperately to close, and now that I'd done what I could, I let them. Reyes might not get me, but she could tell him what was going on and Apollo could probably fill him in on the rest.

17

———

I woke when they were pulling me out of the ambulance, my vision blurry at first, like an old television that had to resolve the pixels, but then everything snapped into perfect clarity. Unfortunately, my brain didn't come on-line quite as quickly, and I immediately tried to rise, only to find that I couldn't ... but because of the restraints, not because my muscles failed to obey. They'd tried to snap me free, but even at my best, I wasn't exactly the She-Hulk.

"I'm fine," I said to the EMTs as they unloaded me from the ambulance.

The woman gave me a pitying look, but didn't immediately answer, too busy lowering the wheels and getting them all to move in the same direction.

"We'll just make sure of that," her partner said. The radio on his hip buzzed, and he helped maneuver me with one hand while he answered with the other. I didn't understand the codes, but there was no missing that it was another call-out. And, it seemed, right back to the mess we'd driven through.

He and his partner exchanged a look, her with a groan, and they handed me off as soon as we were inside, their paperwork signed off on and a copy given to the nurse. Reyes followed me in but then disappeared with her phone, only to reappear once the nurse had me in a ... well, "room" was being generous. Had me in an area of the emergency room partitioned off by perky polka-dotted curtains in shades of blue and purple.

Reyes grabbed the nurse as she was leaving. "Keep me apprised of her status?" she asked.

The nurse looked startled. "Ma'am—Detective—I don't know how much I'll be able to tell you."

"It's okay," I said from the gurney.

"Oh, well, if you'll sign off on that ..." And she disappeared, presumably to get the paperwork necessary to cover her butt.

"I have to go," Reyes said, not unexpectedly. She grabbed a card from her pocket and put it into my hand, which made me think of Eros's business card tucked into my cleavage. "Call me if you think of anything. Or, anyway, have someone here call me or Detective Armani."

I tried to nod and cursed myself. I'd forgotten again that I was all bound up. Now that I could move, there was nothing I wanted to do more. Although, the fact that my muscles had responded didn't mean they were in any condition to actually coordinate with each other.

"Okay," I said.

She nodded, and I tried not to be jealous of her freedom of movement.

Five minutes passed. Ten. A million for all I could tell. Paralyzed boredom minutes were about a zillion times longer than regular minutes. Finally, a nurse came and shined a light into my eyes, took my blood pressure and temperature, asked me a few more questions to add to the info on her clipboard and then told me they'd be taking me into x-ray any time.

I started to ask about releasing my restraints, but she was gone before the question died on my lips.

She was back a second later, and I thought maybe she'd

heard me after all. "Can I get out of here?" I asked as she came through the curtain.

"Oh, you're getting out of here," she answered back. Only it wasn't her voice.

"Neith?" I asked, half sure I had a concussion after all.

"Shh," she said quietly. "That's Nurse Nancy to you."

I realized my jaw was hanging open, and I shut it. She came around to the side of my bed and raised the protective bars up into position.

"What are you doing? You've got to get me out, not fence me in."

"Don't worry, I've got this. Play groggy."

I glared.

"Come on, shouldn't be too much of a stretch."

I glared until she ducked down to see where the brake releases were on the bed, and then she slid the bed out from the wall and disappeared around behind me. With my head bound to the board, I couldn't rotate it to see her, and anyway, I didn't seem to have much choice but to play along.

I let my eyes go vacant and willed my body to go slack.

She rounded the gurney long enough to push the curtain out of the way and then pushed me through.

No one stopped her. No one even gave us a second glance.

The real Nurse Nancy came out of a curtained area just in front of us, and I willed her not to turn around, not to see her second self. The chaos field must have been far enough away to give us that turn of luck. She immediately headed off in the direction that was away, and we slid right through the ER and out into a hallway without anyone taking notice.

The hallway was too well-trafficked for Neith to do whatever she was going to do ... or so I presumed, and so I held my peace while she wheeled me around a corner and down another hallway, stopping us in front of an elevator. I hoped to Hades she knew what she was doing and that the gurney would actually fit into the elevator. The doors looked wide enough, but ... when they opened, I was thrilled to see the elevator was even deeper than it was wide.

We slid in, and as soon as the doors closed, Neith set my brakes, stripped off her jacket, and hung it on the control panel, which wasn't quite flush with the elevator wall. Then she undid my head restraint and I instantly rocked my neck back and forth, thrilled to have movement, even if my muscles screamed with it.

She flopped the strap back over my head without a word and took her jacket as the elevator beeped to let us know we'd hit a floor. Two men in lab coats stood aside holding the doors as Neith wheeled me out again. I reassumed the dazed look and didn't ask any of the million questions running through my head, like, "Why the elevator?" The emergency room was already on the ground floor. Going up seemed to be the opposite of progress, but I assumed the goddess of strategy knew what she was doing.

Halfway along that hallway, she stopped at a door with a film over the inset window that made it look like stained glass. It had a small gold plaque where a room number might be that said, "Chapel."

She left me in the hallway momentarily to check whether anyone was inside, then propped the door open as she wheeled me in. We seemed to have the place to ourselves.

"What are you doing?" I finally asked as the door closed behind her.

"No cameras in here. Let's get you free."

I was absolutely on board with that. I'd never have guessed Neith was the answer to my prayers, but then, the gods worked in mysterious ways. After she got the strap across my chest unbuckled, she moved to the one around my lower arms. Once they were free, I was able to help with my own legs.

I felt as weak as a newborn colt on spindly little legs as I tried to stand, and I had a moment of vertigo where I fell back against the bed, but once that passed, I was able to stay upright more or less reliably.

"You got this?" Neith asked. Not coddling. Not offering help. Just watching. Assessing.

"Yeah, what next? Why up?"

"Because they'll search everywhere else when they come to take you to x-ray and find you gone. They'll check cameras, starting with those around the exits ... Since you came in as the victim of an attack, the first thing they'll think of is foul play. Neither one of us can afford to get caught. We've lost too much time as it is."

It made sense, but ... "What now?"

"You have wings, don't you?"

"Yeah, but ... it's broad daylight. Anyone could see me use them."

"Uh huh. There are superheroes and supervillains battling it out on Hollywood Boulevard. The waxworks at Madame Tussauds are coming to life. The replica of the tallest man in the world at the Ripley's Believe It or Not Museum just stood up and dented the ceiling ... I don't think anyone's going to be too concerned about your wings."

I stared at her, stunned. Maybe I really was concussed. "Seriously?"

"And that's just what I know of."

"We've got to stop these boys before things get any worse."

"Well, duh."

My mind boggled. Of all the things you didn't expect to come out of a goddess's mouth. "Besides," she said, "what good is a superpower you're afraid to use."

That steeled my spine. I hadn't thought of myself as being afraid. Cautious, yes. Considerate even, thinking that if the world found out about me, they'd go looking for others. But my family had been in the glare of the circus lights for generations.

And the gods, Fates, Titans and others had been avoiding detection for ages. They were clearly better at it than I was. Was I really hiding out for them or for myself, not wanting the attention, afraid of what it would mean for my life? I wasn't a big fan of change. Chaos was right out.

Damn it, these boys had to be stopped.

"Fine," I said with admittedly bad grace. "What about you?"

Neith gave me a pitying look, and then shook herself. As she shook, her body rippled and transformed. Her hair darkened and gathered up into her former braids, color spread across her face and over her skin in a wave, pounds melted off, her shape changed ... And then Neith was standing before me. She shed the lab coat, dropping it onto the hospital bed. No one would associate her with Nurse Nancy. No one would have seen us together. She could just walk out. I should have thought of that.

No wonder the gods and goddesses had been so good at hiding all these years. They could be anybody. If the boys channeled enough power to Set for him to break loose, we were going to be in a whole world of hurt.

"We're all meeting at my hotel, the Loews Hollywood. You know it?"

"Yeah, but shouldn't we be going after these guys while the trail is hot. Thalia—"

"Are you ready to get your ass kicked again? Maybe this time the boys will do some damage you can't come back from. The police are on Thalia's kidnapping. Let them do their jobs. At this point, with a kidnap victim, they're not going to go in with guns blazing, but maybe they can keep the boys busy long enough for us to come up with a plan. We need something that will neutralize them."

"We need Sigyn," I said.

It popped out of my mouth before I even realized I'd formed the thought. She'd "neutralized" me back when we'd been on opposite sides. She was a runemaster ... mistress ... whatever. If anyone could come up with a countermeasure ...

"She's already in. She and Hermes are meeting us there."

"Great." Already I wasn't so certain about my brainstorm. What if Sigyn was ready to switch sides all over again? If she joined forces with Set we were sunk.

But who on earth would join forces with the god of chaos? It was the same thing I asked myself about satanic cultists. Why would people pledge themselves to the Prince of Lies? Did they really think he was going to live up to his end of any bargain? Or that there wouldn't be a buttload of fine print?

And that was the very moment it occurred to me that the devil might be real and ...

I couldn't even think about that. One crazy crisis at a time. If I ever came face to face with a pitchfork-wielding, cloven-footed menace, I'd spit in his eye. Until then, I had to focus on the demons that came to my town spoiling for a fight.

"Meet you there," I said.

I let her leave the chapel first, since my wings would be faster than driving in LA traffic, especially with roads likely blocked off around whatever insanity had spilled out into the streets. I left a minute or so later, all my lack of patience could handle. Nobody stopped me. Nobody questioned me. But then, my wings were still safely hidden away. The real fun would come when I tried to jump out a window.

I looked at the signs as I stepped out into the hallway. In one direction lay pediatrics. In another, obstetrics. I was sure those sections were watched fairly closely, and that I'd be a little ... apparent. I turned around and found a sign for a visitor's lounge.

It was empty as I entered, lights out since it wasn't in use. I didn't flip the switch. The only light came from the two sliding glass windows. There were screens on the other side. And that weird prickly stuff that was supposed to discourage pigeons and gulls. But there were no bars on the windows.

I undid the latch and slid one open … until it stopped only halfway to home. There was a stopper jammed into its track to keep it from opening all the way, probably to keep people without wings from doing the very thing I contemplated. I checked out the stopper and found a nail. A simple nail, but smashed in so well, I didn't see any way to pry it out. I didn't have super strength or laser vision or anything that would help me with the problem. What I did have was the willingness to cause myself bodily harm, knowing I would heal. Still, I'd need something thin and strong enough to wedge under the nail head to pry it loose.

There was nothing, of course. A table, chairs, a couch, a smaller table, some magazines. I started there, grabbing the toughest looking of the bunch and sliding the middle staple on the spine under the nail head. I thought I felt it start to give, but it was only the staple buckling under the pressure. I cursed and tossed the magazine down.

I wondered if the buckle on my cursed sandals would do the trick. It seemed worth a try. I took both shoes off, so that if I was caught, at least I'd be flat-footed, which messed with the cliché, but there it was. Then I stabbed the buckle up under the nail head, angling it so that the head was caught in the corner and ripped at it with all the anger I felt at those shoes. Because yes, dammit, anger at inanimate objects could be productive, thank you very much.

Slowly, the nail pulled forth. The angle was awkward, but I repositioned myself and kept pulling and finally the nail popped free, setting me back a few steps.

The light came on suddenly, and I whipped my head around to see a nurse as surprised to see me as I was to see her.

"Hey, what are you doing?" she asked, stepping into the room.

I quickly tossed the nail down and yanked open the window. Now she wasn't walking, she was racing, and the room wasn't large. In a flash, I hopped up onto the sill, shoved out the screen, and jumped out, chanting the words to free my wings in midair.

She called out after me, but I soared away, hoping she hadn't gotten a decent look at my face and wondering whether her next move would be to call security or have her eyes examined.

18

I started low, since the window I'd jumped from was only on the third floor, and since I'd fallen even farther before my wings had engaged, but I quickly found myself soaring over the city. I knew where Neith's hotel was, but before heading there, I circled the hospital in an ever-widening spiral, hoping to feel another zing, another tug, blood to blood. I wanted to pin those boys down, so that when the time was right, I could swoop in.

But either the chaos field was interfering with my power or they had fled somewhere outside the city. I couldn't spend any more time on the search. Maybe Nick had tracked them down. Or maybe one of the others had something to contribute, but Neith was right. We needed a plan.

I veered off toward the hotel, landing on the roof of the building, where, luckily, someone had stuck a loose piece of cement in the path of the roof entrance door. Maybe Neith. Maybe some smoker who'd doggedly resisted all the anti-smoking campaigns. Whoever it was, I thanked them silently, tucked my wings away, and took the offered entrance. A minute later, I was standing in front of the room number Neith had given me, knocking on the door ...

Which opened to the sight of a boyish face with overlong curls. There was no dimple currently in evidence, and the face was as grim as I suspected it got.

"What are *you* doing here?" I asked. I hadn't meant it to come out quite the way it sounded, but this was no time for fun and games. Matchmaking or ancient feuds.

"One of Aphrodite's girls has gone missing as well," he said, opening the door wider and stepping aside so I could enter.

"Girls?" I asked, bristling. Not bad enough she ran Hollywood's premier "escort service," but not to even grant the women who worked for her the status of adulthood ...

"Women," he said, "is that better? Well, actually, nymph in this case."

I stared. "Nymph? Do the customers know?"

"She doesn't exactly advertise. I mean, a select clientele might be aware, but otherwise ..." He shrugged. "You know how it is. Kingdoms fall and so do fortunes. It's a living."

I moved dazedly into the room. Neith had what was probably referred to as a junior suite. It wasn't hugely, incredibly grand, but it was impressive enough. It probably would have looked a lot bigger without all the bodies taking up space. Hermes, Sigyn, Apollo, and Neith had beaten me there. Aphrodite was present too, pacing. It looked odd on her.

She should be lounging. Or slinking. Flirting or flattering. Instead, she looked honestly concerned, enough to allow a wrinkle to form on her brow.

Apollo rose at the sight of me and came over to fold me into his arms, flat against his body. As always, it radiated heat. I drank from it. His closeness or some radiant energy he gave off seemed to give me back a little of what I'd lost in the battle back at the theatre.

I held him close, but only for a moment. The comfort was too indulgent when others were in danger.

As soon as I pulled back, Aphrodite closed in on me. "You have to save Genie," she said, her gaze boring into mine.

"Genie?" I asked. It had to be the name of her nymph, but it seemed an odd one to me.

"Iphigenia," she said impatiently. "She's an innocent." She waved away whatever emotion showed on my face. "That aside. She doesn't deserve this. And I promised to protect her. I promise that to all my girls."

"Women," I said automatically.

"Sure, fine. Women ... whatever. You have to help her."

"We will," I said.

I didn't know I had the parts to a plan until they started coming out of my mouth. "Neith, I need you to check on Set. Look in on the security arrangements. See what needs to be bulked up. Take Hermes with you. He thinks like a trickster. If there's a flaw in the precautions, a way out, he'll find it. Right?" I asked him.

He saluted me with a three-fingered gesture that suggested I read between the lines. I knew I had extreme cheek ordering around gods and goddesses, but it wasn't the first time and probably wouldn't be the last.

It was Neith who protested. "I suppose you'll be going after the Roland twins. They've beaten you once. What makes you think they won't beat you again?"

"Sigyn," I answered.

The goddess looked up at me in confusion. "What can I do?"

"Your runes. I've been on the receiving end, and I never want to be there again. You want to even the score between us, then you'll devise some runes I can plant on the boys to neutralize them. You paralyzed me. Maybe you can do the same for them. Then Jessica can call in an exorcist or whatever to free them from whatever psychotic spirits have taken over, and they can turn themselves in to the police. I'm sure with the kind of lawyers they can afford and a good insanity defense ..."

Jessica ... I hadn't heard from her since this morning when we'd dropped her off. It was now fairly late in the evening. She'd been the nervous type so far, calling regularly for hand-holding and updates. A bad feeling started to grow in the pit of my stomach at the realization that no news wasn't always good news.

Sigyn's lower lip had nearly disappeared as she chewed it in thought. She had to let it go to answer. "It'll take me a little bit. I can't just turn any old object into a rune stave. The more transitory, the weaker it is. Paper, for instance, is right out. Carving the runes into wood or stone works best."

"You do what you need to do."

"And I'll need to be present to activate them."

"Fine," I said, hoping it was. Part of me truly believed in her rehabilitation, but a deeper part of me that still smarted from Hecate's betrayal had some serious trust issues. "Apollo, maybe you can give Artemis a call? She and her gang might want to reinforce the guards for Set until all this is over."

A feral grin spread across his face. "Knowing my twin, she'd give her left arm for the chance to shoot Set."

"Would make it awfully hard to draw a bow," Hermes observed.

Apollo didn't respond. To me, he said, "Don't even think you're going to send me away. I'm sticking to you like glue."

"Like you did back at the theatre?" it slipped out. I knew there had to be a good reason he hadn't seen that the boys were closing in on the ladies' room and given warning. But there hadn't been a private moment to ask him about it and now it was out there for everyone. Even I heard the accusatory tone.

"There was a huge commotion at the theatre doors, like some crazed superfans had stormed them. The doors rocked like they got hit by a battering ram. There were screams. I ran toward them, thinking it might be the Roland brothers and that someone needed help ... It turns out it was either a perfectly timed coincidence or a planned distraction. Either way, it worked. Security and I were both pulled away."

Well, that explained that. I could tell by the look on his face he felt like hell, and I didn't make it any worse. "I didn't mean that to come out the way it sounded. Yeah, you're with me on team 'Rescue Thalia.'"

"And Genie," Aphrodite inserted.

"What about me?" Eros asked. "Contrary to popular belief, I'm both a lover and a fighter."

I rolled my eyes.

"He's all yours," Neith said.

A snarky comment was on the tip of my tongue, but, after all, Hermes had proven himself useful, and if I turned down the help of every overly flirtatious Greek god ... well, I'd hardly have any allies at all.

I was ignoring the fact that Apollo had once fallen into this category. It was one of the things that had kept me from giving in to my feelings for him for so long. Yet he'd come through for me time and again. And anyway, change was squarely in his nature ... in all their natures. Belief fueled reality. Maybe if I believed hard enough ...

I was either a fool or a visionary. "Fine," I said again, thinking clearly of Inigo Montoya from *The Princess Bride—You keep using that word. I do not think it means what you think it means.*

"Sigyn, you work on the runes. Neith and Hermes, you work on Set. Apollo and Eros, you're with me when the time comes. I need to check in with Jessica. Maybe she's heard from her brothers."

"Jessica?" Aphrodite asked. I realized she'd neither asked for nor received a part to play in all this.

"My client," I answered shortly.

I moved a bit away from the others so I'd be able to hear, and I called Jessica.

Her phone rang and rang before sending me to voicemail. I tried to tell myself that it was only an unanswered phone, but that feeling in my gut rose up like Godzilla storming out of the ocean to trash Tokyo. I regretted now that I hadn't gotten Mrs. Barbarosa's number. At least I had her address. I quickly used my browser to look up her number on-line, but no one answered my call.

When I looked back toward the others, Apollo was already glancing my way, alerted by the alarm radiating along our link ... or maybe by his own precog.

"We've got to go now," I said.

"The limo's outside," he answered, not even asking for an explanation.

I ran for the door. I didn't have time to protest about the limo being too conspicuous.

Given the violence of my reaction, we might already be too late to save Jessica. "Shotgun!" called a voice behind us.

Eros. Curse him.

"There's no 'shotgun' in a limo," Apollo bit back.

"Well then, whatever. I'm coming with. Most action I've seen in ... Wait, don't get the wrong idea, I've *seen* action. Just not the *Terminator*-type stuff."

"This isn't a movie," I said. I'd hit the hallway and made a command decision to give up on the elevator and take the stairs. We were only five floors up.

Apollo and Eros pounded down behind me. I only hoped the others were doing what I'd told them to do. We needed to nip this whole thing in the bud, dammit. If not, we'd have another clash of the Titans or battle for New York or ... I'd had enough of near apocalypses.

The limo waited for us in the covered portico in front of the hotel, off to one side so as not to block traffic. We raced for the door before the porter could grab it for us, startling our poor driver, who was cracking pistachios and flipping through messages on his phone when we jumped in.

Or maybe I startled him more than we, given my barefoot state and disheveled appearance. My gown might never be the same. I didn't give him time to ponder it, but rattled off Mrs. Barbarosa's address, which was still saved in my phone's GPS under recent searches. He looked to Apollo in the rearview mirror to confirm he should listen to the crazy woman, and Apollo answered with, "Move, dammit. This isn't a drill."

The driver didn't need to be told twice, but put the car into gear and pulled out into traffic.

"So, what's the haps?" Eros asked, sounding eager.

I had the sudden urge to share crime scene photos, the especially bloody kind, to take his enthusiasm down a few notches.

"Does anyone still talk like that?" I snapped instead.

"Don't they?" He thought about it. "How about: what's the 4-1-1?"

"We'll find out soon enough," I said.

We seemed to be catching every single light. Every one of them. I was leaning forward in my seat, straining as though it would get me there any faster. Hell, I could probably run there ahead of the limo ... Or fly.

"Pull over," I said.

The driver again glanced into the rearview mirror to check in with Apollo ... the man paying for his services.

But Apollo was looking at me. "There's no time to stop," he said, which the driver took as a sign to ignore me entirely.

"I'll get there faster on my own," I said, reaching across for the door handle.

He put his hand over mine to stop me. "You're not going off alone. I'm not going to lose you."

"No, you're not," I said. I kissed him hard in good-bye and to put him off kilter, then yanked on the door handle even with his hand on mine and threw myself out of the car, rolling and scraping across the asphalt as the limo went on without me. I heard the brakes squeal as my cursing died down and a curb stopped my roll, but I quickly jumped to my feet ignoring the fact that I was in pain and still wobbly from my earlier defeat and bolted down a side street, though only a few steps before I unleashed my wings and achieved lift-off.

Only this time it took a monumental effort. All action and no recharge was taking a toll on me. I felt like I needed a big, fat, bloody steak to build my blood back up and then a twenty-four hour nap. I wasn't getting either one any time soon.

I had no idea how to get to Mrs. Barbarosa's as the crow (or Gorgon) flies, so I had to follow the roads, sometimes swooping low enough to read the signs. I could see people down below, wondering if I was a bird or a plane or yet another Superman reboot. Cell phone cameras pointed my way. By tomorrow I'd probably be a YouTube sensation. Not my favorite idea ever, but I'd survive.

At last, I hit Mrs. Barbarosa's street and spotted her tidy, one-story house—yellow with green and white trim. The roof was too steep for me to land on safely, but luckily, she had a fenced-in backyard for her cats, and I landed there, startling two of them, who disappeared as though they'd never been.

I took the two steps up to the shaded back porch. As I approached the back door, one of the in-house cats scared the hell out of me by leaping at the door and clawing at it for all she was worth. I expected the screen to shred, but she must have been declawed, because all that happened was a shooshing sound and a plaintive mew like she was begging to be let out.

Something was wrong, but I didn't need her to tell me that.

I tried the door, and the cat paused in her batting at the

screen to stare at me. It was locked. I debated going around for the front to try that door, but my sense of urgency wouldn't allow it. Instead I grabbed an empty clay flowerpot and swung it for the window. Both shattered on impact, and I punched out a few remaining shards to stick my hand through and push in the screen as well. If her neighbors were on guard, they'd have heard the sound and should be calling police right about now, but that was okay with me. I might need the backup.

I stood on my tiptoes and reached in to undo the locks to the inner and outer doors and let myself into the house, closing the screen door behind me so the clawless kitty didn't get out of the house and into some trouble she couldn't fight her way out of. But the cat had vanished at the racket I'd made. Other cats, though, peered out of everywhere to see what all the fuss was about.

Or maybe just whether I had the kitty kibble. I had, after all, just let myself into Mrs. Barbarosa's kitchen. It smelled of canned cat food and ammonia, as though the kitty litter tried and failed to keep up with so many cats—at minimum the clawless kitty who had dashed away, one thinking she was thin enough to hide behind the legs of the kitchen table, another peering from the wall separating the kitchen from the next room, and yet another, a huge orange longhair, making a bee-line for me, rubbing herself against my legs for all she was worth, as though she wanted to weave me legwarmers with all the excess fur.

"Jessica!" I called.

The walls ate the sound. My precog lay dormant. As silent as the house that gave me no answer.

I stepped forward, toward the next room and the half-pink, half-black nose of the multi-colored kitten who stared at me from around the corner. My new friend, the ginger kitty came with me, pressed tightly against my legs as I walked, making it a special challenge.

The kitchen led to a hallway that had a staircase on the left and a living room/dining room combo on the right with a half-wall separating the two. Not separate enough. From where I stood, I could see the body and the blood. So much blood.

I took a step closer. Then a few more. The dining room area wasn't large, and I was to the half-wall when the world went wackadoo again like it had back at the Roland mansion. The air around me seemed to thicken, but still I could see through it like old glass. The room lit up, sunlight streaming in through the front window where yet another cat basked in the warmth, eyes closed contentedly. Based on the angle of the light, it was no later than mid-afternoon.

Through the veil of my retro-vision, I could still see Mrs. Barbarosa in her flowered housecoat lying right where she was now, but unbloodied. Peaceful. Her chest rising and falling as she slept and a slight whistle coming through her nose. A long-haired black cat with a smudge of gold on its forehead perched above her keeping watch. One of Mrs. Barbarosa's hands rested on her chest, the other hung to the ground where another cat—the big orange beast pressed up against me now—licked at her fingers.

When Jessica entered from the front hallway, the orange cat took off like a rocket, right between Jessica's feet, as though to trip her up, but Jessica kept her course, moving almost like an automaton. The cat basking in the sunbeam startled awake. The watch-cat perched on the back of the couch hissed, her hackles rising, as though she sensed something wrong. She leapt to her feet, her back arched, her eyes trained on Jessica. She hacked in warning.

Jessica hissed back, and my knees started to buckle. I reached out blindly for the half-wall and held on to it like a life-line as the vision played out. I knew what I would see.

Jessica ... when had they gotten to Jessica? I'd failed to protect my client. Worse yet, I'd sent her right to sweet old Mrs.

Barbarosa. I'd practically signed the cat lady's death warrant. Jessica reached the sleeping lady, and the watch-cat leapt from the back of the couch, claws out, slashing at Jessica with a screech I knew from back alley fights. Jessica caught the cat, but couldn't hold her. The cat fought like Mrs. B's life depended on it, which I was pretty sure it did. The cat from the window launched at Jessica as well, catching her on the shin, right through her jeans. Both drew blood, the pain seeming to bring Jessica momentarily back to herself. Life seeped back into her eyes, which filled with horror at the realization of what she'd been about to do.

Then two things happened at once—there was a massive crash from the front of the house and Mrs. Barbarosa bolted upright on the couch, finally alert to the danger. In that instant, the Roland brothers invaded the living room. Mrs. Barbarosa's eyes went wide with fear, but she only had a second to live with it before one of the brothers plunged a knife into her chest.

The vision winked out as the bile rose in my throat and I needed someplace for it to go without contaminating the crime scene. I stumbled out into the backyard and burned my throat out coughing up the vile stuff, wishing I could expunge the vision along with it.

I heard a car pull up outside and forced myself to stumble toward it on unsteady feet. I had to keep anyone else from coming in. I needed to preserve the crime scene. To call Nick and Reyes. I needed ...

Hells bells, no one knew to be wary of Jessica. She could waltz right into the police department and ...

I held out my arm to stop Eros and Apollo from going any further than the front yard and made the call. Nick answered on the first ring. "Tori? My God, Tori, where are you? The hospital said you disappeared."

"I'm all right. I, uh, disappeared under my own steam." Mostly. "You can scold me later. For now, you need to know—

Ian and Richie have Jessica Roland. And ... you need to watch out for her."

With my throat still burning from the bile, the speech cost me.

"Watch out for her how?" he asked.

"They've gotten to her. Infected her somehow. She can't be trusted. Right now you have to consider her armed and dangerous."

"Has she—"

"Not yet. At least, not that I know of. But you do have another body." I gave him the address.

"How did you find out about the murder before the police?"

"I came to visit my client and found the body of the woman she was staying with. From a distance it looks a helluva a lot like the bodies of Ma and Pa Roland."

"I'm on my way. Reyes can handle things here."

"One more thing—you might want to call animal control. The woman has a lot of cats."

"Great."

19

———

Nick was not excited to see Apollo and Eros when he pulled up, both of them sitting on the hood of the limo, the latter tinted blue in the glow of a vapor cigarette—cinnamon scented.

I met Nick at his car. "No one touched the body. No one disrupted the crime scene. Well, I mean, I broke a window and screen at the back of the house to get in, but aside from that ..."

Nick took a deep breath and seemed to count to five before letting it out. "Anything else to confess?"

"I had another vision. That's how I know it wasn't Jessica who killed Mrs. Barbarosa. Not that she wouldn't have, but ... the cats didn't give her the chance."

"*The cats?*" he asked.

"Yeah, she was in a trancelike state until one of the cats attacked and drew blood. It snapped her out of things. I don't know for how long. The vision ended after one of the brothers plunged a knife into the old lady's chest." I paused for just a second. It wasn't relevant to the investigation, I knew that, but what came out next was. "It's all my fault."

"How? Did you put the knife in their hands?"

"I put Jessica in that house. I didn't do enough to make sure things were safe, and now you've got about a dozen cats with no nice old lady to feed them."

Some of them were watching us right now, actually. My friend the big, fluffy orange cat had retreated when Nick's car pulled up, but was cautiously approaching again. She seemed to be my new shadow.

"Did either of you see anything?" he asked, nodding to Apollo and Eros, who I let introduce himself, since his current name hadn't left much of an impression on me. Roman ... something.

"Not a thing. She never even let us get out of the car," he said in answer. Then, realizing he *was* out of the car, added, "I mean, not to go inside. This is the farthest we've gotten."

"Good. Stay here."

"Sir, yes, sir," Eros answered, flipping him a casual salute.

I hoped he and Apollo could play nice long enough for me to walk Nick through the crime scene.

"Take me around back," he said.

"Sir, yes, sir," I mimicked.

He rolled his eyes and didn't say a word. I led him around back, watching as his lips thinned and the lines around his eyes deepened at the sight of the window I'd smashed and the busted in screen.

"Subtle," he said.

"Thanks, I try."

"Did you touch anything inside?"

"The half-wall between the dining area and the living room. I had to hold myself up when the vision hit."

"Okay, we've already got your comparison prints on file."

"Wait, before you go inside, did Reyes give you my message? Were you able to track the chaos?"

He looked back at me in the darkness, but, of course, in the ambient light of the city, nothing was ever truly *dark*. "Yes and no. It seemed pretty straightforward at first, but then ... there was a ripple effect, like the butterfly flapping its wings in South America that causes a tsunami in Asia or however the saying goes. By now, there are reports coming in from all over the city. Fights breaking out, galloping topiaries, traffic lights gone wild."

Little things that could snowball out of control. LA with its car culture would practically shut down with its traffic system on the fritz. There'd be accidents, gridlock, patrol units tied up directing traffic and giving out tickets for blocking the box. And with the area's history of road rage and other violence ...

"Damn," I said.

"Tell me about it. Are you any closer to stopping this craziness?"

"We're working on a plan."

"If I could make a suggestion?"

"Shoot."

"Work faster."

"Gee, why didn't I think of that?"

"I've missed bantering with you," he added after a second.

"Me too." The moment turned awkward.

"Well, I have to go see about a dead body," he said. "And call it in. And wait for the forensic team, which with as many calls as we've had tonight might be a while. Go. You're of better use elsewhere than sticking around for a statement, but you'll have to come in for one tomorrow."

I nodded and watched him go. It was getting a little easier every time.

My phone rang as I got back into the limo, which was good. It put off the moment of decision—where to go next when I had absolutely no idea. No direction. I'd lost Richie's blood trail and time was running out.

The read-out told me it was Yiayia before I even answered.

"Tell me you found Ichnaea!" I said as I punched the button to accept the call.

"Well, hello to you, *Egona*."

"Kind of in crisis mode right now," I said impatiently.

"We are certainly at the breakdown of human society if—"

"*Yiayia!*"

"Sheesh. Fine, fine. I can take a hint. Do you want the good news or the bad news?"

I groaned. I didn't have time for games. "The good news?" I ventured, knowing it would take longer to argue.

"I found Ichnaea!"

"Hallelujah."

"The bad news—she's over in Asia, helping track those still alive under the ruins from the last tsunami."

My joy evaporated. I should have known.

For a second, a small part of me considered that Asia wasn't impossible. We could bring her over as we had brought Panacea from Africa to combat the plagues the demons unleashed on Earth. Hermes could open a window, which boosted by Apollo's power could become a portal, but ... did I have the right? The brothers were killing people one at a time ... for now. Ichnaea might be rescuing hundreds ... thousands ... finding pockets of entire families trapped in the rubble ... No, I couldn't take her away from the rescue efforts. Not now. Not unless things became dire.

"Damn," I said.

"Tori, you will not curse. Your mother would wash your mouth out with soap."

"Damn's only a curse if you believe in hell," I countered.

"I believe in Tartarus," she said, "and I wouldn't wish anyone there."

I didn't have an answer for that.

"Is it true that you were at the same premiere as Thalia Day tonight? And that she was kidnapped?" Yiayia asked.

It was as though she'd run an icy finger down the center of my back.

"How did you know about the premiere?" I asked.

I hadn't mentioned it to anyone in the family. I hadn't even thought to mention it. To me the premiere was a chore, something I had to get through without falling on my face or saying anything stupid. It wasn't brag-worthy.

"I teased it for the *Goddities* blog," she said proudly. "Oh, not about you, of course. I didn't know about that until I saw you on the news. But about Thalia. She's got a supporting role in that new movie. I knew she was going to be there. And of course, as one of the Muses, I knew she'd be of interest to my readers."

"What about Aphrodite?" I asked, trying not to jump to any conclusions.

Eros was already leaning forward in his seat, trying to catch both sides of my conversation. At this he practically fell into my lap.

"Now she was a surprise. I had no idea she'd be attending. And with that handsome son of hers ..."

Eros flashed me his dimpled grin.

"But you stay away from him. Far away," she added. "That one's trouble." His grin didn't fade.

"So you didn't say anything about Aphrodite on the website?" I asked, just to be certain.

"Not as far as the premiere," she said defensively.

"As far as what then?"

"Nothing recent. It's all old news. You know how I run it, 'Rumor has it that a certain goddess of love is La La Land's latest Mayflower Madam and that those in the know can request some very special services from certain nymphs and naiads who've been chased out of their elements by encroaching civilization. Naughty, naughty!' Nothing too specific. Why, what are you thinking?"

I was silent for a second. I had a bad, bad feeling. A really terrible feeling. And I didn't want to share it with Yiayia in case I was wrong.

But what if I was right?

"Yiayia, would you send me whatever you've written on gods and goddesses in the LA area?"

"Do you ...?" She gasped. "Do you think they found out about Thalia from me? But ... but it was the premiere for her very own movie. Lots of places would have talked about it."

But lots of places wouldn't have known that she was one of the Muses. If I was right—and the monster pinging of my gut said that I was—this was all my fault. Even more than leaving Jessica with Mrs. Barbarosa.

Based on the shocked look on Richie's face when my wings had come out during our battle, he hadn't known about me. Maybe he knew the gods were real, if he was aware of his connection to Set, but he might not have thought about other mythologicals walking around ... And if he or the force that drove him had gotten curious enough to do some poking around about me, it could very well have led him to the *Goddities* website. I knew for a fact that while Yiayia had kept my name out of things, she hadn't been able to resist certain teasers. My life of late had been the ultimate fodder for a godly gossip site. Witness my relationship with Apollo.

And if they'd decided that humans weren't enough of a challenge or that killing immortals would facilitate Set's greater glory ... or power ...

Apollo, feeling my turmoil, even if he couldn't read the cause, reached over to put a hand on my knee and squeeze in support.

"Yiayia, it's not your fault," I said with complete honesty. "But sending me that list will be a huge help."

"I'll get right on it."

I let my head fall back against the seat as we rang off. How on Earth was I going to protect all the gods and godlings in the

LA area? It seemed rife with ancients—so many of the old gods were attracted to influence, fame and fortune, longing to recapture a little of the power they'd lost. Hollywood alone had far more than its fair share.

There was no way to protect them all individually. I debated what to do. I could have Yiayia put out a warning on the *Goddities* website. Not everyone would see the site, but surely word would spread? But was that the way to go or should we reserve the site for setting a trap, since I suspected the brothers were checking in? There was no way to know, and it wasn't a decision I wanted to rest on my shoulders alone.

I asked the driver to put up the privacy shield before I told Apollo and Eros what I suspected.

We all stared at each other momentarily.

Then Eros chimed in, "Why didn't I know about this site? What does your grandmother say about me?"

I rolled my eyes, called the site up on my phone, and handed it over. "No idea. See for yourself."

He scanned the site, clicking around, and Apollo said thoughtfully. "We still have the option of Hades and the hellhounds."

"With the chaos spreading, I'm worried about controlling them. What if they're affected and go on the attack? We can't risk it." We both lapsed into silence.

"You're the god of foreseeing," I said to Apollo. "Is there any way you can kick-start a vision? Maybe tell me where to find the boys or what they'll do next?"

His sigh didn't seem like a good sign. "I'll try, but chaos is, by its nature, chaotic. Unpredictable. With the Roland boys tied to Set and not working off any script, I'm not sure we'll know anything before it happens."

"But there must be a way ..."

Inspiration struck like one of Zeus's lightning bolts. If anyone had a direct line on the future, it was the Fates, the sacred sisters who measured out our time on earth, wove our destinies, and cut us off at the point of death. Surely, they had a pattern in mind, a vision of how the weave would flow. If something disrupted their pattern, took power out of their hands, and cut off threads before their allotted time, they'd have a vested interest in helping us restore order.

I didn't exactly have them on speed-dial, but I'd been on the point of death more than once in my life and in that Schrodinger's state, I'd heard them arguing over me. Specifically, Atropos, who'd been ready to come at me with her shears and cut me from the great weave. I'd been saved only by her sisters intervening on my behalf. It turned out they watched my thread as avidly as some people watched soap operas or their favorite sports teams. Which said pretty significant things about the amount of drama in my life.

I wondered whether they still watched, and whether they'd answer if I called to them. "Ouch," Apollo said suddenly, rubbing at his temple.

"Sorry! Was I thinking too loudly?"

"You fairly well screamed. What do you have in mind?"

"I'm calling for the Fates."

There was a pause. "And you just expect them to answer."

"No, but ... Well, yes, actually. They've done it before. Kind of."

"You've met the Fates?" he asked, an odd note to his voice. "And lived to tell about it?"

"Uh, I was in pretty bad shape at the time. I'm not sure they expected me to remember."

"Tori!" Apollo said.

"Hello!" a female voice piped up from the front seat.

I whipped my head around. The privacy screen was down, and instead of the driver, who'd been most decidedly male, there was a woman in his cap and coat craning around in her seat to face us, dark corkscrew curls spilling around her face.

She had olive skin, a pert, upturned nose, and a look of girlish glee.

I recognized the voice. I didn't know which of the sacred sisters she was exactly, but I had a good idea from the smile on her face she wasn't my nemesis Atropos.

"Well hello," Eros said, his voice dropping seductively. "You here to even out our numbers? Not that I was threatened by the odds, mind you."

The goddess blinked at him. "Eros!" she said delightedly. "You do keep us guessing. It's so good to see you … in the flesh. Not enough of it, I'm afraid, but then, I've seen it all before."

"How are you here?" I asked. "And … which one are you?"

I was worried she'd take offense. It seemed pretty ungracious after I'd called her, but with Hermes popping in and out whenever he pleased, I was starting to get the sense that I was never quite alone, which put a completely different complexion on the things I did with Apollo in our free time. I blushed just thinking about it.

"Oh, please," she said, cheerfully. "Gods and goddesses have been possessing mortals for time out of mind. Plus, this isn't a real possession. I'm just … borrowing him temporarily. I'm Clotho, by the way. I don't think we've ever been formally introduced."

She reached a hand through the privacy window and I took it to shake, fairly bemused. Apollo did the same, but Eros kissed it, hairy knuckles and all. She hadn't bothered changing the driver's appearance down to the knuckles.

She giggled a little on contact, "My sisters are going to be *so jealous* to have missed you. Lachesis, especially. She's a big fan. We don't get out much, you know, with all our extra duties. Theatre hours, you know."

I vaguely remembered from my past visions of the Fates that their day jobs involved costuming for Broadway shows. I didn't know how they found the time, but maybe it let them flex their more fanciful sides. Clotho, if I remembered right, was the spinner, Lachesis the measurer, and Atropos, the old hard-ass, was the cutter. All three played a hand in fate, in setting the weave.

"Clotho, you must have been watching, following along, since you showed up so ... fortuitously. We need your help."

"Ooh, do I get to go undercover?" she asked, clapping the driver's hands together gleefully. "Or spy on someone? Or, oooh, maybe serve as a diversion while you neutralize a threat?"

My mind boggled, just like in the game where you shake up all the letters and they spill out nonsensically. I was still trying to form words. "Uh, do you *want* to do those things?"

"Oh yes, please!" she answered, every bit like a five-year-old asked if she'd like a puppy.

"We'll, uh, keep that in mind." I exchanged a glance with Apollo, who looked a little dazed. "What I need is actually a little more in your wheelhouse."

She looked hopelessly disappointed at that. "Oh."

"It's ... there are two brothers on the loose, killing people. Now they've recruited others. One other at least. You must have seen all of this. Your weave may be getting out of control. Worse, the brothers are tied to Set, and if he gets loose ... We need you to tell us what you can of their threads, where they're going. Where we can find them."

She had the most expressive face I'd ever seen and now it was the model for dejection. "I can't. The future isn't set. Even at the best of times, and these ... aren't. We can nudge, guide, but there's free will. And humans are such contrary creatures. Plus ... it just wouldn't be fair."

I boggled at that. Again. "Fair? Since when is life fair?"

"Life might not be fair, but the Fates—we play with everyone in equal measure. Test, challenge ..."

"What about help or hinder?"

I remembered how ready Atropos had been with her scissors when I was hovering between life and death. I remembered Clotho and Lachesis intervening. They might not play God with a capital G, but they did play favorites. She couldn't tell me they didn't tinker. Clotho sucked her lips into her mouth, chewing on them in thought. "I can't, I'm sorry," she said finally. "My sisters—"

"Do they know you're here?"

She looked away. "I can't," she repeated rather than answering. "Even I don't know how this pattern will complete. It is ... chaos."

"If you don't want the chaos to grow, you have to give us something. Perhaps what strands ... whose strands are closest to the Roland brothers. Something we can use to track them."

She considered. "I will do what I can. Also, I may be able to put others in your path. Look for—"

Her head whipped suddenly around, and she stared out the front window of the car, though I had the idea what she was seeing was half a world away. "Coming!" she called in a harried voice. "Just ... finishing up!"

She turned back toward us all. "I have to go," she said. "Back in New York, it's nearly show time ... Yes, yes, I'm coming!"

Without so much as a goodbye, she winked out, leaving the baffled features of the chauffeur staring back at us.

"Sir?" he asked Apollo.

"Drive, please," he said. "Back to ..."

There was a sudden echoing shout in the car, and we all looked at each other. It hadn't come from any of us. And then a tiny little window none of us had noticed expanded to the size of a dinner plate, revealing a scene that looked like someone had gotten heaven and hell confused. There were clouds all around, so thick they were more a mist than separate entities shaped into nice safe puppies and bunnies. And in the midst of them, a dark figure fighting its chains in the form of ... a giant serpent, then a crocodile, then ...

Hermes's face appeared in the window. "Come quickly. I'm not sure how much longer we can hold him. He's—"

In the background, the figure—Set, I assumed—had taken on yet another form, that of a giant bristle-backed boar. Another figure, barely seen in the mist, leapt onto his back like one of the bull-riders of old. And like those ancient bulls, the great boar thrashed, trying to throw her off, growing tusks that looked more like scimitars.

"Apollo!" I cried.

He knew what I was asking. It was night. He wouldn't have the power of the sun to draw on, but I hoped he'd have enough stored up to turn Hermes's window into a portal as he'd done in the past. There was just one other problem, we were geared up for the red carpet, not for war.

"Just a minute," he said. "Christian, pop the trunk? Hermes, hold the window, we're coming!"

Our driver popped the trunk, as asked, looking somewhat stunned as Apollo ran around to the back of the limo and grabbed out weapons he must have arranged for earlier. To my shock, he lifted out a classic recurve bow and a quiver of arrows and then ... a sword. Not Perseus's famed sword, still magically coated in Medusa's blood, which I'd used to take down Hecate and her cabal. That one had been anonymously returned to the Greek government. But this one was about the same size and shape, its hilt wrapped in leather for a sturdy grip rather than carved of bone or uncomfortably inset with gems. It had an equally plain cross-guard and a blade with a lovely channel down the center for the blood to run. This blade meant business.

Apollo appeared back with them, looking to Eros. "Sorry, I didn't realize we'd have you along." Then he did a double take, making me look to Eros as well.

"No problem," Eros answered with a chilling smile. "I always come prepared."

Sure enough, he now sat awkwardly in his seat, a quiver of arrows strapped to his back and a bow in hand. The arrows had three different fletchings—gold, silver, and black. I understood two out of the three. Myth said the gold arrows inspired love ... or at least lust. The silver fletching probably indicated the lead arrows, meant to cause revulsion, but the black ...

"What are the black arrows for?" I asked.

"War."

Well, okay then. I hoped he could make more of them appear as he'd made the bow and quiver appear out of nothing, because there didn't seem enough to do reasonable damage to that giant boar ... not unless he got in a really lucky shot.

Apollo strapped on his own quiver and leaned into the car to hand me the sword. I tested the balance as well as I could in the close confines without cutting Eros off at the neck, and Apollo reached his freed-up hand out to Hermes's window, closing his eyes in concentration. It began to expand, but not quickly. When it reached about the size of a doggie door, his eyes popped open.

"Go," he said. "This is the best I can do right now and with Hermes so far away. I'll ... hold it."

I could tell from the sweat on his brow and the difficulty of his speech that it was costing him, and I didn't waste his effort arguing. I plunged through the portal, careful to keep everything I had within the confines, not sure what would happen otherwise. I didn't want to be cut off at the toes or anywhere else.

I hadn't thought about the fact that I was stepping out into nothing. Nothing but clouds, anyway.

Sheer terror hit me as soon as I was through and I started to plunge, my fear of heights coming back with a vengeance. It was one thing to overcome it while standing on a mountain or a few flights up on a hospital ledge, but ...

I started to mumble a prayer and turned it into the spell for my wings, which were already unfurling, called by my necessity. I pulled up short, looking around in case anyone needed my help. Hermes called my name, sounding terrified.

"I'm here!" I called back, choking down the bile that had risen in my throat. I forced my stomach to unclench and my hand to loosen from the death-grip on my sword threatening to imprint the hilt permanently on my hand. Paralyzing fear wasn't going to get me or anyone else through this fight.

I flapped back upward toward Hermes's panicked call. I lied to myself that there was no such thing as down. No buildings or cold hard earth waiting to break my inevitable fall ... and every bone in my body.

I rose up, through the mist-like clouds, up until I saw dark shapes above me and then to the point where I could make them out—Eros and Apollo standing on the clouds as though they were something solid, both taking aim at the great boar, concentration hard on their faces as they analyzed which way he might jump and how best to attack without hitting Neith, who had grown to match Set in size, as I'd seen some of the older gods do. She now clung to his back like a champion bull-rider, hands wedged under his chains to the point where they cut into her hand. She had a javelin or spear in the other, and jammed it down into his red bristled back every time his bucking allowed. Each time he squealed and bucked all the harder.

Apollo let his first arrow fly, and in a blink Set changed again, this time into a flame-red scorpion, darkening to black at the tip of his deadly tail, which glistened with venom. Apollo's arrow bounced off his tough exoskeleton.

The chains had tightened magically around Set's new form, so there was no slack. Neith's hand was still trapped under the chain where she'd wedged it, and she had nowhere to go as Set's stinger arced toward her.

I yelled a warning to Neith, hoping there was something she could do to break free, but I didn't count on that. I flew straight for that stinger, sword out before me ready to cut it off. But my cry caught Set's attention, and he whipped one of his front pinchers at me, catching me hard in the stomach. Given our relative sizes, it felt like I'd been hit head-on by a Mack truck. I went flying, and this time not of my own volition, headed straight for Eros and Apollo.

Apollo transferred his bow to his off hand and caught me before I could fly too far, as if leaving the cloud would be stepping off the edge of the world. Maybe for him it was. I didn't understand the rules here and didn't have time to learn. Maybe it was more of that belief-based reality I kept hearing about. Apollo and Eros saw the clouds as physical manifestations and thus they were. I had no faith in their ability to keep me from falling to my death and so they'd almost certainly let me down. As much as I liked being right, I liked being alive even more. I wasn't going to test my theory.

Instead, I flapped my wings to regain control and keep myself aloft, afraid my extra weight or my lack of belief would sink Apollo. Every movement was agony. Something bad was happening inside. Maybe internal bleeding from the blow Set had dealt me, but it wasn't as bad as what Neith faced.

Neith! I shot back toward her, afraid I wouldn't be in time to do anything but witness her death.

To my shock, she'd heeded my warning and thrust the javelin deep into the scorpion's tail. Her muscles strained visibly as she fought to hold that tail at bay on the end of her javelin. Meanwhile, the bead of poison on the end of the stinger grew and gathered. It had about reached critical mass and was ready to drip straight into Neith's face. It probably wouldn't kill her—not right away—but at best she'd be burned, maybe blinded. At worst, well, there were too many ways into the blood stream from there—tear ducts, mucus membranes ... If the poison didn't kill outright, the pain would certainly distract, maybe even critically.

I cut myself with my sword, a small slice across my arm, just enough to coat the blade with my blood. My gorgon glare didn't work with the old gods. I knew that from experience, but the petrification power in my blood was a lot more concentrated. One slice with the bloodied blade and Set would start to go stony. I hoped. It had worked on Hecate, but I still didn't know if it would last ... or if it would work on a god of Set's stature. There was only one way to find out.

I swung for that stinger with all I was worth, and the blade sank deep. Blood and ichor burst out, joining with the drop of venom at the end of the tail to gush over my blade, racing down the runnel meant for other things. I thrust the sword away just as the ghastly flow reached me, but I was too late to save myself. The venom that hit had me screaming in agony. It felt like my hands been burned in acid, set on fire, and crushed into claws all at once. They shriveled, the effects then racing up my arm.

Set gave an inhuman cry of pain as well and swung his stiffening tail in reaction, catching me in the temple with his hardening stinger and knocking me a great blow, sending me spinning out into space. I couldn't grab on to anything. Couldn't even see, I was so blinded with pain.

I fell—felt myself falling and couldn't even gather enough sanity to care. My biggest fear was no longer heights. It was that I wouldn't crash and die and would have to endure this agony forever.

The wind screamed in my ears as I fell or I screamed to the wind, my wings now dead weight. The only messages getting to and from my brain involved pain and the ending of it.

And then something halted my fall. It wasn't the ground.

The pain was still as horrifying as it had been. The source hadn't changed. Or cut off.

Something was trying to reach me through the screaming. Some still-sapient part of me stopped it long enough to listen.

"I've got you," said the voice. Hermes?

"Dying," I said. I thought I said it. Maybe it was only in my head.

"It feels like that, I know."

I worked hard to focus. The battle wasn't over. I couldn't check out and leave the others to fight it, but I couldn't hold a weapon. Couldn't—

"Tell Apollo and Eros to coat their arrows in my blood," I said.

"Tori—"

"Do it," I ordered.

I forced my eyes to open. They'd been squinched shut against the pain. I'd thought I'd gone blind, and certainly the world was vague, watery. From tears in my eyes or the creeping venom, I had no idea, but I saw that we were back in the clouds, saw Set change yet again, his stone tail now weighing him down, a liability. He took a shape in which his tail was negligible, at least for maneuverability. He was back in the form of the red boar, with bristled fur instead of tough exoskeleton. The arrows would penetrate, and while he could thrash, the chains still held him in place. He wouldn't be able to dodge.

But before the gods could drench their arrows in my blood, I saw Neith leap up from the far side of Set where she must have fallen or dodged during my attack. She dove under Set's tusks as he would have gored her and thrust her javelin through the soft base of his throat straight up through his jaw. The point came out through the top of his muzzle, pinning his jaws together like a toothpick through a club sandwich.

He twisted violently through his forms—crocodile, serpent,

scorpion and back, but in none of those forms was he able to open his jaw and loose the javelin.

He seemed to realize it, and his head drooped momentarily before he slowly seeped into his more human form and yanked the javelin out with his hands. He stood glaring us down, dressed in nothing but a short black skirt belted at the waist, his skin as white as old ash, the chains stark against it, and his hair as red as the coat of the bristle-backed boar. It flared outward around his head like wildfire and matched the red still dripping from his jaw and in the furrows scraped raw by his chains.

I burned with hatred even fiercer than the pain in my hands. I didn't know why we all paused. He was vulnerable now. Or at least more so than he'd been in any of his other forms. If we struck now we could rid ourselves of a lot of trouble later on. But he was still wrapped in chains. They'd morphed along with his every shift. Maybe it was the captivity, or the fact that he stood before us in human form or that he'd already been beaten ... for the moment ... but we couldn't strike him down. Not in cold blood.

Then he started to laugh. It made my skin crawl as if I'd been overrun by a swarm of fire ants. His very laugh was chaos —somewhere between that of the creepy bad guy from *Who Framed Roger Rabbit* and ... I couldn't think of a suitable comparison ... As if the bad guy had laughed down into the abyss and the abyss had laughed back.

"I suppose we are at an impasse," he said. "I am not currently in a position to kill you. You cannot kill me, for without chaos there is only order and, ultimately, atrophy." He shuddered, and, oddly, I felt an answering shudder in the depths of my soul. "I am already imprisoned. You can do nothing to me that has not already been done."

"We can petrify your ass," I said, glaring through my pain.

That laugh again. "You tried that, little gorgon girl. Only it was not quite my ass you stung. And so, we have all tested my chains. We have found that I cannot break free." Yet, I supplied mentally. But he'd sure as hell tried. Hermes had sounded nearly panicked when he'd called us in, and Set had been more than a match for all of us combined. The moment he gathered enough power ...

"Will you stay?" Set continued. "Are you to be my new jailors? I get so tired of seeing the same old faces day in and day out, and you really have been quite amusing. Something different to while away my days."

"Where's Taweret?" Neith asked, challenge in her voice, as though she'd jump him again in a New York minute with or without her weapon.

"Merely sleeping," he said, waving vaguely into the cloud cover, "after a vigorous night. You see, I am not totally without my charms." He adjusted his skirt in a way that left no doubt about what he considered his charms. I wondered if Taweret felt the same way. I didn't plan to take his word for it that she was "merely sleeping," especially through the noise of our battle.

"Can someone check on her?" I asked ... anybody in a better position than I was. The burning sensation had moved up my arms, leaving my hands behind feeling merely numb ... disconnected ... useless, as though the strength to move on had been drawn straight out of my own muscles and sinew.

Neith started in the direction Set had indicated and called Hermes over almost instantly. "You're going to have to hold her down while I realign this break."

"Field medicine," Apollo said to me. "Neith's well-versed. Don't worry, Taweret's in good hands." To them, he called, "You two good here? Can you handle things until Artemis and her huntresses arrive for reinforcements?"

Hermes nodded distractedly, and a second later, I heard the snap of bone and a cry of pain I felt in my soul. And then I had my own pain to distract me as Apollo scooped me up. I mumbled the spell to draw my wings back, and he cradled me to his chest, my burned hands bumping against him, sending agony screaming up my arms. I blacked out for a second, the world gone purple with pain.

"Where are you taking me?" I asked when I was able to form the words.

We didn't know any healers. Panacea was off battling a new and virulent outbreak of the flu. Hecate was no more than a living statue.

"To Sulis," he said.

It didn't make any sense to me. She mentioned she'd been a localized deity and that her healing waters were back in Bath ... hadn't she. I couldn't remember anymore. Everything was pain.

20

I was only dimly aware of things after that. Together, Hermes and Apollo must have opened a portal to the spa, because the next thing I knew I heard voices—someone shrieking in surprise, demanding to know what we were doing there. Apollo asked for Sulis, and the response came that she'd gone out mid-afternoon and never returned. None of it made any sense. It was still night, wasn't it? I couldn't understand why anyone should be at the spa at all.

There was more discussion, and jostling and pain like my arms were all funny bones that someone kept striking with a fire stick. And then I was lowered into something warm and enveloping like a hug. It didn't make me hurt any less, but it relaxed my muscles enough to drive me into something like sleep so that the pain seemed part of a nightmare rather than my reality.

"Poison," I heard Apollo say distantly to whoever was listening. "This should draw the impurities out, right? Give her the chance to heal."

"If she's been poisoned, she needs a hospital, not a mud bath," the voice protested. Female. Kind of stick-up-her-butt-y.

Like an accountant. Or a librarian. Maybe that was it, someone burning the midnight oil working on the spa's books.

"Trust me, I know what she needs," Apollo said.

"*Of course,*" she said with derision, "being a man and all. Maybe we should ask *her*. Anyway, the spa is closed, and I can't be responsible—"

"*I'll* be responsible," Apollo answered, power in his voice. I'd heard him use that voice before with the slight godly resonance. "Sulis is an old friend. She'll understand. Get her on the phone."

There was a pause. "I told you, she went out and never came back. We've been trying to reach her all day."

That didn't sound good. Not at all. Not with one of Aphrodite's nymphs missing and Thalia kidnapped.

What if, I wondered ... and then my thoughts wandered away. I'd been going somewhere with that, but the pain ... I worked harder to focus. This was stupid. I was made of sterner stuff. Definitely not sugar and spice and everything nice, but maybe salt and spice and a cockatrice ... it seemed to fit given that we both had a paralyzing effect. But I was digressing.

What was I thinking about?

Nice ... cockatrice ... ah, mythologicals, that was it. What if the brothers had decided that killing more powerful beings gave greater glory to Set? It seemed logical that the longer-lived might leave behind a greater gap in the world ... or the weave, as the Fates would have it ... with their passing. Or that they'd have more power to be channeled for Set's use.

But that assumed the brothers even *could* kill them. Gods were tough. The gods had condemned Prometheus to have his liver eaten out again and again by a giant eagle for the sin of bringing fire and innovation to mankind. Atlas supposedly held the weight of the world on his shoulder, which I knew to be as true as the myth of the world tree or the earth growing on a turtle's back, but the point being that he could lift things that would crush a mortal man. I myself should have been dead at least ten times over.

But ... what if Thalia and Genie and possibly even Sulis were being sacrificed over and over? I tried desperately not to remember the crime scene photos Neith had shown me of the poor woman back in the museum in Egypt, but ... What if they were being sacrificed and worse. I couldn't forget that Set wasn't the only psycho in the mix here. There were those two sarcophagi and Neith's theory that they'd been bound with restless, evil spirits denied the afterlife who may have found new homes in the Roland brothers. They'd undoubtedly spread chaos and destruction in life and now, it seemed, were driving it in death.

The mud no longer felt warm or soothing. It felt restrictive. I had to do something. Before I even remembered about my hands, I tried to use them to pull myself out. The pain that shot through me blacked my sight for more than a second this time, and I felt Apollo's alarm like a zap from an electric fence.

"M'okay," I mumbled when I could speak again. "Do what ya gotta do."

At least, that's how it sounded in my head. In the real world, it might have been sheer gibberish.

I sank back into the mud and prayed that Apollo was right, that it would leach out the impurities and help my body heal that much faster.

In my semi-conscious state, I heard him making calls—to his sister Artemis, to Hermes, to Nick.

And then he was waking me. "Tori, how do you feel? Are you ready for the baths?"

I blinked my eyes open. A bath sounded pretty good, especially if Apollo was volunteering to wash my back or any number of other areas, but then I remembered about my hands. I tried to move them, and to my surprise, they clenched and unclenched. It hurt, but in a way I could live through.

"Yeah," I said. "Thank you."

"No problem." He reached down, and I reached up with my muddy arms, looking like some kind of swamp monster.

"*Sexy,*" he said.

"Thank you, I try," I answered wryly.

This time when he grabbed my arms—going for the upper arms where the venom hadn't quite reached—I didn't black out. My quick intake of breath was more about the pain I expected than the reality. Between us, we got me to standing.

"Let's get you cleaned off."

I stepped out of the mud bath onto the tile. My brain started to click, as though now that the pain signals weren't jamming the switchboard, other things were coming back on line.

I let him towel me off, but *let* was about all I was doing. I wasn't helping, because something was nagging at me. Something else needed to be done. I flipped mentally through the calls he'd made.

"We need to call Yiayia," I said suddenly. "Right away. The other gods and godlets, godlings, whatever, need to be warned. If the Roland brothers are finding them through her site ... or even if they aren't. I think they're hunting more-than-human prey now."

The towel froze in Apollo's hand.

"If we post a warning, the brothers will know we're on to them. We lose any advantage of knowing something they don't know we know."

Apparently, I wasn't yet together enough to process that. "What?"

Apollo started up again with the towel. Faster, and more vigorously, catching my urgency. "I mean, we need to warn them, yes. But what if we can use the site and the fact that they're watching it to set a trap."

"I like the way you think," I said. "Go on."

"Let's get you to the baths."

"Fine," I said, "if it will move things along, but keep talking."

He steered me through a quick shower and into a room I hadn't gotten to before—one with several round pools, more like hot tubs than the original waters at Bath. But I wasn't complaining. I groaned in relief as he lowered me in. The spa might not quite have the healing waters of the famed Roman bathhouse, but something was definitely at work to finish drawing out impurities and to renew and invigorate. Herbs? Oils? I had no idea, but if they had a shop where I could get a consumerized version for my bath at home, I was going to treat myself when all this was over.

"So," he continued, "if we know they're looking for gods, that's what we have to give them. Plant a new story that gives them a target they can't refuse."

"You mean use someone as bait? They already know about me. And you. And Neith, through Jessica. If we make it any of us, they'll see it coming and know it's a trap."

"I was thinking about Eros." He gave me an evil grin.

"Might work," I admitted. "If he'll agree, but ... I think they prefer more feminine targets." I was not going to say softer, because I knew plenty of women who could rip a man's head off—and would at any suggestion that they might be the softer sex. Some might even eat their innards. The Grey Sisters came to mind.

"What about Sigyn?"

That question, those three words hung there for a minute. "Maybe."

I knew from painful experience that Sigyn could take care of herself. Her runes were powerful. If we could draw the brothers out ... or get them to capture Sigyn while she was armed with some kind of tracker, magical or otherwise, like a signal rune that could be triggered that we could trace back to her and the other kidnap victims ...

"We need to talk to Sigyn. Also, I need to call Yiayia. We need to warn the others in the LA area. Not overtly," I said, before he could protest again, "but maybe she's got some kind of code she could use or maybe even a phone tree."

Apollo snorted.

I stood and started to wade out of the pool, ignoring Apollo's disapproving look. "We need a council of war. We need to call those boys out and put them down before they can do any more damage."

My arms felt merely weak now. And tingly. And still numb, but no longer totally useless. I'd take it over the mind-sucking pain any day. I tried to raise them to grab a towel for myself from a shelf on the wall, but they'd only rise so far, and actually gripping and lifting a towel was still beyond me. It would come.

I missed the old days when I could down ambrosia and be miraculously healed. Oh sure, ambrosia had come with an addiction, complete with horrible withdrawal symptoms and the very real possibility of death, but ... Well, I supposed I was an instant gratification junky. Now that I'd experienced healing at ludicrous speed, merely super felt like a come-down.

Apollo had to towel me off again. I barely even had time for a wistful thought of how we could defile the pools while we had the place to ourselves.

"Everyone's meeting at my place for a council of war," he said, handing me a fluffy white robe.

"Your place?" I asked.

"It's the only one big enough."

21

A pollo must have called the doorman at his luxury apartment building and let him know to let people up, because his living room was nearly full when we arrived after calling a cab to take us home from the salon.

I was almost recovered by the time we got there, but the sight that greeted us when we stepped into the fray nearly set me back in shock. I hadn't really understood why we couldn't meet in Neith's hotel room. We'd all fit before, if barely, but now ... it was like a godly multiplication dance, as though everyone had grabbed a friend or two.

My gaze caught and held on a green man with the usual squared off beard of a pharaoh. Not slightly green, like a blond who'd spent too much time in chlorinated water, but the true green that came in every box of crayons. I tried not to stare, even as he caught my eyes and blinked slowly, as though time moved differently for him.

"Who?" I asked.

"Osiris," Apollo said, following my gaze. "I haven't seen him topside in ages."

"He's not, like, a counterpart for Hades or anything like that?"

Apollo looked at me like I'd asked something odd. I'd thought it was a perfectly valid question. "Hades mentioned to you about the various underworlds, right? All those different beliefs ... no one could govern them all."

Plus, as far as I knew, *Hades* had never been cut up into a million parts, scattered all over the world and resurrected, though there'd been days when I'd gladly have performed the first two parts of that myself.

"Wait," I said, "aren't you associated with—"

"Horus, his son," Apollo finished for me. As I watched, he changed. I'd never seen Apollo shift before. He'd always told me that it wasn't really his area. At least, not as a sun god. The sun was constant. Unchanging, if one didn't consider solar flares and sunspots.

But Horus had come before Apollo, and in that other aspect, in his association with the moon, he'd been changeable. He'd been ... It was all I could do not to take a step back when he turned a hawklike head toward me. Not because I didn't still sense him inside, but because being that close to a raptor's beak and his piercing predatory eyes was slightly unnerving.

Reassurance radiated out to me, but still I stood speechless as he stepped forward to greet his ... father? I'd never understood the Horus myth. I'd always heard that when Isis put Osiris back together she'd managed to find every part of him but the one essential to procreation. Myths were full of births that didn't seem to have anything to do with the natural order of things—Athena springing fully formed from the head of her father, women being impregnated by gods who weren't in human form at the time and bearing unlikely offspring like the Minotaur, immaculate conceptions ...

I made myself move on. Osiris was not the only newcomer.

Hangings on Eros were a gaggle of girls ... *women* ... who looked like the Real Housewives of Hugh Heffner. No, that wasn't quite fair. One looked like a Fembot out of *Austin Powers* in a pale pink negligee, complete with sheer overcoat. The others were in varying shades of black and in one case a whiskey-colored cowl-necked sweater where the cowl dipped so low between her breasts I wondered how she got it to stay up on her shoulders. Maybe she and Aphrodite shared boob tape ... or possibly defiance of gravity was her superpower. Then there was the girl with the beautiful brown skin and the darker hair flowing into full on green in an *ombré* effect that I first thought was salon created ... until I noted the pointy ears that jutted slightly from the cascade of hair and fingernails that looked more like bark than keratin. A dryad then? I'd never seen one before. I stared in fascination.

I'd known that Yiayia's blog wasn't the only godly grapevine out there, since word had somehow spread labeling me "PI to the Pantheon." But I'd never expected word about Set and the trouble we faced to get out this fast or to achieve such a response. Apparently, renewed attempts to unleash chaos into the world warranted an all-hands-on-deck approach.

There came a knock at the condo door, and I went to answer it, needing a moment to process in any case.

I hit the button first on Apollo's video monitor to see who stood outside and received another jolt. I recognized the woman peering back, looking straight at the camera with a determined stare.

It was Demeter ... Ceres ... the mother of Persephone, Hades's previously pilfered bride. She'd liberated herself at long last, but I'd made sure it took. The god of the Greek underworld did not take well to having his will thwarted. I thought that was just too damned bad.

I opened the door, pleased to see another familiar face ... not to mention a goddess I knew to still have quite a lot of power.

"Demeter!" I said, not holding my arms out to her. She was *not* the huggy type. "Thank you so much for coming."

Last I'd seen her and Persephone they'd been up in the Napa region of California, but after all that had happened there, I had no idea where they'd finally settled. "I had to come," she said, stepping inside.

I closed the door behind her, and by the time I turned, she'd changed completely. Her hair was no longer wild and white. She no longer wore a natural-tone hemp skirt and over-sized top like an aging hippy/earth mother, but was in a sleek white gown that stopped just above her knees. Her hair had darkened and now lay straight and glossy down her back, hanging all the way to her backside. Her features too had smoothed out. She was still nearly the same earth-brown, but now it seemed more her natural skin-tone than from years and years spent out in the elements. Wrinkles and decades had fallen away, and she now looked as perfect and polished as though she'd walked off a Hollywood set ... one where she'd been playing a modern-day Cleopatra.

I watched her with wide eyes as she strode toward Horus/Apollo and Osiris, holding her arms out to them and enfolding them in her embrace when she got within range. I ... my brain stuttered. Demeter was Isis was ... Apollo's mother? She hadn't exactly been warm and fuzzy the last time we'd met. But then, she'd been a little focused on her domesti-cally abused daughter. And Apollo had never mentioned other siblings beyond his twin sister Artemis. I was ... stunned didn't even begin to cover it. Where did the myths stop and the reality begin? How did I know who was who from one minute to the next when it could all change at the drop of a hat?

For a moment, it didn't seem as though the three of them—father, mother, child ... Osiris, Isis and Horus—were aware of anyone else in the room. They were complete in and of themselves. And then, slowly, Horus and Isis opened their arms to me. I didn't know what on Earth to do with that.

I approached, but stopped short of the hug fest until they came out of it and looked at me askance.

"Demeter is Isis?" I said, just to be absolutely certain I understood it all.

Apollo must have sensed my minor freak-out through our link, and seeped back into ... I couldn't actually say "himself." He was Horus, apparently, as much as he was Apollo ... or any of his other incarnations. Geez, you think you know a guy ...

"Is, was, will be," he said. "Mother and fertility goddess under whatever name she's known."

Neith stepped up to our little group and drew my attention. "As those most affected by Set in the past, I thought they had a right to know. I thought they'd want to help."

"You did the right thing," Demeter-Isis said. No, that was going to get complicated. She appeared now as Isis, and that was what I'd call her. Just like Neith-Athena (or vice versa) was simply Neith. "We'll do all we can. What is the plan?"

Neith and I looked at each other. "You're the goddess of strategy," I said. "Now you have troops. I defer to you."

Apollo looked at me in utter amazement. "You've never deferred to me," he said quietly enough so that it might not have been heard in a room any less filled to the brim.

Everyone seemed prepared to ignore it ... except Eros, apparently. "Well, I guess that answers the question of who's on top," he said at full volume.

Two of the nymphs ... or whoever they were ... tittered.

Apollo looked like he was prepared to take Eros's head clean off.

I fixed Eros with a look, "Top, bottom, upside down, right-side up ... don't you worry, Apollo's got all the moves."

"Oooohhh," chorused the girls surrounding him. I noticed half of them edging closer to Apollo.

"Don't even think about it," I snapped.

It stopped them in their tracks, all but the Fembot, who said, "Surely he's god enough to go around."

I looked up at Apollo, wondering if he was going to chime in and found his gaze riveted to her more obvious attributes. Power flowed out of her in waves; even I caught the edges of it as it lapped against Apollo and flooded our link with desire.

My breath quickened, and I felt ... heat and readiness swept through me like a wildfire.

I wanted. He wanted—

Apollo tore his gaze away from the nymph and looked to me. He wanted to act on the impulses she'd inspired, but with me in her place. I could read it in his eyes, feel it through our link. He wanted to order everybody out and take me in every room and in every position I'd mentioned and then some. Possibly invent some new.

"Enough," snapped Neith. "Vega if you're not part of the solution, you're part of the problem. Step back."

The Fembot, Vega, I presumed, pouted prettily and took a step back, though she didn't look the least bit chastened. In fact, she turned her gaze on Hermes.

"What about you, handsome?" she asked.

Sigyn hissed. "Over my dead body."

"Oh, is that how he rolls?" the nymph asked.

"This was a mistake," Eros said. "Vega, go back to Aphrodite. Explain to her how you couldn't control yourself."

Vega rolled her eyes and blew out a breath. "Oh, you're no fun."

"No fun at all," Sigyn agreed. Hermes shot her a dirty look.

"Plan?" I asked Neith.

"We're waiting for one more."

As if on cue, there was another knock at the door. This time Apollo went to answer it, possibly needing a modicum of space to cool down so that his pants might fit properly again.

He came back with Nick, looking ... stormy. Haggard. I wondered if he'd been home at all between crime scenes. If he'd even slept since the Roland brothers had killed their parents.

He nodded quickly to everyone, eyes widening at the sight of Osiris, narrowing at the nymphs—clearly recognizing trouble when he saw it. Then his gaze came around again to Neith and settled there. Something passed between them.

"Any sign of the Roland boys?" she asked. "Or their sister?"

I could see the answer on his face. "No sign. Not of Thalia or Iphigenia either. And now you say another woman is missing? Sulis?"

"Yes," I answered, "missing, though not a confirmed victim. Her assistant says she went out and never came back, never called and no one can reach her. It's not like her."

"Noted. The chaos, by the way, has spread. You won't believe the reports we have coming in. Dispatch is swamped. HQ is authorizing all kinds of overtime. Don't know how they'll find money in the budget, but ... Not my problem. I don't really have the time to be here at all, but I've been on shift from the beginning. Captain ordered me home for a shower and a few hours of sleep before reporting back."

"What kind of reports have you received?" Apollo asked. "Anything we can use to pinpoint the trouble?"

"You have a map?" Nick asked.

Apollo looked blank. In the days of GPS and navigation apps, no one had maps anymore.

Hermes sighed, snapped his fingers, and produced one out of thin air. It was a real map of LA and the surrounding areas, not one of the touristy kinds with attractions or stars homes marked off.

Apollo went into the kitchen and came out with a Sharpie.

He and Hermes cleared the coffee table of the decorative

bowl of balls that I'd virtuously never commented on and spread out the map.

"You know about Hollywood Boulevard and all that?" Nick said, getting nods. "That's where it seemed to start. It spread out from there. At the Page Museum, the mammoths have pulled themselves out of the muck and gone on a rampage. A five-year-old boy was nearly trampled to death. Trouble on a film set where one actor took his stalker character a little too far. And then there's the gangs …"

I hadn't even considered the gangs. Oh, hells bells, we were in trouble. Hollywood was insane at the best of times. With chaos leaking out, we could easily descend into madness. It had happened before even without Set's influence.

"Yet they sent you home?" Hermes asked.

"Tired officers make mistakes. We can't afford that right now. Not ever, really, but at the moment … LA is a powder keg. One misstep, one overzealous cop, and it might well explode."

Apollo handed Nick the Sharpie. "Here, show us on the map."

Nick got down on his knees so that he could reach the map and circled a bunch of areas. By the time he was finished there wasn't a whole lot left untouched. The chaos field had headed away from the Boulevard, out past LACMA and the Page Museum, and on out of the city. I'd guessed that much—that they'd gone beyond the bounds of LA proper—from my earlier flying reconnaissance. Now, at least, we had a direction.

"Got it," Neith said, sounding strong, decisive and not the least uncertain. "We need two teams. One to draw the brothers out, get them away from their victims so that we can rescue them. The boys aren't going to stop here. They'll want to capture and kill again. We need to control their next targets, the where and the when. We need to be ready. The second team will hunt down their lair while they're lured away, free those they've captured and get them medical help. We need to steal the source of strength they're sending Set right out from under them."

"We don't want to spread ourselves too thin," I protested. "Wouldn't it be best to let them take whatever bait we dangle and then follow them back to their bolt hole?"

"And if they escape us? If we lose their trail or they decide to slice and dice their captive along the way? Then all we've done is throw someone to the wolves. Remember what you said back at the movie set—divide and conquer. There's a reason it's a classic."

I hated her throwing my own words back at me, but I wasn't prepared to argue. She was the goddess of strategy. She had ages of experience on me. But ... I was usually the one to come up with the plans, even if they generally amounted to "find trouble, smash it to bits, try not to die."

Okay, so I was no master strategist, but I'd always gotten the job done ... and I guess I'd gotten used to leading the charge. I never thought my ego had gotten wrapped up in it. Maybe PI to the Pantheon had gone to my head. Maybe I was more competitive than I realized. Maybe even I was never really who I'd thought I was.

If Neith played my role better than I did, where did that leave me? Had I been an understudy all along, poised to be pushed aside when the diva arrived for her starring role?

Apollo reached out and took my hand, sensing my emotions, even if he couldn't know the reasons behind them. Hell, I barely understood myself.

"Okay, fine. I can do the tracking," I said. This was something I was designed for. With my bizarre directional precog and my strange blood call, this was a team I could lead. I'd let Neith handle the takedown, even if I wanted to be there as well. "I just need to figure out where to start."

We all looked at the map. It was clear the chaos had swept through the center of the city and out toward the freeway. I was willing to bet the insanity hadn't stopped there, but accidents and road rage were so common around LA, I wasn't sure any uptick would be immediately evident. And once on the highway, the brothers could have gone anywhere or even circled back.

"I can help you there," Sigyn said, stepping forward. At some point, probably while everyone else was fighting to keep Set down, she'd found time to change out of her red carpet clothes. She now stood there in designer jeans and stylish half-boots in a sheer, flowy shirt with a camisole underneath. She looked like she should be strolling down Rodeo Drive with an armful of shopping bags, not attending a counsel of war, but I knew how looks could be deceiving. The first time I'd met her she'd been in a girly blue dress and she'd kicked my sensibly styled behind. Or, anyway, had minions to do the dirty work. I still didn't like counting on anything she might come up with, but I didn't see that I had much choice.

She reached into her little black-and-leopard-print purse and came out with something that looked like a small sundial, only instead of numbers, it was inscribed in runes.

"Here," she said, handing it forward. "It just needs a bit of your blood to link to your desires. Then you hold what or who you're looking for in your mind and it will point you there."

"So if one day I'm in the mood for a real Philly cheese steak …" Hermes asked, reaching out for it.

She slapped his hand. "Down, boy. They've got Yelp for that."

I took the tiny sundial, not at all tempted to admit that my mind had gone momentarily to the mother of all margaritas. It had been a rough night.

Nick's phone buzzed loudly, and we all looked to him. He pulled the phone from the holder on his belt and checked the read-out.

Then he looked up to us gravely. "Turn on the television."

No one asked why. Apollo stepped up to the cabinet under his large wall-mounted flat screen and turned it on. "What channel?" he asked.

"Just about any channel, I'd think."

He was right. The first one that came up was a ten-year-old sitcom that had long since gone into syndication, but even there a bar ran across the bottom of the screen, warning of riots and listing areas to avoid ... It might have been shorter to list what streets were still safe.

Apollo flipped to a local news station, and what we saw ... They could have been replaying footage of the infamous 1992 LA riots if only the fashions hadn't changed.

Nick swore under his breath. "I have to get back to the station," he said.

"No," Neith responded, twice as adamantly. "They sent you home for a reason. At some point, they're going to need you fresh ... or we will. You cannot afford to fail when they need you most."

"And, as you said, tired cops make mistakes," I added.

"I doubt I could get home through this anyway."

"Then you can stay here. I have a guest room," Apollo offered.

I didn't have to be linked to Nick to see what he thought of that. It was written all over his face. And then a complete shift of scene and a new but familiar voice arrested our attention. I whipped my head around to see Susie Tallios, my reporter friend from back at the Roland mansion, this time in a royal blue power suit with black piping, her hair pulled severely back into a no-nonsense ponytail. With her was a man in a thousand-dollar suit with a pricy haircut, unnaturally white teeth, and a zealot's smile. Everyone in LA knew him. He seemed to attach himself to every controversy and tragedy ... as long as they were newsworthy. Why his fifteen minutes of fame weren't up yet, I had no idea. Sheer force of narcissistic will.

I'd missed the beginning of what Susie had to say, but tuned in at, "... here with Reverend John Moses Smith of the First Church of the Holy Believer, who has an interesting take," I thought I caught a twist of her lips, like maybe she wanted to say angle but wasn't allowed, "on the spate of troubles that have hit Los Angeles."

The reverend thanked Susie and then looked straight into the camera, dismissing her and talking as if to his congregation. "I have not wanted to believe it myself, but I have studied and I have prayed over it, and I can come only to the conclusion that we are in the End Times." The way he said it, End Times was very clearly in caps and if he'd been on a sound stage, probably would have had its own reverb.

"They call this news?" Neith spat.

"Shhh!" I insisted. My precog was kicking me in the gut. Susie ... the reverend ... there was something here.

"Revelation 6: 7-8 'Then the Lamb broke open the fourth seal. I looked, and there was a pale colored horse. Its rider was named Death, and Hades followed close behind. They were given authority over a fourth of the earth, to kill with war, famine, and disease, and with the wild animals of the earth.'"

I startled at Hades's name. In a Bible verse? It couldn't be real, could it?

"I think he's paraphrasing," Osiris said. I thought it was Osiris, anyway. I didn't turn to look. My eyes were glued to the screen. I shushed the room again.

"Does this not sound like what happened in New York? No doubt a modern-day Sodom. Plague and pestilence affected the city. Animals turned on their human hosts. Brother struck at brother." Which was true if one of those brothers was a freakin' zombie. "Have we not already seen the signs? Dragons and strange beasts appearing in the sky."

He gestured, and the studio must already have had footage cued up from New York. A window opened beside him much like one of Hermes's creations, but this one showed rain-slashed footage from the huge storm conjured up by Poseidon's queen, Amphitrite, armed with his powerful trident. Through the rain pelting the cameras—police cam? traffic?—there was the impression of wings and a huge golden shape moving through the skies. Much like the "evidence" enthusiasts put forth for the existence of Big Foot and the Loch Ness Monster, it was grainy, but ... maybe not quite as grainy. Not quite as easy to dispute. And I knew for a fact that it was Eu-meh, the huge, gold-bronze dragon ridden by Nick's former partner who'd helped us defeat the plague demons and Amphitrite as well. And that this dragon was absolutely no satanic symbol.

The next clip showed one of the videos I knew had been taken of me in New York. I was practically falling out of the sky, my wings shredded after getting in the middle of a fight between two gods—Hecate and Janus. It had been played and replayed. Through most of it, my crazy, unruly hair covered my face, but for one brief moment, it blew away, leaving me exposed. That had been the image all the stills had been drawn from ... for the tabloids, in particular. The mainstream press had been mostly about the real news—tragedies, body counts, destruction, and where people could go to find help. If my picture or any others were picked up, the articles were carefully non-committal and most likely to be in back pages, as if they didn't want to get egg on their faces when the pics were revealed to be a hoax. Even the *Daily News*, which could always be counted on for the absolute worst headlines, chose a flesh-eating zombie over me. It was still fully human in form, though worse for wear than your average man-on-the-street. It was something they could grasp, write off as a particularly nasty virus, and one that had since been cured. I think it had said something like, "Man ... the other white meat." Boy, had that raised a stink ... but it had sold papers.

But this was mainstream news ... on a major network.

Millions would see and maybe believe. Sure, the network was allowing the reverend to intro the footage and its possible implications and could easily disclaim, "Views expressed by our guests do not necessarily reflect the views of this station" or some such, but …

He was continuing, "And now war has come to our very streets and a strange winged woman has been spotted in our skies."

I gasped as a new video segment played. Crystal clear. No lashing wind and rain. No grainy traffic camera. It showed me, wings flared, sweeping low, and then climbing higher into the sky. Luckily, it didn't show my face. Whoever had taken the video was above and behind me, but … from the vantage and from the fact that I wore my red carpet gown, I realized it had to be the nurse who'd seen me jump out of the hospital window who'd taken the video. She must have run to the window to try to stop me or to follow my fall and seen me take wing. I could hardly blame her for whipping out her cell phone camera. But to send the footage to Reverend Smith …

"From the wings, she is no angel," the reverend continued. "A demon, perhaps, sent from Hell to fight for dominion over earth, her dress the color of blood. Or perhaps one of the locusts Revelation warns of, who wear the faces of man. 'Their hair was like women's hair, their teeth were like lions' teeth,'" he quoted.

Susie, I thought, had had enough. She tried to take the microphone back to ask a question or put an end to the segment, but the reverend wrapped his hand around hers and held it in place.

"'They have tails and stings, like those of scorpion,'" he continued, eyes burning into the camera. I expected froth to start forming at his mouth, "'and it is with their tails that they have the power to hurt men for five months. They have a king ruling over them, who is the angel in charge of the abyss. His name in Hebrew is Abaddon; in Greek the name is Apollyon, meaning "The Destroyer.""

We all looked at Apollo.

"The Destroyer?" I asked, sotto voce.

"Locust?" he responded, raising a brow.

"Touché."

It would have been funny, except that it wasn't. It was far too easy to see signs and portents in what had been going on these past few months. I couldn't imagine the Reverend Smith was the only one. In fact, the description of these End Time locusts —and surely there was an alternate translation—sounded eerily like Namtar, the god of all plague demons. He'd been human-esque with bulging muscles, covered in leonine fur with back-bent legs much like a lion rampant. He'd sported a scorpion's tail complete with deadly stinger. If I'd met him fully versed in two-thousand-year-old prophecies, I might have been half convinced myself that the End Times were upon us. Hell, I'd thrown around the word apocalypse at the time and ... No, surely not.

"Oh, Hades's flaming phallus!" I said. "Now everyone and their brother will be watching the skies. I'll be lucky if some gun nut doesn't blow me out of the air, thinking I'm a demon or something."

"Actually, I believe the locusts are sort of like the old Biblical plagues, sent to torment the unfaithful. So, in a way, you're like a hand of god," Eros said helpfully.

"Great," I answered wryly. "I'm absolutely certain everyone in LA will appreciate that distinction."

Reverend Smith had gone on to talk about some kind of meeting to pray for our city's salvation. Susie just barely let him get the details out before reclaiming the microphone.

I shot a glance at Apollo, who nodded solemnly at me. He'd felt it too. There was something here. Some danger or ...

My eyes shot wide open and my heart started pounding

double-time. Damn and double-damn—the number of times I'd heard it, you'd think I'd get it instinctively by now. Belief fueled reality. If enough people believed, truly believed in the reverend's fearmongering ... believed we were in the Biblical End Times ... It could affect how this all played out. At best, some would certainly prepare for the rapture. At worst ... well, I wasn't sure Set could cause greater chaos than crashing some other god's homecoming bash. But would he come masquerading as the guest of honor or crashing the party like a jilted ex at a wedding?

Either way, my gut said clearly we'd come upon this for a reason. Maybe chaos, like every other force in the universe, had an equal but opposite reaction, like fate ... or The Fates. Just in case, I closed my eyes and said a tiny prayer of thanks to Clotho.

"If Set escapes, Reverend Smith's prayer meeting is where he's going to go," I said aloud.

There was no room in my mind for doubt.

"Then we have to make sure he doesn't," Neith said, kindly not pointing out that this was what she'd been trying to orchestrate before I shushed everyone.

"Great," I said. "I'll track, you trap. Now, who do we use as bait?"

22

I was very afraid that Neith might become my hero. Her plan for luring the Rolands was, I thought, nothing short of brilliant. Not that I admitted it in so many words.

Since the misadventure had all started with Ian and Richie's trip to Egypt and their larcenous fascination with Egyptian antiquities, and since we had Isis and Osiris right to hand, Neith proposed to plant a wonderful story. A decade or so ago, the LACMA—Los Angeles County Museum of Art—had hosted the famed King Tut Exhibit that had traveled the world. It wouldn't be a stretch for Yiayia to suggest on her blog that key members of the Egyptian pantheon might be consulting "in person" that very day—because it had long passed midnight and slid into the early hours of the morning—on a new exhibit on Egyptian mythology and magic. She could even drop a hint that they might be presenting certain special artifacts that couldn't be trusted to travel any other way. Yiayia never mentioned names, but posting beside the story a picture of a classic fresco of the green god or of Isis with the sun disk and horned headdress would be hint enough.

I did worry that it might be too obvious a ploy, but then, I wasn't sure the brothers could resist the lure either way. But ... we had to plant hints elsewhere as well. If the only whisper of such an upcoming exhibit was on Yiayia's blog, the deception would be as clear as day.

Hermes, in his alter ego as humor columnist Thom Foolery, had certain media contacts, but they were mostly on the other coast and mostly not of the right sort. Still, he was going to do what he could. Apollo had a few contacts of his own.

I had the business card of a certain reporter who'd been waiting to hear from me. She might be willing to help, but I'd likely have to give her something in return. Like an exclusive. It seemed that my secret was already out anyway. Too late to worry that exposing myself would a) skyrocket me to instant unwanted fame, and b) lead to the discovery of others and further belief, which would fuel myth-hunters (downside) and potentially feed the gods themselves (upside, as far as they'd be concerned). In these days of cell phone and other cameras everywhere, discovery was probably only a matter of time anyway. That didn't mean I wanted to bear the responsibility.

Of course, there was a better than even chance the jig would be up before it ever came time for me to pay the piper. Chaos I could stake no claim to was already busting out all over, and Susie wasn't stupid. If we planted the LACMA story with her, she was going to sense that's where the action would be. If she could convince the network to send her with a cameraman ...

Not my problem. My job was to plant the story with her and with Yiayia. It was up to Neith to arrange things on the LACMA end. She really did have contacts with museums through her freelance insurance investigation gig.

I just hoped that by the time all was said and done, the museum would still be standing. Although, with the Page Museum and their rampaging mastodons right next door, the danger was real one way or another. In fact, I was half-surprised nothing in the LACMA had yet made the news.

Weird modern art statuary grabbing at the unsuspecting smacked of something out of *Beetlejuice*. Perhaps not chaotic enough? Maybe the paintings or statuary would come alive to argue their own merits. Perhaps they already had and no one had realized it wasn't a new form of interactive exhibit.

For about half an hour, there was great sound and fury, everyone walking off to quiet corners to make their calls and then, suddenly, there was nothing to do but wait ... for callbacks, for action, for dawn.

"Okay, all," Apollo said finally, "you don't have to go home, but you can't stay here. Everyone should get a few hours of sleep, gird your loins, whatever." He looked over at me, and I didn't want to show the relief I was feeling, but between the earlier battles, their damage and my healing (still a work in progress), I was about to collapse, and I really didn't want to do it in front of witnesses.

Nick opened his mouth, maybe to protest again about whether he could make it home, but Neith stopped him. "Come with me," she said.

"But—"

"Don't worry, I won't jump you," she said quietly, probably for his ears only, but she had a voice better suited for battle commands than intimacy, and even her murmurs carried, "I know a warrior needs to save his strength for battle."

I couldn't help but watch Nick's face, and for the first time, I understood why the Fates might watch us mortals like others would watch daytime television.

I wasn't sure what expression he was trying to suppress, but his face went through contortions trying to rein it in. "Uh, okay," he answered finally, "thanks."

I wondered about the sleeping arrangements. I'd been in Neith's hotel room. There was only one bed, though being a junior suite, there was also a couch. I couldn't remember whether it was big enough for a six-foot cop to stretch out on, but ... I was sure they'd work it out, and I was just as certain that I didn't want to know a thing about it.

Nick flashed me a "Help!" look on the way out, which was totally gratuitous, because he and I both knew that he was a big boy and could take care of himself. If he was going along, it was because he wanted to. Or didn't not want to. Or didn't have any clue what he wanted but was willing to find out.

Gah, my brain hurt. I needed sleep. And come to think of it, I also needed to pee ... not necessarily in that order.

We got everyone out, and I locked myself in the bathroom. By the time I was onto washing my hands and then face, I unlocked the door so that Apollo could get in alongside me. I secondarily debated going facedown in his bed without even brushing my teeth. I was that tired. Dragging a toothbrush around for thirty seconds in each quadrant as Yiayia had taught me, seemed like a monumental task. But in the end, programming won out, and while I might have skimped just a bit, I did end up with fresh breath and a lack of fuzzies on my teeth. All hail the great goddess Hygenia, who I'd just made up. At least, I thought I had. It sounded good though.

I left Apollo behind performing his own routine, and was asleep the second after I slid between the sheets. Then I was awake again as his arm slid around me, and his hot body pressed up against me. I swear that Apollo ran a full degree hotter than the rest of us, probably the whole sun-god thing. It made him impossible to ignore. Even if I wasn't suddenly aware of ... oh! A shudder went through me, as I felt him hard against me. He tried to be good; I could feel it through our link. He meant just to cuddle up, breathe me in, and let me sleep, but the fact that he couldn't, the fact that just pressing up against me raised his ... interest ... that was about the sexiest thing I could imagine.

Lazily, I started to turn toward him so that my body could have more access to his.

There wasn't much I could do turned away as I was.

"I thought you were tired," he said, his voice husky.

"So did I," I answered, running my hand down his chest slowly, circling a nipple on the way down to stroke lower, over his hard, flat stomach, molding to his tight abs, teasing downward. "You're not saving your strength for battle?" I asked him.

He gazed down into my eyes and the intensity of his feeling hit me through our link, turning my core molten. "Saving myself for you," he said. "You scared the hell out of me tonight, and the thought that I might lose you ..."

"Not going to happen," I told him. At that moment, I meant it. I felt invincible ... unless he made me wait too long to come together, in which case I might spontaneously combust. He took my mouth then, devouring it. The hand on my hip slid over it as smooth as an air hockey puck on a working table. I giggled at the metaphor, knowing I had to be loopy, knowing I needed that sleep ... but needing him more.

His hand circled around to my backside, and he grabbed a good handful and pulled me into him, squashing my chest up against his as he raided my mouth. He shifted his weight to free his other hand to slide his fingers through my hair, nails raking gently against my scalp until he could cup the back of my head and hold me to him like he might never let me go. All the time, his cock pressed between us. The hand I'd been using to stroke him had gotten trapped when Apollo pulled me tight, but now I squirmed to put enough distance between us that I could slide it down and ...

My eyes rolled back into my head as my hand closed around his shaft—iron hard and yet as smooth as silk.

He groaned into my mouth as I stroked him, one long stroke from base to tip. Then another.

And then neither of us could wait. I was already wet and aching for him, he was already hot and ready, which made him sound like a pizza, but ...

I opened my legs, and he rolled me under him, raising himself to plunge inside ... and then all metaphors and coherent thought went right out the window in the face of amazing, explosive sensation. He put his forehead to mine, eyes closed as he slid inside me the first time and the second, over-whelmed by the feeling. And then he pulled back to look deeply into my eyes. I stared back, gasping as he thrust into me again, feeling as though my soul had escaped on the exhale and he'd breathed it in.

Something significant was flowing between us. Through our link, through our look. It felt ... It felt ...

My body took over where words failed, exploding, fractur-ing, each shard a whole being's worth of ... everything. And when I came back together, it was though some of his shards had bonded with mine. Or vice versa.

We were more. Filled up. Replete. Not depleted. Not even a bit. I had no idea how the Spartans or any warrior could forego that.

I felt like I could run marathons. Leap tall buildings in a single bound ... Tomorrow.

Tonight ... my eyes had already started to close and all of my muscles to relax. Apollo let his forehead drop to mine again, and while we lay there contented, both our eyes shut because we were just too close, he whispered, *"S'agapo."*

My heart gave a hard knock and my eyes flew open. I pushed on his chest to give me enough distance to see his face, and he opened his eyes to stare down into mine.

S'agapo ... I love you.

I kept pushing until Apollo rolled himself to the side and let me escape. Not far. I didn't go far but I needed ... a minute.

I knew ... I mean, I thought I knew how he felt about me. How I felt about him. But saying it, *admitting* it ... If we said it there was no going back. If I internalized it and trusted it and things went wrong, it would ... It felt so melodramatic to think "kill me," and I'd never been melodramatic like that. Not even as a teenager, but ... I realized even as I protested, logic flapping around like a bird in a steel cage trying to find the out, that it was already too late. I'd given him my heart. I had no control now of what became of it.

It was what I'd always feared.

"Tori," Apollo said softly, hand to my shoulder turning me gently to face him. "Talk to me."

"I love you too," I said, not able to look him in the eyes. "Dammit."

He froze for a second, and then his laugh shocked the hell out of me. I finally looked up to glare, which only made him laugh harder. "Not exactly how I imagined it," he said, his entire face lit up like I'd ... okay, like I'd declared my love for him, but better. Bells and whistles and doves exploding into the sky. "But it'll do."

"Good," I said, cranky. "Now can I get some sleep?"

"I don't know," he said, "can you?"

I glared and rolled over, giving him my back. But my body still hummed from what he'd done to it and my soul still quaked. Worse, as soon as I let myself relax again, a smile crept over my face.

He loved me. Damn, damn, damn.

23

A pollo, unsurprisingly, was up with the sun.

He tried to get up without waking me, but my body was apparently on high alert. I jerked awake as soon as his weight shifted, looked over to see what was going on, and groaned at the realization. I kept my eyes open only long enough to watch his naked form head for the bathroom, glorious in the light teasing through his sheer curtains. Then I grabbed his pillow, yanked it over my head, and rolled with it into my favorite position.

I must have fallen back to sleep, because the smell of bacon woke me up some time later.

Bacon ...

I lay there a moment longer. The bed was so comfortable. And warm. And easy to face. Apollo not so much.

But ... bacon.

I groaned again, even though there was no one to hear me, and reluctantly I tossed his pillow to the side and made myself get up. My body no longer ached. On the contrary, it felt alive, healthy, like I'd just gotten a B-12 shot and lived on a diet full of protein shakes and fruit smoothies with wheat grass kickers ... or whatever the starlets-in-training were drinking this week.

I cursed, went to the bathroom to take care of a few things, like personal hygiene, and walked out into the living room wearing a robe meant for someone Apollo's size rather than mine. I swam in his robe, feeling small and yet sexy. What *was* it about wearing a man's shirt ... or his bathrobe? I'd only sniffed the collar, which, of course, smelled like him, once or twice while slipping it on.

The television was going in the living room, but I barely noticed.

A stupid smile crept over my face as I peered over the breakfast bar into the kitchen where Apollo was heaping plates full of food.

He turned when he heard me or sensed me, flashing me his million-watt smile. "Good morning, beautiful."

The food wasn't the only thing that looked good enough to eat. Apollo had left the robe for me, and stood there shirtless in nothing but black drawstring pants riding a little low on his hips.

I heard myself gasp and tried to play it off. "The food smells good."

"I figured that after last night ... Well, we'll certainly need our strength today."

He turned with the plates and put one in front of me. Omelets. Honest to gods omelets, complete with diced tomatoes, onions and green peppers, and folded over a nice thick layer of cheese. On the side, three slices each of thick-cut bacon and two slices of dry toast.

I raised a brow at the sight of that, and Apollo shoved forward two little jars of jam and a stick of actual butter on a cut crystal dish. Silverware and placemats already sat in front of two of the stools, so I propped my butt up on the one in front of me and asked, "Coffee?"

"But of course."

Apollo set his plate down and headed for a carafe full of the most wonderful scent in the world, second only to bacon and the smell of Apollo himself, especially when a little bit sweaty with exertion....

I had to close my eyes and breathe. In through the nose, out through the mouth. Too much. It was all just a little too much. Too perfect.

He set the mug down in front of me, the sound popping my eyes open.

He watched me as he also placed down a half-gallon of milk and a glass container holding packets of every sweetener known to man. White, pink, yellow, blue ...

"Green?" I asked.

"Stevia in the Raw," he said. "All natural."

"Sounds dirty," I said.

He grinned and leaned in for a kiss, stopping right before our lips touched to say, "So it does."

My libido and my heart were both doing jumping jacks, vying for attention, and I shoved them both aside for bacon. I always liked to save the best for last, but with *three* slices, I didn't have to entirely delay gratification. The first bite was almost better than ambrosia, better than nectar. I knew, I'd tried both. It was crunchy and salty and applewood smoked and ... just the way I liked it.

"Marry me," I said. It slipped out of my mouth, which immediately fell open in horror. "I mean ..."

Apollo laughed. "If I'd known bacon was all it took to make you fall for me, I'd have cooked for you sooner."

I made sure my mouth was free of food and then stuck my tongue out at him, glad he was making light of the moment. "Now you know my Achilles's heel. I'm sorry, it's too dangerous for me to let you live."

"I understand. If I could have one last request?"

I flashed him a considering look. "Perhaps. Ask."

"Wait until after breakfast to kill me? No point in wasting all this good food."

"You just want to lull me into a food coma," I protested.

"Guilty as charged."

I cut into the omelet and took a bite. It was ridiculous. Really. An omelet was an omelet, right? Maybe it was whatever kind of cheese he used. Nothing should be allowed to taste so good.

If this ... if we continued, I wondered if he'd keep cooking for me or whether he'd start to take me for granted. Or expect quid pro quo.

"Stop," he said.

"What?"

"Sometimes an omelet is just an omelet," he said.

"And if it's the best omelet I've ever had in my life?"

"That's a metaphor for sex, right?"

I gave him a look. "You fishing for compliments?"

"Honey," he said, bringing a warm hand to my leg where the robe had fallen away, "I was there. I don't need you to tell me it was amazing."

His hand slid up my leg, and he leaned in to kiss me again ... when suddenly Hermes's face appeared right between us, shocking us both back.

"Am I interrupting something?" he asked, glancing at the little vee of skin at my throat revealed by the robe. I pulled it tighter around me and he clicked his tongue against the top of his mouth, the sound carrying through the window he'd created. He turned his gaze on Apollo and swept him bare stomach to chest. "Nice. Very nice. You know, Sigyn and I have an awfully big bed ... No?" he said at the look on Apollo's face. He glanced down at himself, even though we couldn't see the rest of him through the small message window he'd created. "Perhaps I should get to the gym a bit more. Or maybe I can get the abs airbrushed on, as they did in that *300* movie, hmm? That certainly sounds like a lot less trouble."

"Hermes," I said, exasperated. "Do you have a purpose in calling?"

He sighed. "I do. We're all set up. Sigyn has set runes to trap the brothers when they come through the central hallway. You might want to get dressed ... or not. We'll let you know as soon as they take the bait."

He winked out, and I stared at Apollo in disbelief. "Did he really just ..."

"He really did. It's Hermes. Are you surprised?"

I didn't answer, because the truth was I probably shouldn't be. I had no idea what my friend Christie had seen in him, even if, despite his comment about the gym, he was built like a Greek god.

I turned back to my food, not about to let it go to waste. "Guess we'd better eat fast. As you said, we're going to need our strength."

I was used to eating on the go or wolfing down fast food during a stakeout, so it was hardly difficult for me, and with Apollo's size, he had his omelet finished off in about three bites. I then took the world's fastest shower to get rid of the remains of yesterday's sweat, grime and any possible remains of poison and dressed in a tracksuit I kept at Apollo's place—black with a hot pink stripe up the side of the pants. I decided it was too hot for the jacket, and I was just going to have to go with the matching jog bra. LA camouflage when you couldn't afford high fashion. Everyone was always coming from or going to the gym, off on a jog, doing pull ups, weights, yoga-lates, or crazy acrobatics on Muscle Beach ... All I needed was a high ponytail, which I managed, and a sheen of sweat, which I knew would come the second we stepped out into the LA heat.

Apollo took his cue from me, changing into dark gray sweatpants, a lighter gray tank top, a baseball hat, and sunglasses to hide his identity. I didn't suspect it would matter. Apollo had a certain presence, even when he damped it down. He'd draw attention wherever we went.

I grabbed my phone, the pepper spray, and my ID out of my small clutch from the night before and shoved them into pockets.

"Anything on the news before I got up?" I asked. The television had been tuned to one of those soft news morning shows when I'd trudged through the living room seeking bacon. Apollo was standing in front of what looked like a buffet table —flat on top, just the right height for serving, drawers in front. I wondered why until I saw him lift the top to reveal satin fabric inlaid like the padding of a coffin, only instead of a body, short swords were strapped to the top, and more weapons gleamed from the inside. "Ooh," I said, approaching.

"Nothing much on the news," he said, answering the question I'd nearly forgotten I'd asked. "A lot of confusion about what went on yesterday, everyone with theories—including mass hysteria, something in the water, killer-slash-hallucino-genic smog like something The Joker might cook up, Mercury in retrograde ..."

"Is it?" I asked.

"How should I know? I don't keep track of these things. Anyway, choose your weapon."

I tried not to feel like a kid in a candy store, but, really, the array of weaponry was pretty impressive. But then I remem-bered ... I looked down at my sports bra and tight track pants. I didn't exactly have anywhere to conceal anything. Damn, I guessed I was going to have to deal with my jacket after all.

I reached for a triangular sort of dagger that called to me and a blade not quite long enough to be a sword or short enough to be a dagger.

"The xiphos," Apollo commented. "Good choice."

Xiphos. I'd have to remember that.

I gave it a few test sweeps, checking out the balance, how it moved in my hands. It felt good. Much better than my gun ever had. Practically like I'd been born to the blade.

Ours was a rescue mission though. If all went well, I'd never have to use it. I didn't want to examine the fact that it disappointed me the same way I didn't want to examine our relationship.

"We should get started," I said to Apollo, retrieving Sigyn's sundial/compass. "That way we can be on the spot to rescue Thalia and the others as soon as the boys take the bait."

"If they see us, that will blow the whole thing," he said.

"They won't. Besides, we'll need to do some recon, and I'm antsy."

He studied me. "Okay, fine, but I'm taking a cup of coffee for the road."

"Get me one too?" I asked. I went back to the bedroom for my jacket and came out to an offering of a travel mug's worth of Apollo's amazing coffee made just the way I liked it. I tried not to tear up, but after the bacon and omelets, I was feeling a little emotional.

"Okay, already, you're perfect," I grumbled. "Will you just stop?"

"All right, more coffee for me," he said, reaching to take back the mug.

"Do it and die," I said, hugging it protectively to me.

He laughed. "Thought so."

Then my phone buzzed in my pocket, and I saw Apollo reach for his as well. When I drew mine out, I saw I had a new text from Hermes. *Boys have breached perimeter.*

"Looks like we're on," I said.

WE DIDN'T WASTE any time getting to Apollo's car in the garage beneath his building. It was a silver Lexus and a thing of beauty, but it was going to be a tight squeeze getting all of our rescuees inside. I shrugged. If need be, I could fly back, even bring a passenger if the brothers had kidnapped more than our count. I let Apollo drive, since he was most familiar with the car ... and anyway, I had to concentrate on the tracker.

As he pulled out—only one exit, so no mystery which way to go until we were out on the street—I nibbled on a hangnail until it bled. Mom would have slapped me upside the head for it, but she wasn't here, and Sigyn had said the little rune disk activated with blood. I smeared what little welled up on the dial, closed my eyes and thought really hard about Thalia, the one missing person we were absolutely certain the brothers had taken. If they'd managed to kill her and dump her body this whole thing would be in vain, but I couldn't think that way. As Set had shown, the old ones were fiendishly hard to kill, and anyway it seemed like the world would be a sadder place if such a light had gone out of it. I couldn't believe we wouldn't all feel the loss.

When I opened my eyes again, it was to see the dial turning, turning ... "Right out of the garage," I said.

My precog hit me like a physical thing, like a slap in the face, wanting to whip my head around to the left.

I looked to Apollo.

"I feel it too," he said. "What do we do?"

"We already know the brothers are at the museum, maybe Jessica too. We know there's danger. Hermes will call if they need us."

The dial in my hand swung a complete one-eighty. "Turn left as soon as you can," I said. I hoped Sigyn's little dial would work. It was something like a GPS, but with no warning at all on upcoming directional changes. Worse, it pointed the way, but that only went so far. Roads weren't straight lines. They veered or dead-ended, became one-way streets. I really didn't like this plan. My precog was only amplifying my need to be in on the action, on the capture.

Even as Apollo drove, looking for the next left, I pulled out my phone.

"Eyes on the prize," he said. "You don't want to lose focus on the kidnap victims. If you start thinking about what's going on back at the museum, that dial might lead us right there."

"So I'll multitask. Women can do that, you know. I'll focus on Thalia while I put in a call to Hermes, just to make sure everything is okay. Plans can change."

I dialed Hermes, but the phone just rang and rang. I hung up before it got to voicemail. "No answer."

"He might be busy," Apollo said.

"Might be."

"But you don't think so."

"I don't know what to think," I said. "This precognition didn't come with a training manual. But I guess you're right. They'd call. Hermes might even drop in. We stick to the plan. I guess. But I feel like a mama whose teenage daughter missed their meet-up at the mall. Or blew curfew by a huge margin. Something's wrong."

"Danger doesn't mean destruction."

"Doesn't it?" That had certainly been my experience.

"Right!" I said suddenly, as the road started to veer left and the needle on the blood dial swung pointedly in the other direction.

"Highway entrance coming up. Should we ignore the dial momentarily and get on the highway, since it heads that way?"

"Yes." I didn't even have to think about it. Both Nick's map of mayhem and my flying canvas had indicated that the brothers had fled somewhere outside the city.

At the highway entrance, the dial pointed us distinctly northbound and then seemed fairly happy with our progress until we were right on top of an exit. All the while my gut was churning, no longer sure which way the danger lay—forward or back. Now that we were getting close to our quarry, it was clear that not all the trouble was behind us back at the museum.

A few more hairpin twists and turns and one long stretch where we blew past anything commercial and even the real residential areas. Houses grew farther and farther apart. More isolated, more run-down. Finally, the dial pointed us not toward another turn but toward a house standing off all by itself. It was an old Mexicali style one story that had seen better days. A great golden-orange wall of crumbling stucco with the crumbled parts still lying in the overgrown grass blocked the view of the house except through an arched entrance into the courtyard. It looked like a home time had forgotten.

Apollo and I shared a look. "Doesn't seem like the kind of place you'd find the Roland heirs," I said.

"The police would have investigated any property linked to them."

"Do you think—" *that the owner was one of their victims*, I thought but didn't finish.

We'd find out soon enough. "Never mind. Let's go."

The nearest neighboring house was probably a quarter to a half mile away and there was no one strolling the street. No reason to wear the jacket any longer to hide my weapon and risk it getting in the way. I left it behind as I got out of the car, took firm hold of the xiphos, and slid the dagger into my waistband at the small of my back, hoping not to stab myself before anyone else. I wanted my dagger hand free to open doors or hold back cobwebs. I didn't absolutely know we'd be faced with the latter, but from the state of the house, I couldn't rule it out either, and with both hands bearing weapons, I was in danger of slashing myself if something multi-legged dropped on me from above.

I'd gotten better about heights. Spiders were never going to give me the warm fuzzies.

Especially not after Arachne and her minions had scarred me for life.

"Watch yourself," Apollo said as we approached the arch. "It could be warded."

"Can you tell?"

He edged a little closer and went very still, sensing. "I don't think so, but there's something off here. I can feel it."

I felt it too. I waved my xiphos through the archway first, figuring that if anything was going to trigger, better on the blade than on us, but nothing happened, so I let it lead the way, following it onto a cracked walkway with grass growing up through the fractures. The yard itself was more weeds than grass, all overgrown, almost to the point of swallowing a child's three-wheel bike that tilted up against a large palm with drooping fronds. If it hadn't been bright blue, it would have blended right in. Two big, colorful pots of agave plants stood as prickly sentinels to either side of the doorway—a smaller stucco arch over a staunch wooden door. Bright blue and gold tiles inset over the doorbell to the left labeled the house number 207, which seemed odd, since there were less than a dozen houses on the whole street.

My precog kicked me again. Inside, it insisted. As if we didn't know.

"How do you want to handle this?" I asked quietly. "You want the front and I'll take the back? Vice versa?"

He looked around at all the high grass and higher weeds. "I'll take the back," he said. "Give me a thirty-count."

I knew he was being chivalrous, thinking of what might be lurking in and among all the growth. Spiders, fire ants, sharp, rusty pieces of metal. Tetanus I could handle, but the rest ... I didn't argue.

But as instructed, I did wait, none too patiently. My precog didn't understand caution. It understood danger, and whether I chose fight or flight, it wanted me to give some indication I'd gotten the damned message already. Passivity was not an option.

My thirty-count might have been a little fast. I might have rushed my Mississippis. Still, on thirty I tried the knob, which —no surprise—did not conveniently turn in my hand. On thirty-one-and-a-half, I backed off far enough for momentum and kicked the door in with a great, huge blow right above the knob where I'd found it did the most good.

The door bucked and gave, and in the next instant, I heard glass break from the back of the house. Anyone inside would know they were being invaded.

I entered cautiously, xiphos prepared to slash. The front entrance was crowded with shoes—sneakers, sandals, flip-flops from kid-sized to adult. Enough to trip over. I brushed them aside with my foot and kept going. The foyer opened immediately onto a small living room covered in laundry, as though someone had been folding and sorting when they'd been interrupted.

Apollo met me a second later, coming from the back of the house, the kitchen entrance. He shook his head as our eyes met to let me know there was no one back there. Together we stopped and listened to the rest of the house. All was eerily silent, but my precog insisted that to be misleading.

At least we didn't have much to search. There was only one way to go. Off the living room was a hallway lined with closed doors. Four of them. Two on one side, one on the other and a door at the end which was probably the master bedroom.

I took the lead. The first door I came to was on the left. I opened it quickly, poised with my xiphos in case anything jumped out, but it was just a bathroom ... with a patina of red staining the sink and suspicious dark stains on the towels tossed to the side of the sink and onto the floor. The incongruously cheerful ducky shower curtain was yanked back and half off its rings, so it was clear no one was hiding behind it.

I didn't venture any farther. The police forensic team would want to sweep it for clues, evidence to wrap their murder cases up with neat little bows. I was interested in saving the survivors.

Apollo looked over my shoulder, saw that there was nothing to see, and moved on to the next room. I closed the door behind me to maintain the scene the best I could and waited to one side of the next door while he stood to the other side. My precog was going crazy as he turned the knob, but there was no need to say a word. His senses were even more developed than mine and we couldn't be any more ready than we already were.

He thrust the door open as soon as the catch released. The sight that greeted us was horrendous. Inside what was clearly meant to be a kids' room—red with auto-racing details every-where from the race car runner to the checkered and yellow flags crossed decoratively on the walls—were twin beds sporting material that would definitely be disturbing to younger viewers. Bodies. Two of them. Both female. One with golden curls falling over the pillow and onto the floor like abandoned party streamers. The other with scads of dark hair that glistened wet with blood.

Both had their chests laid bare. Not in the sense of clothing pulled back or ripped off, but in the sense of *flesh* rolled back like sod to reveal what was underneath—only I couldn't see what that might be through all the blood. The sternum ... the heart ... I couldn't tell what was still there and what wasn't. Bile rose, and a vision started to rise up. I fought it down. My precog was still going insane, alarm bells now ringing loud enough to rattle my brain. I couldn't afford to be distracted or out of time in my own little blood-slicked world.

Apollo stepped toward the beds. One step, then another. My alarm bells were deafening. "Don't," I called, not sure why. Surely neither of these women—Sulis of the golden curls and perhaps Aphrodite's missing nymph with the darker hair—were in any condition to harm him, but as he reached them, something whipped out from beneath the one bed and grabbed Apollo around both ankles, yanking his feet out from under him.

He cried out as he toppled toward the other bed, about to, literally, fall on his sword. I lurched forward to catch him, knowing I'd be too late, when a shriek from behind warned me of my own danger. I whirled, instinctively raising my xiphos to ward off an on-rushing blow. A cartoonishly large kitchen knife caught on the cross guard of my blade just before it would have buried itself in my neck.

I forced my gaze past it and looked beyond ... straight into the crazed eyes of my client. "Jessica!" I cried, shocked.

She answered with a snarl that sounded anything but human, crushed my hand around my hilt with her free hand, and ripped loose her kitchen knife, swinging her freed blade for my gut. I tried to leap back, but she held me there with that hand bruising mine, and I only managed to get enough distance to lessen the depth of the slash, but the sharp pain in my abdomen and the sudden heat of gushing blood shouted that I hadn't done enough. I whipped the dagger from my waistband, now doubly armed, and slashed it at her knife hand as she pulled back for another attack.

I felt my blade slice, and took instant advantage of her reaction by pressing my trapped hand and xiphos toward her. She was prepared for me to try to yank the blade free, not to swing for her and she wasn't able to adjust quickly enough. I twisted as I pushed so that if I hit her it would be with the blunt of the blade rather than the edge. She was *my client* and clearly not herself. I didn't want to kill her. It wouldn't do good things for my professional reputation or my conscience.

The blunt of the xiphos struck her dead center of the forehead, and her eyes seemed to roll up to look, but I hadn't hit her hard enough to knock her out. Not with her own hand still crushing my fingers to the hilt.

I didn't wait for her to recover, but jammed my foot down hard on her instep, whirled around, torquing to the side so her hand and body would have to move in unnatural ways that would put her off balance if she wanted to stay with me. She let go instead, which was what I'd been hoping for. I finished my spin, coming full circle and slashing the blade down toward her calves. Hoping for hamstrings or her Achilles's heel, willing to settle for anything that took her down.

But she wasn't where I'd expected her to be. She danced back and now held her knife in front of her like a street fighter, the look on her face just as feral.

"Jessica," I said sharply, trying to break through her Set-induced fog. "Jessica, this is Tori. I'm here to help. Don't—"

She ran at me, stabbing with her knife, going for my center of mass. I jumped back, but there was no space to maneuver in the small room, and I didn't want to trip over Apollo, who was fighting his own battle, kicking and flailing, but seeming as reluctant as I was to use his blade. I thought I heard him call, "Thalia!" but I couldn't spare the attention to look. Anyway, it couldn't be. Couldn't.

Dammit, there was not going to be any reasoning with Jessica. I waited for her crazed gaze to meet mine again and yelled, *"Freeze!"*

She stopped dead, not so much as a twitch to her snarl. I didn't wait to see if she'd shake herself out of it. If chaos could trump paralysis with her as it had with her brothers. I quickly stepped behind her and cold-cocked her with the hilt of my blade. She dropped like a stone and I whirled to help Apollo.

His upper body was still free, but some slasher film version of Thalia had climbed her way up his legs from the ankles she'd grabbed to his thighs, her face now level with some very sensitive spots.

Apollo had called on the force of the sun, which burned straight through the lowered shades of the room's solo window and were focused on Thalia's back as though she was an ant and someone outside held the mother of all magnifying glasses. I could see the smoke rising from her skin, but she didn't appear even to notice. Her hands were covered in blood, which made me wonder whether she'd opened the other women's chests with her bare hands ... but then I noticed that her red carpet dress itself was laid open at the chest. Blood covered the skin and the fabric that now hung in shreds and yet ... and yet, she still lived. Moved, anyway. But she, like Jessica, was not herself.

I walked over and brained her like I had Jessica, feeling terrible about it. I could only hope I hadn't given either of them a concussion, but at the moment, it seemed the least of their problems.

"My hero," Apollo said with no discernible resentment at being rescued by a woman.

"It was my turn," I said with a shrug.

I helped him roll Thalia off his body and then crouched down to study her. The huge gash in her chest was bloody, but no longer raw. Already the skin at the edges showed signs of reknitting, the scars pink and raised. But in the midst of the wound itself, something caught the bright stream of sunlight just as Apollo shut it down.

"Wait!" I said. "I mean, don't burn her, but can you kind of shine a beam right at her chest."

I realized how that sounded the second it was out of my mouth, but neither of us made a joke of it. The light hit something again, and held there. I leaned in, careful not to overshadow her, and ... I started to reach for the spot.

"Don't touch it!" Apollo said, grabbing my hand back. "Just wait."

He looked around for something and apparently didn't find what he was looking for. "I'll be right back."

I didn't protest as he left me there with the four unconscious women. Instead, I did a little exploration of my own, looking for something to tie up Thalia and Jessica before they could come to. I really wanted to check on Sulis and Iphigenia, but there was time for that once I made sure our threats were neutralized. I found two boys' robes shoved into the bottom of the closet—one brown and one blue—and used the belts to bind Thalia and Jessica's hands. Apollo was back before I found anything for the feet, and he carried a pair of those yellow plastic kitchen gloves that made the hands sweat but supposedly protected them from the rigors of dish detergent. He also came with a pair of tongs, the kind used for turning meat on a grill.

"What are you going to do with those?" I asked, afraid I already knew the answer.

"Here," he said, handing me the tongs and donning the gloves himself, thank goodness. "I need you to use the tongs to hold back the edges of the wound," he said. "I'm going in."

So we were playing a real, live game of Operation. My stomach rebelled. For the second time in not very long, I swallowed back bile.

I squatted down close to Thalia and forced myself not to squinch my eyes shut to protect myself from the sight. Instead, I eased the tongs into her chest cavity. Apollo crouched on her other side, reached in gingerly with the gloves, and tapped something hard. Her sternum, I thought at first, but then ...

Oh no, I was not *going to lose my lunch.*

I fought it down. I was made of sterner stuff. I repeated it to myself like a mantra, but myself was unconvinced.

He curled three fingers into his palm and used just the thumb and forefinger to grab at something inside her chest cavity.

"It's not coming loose," he said. "It's like it's become part of her."

"What?" I asked.

"A coin. Small, about the size of a nickel."

"One of the Set coins."

"At a guess."

"Embedded into her chest?" I said, just to be clear.

"More like her heart," he answered. "It's—"

"Barbaric," I finished.

He nodded. "I can't just yank it loose. It's really in there, and I don't know what it will do to her."

"We don't know what having it there has already done ... or what it will do. Already she's not in her right mind."

"We need to get her to a healer. A real one this time. The mud bath at Sulis's spa is not going to cover this."

"Speaking of which—"

I rose, my knees protesting the time I'd spent squatting, and went over to the bed with the blonde hair shining in the sun. It was Sulis, as expected, and her chest wasn't the only part of her covered in blood. More had seeped out of her nose and coagulated on her upper lip, and ... I concentrated on her chest, watching to see if it rose and fell. There was no movement. I put two fingers to the pulse point at her neck and didn't feel anything there either.

"Apollo," I said softly.

He gave Thalia a tortured look and then stood, stripping off the rubber gloves and following my gaze.

"She's gone," I said. "At least I think so. I don't know what the rule is for you gods, about resurrection and all that."

He rose to look at Sulis himself and did something I hadn't even thought to do. He took an untouched hank of her hair, separated out a few strands, and held them in front of her nose and mouth to see if there was any air passing at all to stir them, but there was nothing. With a heavy heart, I walked the few paces to the other bed.

The woman who lay there—Iphigenia?—had clearly been through torments I didn't want to fathom. She was all torn up. I could see her chest rise just slightly, and heard a single breath escape. Then, as if it had taken her soul with it, she lay still. I cried out and readied myself to do chest compressions and CPR when another breath issued forth, no less heart-wrenching. It was too shallow and far too slow. I didn't know how much longer she'd hold on ... And that was when I noticed that there was something glinting inside her chest as well. At a guess yet another of the insidious coins. I picked up the house phone and dialed 9-1-1 then held my hand over the receiver as it started to connect. "What do we do about Jessica and Thalia?" I asked. "Do I tell them two victims or four or ...?"

Apollo looked away from Sulis to me. "I don't like this. Any of it. But ... you'd better tell them four. These ladies need medical help and right now we're not in a position to give it to them."

"What about the Set disks? We can't just leave them behind for anyone to touch. We don't know if they're a one-time-use sort of thing or if they can still infect others."

"What choice do we have? Doctors use gloves and all that. They should be safe enough."

"But what if—"

"Hello? Hello," came a voice. "What is the nature of your emergency?" Time was up. Even if I had the leisure to think it all through, I wasn't sure Genie had that kind of time. I explained everything to the dispatcher as best I could, which was to say "not very well." I told her we needed medical help, stat. I told her it was pretty clearly a crime scene and that based on the violence it might have something to do with that case in the Hollywood Hills and that the police might want to come along. I could only hope that this would be enough to get the disks handled with care and with kid gloves, knowing they could be evidence and all that.

I was told to stay on the line and had every intention of doing so, but just then Hermes's frantic face appeared in the air right before me.

"We need you!" he said, looking around and catching my gaze. "Bring Sigyn's tracker."

"What's happened?" Apollo asked, at the same time the dispatcher said, "Is there someone there with you?"

I ignored her, hitting the Mute button and waiting for Hermes to continue. "We've got Richie." I didn't even have time to process relief at that before he went on. "But Ian's got Neith."

"What? What happened?" I asked.

"Another blast from that chaos amulet or whatever it is the one is wearing. You do not want to see modern art come to life."

Crap, crap, crap. "We're on it," I said. "Apollo, do you want to work with Hermes to turn his window into a portal?"

"No!" Hermes said instantly, fear in his voice like I'd not heard it before. Mischief he was up for ... mischief he could control, but it seemed chaos had him spooked. "Not with this field going here. You might get turned inside out. Or end up two-dimensional or ... Just no. Wings or wheels," he said.

I looked at Apollo and he at me. "Wings are faster," I said. "Want to go for a ride? We can be like Superman and Lois Lane. Only, I wear the tights in this family."

"Good. No one wants to see my hairy legs in tights," he said.

The banter was a reflex. Neither of us felt very funny. I could feel his concern through our link. And it only got worse when I said, "Wait, what about Jessica and the others? We can't just leave them. What if Ian comes back? Or Jessica and Thalia get free? Or Genie stops breathing ..."

"Poseidon's puckery posterior! Fine, I'll stay. You go. Anyway, you'll be faster without me. Track Ian, save Neith. But be careful."

"But—"

"Go!" he said. "I've got this."

There was no time to argue. I unmuted my phone and answered the dispatcher's increasingly worried questions. "Sorry, I'm here! I just ... I have to get out of here. So much blood ..." I quickly told her about Apollo so the police wouldn't shoot him on sight, thinking he was a danger, and handed the phone over to him.

"I'm going to check the last two rooms before I go, just to be sure ..." I said quietly. By my count, at least three of the Set coins had been used—one on Viktor, one on Genie and one on Thalia. Four coins, actually, because there was no way Jessica would have attacked if she hadn't been under the influence, though at least her coin hadn't been implanted straight into her chest. I didn't think so anyway. For one, there was no blood and for another, she was still kicking, while Sulis, a goddess if not one of the biggies, wasn't nearly so lucky.

What I didn't understand was why the brothers had mutilated the goddesses. Because they were more than human and theoretically able to take it? Because with humans Set could get into their heads, but with someone stronger he needed to seize control of their very hearts? Had Genie and Sulis been earlier experiments, before the system was perfected with Thalia? Had the shock to their bodies been too great? Too many questions, too little time.

I walked quickly through the rest of the house, toward the back two bedrooms. The one at the end of the hall, the master, was a disaster of beer cans and bottles of even harder stuff. The comforter had been yanked off the bed to create a kind of nest or pallet on the floor. The bedding reeked with the acid bite of ammonia that signaled night sweats. The scent was strong enough to reach me even at the doorway. I stepped in quickly, careful to avoid landing in or on anything, and checked under the bed before moving to the accordion doors of the closet. I opened them in a flash, flailing inside with my blade, stabbing nothing but women's clothing.

The next room ... I closed the door to the next room without ever stepping inside. In fact, I raced for the outside and only made it as far as the tall grass before losing everything in my stomach. Newsflash: bacon does not taste as good coming up as it does going down and coffee downright burns.

I was gasping for breath by the time I was done, and then blowing air out my nose, hoping to get rid of the stench of death. The horror of that third room would haunt me forever. Three bodies stacked ... But no, that would imply precision or order. They weren't stacked, they were thrown aside, one on top of the other, their blood mingling and pooling on the floor.

I bent double for another heave, this one producing nothing but a thin trickle of pure stomach acid. My gut hurt, my brain hurt, my heart hurt most of all. Three more dead. Three innocents ... a woman and her two young boys. Ian was going down. Hard. I'd rip his heart out. I'd ... No, I wouldn't do any of the things I sorely wanted to do. No more death or destruction or chaos. Not if I could help it. No more glory to Set. No. This needed to end.

I wondered how close the brothers were—brother now, singular—to freeing Set. One more death, say the murder of a major Pantheonic player like Neith?

My precog didn't just kick; it performed feats worthy of my family's acrobatic troupe.

Could Neith be the final brick in the wall ... or, rather, the final blow that busted Set's chains?

24

———

As soon as I had my feet under me again and could be sure I wouldn't spew all over the good people of LA, I consulted Sigyn's blood dial, hoping it would hold, since I couldn't count on my knack. I had the taste of Richie's blood, but not Ian's. I couldn't trace him on my own.

But as I focused on Ian, a vision began to form. I knew it for that and not a memory because I'd never seen him this way—face half covered in blood from a slash that had gauged a deep furrow from his hairline down across his nose. Combined with the snarl that twisted his features, he barely looked human. I could see only the top of Neith's head as it lolled in his grip. I didn't know what he'd done to her, but he had her now in a half nelson, his other arm seeming to hang useless at his side. Whatever had gone down at the museum, our side had gotten their licks in.

The dial spun in my hand, pointing back in the direction I thought led to the museum, but then hesitating and pointing off to the east. I'd more than half expected to intercept Ian, but east meant he wasn't bringing her back here. Did he already know the house was compromised or had he intended something else all along?

It didn't matter. Not really. Either way, I had to hunt him down.

My wings were out before the words to summon them had died on my lips, as if they'd been poised and ready. It freaked me out all over again that they seemed practically to have minds of their own. *Instinct.* I was going to call it instinct and leave it at that.

The media already had pics of me—stills and now actual video. I couldn't worry any more about being seen. Set had already blown the doors of the bizarre and unexplainable wide open. Unexplainable unless a person believed Reverend Smith's End Times explanation.

I took off, feeling a brief, fluttery moment of panic, as always, as I cleared the tops of the houses, but exposure therapy was getting me over my fear of heights.

I had no idea how Ian was getting anywhere with Neith. Motor vehicle, I presumed, which meant he had to take roads and deal with traffic. I could get wherever he was going as the crow flies ... or Gorgon. Which meant, hopefully, I could head him off.

My precog was going all sorts of crazy, practically shooting off fireworks in my head to get my attention. I told the precog to Shut It! in no uncertain terms and the fireworks died down to those firecrackers kids set off in the street. Still, the urgency drove me, almost straight into the back end of a pigeon, which squawked indignantly and veered sharply out of my way, eyeing me reproachfully out of its beady orange eyes.

The path took me wide of the LACMA, but a plume of dark smoke roiled out of a gaping hole in the roof that hadn't been there before. I hoped the museum's insurance would cover it ... along with the medical expenses of anyone caught in that cloud. Something in the way it churned said that it was something far more noxious than mere smoke.

I was glad Sigyn's device had taken me wide of it. I checked the dial again, adjusted my path and headed for the downtown area. Back toward my office and all the old theatres from the heyday of Hollywood—The Roxie, the Tower Theatre, the Rialto ... the Orpheum ...

The alarm that went off at the thought of the Orpheum nearly blew me out of the sky, but I couldn't figure out why at first. Why would Ian have headed for the old theatre rather than for his house of horrors? And why ...

The question was answered a moment later when I came within sight of the theatre itself and spotted the marquee. The Orpheum was one of the few old theatres that actually still operated like a theatre, featuring traveling acts—plays, musical performances, screenings, comedians, even the occasional motivational speaker or big business seminar. Whoever could pay or bring in a big enough audience to fill the seats. Tonight, the featured "performer" was none other than the Reverend John Moses Smith with *Reflect and Redirect*. I could only guess it was the name of his program. Catchy. Alliterative. Positive-sounding and spiritual without being in-your-face with any particular credo that might alienate his audience.

But ... this couldn't have been thrown together just since this morning when Reverend Smith had invited all of LA to pray with him. The Orpheum booked up months in advance, which meant that either they'd had a very coincidental cancellation or the reverend's revival had already been in the works and he'd merely taken advantage of the insanity that had hit LA to promote his message and fill seats. At this rate, it was likely to be standing room only. I circled the theatre from the air. The blood dial confirmed what my precog had already told me. This was the place. It was quiet yet. The actual revival, according to the sign, was hours away. I needed to get in and get Ian before he could do any damage. Before there was an overwhelming chance of civilian casualties. I couldn't wait for back up. That didn't mean I was stupid enough not to call for it or to let everyone know where I was.

I texted Apollo, even knowing he'd still be tied up with the police. *At the Orpheum.*

Urgent.

Send failed, my phone said almost immediately.

Oh holy hells.

Cursing, I next voice-dialed Hermes. It seemed to take forever to start ringing, but once it did, the connection was terrible.

Hermes answered, but we could have been two kids using Dixie cups connected with string for all the reception we had.

"Tori?" he called through the phone line. "Tori?"

"Hermes," I yelled. "The Orpheum. Get here. All of you."

"What? Tori, I can't hear you. I'm going to hang up and try you again."

No call came back, and when Hermes's window appeared in front of me, it was barely the size of my thumbnail. "Quick," he said, "something's interfering."

I could see part of his eye, that was all, and it was completely disconcerting. "Orpheum," I said loudly and clearly. "Get here."

"Opium? Tori, what—"

"Orf-E-Um," I said, enunciating. The window snapped shut with an audible pop just as I hit the last syllable, and I cursed again.

The chaos field? I wondered. But if the blood and tribute the brothers had offered up was powering the field, how much was getting to Set? Or was there a great big feedback loop with chaos itself fueling the god and the god fueling the field? Damn and double damn.

I tucked the blood dial into the pocket of my track pants and tucked my wings away. I should have done it already. I was not exactly inconspicuous perched on the roof of the Orpheum in downtown LA. It was nothing short of miraculous if I hadn't been spotted already.

I started looking for a way off the roof and into the building that didn't involve property damage or charges of breaking and entering.

My precog hit me just before the sound of electricity had me whirling around. I'd been so focused on the paranormal threat, I hadn't even considered all-too-human security. They seemed to have come out of nowhere—two men, one about the size and shoulder width of Apollo and one tall and whipcord thin like a long-distance runner or pole-vaulter. That was all I caught in the split second before I was diving out of the way to avoid the Taser blast I knew was coming. I dodged the one, but the other ...

Suddenly it was as if I'd been struck by lightning.

Electricity shocked through me, arching my back, contracting my muscles. My whole body went rigid and paralyzed with the jittering. My teeth clacked together, eyes rolled into my head. No thoughts but pain. No control. No ...

I fell away from myself, my brain's electrical system fried like a power surge to an unprotected computer.

I COULDN'T HAVE BEEN out long, but I'd lost time, because when I jerked awake, the guys with Security emblazoned in bold yellow letters across their chests were standing over me. My body was still shaking, a million volts seemingly still running through me, making it hard to get my thoughts together. I wanted to kick out, knock them both to the ground, catch them by surprise, but my legs wouldn't obey. Nothing was obeying.

One bent down to examine me. "I think she bit her tongue," he said.

I must be bleeding. The urge to spit it at him was almost overwhelming, but as useless as my body seemed, I was more likely to dribble it on myself. Anyway, he didn't deserve to be turned to stone just for doing his job. If I'd been purely human and a winged woman had landed on the roof of the building I was hired to protect, I might stun first and ask questions later as well.

Still, I wasn't going down like this. I rolled my eyes until I could catch his gaze and said, "Freeze."

It came out more like "Fee" along with a little of that dribble, but the intent behind it came through. He froze.

The other guy, not aware yet that there was anything wrong with his partner, circled behind me to cuff me or zip tie me or whatever he was about to do, and I tried to twitch myself into a position to get him too. Only my body wouldn't move.

He grabbed one hand behind my back and had to roll me to grab the other. But he wasn't looking into my face. He was focused on my hands and getting me locked down.

My lungs felt seized, my heart beating way too fast and so strongly I thought it might explode with the effort. I mustered what energy, what control I had to force air out of my mouth, to make a sound to get his attention. I managed something like a honk. It startled him enough to look up, and I said, "Fee" again. He froze in place. I didn't know how long it would last, especially not as weak as I was. I felt like a newborn ... without the strength, muscles, or coordination to get myself up off the ground. With no choice, I gave myself another second to lie there, hoping that with my advanced healing I would overcome a Taser charge faster than the average person, but ... damn, it hurt. And the helplessness was something I never wanted to feel again.

Again? I was still feeling it now. I might have felt a finger twitch, but I couldn't even be sure of that. Or that the twitch was in fact voluntary. Randomly, my knee would still jerk up or my foot would flick ...

Rise, I told myself. Myself would have laughed if it had even that much motor control. Nothing happened. I decided to focus in. Small things first ... Roll to my side, get my legs under me, use my hands to push myself up ... Nothing.

I counted to five, watching the security guys closely for signs they were coming out of it. I could freeze them again if they started to move ... if I could get them to meet my gaze again and if some instinct hadn't taught them better. But the sooner I could get moving, the better. I didn't want Neith to turn into ... whatever Thalia had become. Herself, but not. Would it feel like my helplessness, only a million times worse? Would she fight the control yet be powerless against it? Or would the disk subsume her, taking away her will, turning her wants to his?

On five I tried again to move. This time, I was able to rock to my side, only to see the first security guy blinking down at me. Blinking. He was coming out of it.

It would be a race to see which of us could recover first. I got up as far as my knees when his partner's hand twitched. Oh crap. I nearly fell trying to get my feet under me too fast, but then I was balanced, making sure of myself before I started to rise. The first security guy reached for me, but in slow motion, still shaking off the effects of my gorgon glare.

All I could think was that this was going to be the lamest fight in creation. A battle in super slo-mo, like something out of a low-budget Matrix. I hoped I was going to be Neo. Or at least Agent Smith. He was, after all, pretty cool. Evil, of course, but cool.

At least my sense of inappropriately timed humor had returned.

Sec Guy connected, knocking clumsily into my shoulder,

but it was enough to overbalance me, and meanwhile his partner had shaken off his paralysis and raised a foot, ready to stomp down like a puppy eager to keep his ball from getting away. Only, I was the ball. I rolled out of the way, into the first guy, acting like a bowling ball and treating him as the pin. It wouldn't have worked if he'd been moving quickly enough to adjust, but he wasn't, and as he started to topple, I had a burning urge to yell "Timber!" except that he was falling at me.

His buddy, coming down on the foot that had failed to connect, was off balance as well, and the two met in the middle, holding each other up like a tent over me. I alligator-crawled out from between them, grabbed the zip tie cuffs off the one guy's belt and grabbed hands together before they could disentangle, locking them tight, weaving the zip ties together.

They looked at their bound hands, at each other, at me ... both faces promising serious retribution. Personally, I wasn't even sure we were even from that Taser blast.

"Sit," I ordered.

They stared at me in defiance.

"Fine, try to get somewhere and fall down. Up to you."

I patted them down. Came up with keys, personal radios for communication with each other, their cell phones, and more zip tie cuffs. I tucked the latter into my waistband, hoping I'd have the chance to use them later. Soon.

"Now, freeze," I said, while they were both shooting daggers at me with their eyes.

They froze, of course. I'd been trying to save them the inevitable bruises to their butts when they unfroze again and overbalanced each other, but, well, I couldn't be too torn up about it.

Then I headed in the direction from which they'd appeared, knowing there'd be a way into the theatre, hoping I'd get there before any reinforcements. Because for certain they weren't the only security, whether hired by the venue or the revival.

Sure enough, they'd left a door propped open. More of a hatch, really, but the effects of the Taser were wearing off, and I thought that I could handle a ladder. Maybe. My legs still shook and wanted to accordion like those of a Jack-in-the-box who'd just sprung. But they held. I was down the ladder before I heard voices and readied the gorgon glare again. As long as they kept sending humans at me, I'd be okay. And as far as I knew, they didn't have any gods on their side ... yet. I planned to keep it that way.

The two new security guys were loud enough to wake the dead, so I heard them in plenty of time to duck out of sight until they were right there and then surprise them with the gorgon glare. Their Tasers weren't even out of their holsters. I continued on down the stairs and through a door out onto a quiet room not in use. The lights were out, and it was completely dark. I could use the light app on my phone, but if anyone was watching security cameras, it would tell them right where to find me. Of course, it was also possible that ship had sailed. In the end, I used it, doing my best to shield the light with my hand. I didn't know what this room was used for regularly, but for now, it was empty, and I made my way to the door that luckily locked from the outside, and so I didn't have to go through the jumble of keys I'd taken off the security guards on the roof.

I pulled the door open just a sliver and looked out into the hallway, which was a helluva lot better lit than the room where I stood, but just as empty. I slid out, closing the door behind me as quietly as I could. It was crazy, I now realized, to have worried about whether my light would appear in the empty room. Now that I was in the brightly lit mezzanine that overlooked the main floor of gleaming white marble, I realized I stuck out like a sore thumb in my black tracksuit and sports bra. I had to get into a security shirt or a suit or whatever it was the reverend's lackeys wore if I wanted to be less conspicuous.

Luckily the mezzanine was designed like an arcade, like something that might have come out of a *palazzo* or manor from another time. It meant there were columns here and there to duck behind and ...

My precog and the voices warned me that there was someone coming, and I quickly dashed behind the nearest column and up against the wall. My precog wasn't kicking like the danger was going to come flying at me at any moment, but more like spiders with zappy little Taser feet were crawling all over my spine. Maybe it was an after effect of the actual Taser blast, but ... I didn't think so.

Even without an audience to project to, Reverend Smith's voice carried, echoing off the vaulted ceiling. "Well, of course, I'm always happy to meet with a true believer who wants to contribute significantly to the cause. It's just that there's so much to prepare before tonight. Other VIPs should start arriving any time now. Perhaps my assistant ..."

His voice fell off as someone else spoke, this voice not meant to carry over crowded auditoriums, with or without microphones. I desperately wanted to know who he was talking with, but if I peeked out in time to see faces, they'd be able to see me as well. I was going to have to wait until they passed and hope I recognized the back of a head.

I was terrible at waiting. My leg wanted to thump impatiently, but I forced myself to stay still. To wait. As they passed, I edged around the column. I didn't recognize the woman walking with Reverend Smith. She was tall—nearly six-foot— with her black hair braided into many rows which were in turn interwoven. She wore black pants that fit her like gloves or, since that seemed a really terrible analogy, riding pants, and boots all the way to her knees. Her jacket came to points at the back, cinched in at the waist and broad at the top, either stylistically or because of a really impressive breadth of shoulders. She looked badass. For a moment, I thought of Hecate, but as far as I knew, she was still a statuesque block of stone, and anyway, if it had been her, the outfit would have been entirely of leather and her hair would have never have been tamed.

I whipped my phone out for a quick picture, thankful I'd silenced it so the totally unnecessary shutter-sound that designers kept to alert that a picture had been taken wouldn't give me away.

I quickly texted it to Hermes with a message, *Anyone recognize? When to the Orpheum?*

I waited only a second for it to go through, cursing when again I got the *Send failed* message. *Tap to try again.* I knew it would be futile.

Plus, the reverend and the woman were getting away.

I slipped out, keeping behind columns as much as possible, but if they turned, they would see me. If there was any security still manning the cameras, they would see me. Unless chaos was on *my side* for a change ...

The woman stopped in front of a closed door and opened it for the reverend, stepping aside to let him precede her. I tried to catch a glimpse inside, but her body blocked me. She scanned the hall before stepping in herself, and while I was half behind a column, I was also half out. She was going to see me. There was no way she wasn't going to see me.

Her gaze passed me right by, and she followed Reverend Smith into the room, closing the door behind her.

I blinked. There was no way I'd gotten that lucky.

There was also no way to see or hear what was going on in that room without giving myself away.

Still, my precog and my intuition—not that it was possible to separate them anymore—told me it was important. And Ian fit the profile of a large potential donor ... or would if his accounts weren't frozen by the murder charges hanging over his head. There was no way he could think Reverend Smith would cement any kind of association with a killer. It would ruin him. Of course, there was no knowing what tale Ian would tell ... or even if the reverend knew who he was dealing with. Maybe Ian could convince the reverend that his mother and father had been the ones possessed—the pot calling the kettle poltergeist. Of course, if he used one of the remaining Set coins, he might not need any story at all to influence the reverend.

It didn't really matter how things were set to go down. If Ian was in there, that was where I needed to be.

I dashed out and tried the door, but the tall woman had locked it behind her, which didn't bode well for the reverend. Reverend Smith wasn't one of my favorite people, but still ... no one deserved to have their free will usurped, and the trouble he could wreak as an acolyte of the chaos god....

Something in that room thrummed against my head and plucked at my already abused nerves, causing them to jitter just like my entire body after the electrodes from the Taser had struck. And so I missed the danger creeping up behind me until my upper body was slammed into the door and another body pressed in on me with all her weight.

Instinctively, my wings lashed out to throw her off, but the woman pinning me down gave no quarter, and they only half-unfurled, crushed and trapped between us. I hoped they poked her at the very least, maybe even leaving unsightly bruises. "Gotcha," she said.

"I'm just here to see the reverend," I said desperately. "About his prophecies."

"Nice try, Ms. Karacis."

I froze. I didn't know the voice, but it had the same exotic accent as Neith's. What in the unholy hells was going on?

She pushed my head against the door again, banging my skull against it, I supposed by way of knocking. The latch clicked and it gave way, revealing the woman I'd seen with Reverend Smith, only from the front this time. With her height and those boots, I had to look up to take in wide, prominent cheekbones, a flat nose, generous lips with just a touch of color. Her only other makeup, as far as I could tell, was the kohl lining her eyes. She was so striking and so regal; she could have stepped right out of one of the ancient Egyptian frescoes.

"Welcome," she said, gesturing us in.

The woman who'd attacked had me by the hair and also with a hand around my throat. She pushed me inside and I let her for a moment, needing to get a handle on what I was facing. The door slammed and locked behind me, and I stared at two slabs ... no, not slabs, long narrow tables of the kind brought out for trade shows and banquets but usually covered up by nice fabric table cloths. The only thing covering them at the moment was two bodies, both breathing, thank the gods.

Those I recognized—Neith and the reverend. Wow, they'd worked fast. And standing at the reverend's head, pressing a coin right into the center of it, between his brows and into what I was fairly certain was one of the chakras, was Ian Roland. His hands were covered in blood up to the rolled-up sleeves of his white and blue oxford.

And it was clear enough whose blood that was. Neith had apparently opted for bounty-hunter black for the ambush at the museum, and it soaked up the blood pretty well, but there was no disguising the shine or the scent of fresh blood. Fiction always equated the smell with the copper of new pennies. An outdated notion now. To me it had the tang of an aptly named Bloody Mary. There was a bite to it. It nipped at the nose.

Either it or the menace in the room stood the hairs at the nape of my neck on end.

The woman who held me suddenly let go of my neck to frisk me for my phone. I took advantage of her one-handed hold to rip myself away from her, leaving some hair behind by its roots.

I spun, my wings flaring, stretching, glad to be freed, again like they had minds of their own. With Ian distracted by his victims, I glared down the two women, centering my weight in a fighting stance. The woman who'd held me had hair as free as the other's was controlled. It was bigger than mine even in the highest humidity. Nearly as big as Hecate's when it rose with her winds. Otherwise, the two could have been sisters. Very nearly twins.

And that clicked everything into place. There were only two sisters I knew of in our little tableau—Anat and Astarte. Sigyn had referred to them as Set's sister-wives. It occurred to me that she might have meant that literally. She'd sworn to their trustworthiness, insisted that they wouldn't want Set to get loose.

Neither my precog nor the fact that they hadn't stopped Ian suggested it to be the truth. Either Sigyn was sorely mistaken or she and her blood dial had sent me straight into their hands.

"Oh, that's cute," the wild one said. "She wants to fight us."

"She'll get her chance," said the more-contained one, leaning against the door, but keeping her arms uncrossed, at the ready, in case the lock might not be enough. As though I'd just run.

"Anat? Astarte? Why are you doing this?" I asked ... because everyone in the room with exception maybe of the two on the tables knew exactly what was going on but me. And when and if help arrived, I had to know who to trust. I had to know what the hells was happening.

The wild one laughed. "We were not meant for jailors; we were meant for war."

"Yet wars have come and gone," said the other. "Always and ever we have our fun, only to be called back to our duties." She sneered. "To our husband."

"But we have seen the signs."

"Titans arisen, the plague demons awakened. Gods and dragons stirring."

"If the Great War isn't upon us we will make it so," the wild one said, her voice rising with her hands as she threw them into the air and whirled with the anticipated joy of battle.

"But—" I started.

"Just think," said the braided one, who I decided to think of as Astarte, because they hadn't seen fit to introduce themselves, "the arguments over the signs and portents. The hysteria. The battles that will ensue."

"The Chaos," said the other, embracing it.

It hit me then right between the eyes. It was a wonder this plan hadn't hatched sooner. Chaos and battle—they went hand in hand, just like husbands and wives. Or did they? My mind argued with itself even as the thought occurred. Neith-Athena was a war goddess as well. The big kahuna of war goddesses, and she was pretty much the antithesis of chaos. She was about strategy, discipline, order and yes, the fighting sometimes needed to create or restore it. Anat and Astarte must have subscribed to this discipline once. Long enough to grow heartily sick of it. It had gotten them exactly nowhere. A dead-end job with no possibility of parole. And so they'd broken free.

It all made a horrible sense.

But there was one wife missing, and when I thought back to the battle with Set, I thought I knew why. "Taweret," I said. "She wouldn't go along with you, would she?"

"Taweret," Anat scoffed ... or at least the one I'd decided was Anat. "So gentle. So useless. She was never even asked. She would have blown the whole thing."

"And now," said the other, tapping a finger against her lip contemplatively, "what shall we do with you until show time?"

My mind was whirling. Until show time? That implied I was somehow part of the spectacle. What on earth did they have in mind? A gladiatorial battle? The old Christians versus the lions? I wondered which I was meant to be.

I readied myself, not about to go down without a fight, but there were two of them and one of me, and when I swung to fight the first, the other hit me hard in the back of the head and everything went dark.

25

I came to in the same room where I'd gone down, only instead of facing off with the warrior goddesses, I was practically eye to eye with someone a helluva lot scarier ... at least at that moment.

Ian Roland.

I'd seen what he'd done to that woman back at the museum in Egypt. I'd seen the bodies of Mrs. Barbarosa and his parents, at least in my vision. And now I looked around wildly, hoping there was someone left behind to rein him in, but there was no one. Anat and Astarte, the reverend and even Neith, all gone.

I glanced back into Ian's psycho-eyes. "Alone at last," he said. Then he licked his lips, very intentionally, and raked his gaze over me.

I yanked at my hands, tried to get my feet under me where I lay sprawled on the floor. My legs obeyed, but my arms were zip tied behind me. Ian let me get all the way into a sitting position before he knocked me back down, hand to my chest, keeping me there.

"You don't—You're not—" I started, realizing I was stuttering, showing fear. I didn't want to, but I knew from trying it with Richie that the gorgon glare couldn't penetrate crazy and possessed. That was one weapon down. But helplessness wasn't my real fear. It was those Set disks, being turned on those I loved. I did a quick rundown in my head. Neith had said there'd been half a dozen. Six disks. One for Victor, Jessica, Thalia, Neith, and the reverend. They'd tried a disk on Iphigenia and maybe Sulis, possibly the same one on both. That was all the disks accounted for, right? Unless they'd done double-duty with one of the other disks.

But I didn't feel any different.

I must have crossed my eyes trying to see the top of my head. I'd have known immediately if someone had cracked open my chest. Ian laughed at my look.

"Oh, Tori … Can I call you Tori?" He didn't wait for me to respond. "We don't need to control you. You'll fight because you're a fighter and because, well, you'll see. It's not as though you'll have any choice." His laugh was like a stampede of snakes slithering up my spine. "Best of all, I get to play with what's left of you."

The hand holding me down was suddenly stroking, straight over to one nipple, which he grabbed and twisted. Pain shot through me, but it was nothing to the fear—not so much for me. I'd fight whatever or whoever they intended for me to fight to the death if I had to before I'd leave anything behind for Ian to "play with." The fear that swamped me was that even dying for the cause wouldn't be enough. Unless the others could figure out where to go and get here in time … Even then, with Neith and the reverend turned; Anat and Astarte traitors and no idea which side Sigyn played for … The deck was stacked against us.

I had to believe that at least Apollo and the others would find their way here. All had been there when Reverend Smith had spouted off. They'd heard me predict that if freed, Set would make an appearance. The revival meeting would have been advertised. Plus, Apollo still had his own oracular powers.

Ian's head jerked up suddenly, as if he'd heard a call evident only to him ... maybe in his head, maybe through his link to Set.

"Show time," he said. My heart squeezed.

He manhandled me to my feet and dragged me out of the room and down the hall to an elevator somewhere at the back where no one had bothered to turn on any lights. I went through and debated plans to break free. The gorgon glare might not work so well, but biting my cheek and spitting my paralytic blood in his eyes, or head butting the soft part of his neck or chin followed by a good stomp on his insoles ... But he stayed behind me, holding tightly to my zip tied hands, making any moves difficult if not impossible to pull off.

He was taking me to the heart of the action. I was going to have to wait and watch for my moment.

I heard the reverend even before I could see him. His voice was amplified, but all of the speakers would be pointing out over the auditorium, not to the backstage and back hallways. So I couldn't make out the exact words, but the tone sounded the same—adamant, righteous, a call to spiritual arms.

Ian pushed me through a door, into a backstage area, where I could see Reverend Smith pacing the stage, using up every inch of it, his presence taking it over. Behind him, there had to be a giant screen or screens, because colors were flashing on the back of his thousand-dollar suit. Even my gaze was riveted on him as he spoke, fascinated, choking on his words but gulping them down all the same.

"'... Another mysterious sight appeared in the sky. There was a huge red dragon with seven heads and ten horns, and a crown on each of his heads. With his tail, he dragged a third of the stars out of the sky and threw them to earth.' Strange, horrifying and yet wondrous things, my friends, my faithful, because while it means the end, it is also the beginning. Those who've turned their faces away from God, away from his teaching, those who have not or will not renounce sin, will be left behind to suffer not just a world without His grace, but a taste of the torments that will plague them ever after in the dark place. That is Hell, my friends." His voice rose and fell, sometimes dipping so quietly that the audience would have to strain forward to hear, sometimes rising to an almost physical level where it would knock them back in their seats. His congregation was as invested as though they were watching a favored sports team in sudden-death overtime.

"Mark my words," he continued, his voice ominous as though there was peril in the alternative. "Before the night, week, month is through, you will see all this and more. 'Locusts came down out of the smoke upon the earth, and they were given power like that of scorpions ... they could harm only the men who did not have the mark of God's seal on their foreheads. The locusts were not allowed to kill these men, but only to torture them for five months.... During the five months those men will seek death, but not find it; they will want to die, but death will flee from them.' If you love your husband, brother, son, cousin, neighbor, co-worker, you will bring them to me. They will renounce the Devil and all his works and embrace the Spirit. Later, there will be a laying on of hands, which will inspire you with the divine. Your words will be as His. Your spirit filled with the Holiest of Spirits."

"Not long now," Ian said in my ear, his breath hot like the forges of Hell the reverend conjured up. As I flinched away from it, I caught sight of figures on the other side of the stage—Anat, Astarte, and between them, Neith, her face gone feral. Her eyes burning with fervor as they looked on the reverend. Not Neith as I'd known her, in bounty-hunter black, her own insignia on her chest. She now stood dressed more like her Nike-Athena persona—in a longish gown of white with a blazing gold breastplate molded to her chest. In one hand she held a shield, and in another a sword of gleaming silver with golden etchings.

"But I do not expect you to take me at my word," Reverend Smith went on, drawing my attention back to him. "God sent signs so the faithful should know him, so that they could prepare the way. You have seen some of them," he said with supreme conference. Behind him the screens flickered, and I wondered if he was showing the footage again from the morning show. "But, after all, we are in the land of movie magic. Of special effects. I do not expect you to believe these screens." At a dramatic toss of his hands into the air, the screens went dark. "I will show you your proof. The agents of the end walk among us. Angels and devils. Horsemen and hell beasts . Behold, I present to you one of the agents of our torment and an angel of light."

In an instant, Ian had snipped my ties and pushed me out onto the stage. On the other side, Neith came forth, sweeping her sword dramatically before her. No one had had to push her onto the stage. She came willingly, eagerly, now fixated on me rather than Reverend Smith.

There were gasps from the crowd, screams, voices raised in praise or prayer. I couldn't tell. It was all one big roar. I couldn't distinguish anything but the feeling buzzing in my head. Shock and horror. Apollo? He was here somewhere, I could sense it.

I called out to him mentally, stupidly, because he couldn't hear my words, only feelings. Right now, my overarching feeling—because I refused to acknowledge fear, even though Neith, now linked to the god of chaos, stood before me armed to the teeth—was bafflement, particularly at the fear and awe rolling in from the audience in waves, so thick as to be tangible.

Actors always talked about the energy of a room. This was the first time I'd ever felt it. But why? Neith looked like an avenging angel, which might explain the awe, but I just looked like ... me. I didn't even have my wings out, let alone any other aspects that might be considered beastly. Maybe they recognized me from the reverend's little film clips, but that still didn't explain ...

In an instant, Neith was upon me, no longer wielding her sword for show but with deadly intent. I leapt back, out of the way, and something flapped behind me. Shocked, I whipped my head around, trying to see what was going on, what new threat might have snuck up, and caught sight of shadow wings. Not mine. And something else ... a tail? A barbed tail, like a devil or ... a scorpion. Like one of the locusts the reverend had described. The light bulb was just going off in my head when Neith's sword came down again and I dove to the ground, rolling and rolling as she slashed down a breath away from me. And again.

The Chaos Field. Ian must have activated his amulet again, and just like with the heroes and villains on Hollywood Boulevard, I'd become the thing I was meant to represent, the beast everyone expected to see. Did that mean my tail was real? For now, at least?

I burst up out of my crouch as Neith closed on me, swinging again, and I called forth my real wings, not counting on the representations. I flapped furiously, needing to gain height, the relief of enough time and space to test out what I had at my disposal.

But I wasn't fast enough. Her sword caught me in the calf, laying it open, burning as though it really was made of holy fire. I swiped at the sky with my tail, surprised when it lashed forward at my command. I wondered if it really came with the stinging venom as described or whether that would be going too far. I couldn't count on it. I flapped hard, leading Neith on a chase from one side of the stage to the other as I reached down to my bleeding leg, nearly screamed at the pain as I slid my hand through the wound, covering it with blood. I arched my tail to bring the stinger in close and then coated it with the blood.

And then more blood burst out to join it as an arrow flew out of nowhere to pierce one of my wings. I arched back in pain and looked around wildly for where the danger was coming from now, and saw Anat coming out of the wings, bow in hand.

The crowd roared, cheered to see the side of "good" so easily defeating "evil." And there was some kind of disruption out in the audience as well. I didn't know if it was more of Ian's chaos field or Apollo and any backup he'd brought racing to action, but I hoped to hold out long enough to find out.

Astarte was coming from the wings as well, a spear, or lance or some stick-like weapon with a sharp pointy end aimed my way.

Reverend Smith was chanting something or maybe narrating the whole thing for those in the cheap seats. I didn't think anyone could hear him over all the commotion, but if it kept him from attacking me too, I was all for it.

I flew at Neith as Astarte let her weapon fly, hoping to avoid it and if not take Neith down then at least engage so closely with her the others wouldn't risk firing at me. She blocked with her shield, swinging her sword wide to try to catch me on the back as I went hurtling into her, but my momentum was such that it brought us both crashing to the ground.

Out of the corner of my eyes, I saw others leap onto the stage—believers trying to pry me from their angel of light or reinforcements for me. I had Neith on the ground, pinned beneath her own shield as my weight pressed down on her. I had no idea what to do now. I'd slathered my tail in blood, but I didn't really want to turn her to stone. She wasn't herself. She was an ally. But still, I couldn't have her trying to kill me.

Action and chaos swirled all about us, but no one was pulling me away, by which I knew help had arrived and was keeping the faithful at bay. Neith herself, though, was doing her best to buck me off, snarling, and spitting, like a wild animal.

The entire stage shook beneath us, and at first I thought it was trembling from the weight of the believers storming the stage, but nearly as instantly, the fear of every La La Landian awoke in full force ... Quake!

Either I jerked or the force of the shaking shifted me just enough that Neith could throw me aside, striking me on the temple with the sharp side of her shield as she rolled free. The pain was nothing next to the fear.

The reverend's voice rose above the quake, and I thought I heard him assuring everyone that this was one of the signs, one of the seals opening. "And in that hour there was a great earthquake, and a tenth of the city fell; seven thousand people were killed in the earthquake, and the rest were terrified and gave glory to the God of heaven."

That was supposed to comfort *people?* I wondered.

My precog was kicking up like crazy. Crazier than it had ever gone before. My head spun not with the shaking or the cut to my temple, but with the warning klaxons jittering my very brain to the point where I thought it might turn to jelly.

This was no natural quake. No Biblical seal ripping open. But Reverend Smith had one thing right—this was in no way natural. This was Set, having gorged on the chaos and the force of the communal belief, finally breaking free.

This was a second coming, but not the one the reverend had foretold.

Before people could even get to their feet, they were crawling over each other to get wherever they perceived as safe ... or maybe, to offer a less cynical approach, to take those last moments on earth to try to get out to rescue their loved ones. Others took cover under seats or stayed rooted in place, praying for the rapture. But some ... most ... swarmed toward the stage and the beacon of light offered by Neith.

I heard Apollo, his voice somehow rising above the screams of the panicked crowd. I looked out in that direction to see him rising to resume the fight, along with the others—Hermes and Sigyn, hopefully still on our side, Isis and Osiris, the latter holding a curved staff almost like a shepherd's crook and using it to sweep people out of their way ...

That was all I saw before a blow like an anvil dropped on my back and I twisted my head to see that Neith had come down on me, shield first, and that the metal center was digging painfully into my back. My wings tried futilely to flap, but they were stilled by the weight of the shield. I lashed with my tail, but it was caught under her and the folds of her gown.

The whole building quaked around us. A light from the catwalk that had been pointed at the stage broke free of its mooring and fell suddenly, swinging on its cord straight into a believer as he rushed the stage. I heard his skull crack and saw him start to topple before my vision was cut off by all the people who'd reached us ... grabbing for their angel or preparing to strike blows against her opponent ... me. I was kicked in the teeth. In the ribs. In the eye. Battered from behind. I couldn't protect all of myself at once. I'd no sooner curl or lash one way than a blow would fall from another direction.

In the melee, my tail had come free, and I swung it about like a flail, as best I could, but I didn't dare strike with the stinger. These were *people*. Manipulated, deluded, and endangered, but people. I'd fought gods and Titans, demons and hellhounds, but never before faced such fragile human fall-out.

I only had one good eye left, the other red-hazed, and swollen almost shut from the kick it had taken, but I risked opening it to glare around. I was too low for anyone to meet my gaze, but still I tried. *"Freeze!"* I yelled, imbuing it with everything I had. They thought I was powerful ... they *believed* ... maybe it would amplify my strength.

The set of legs before me started to fall, and at first I thought it had worked and the person had been caught off-balance, but as she dropped to the stage floor, I was able to see beyond her, straight to Eros where he stood on one of the theatre chairs, his bow still aimed.

"No!" I called. These were *people*. He couldn't just *shoot* them.

He gave me a wink and drew another arrow from the quiver at his back.

Gold, I saw. I blew out a breath in relief. Gold was the color of love. I might have a new admirer, but the owner of the legs would get over it. She'd live.

The weight on my back started to lift as the believers got a hold of Neith, but then dropped again as the theatre shook, harder than ever, the violence seeming to start from above rather than below as though a giant hound had the roof of the Orpheum in its jaws and was shaking for all it was worth. Those around ducked or fell to the ground covering their heads against the new projectiles plummeting from the ceiling—lights, acoustic tiles, pieces of scaffolding.

And then the most dangerous thing yet—Set descending from the "heavens" of the theatre on a cloud just like the one on which we'd fought him. Only he no longer looked like the myths painted him—skin white as birch, hair red as blood, terrifying and unnatural. He looked as the reverend under his influence had primed the crowd to expect, as *belief* had painted him. He looked beatific. He looked like an angel or, more on point, like the Second Coming of the Christ himself.

We'd failed to kill Set while he was still imprisoned. What hope did we have now surrounded by true believers who would give their lives for his and who fed his power?

That was the whole thing, wasn't it? We had to strike at the heart of the belief. Which meant first shutting down the chaos field that made us all look like angels and demons.

I struggled to my feet, momentarily ignored as all attention turned to Set. Anat, Astarte, and Neith all closed in to guard him. Believers moved in to touch even the hem of his robe, which was what he'd appeared in, looking like the Western world's sandy-haired, blue-eyed idealization of Jesus that appeared in about every picture I'd ever seen. Biblically, even touching the hem of Jesus's robe would heal a man. What would Set's touch do to his faithful? I shuddered to think.

While everyone moved toward him, I looked away. Into the wings, where the chaos field was guarded only by a sociopathic college boy fused with the disembodied soul of an ancient killer. Because things weren't weird enough.

Like everyone else, Ian was fixated on Set. I leapt up into the air, but my wings, mashed by Neith's shield, barely flapped, and I fell back to the stage with a thud. My attempt had caught Ian's attention, though, and as I raced toward him through the thickness of the oncoming crowd, he lunged for the closest true believer and held her tightly against his body, producing a small, thin knife from somewhere and holding it to her neck. She struggled against it, registering nothing but her need to get to the vision in the center of the stage. Her blood instantly coated the blade, dripping down his hand.

I didn't pause, knowing I couldn't. The life of one versus the fate of the world ... it shouldn't have been any contest, but every step forward the knife pressed farther into her flesh and I felt her pain as though it was my own. I held on to the hope that Ian wouldn't kill her, at least not right away, because then she'd be useless as a shield. Of course, I had no idea how much sanity was left inside not-Ian for logic to penetrate.

When I was nearly close enough to grab for him, Ian shifted the knife, holding it now more like an icepick that he was ready to plunge into the side of her neck. "That's close enough," he said.

"No," I answered. "It really isn't. Ian, what do you think's going to happen here? Set doesn't need you anymore. Already, you've been sidelined, waiting in the wings while Set gets all the real action."

He laughed maniacally. "Is that your plan? You're going to talk me to death? Give it up. Set needs worship. Human worship. And I am his conduit. You are nothing but in the way."

Without warning, he stabbed the knife he held deep into the woman's neck, and yanked it back out. As her blood fountained, he threw her at me and dashed away.

Instinctively, I caught her, lowering her to the ground and pressing my hand hard against her neck, even though I knew it was futile. With the pressure of the blood spray, he'd hit something vital, probably severed her jugular. She was going to bleed out in seconds, and Ian was getting away. I said a quick prayer over her, my hurried version of last rites, before lowering her body to the floor and taking off after Ian.

I didn't see him until a clatter above gave him away. Or maybe he'd wanted me to look, to root me in that spot, because the next thing I knew, I was leaping to the side to avoid a light plunging straight for me ... a big one. It crashed to the ground with an explosion of sharp glass and busted metal flying like shrapnel. I caught a piece of it in my calf, the lancing pain blinding me for a split second. I tried my wings again, and this time they worked a little better than before, healed enough to lift me into the air, if not confidently.

I sped toward the catwalks and grabbed Ian by one foot, holding on to it as I pulled myself up. He kicked at me with the other, but couldn't get much of his foot through the latticework of the catwalk, and the slight impact barely registered over the pain in my calf. But as soon as I'd climbed high enough to haul myself over the waist-high bar, Ian grabbed me by the hair, that wild hair that was the bane of my existence, and I cursed that the chaos field had turned me into the image Set wanted projected rather than emphasizing my Gorgon side. I'd have given anything at that moment for my curls to turn to asps and bite Ian until he collapsed from the venom.

He tried to shove me back, but I grabbed for anything that would hold me there—years of my phobia of heights momentarily blanking out the fact that I had wings and wouldn't plummet to my death. My hand closed around his medallion, which burned icy cold, like touching dry ice. Instinct insisted I let go, but I fought it. Instead, I yanked hard, hoping that the chain would give way, but it wasn't so easy.

Neither was victory. Ian still had the bloody knife he'd used to impale the poor woman below. He'd tucked it into his belt when he'd climbed the catwalk, but now he whipped it out again. I couldn't escape it and keep hold of the medallion. He stabbed it into my shoulder, sending shockwaves of pain all through my arm. My hand spasmed open, and Ian started to pull away, but I forced it to close again, ignoring the pain and the weakening I felt. According to the chaos, I was an agent of evil, a locust, sent to torment mankind. That had to count for something....

My tail ... it whipped uselessly behind me, not thin enough to slip through the catwalk latticework or long enough to reach all the way above me and sting Ian to stone. Despite the fact that he was still human and my client's brother, I was getting dangerously close to not caring.

Ian ratcheted his hand back for another stab at me, and I knew I had to do something fast. I'd never used my wings for anything but flapping, but now I tried to sweep them over the rail of the catwalk, to hold me firm so that I could get my feet onto the rails and use the leverage to burst upward, yanking the chain up and over his head. I scrabbled at the base of the catwalk and latched on with one foot as the knife came back. The second foot caught as the knife struck, and I launched myself up like a rocket taking the knife, now embedded in my forearm, with me.

It took everything I had to keep a grip on the medallion when my muscles wanted to give in, drained of fight and draining of blood, but I kept it clasped in my hand as I skyrocketed, pulling the chain up over Ian's head. He reached for me as I went, but he missed, and had to catch himself on the rail as he overbalanced and would have gone over.

I had to do something about the medallion before my strength gave out—transfer it to my other hand or ...

Put it over my neck. Some kind of instinct kicked in, but I didn't know whether I could trust it. Was it my precog? My oracular powers growing ever greater ... or was it the chaos field itself? I opened my hand just enough to get a look at the pendant within, now slick with the blood that had dripped down my arm. If I wore the amulet, would I have any control over it or would it control me?

I clenched my hand again and looked down at the chaos below. Set was lying on hands, "blessing" his followers. I couldn't see the looks on their faces. I didn't know if they'd been transfixed or transfigured, but I knew a false prophet when I saw one, and I knew I didn't have any other hope to fight Set.

I looked for the others, who hadn't yet been able to get anywhere near him, and for the first time, I spotted Nick. I didn't know when he'd arrived, but he was faced off with Neith, who looked a lot more ready to kill than kiss him.

"Nick!" I yelled, afraid to distract him, but even more afraid he wouldn't last long without help. "Get under her breastplate!"

He didn't spare me a glance. "I don't think now's the time," he growled.

"No, seriously, she's being controlled. If you can break her free—"

Neith got in a blow just then, knocking his head to the side with the tip of her spear and going in with her sword. I couldn't distract him anymore. I had to end this.

My hand started to lift even before I was aware of making any decision, ready to drop the chain around my neck, but the knife in my forearm and the deep stab to the shoulder kept it from rising all the way. As I went to transfer it to my bloodless hand, my good hand, a sudden vision gripped me. Thousands slaughtered. Hundreds of thousands. People dead in the streets. So many there weren't enough left alive to bury all the dead. A whole city of carrion and vultures ... and I wasn't talking Hollywood agents.

And me, flying above it all. Laughing ... having become that which Set had made me. The amulet had to be destroyed. Now, before ...

I looked around frantically for Apollo. The amulet was made of metal, gold in tone, maybe in reality. There was one surefire way I knew to slag metal, and that was with extreme heat.

He must have heard me call for him mentally, because in the huge melee, one face turned toward me. Astarte tried to run Apollo through as he turned, but Sigyn hit her upside the head with something, screwing with her aim and drawing her attention. I guessed that answered the question of whose side she was on.

"Apollo," I called, "slag this!"

I held the amulet aloft in my good hand, up over my head.

Set let out a huge roar and started to rise from his worshippers to come after me, but suddenly all the lights of the stage—all of them—swiveled toward me, flaring and burning with the light of a thousand suns. I had to turn my eyes away, but the brightness burned even through my closed lids. And my hand ... the heat was so intense, it was all I could do not to drop the amulet ... and then that wasn't even an option, as the superheated metal started to flow like oil, coating my hand with the burn.

Set flew into me, sending me reeling, and I reached out

with my burning hand to push him away, the molten metal there scalding him on contact. I ripped away some of his skin when I pulled back, tearing away his illusion with it.

He floated there now, in the heavens of the theatre with me, revealed for his true self—hair flaming, skin unnaturally white, like something hidden for centuries away from the sun, eyes black as night.

Below, people gasped. Some yelled that it must be a trick, that I'd done something to him. Others fell to their knees and wept.

Set snarled. It pulled badly at his burned face, and when I bit my lip and spat my blood at the raw section where the skin had come away, he began to freeze that way ... or, rather, petrify. His face half stone now, set in a perpetual snarl, he lashed out at me, swinging with a hand that quickly became a claw. He was giving himself away now, changing forms. I was no longer the one bearing the scorpion's tail.

People began to scream, and if the earthquake had sent some running for the exits, it was nothing to the new stampede.

"You wanted chaos," I said to Set. "Well, it appears you have it."

The claw never connected with me. As I watched, a form somersaulted into the air, swinging with her glorious silver-gold sword, and the claw was severed clean through, dropping to the stage and scattering the last of the stragglers, who couldn't quite believe ... And that was what it was all about. We'd shattered their belief in their false prophet.

We'd killed his chaos field.

Set was vulnerable.

Suddenly, the force of all those stage lights was shining on Set, and a glow started in his abdomen like an ant under a magnifying glass about to burst into flame. He moved out of the way, but the lights followed him.

I reached down to the shard of glass still embedded in my

calf and with the last of the strength remaining in my stabbed arm, I pulled it forth, dropped onto Set's vulnerable side and drove it deep, complete with its thick covering of my blood.

Set spasmed once, and his legs changed to that of a boar, while his face, half-paralyzed, stayed somewhere between man and scorpion. He started to fall, no longer able to stay aloft, no longer able to fight, his feet scrabbling uselessly like a dog that chases a rabbit in sleep.

And when he hit the ground, he simply lay still. Whether the paralysis spread or he'd simply given up the fight, I didn't know. I watched for him to rise again like a movie monster, but he didn't so much as twitch. Petrified, I thought with relief. Not dead—after all, as he'd said, the world couldn't do completely without chaos—but for now quiescent ... inert. I only hoped he'd stay that way until we could restore his chains.

Finally, I let myself sink down as well, easing myself to the ground. I was a freaking mess with only one good leg to stand on.

26

I sat at the bar with Neith as nervous as a hen in a rooster house, which was a pretty apt comparison, considering the way the guys at the bar were eyeing her. I'd convinced her to put herself into the hands of Spike and Roslyn, the stylists Apollo had hired for me when we'd walked the red carpet, the ones who'd managed to tame my wild hair. Her hair was no longer reined in by rows and rows of braids, but now in a soft halo around her head.

Originally, the stylists had given her smoky eyes, bronzed her cheeks, and done a whole host of other things to her, but she'd washed it all off, saying that she wasn't going into battle and so refused to cake her face in war paint. "He's either going to like me for me or he's not going to like me at all." I applauded her and reveled maybe just a bit in Spike's consternation. She accepted the dress though. Still in bounty hunter black, but now in some kind of silky fabric that molded to her, thin straps crisscrossing her back. They'd paired it with an interesting gold chain with a long dangle that fell right into her décolletage, calling attention to what was there. It wasn't much, but Nick wasn't a breast man or he and I would never have gotten together.

She sat now, nothing but kohl lining her eyes and a little bit of sheer gloss on her lips, looking absolutely amazing. She was completely oblivious to the attention riveted on her, and sat shredding a bar napkin into confetti.

"I can't do this," she said.

"What, dinner? You've faced down enemies. It shouldn't be any harder to face down a friend."

She looked up at me, and I was struck again by her lethal lashes. Nick was going down. "But what if—"

"Neith, there are no guarantees in life, you know that. Don't 'what if' yourself right out of living."

"But—"

She'd been drinking seltzer with lime to settle her stomach. I signaled the bartender for something stronger. When it arrived, a shot of Patrón, she gave it a look and then passed that look to me. "What is it?" she asked.

"Liquid courage."

She snarled at me, again the warrior goddess. "You drink it then. I'll face this sober or not at all."

One shot wasn't going to get her drunk, but I didn't argue it. The drink had already done what was intended, which was to square her shoulders and shore her up. She was not going to back down.

I didn't think Nick was either. Back in the thick of the battle, he'd not only removed her breastplate, he'd had to reach into her chest to rip out Set's anchor into her, his disk. He'd had more luck with his bare hands than Apollo'd had with Thalia and his silly rubber gloves. I hadn't seen the actual moment, but I'd seen Nick and Neith in the aftermath of the battle. Something had passed between them. Something life-altering. Maybe touching her heart had touched his. Or maybe seeing her vulnerable made her a little less terrifying....

Gah, it wasn't even my relationship and I was overthinking it. Maybe it had simply been inevitable. Fate. Or their embodiments.

Or maybe they'd crash and burn. Time would tell.

Neith's head snapped up and swiveled toward the entrance as if she could sense Nick the way I could sense Apollo, because sure enough, Nick stood there, handsome in a suit, his blue tie picking up the blue of his eyes.

I took a deep breath myself. I'd moved on, but the man still had an impact. Presence, the Hollywood crowd might have said.

Well, I'd gotten her up to the moment. Neith could take it from here. And besides, I had security arrangements to double-check—for the still-stoned Set *and* his sister wives with Artemis and her devotees now guarding, giving Taweret some much-needed time off. Then I had my own dinner plans.

I gave Neith's hand a quick squeeze. "Good luck."

I'm not sure she even noticed. She had eyes only for Nick, and she slid off her stool and headed for him like there was some kind of tractor beam pulling her.

Leaving me with the bar tab, but that was okay.

Nick, for his part, had a word with the hostess, but his gaze caught Neith's as he scanned the bar, and I thought I saw him take a fortifying breath.

I paid the tab and then slipped out.

Across town, Apollo waited to take me to the heavens—not nearly as romantic as it sounded—and then a candlelit dinner for two.

Tomorrow I had a deposition with the lawyers on the Roland case, which was going to be ... challenging. The lawyers' strategy seemed to be a variation on Jessica's "curse of the pharaohs" idea. They were even calling in Panacea, as the world-renowned epidemiologist who'd spearheaded the cure for the zombie virus that had struck New York to sell the idea. After all, that had been a case where hundreds of thousands who hadn't been quite themselves had wreaked havoc and brought bloodshed to the city and had never been prosecuted. I hoped that it worked ... and that it would convince the Egyptian authorities as well.

And after the deposition ... my promised interview with Susie Tallios.

There was no question which I dreaded more. I suspected that after tomorrow my world would never be the same.

But tonight, there was Apollo. I'd also make sure of nudity ... and cake ... not necessarily in that order.

ABOUT THE AUTHOR

Lucienne Diver does not actually come from circus folk, though you'd never know it to meet her family. She is, however, in no particular order, a wife, mother, literary agent, book addict, sun-worshipper, mythology enthusiast, travel-junkie, and crazy person. In addition to the *Latter-Day Olympians* series, she writes the *Vamped* young adult novels (*Vamped, Revamped, Fangtastic, Fangtabulous* and *Fangdemonium*) as well as YA suspense. Her short stories have appeared in the *Strip-Mauled* and *Fangs for the Mammaries* anthologies edited by Esther Friesner (Baen Books) and *Kicking It* edited by Faith Hunter and Kalayna Price (Roc). Her essay "Abuse" is included in the anthology *Dear Bully: Seventy Authors Tell Their Stories* (HarperTeen).

More information can be found on her website at www.luciennediver.com. You can also follow her on Twitter @luciennediver.

OTHER WORDFIRE PRESS TITLES BY LUCIENNE DIVER

Bad Blood

Crazy in the Blood

Rise of the Blood

Battle for the Blood

Our list of other WordFire Press authors and titles is always growing. To find out more and to see our selection of titles, visit us at:
wordfirepress.com